BOOK SIX OF THE DEAD HUNGER SERIES

Dead Hunger VI
The Gathering Storm

By Eric A. Shelman

Dead Hunger VI: The Gathering Storm

is a work of fiction by

Eric A. Shelman

All characters contained herein are fictional, and all similarities to actual persons, living or dead, are purely coincidental, except of course, where characters are based on real people, but the personalities and relationships are mostly fiction.

No portion of this text may be copied or duplicated without author or publisher written permission, except for use in professional reviews.

©2014 Dolphin Moon Publishing

ISBN 978-0-9891416-1-1

Cover Art By Jeffrey Kosh

From The Author

Just as a note to my fans and readers, (that's assuming that some have read my crap and are definitely NOT fans!) I was so damned relieved that all you guys accepted Dave Gammon taking a lead role in Dead Hunger V: The Road to California, that I thought you really deserved another chunk of Flex Sheridan telling another story. So I thought I'd send him off on his own for a bit, but since I needed you to know what was happening back at the homestead, I figured Gem could tell that part.

So Flex is going to take off; you'll see who he meets and what kind of trouble he can get into.

As for the dedications, I can't thank my brother, Don Shelman in this one. I didn't brainstorm with him on this particular novel, but that's okay. I've got a project with the working title of "The Camera" that he helped me with. That is now a complete trilogy, also available in an omnibus version.

I'd like to thank all my beta readers again. They are insanely helpful, and I would be remiss if I left them out. So, Cris Berget, Sharon Berget, Megan Sweetness, Carrie Herbel, Debra Allen and Jesse Donovan, THANK YOU! You were all fast and thorough, and you've helped me make a cleaner product for people who deserve one.

I'd also like to thank my wife, Linda, who is so understanding about my writing that it makes it easy for me to create. No complaining about me sitting in my office for two hours every night, tapping away on the keyboard.

She also offers good feedback on my storylines and other things, and she is always willing to lay back and listen to me read her the latest product I've tapped out – as it happens.

So, I hope you enjoy this installment of Dead Hunger. It's going to be the last of its kind – when and if the next one comes, it's going to be a different animal altogether.

Thanks again, all. You're the best. Now go and tell a friend, would ya please?

One last note. If you're listening to the audiobook version of this volume, you're in luck. I re-recorded it in 2023, which is why there are so few reviews – they make you dump all the old ones if you re-release a different recording of it.

The reason I still thought it was worth the re-do is, the original first five books in this series were recorded by another guy … I liked him okay, but he got expensive, and with each new book, he raised his prices.

I had to take over the recording myself. The only problem was, I had never narrated, though it seemed easy enough. Using pillows surrounding my microphones, I bought all different types of gear and no matter what I did, my sound was TERRIBLE. My abilities weren't so great, either.

Still, I recorded book number six (this one) and then seven, eight and nine. By the time I wrote ten, I had gotten good at narrating, and I'd purchased a sound booth. My new stuff was sounding fantastic.

So, after a few complaints about my lackluster performance on this book, I thought it was time. I'll see whether it's necessary to re-record the next three, but for now, I'm letting it simmer.

Enjoy! I hope you have a nice ride here.

Keep calm and zombie on …

Prologue

I'm Flex Sheridan. My wife's Gem, and we have two kids. Trina's almost eight and Flex Jr. hasn't been around two months yet. Oh, yeah. We got Slider, our Great Pyrenees dog.

Slider and my son are the only ones who were born after the world went to shit. Glad they don't know. They'd be pissed at what they got fucked out of. Long walks without firearms, ice cream at the corner shop.

Before some gas started leaking out of every part of this Godforsaken planet, infecting 90% of mankind, I was an electrician. Sounds pretty mundane, huh? Wiring shit up, making everyday life run.

Gem was an artist. Oils and watercolor, everything from still life to portraits to abstracts. Clay, copper. Give her something and she'd make it prettier.

Or at *least* more interesting.

Hemp and Charlie are our friends. Like family. So are Dave and Serena, who were on the road when I started to tell this story. They went to California to see if Dave could find his uncle, and we didn't have a timeframe for when – or even if – they'd make it back.

Back to Hemp and Charlie. Hemp was an engineer and a scientist before all this crap hit the fan and he still is. Charlie was a punk and metal rock lover who is an expert with a crossbow, and she's taught Gem and some others how to use it. She's a cute little blonde firecracker to be sure, and she can rival Gem when it comes to … let's say, *expressing herself.*

Hemp's her husband now – they got married in an Alabama church at the same time I married Gem – and he's

5

the one who figured out most of what I'm about to tell you. 95% of it. Get ready. I'm gonna go through it fast.

Some sort of fissure opened up in the Earth's core, and now a gas is bubbling out through every porous surface of the planet. The makeup of this vapor isn't completely known – some elements in it can be found on this planet, others can't. It's ancient and as old as the Earth. It changes people, kills them, then almost instantly reanimates them. It reanimates the dead, too – so long as the brain wasn't removed.

When they come back, these mutants hunger for human flesh, brains and blood. They don't talk and they can't be reasoned with. They never sleep and they never tire, but they do, far too slowly, rot. Oh, yeah. They hunger. The walking dead hunger.

Another important thing Hemp learned is that if you're immune to a poisonous oil called urushiol, you're also immune to the effects of this vapor. Urushiol is the oil found in poison ivy, poison oak, poison sumac, cashew shells and mango skins. Maybe other places, too. You never have to have seen or even heard of these plants or the urushiol; just know that if you can contact the oil without blistering, you're immune. You're safe.

We don't know why. This means that 90% of humankind isn't immune, because only 10% is. If you're not, what you become is the thing of fiction; of old black and white thriller episodes on midnight television. But they're real this time. We call them ghouls, walkers, rotters, diggers, abnormals, infecteds, stinkers, corpses and biters. Oh, yeah. We call them zombies. We finally started to call them what they *really* are.

A bit about the things themselves. They have offenses and defenses. First, we'll cover the offensive tools in their rotten pouches. The ones we know about, that is.

Their tear ducts emit a vapor that constantly leaks out and give their eyes a pink hue. The vapor isn't the same as the invisible shit coming out of the earth. It's a knockout vapor that paralyzes you and keeps you down until someone touches you. You're just lucky if it's not them hunched over you when you crack your eyelids. If it is, you're likely gonna be dead in short order. When they get close, they can pump the stuff out like a fog machine, but not if they haven't eaten in a while. They've got it real good when they first turn, but it starts to dissipate if they don't get fresh food. Yeah. Us.

One of their defenses is that they recognize things that can hurt them. Like guns and knives, even crossbows. Stuff like that. Maybe it's a little leftover memory from when they were alive, maybe not. Maybe it was inserted in there by one of the red-eyed females.

I'll get into *them* later.

So when they see things that can hurt them, they change up a bit. Nothing dramatic, not so that you'd really notice if you weren't looking for it. But their brains are working when they sense danger, and they will hold up if advancing. Notice I didn't say they'd retreat. These things don't retreat. The red-eyed females do to a degree, but typically they just re-adjust and advance again. You know why I think that is? I think because that particular red-eyed brand of zombie thinks she's gonna win. Every time. I don't think they even consider losing or dying at the hand of us breathers.

They also know when they're deficient. If they've got a broken limb or something else that might make them unable to perform a certain task – they just won't do it. Again, it's instinctive, Hemp thinks. Anyway, let me get into the red-eyes, since I've already whetted your whistle.

At any given time, just in the United States of America – and believe me, I sure wish the old USA meant shit anymore – about 3.13% of all women are pregnant. I won't

7

get into childbearing years at this point, because you just gotta figure that if they're pregnant, they are of childbearing age, whether it's socially acceptable or not.

And yeah, I wish that meant shit anymore, too Since the population at the time the gas started seeping out of our planet was around 317,000,000, and women make up around 50.8% of the population, you can see that we're looking at around 161,000,000 women in the US alone. Now, using that calculation above of what percentage of all women are pregnant, we can estimate that number to be around 503,930. Yep. Over half a million.

Here's a kicker you probably don't want to know about: all the above calculations were based on studies of *live* births. In 2011, there were over a million abortions, just in the US. How about miscarriages? Add another 900,000 to a million. Either way, we're talking some pretty big numbers, considering their frightening capabilities.

If 90% of the population isn't immune to the Earth gas, that means, just based on the numbers I've thrown at you above, that around 2,253,000 women were pregnant when they became zombies. So now you know the scope.

Know what happens when you're pregnant? Suffice it to say that women who were pregnant when this modern-day apocalypse hit now have the advantage. The estrogen levels in their bodies were so off-the-charts high when they were turned, their supercharged brains mutated into something more powerful; they can communicate telepathically with one another. How they do it, what they say and how they say it, we don't know. We do know they can push these mental voices out for about a mile, calling their own, and controlling the idiot, walking dead masses.

All this means when you see a red-eye, you kill her first – if you can.

The vapor from the red-eyes is different from the others. It doesn't have any chloroform-type properties, and

8

they only seem to use it on women of child bearing years. The red-eyes' mist affects these uninfected women by allowing the creatures to take psychic control of them. With this control, they can tell them to open doors or windows, essentially making the rest of their friends vulnerable.

Sacrifice everyone. Again, even the women and girls who have experienced it can't say what they're hearing in their heads, but they do speak aloud before they take action – perhaps so that their brains know what they're supposed to do. Things like *open door*, or *unlock door*, or *break window*, for example. Either way, if a young woman is sprayed with the red-eyes' vapor, she has to be restrained until she receives a dose of a new counteractive wafer we've developed using the properties of the zombie vapor itself.

Yeah. We've pulled a polio vaccine-style trick with that vapor. I'll get into that later, after I tell you about our main defense.

We've come up with a ingestible wafer we call WAT-5. That stands for *Walk Among Them 5-Hour*. It consists of a mixture of the standard zombie vapor, urushiol and the gas coming from the ground – blended together under freezing conditions. We use liquid nitrogen for that, but in a pinch, ice will work fine, too.

Yeah, we've got the equipment to make it. Once it's in its solid, wafer form, it can be taken anywhere in a baggie. Couple of points, though. When you take this wafer, you're going out. I mean dead asleep and that means the moment it goes down your gullet. Sit down before you eat the thing or have a nice bump on your head when you wake up.

You can be awakened moments later, but someone has to shake you out of it. Otherwise, you'll just lay there and sleep for an indeterminate amount of time.

The good news about that is if the zombies show up, they'll pretty much ignore you, because you're on the WAT-

5. They can no longer detect you as food; as flesh and blood. But again, it only works for around five hours.

The bad news? While the zombie masses don't know you're food, the red-eyes aren't as easily fooled. We're not certain if it just doesn't work on them, or if it does work and they just instinctively know you're food anyway. Either way, they'll sick their slow-moving, rotting, zombie friends on you. In a New York minute. (Which to be fair, is probably like any other minute these days, including a Texas minute.)

Their goal seems to be more about controlling their own and killing humans than eating us. Again – if a red-eye is around, kill her first.

As I said earlier, there is another version of the wafers; this is made the exact same way as the WAT-5, only instead of using the regular zombie tear duct mist, these wafers are made from the vapor of a red-eyed female. If a young woman who was doused with the mist from the red-eyes takes this wafer soon after being sprayed, she won't be compelled to follow the instructions transmitted telepathically to her by the strong female abnormals. She'll still utter the word that her brain feels was the intended command, but she'll be able to resist any urge to act on it.

Another word about the red-eyes. They're capable of incredible bursts of speed, but we've never seen it sustained for any period of time. They can jump like a motherfucker and they'll drop down fast to avoid a shot to the brain. To put it bluntly, they're nimble and quick, just like that Jack dude.

Last, but certainly not least, is the urushiol itself. We've developed stills of a sort to extract the oils from the leaves of poison ivy plants. We mass produce the shit. Then we blend it with water and spray zombies with it. They melt, pop, hiss and dissolve when even a micron of it contacts their rotten skin. Fill yourself a super soaker with this solution and you might as well have an Uzi, just so long as a red-eye isn't around.

Them again. They don't much like urushiol, but it doesn't do them near as much harm as it does to the standard variety of zombie. The red-eyes do get a surface burn, but it could just piss them off if you don't put a bullet or ten in their brains, pronto.

Which brings us to the brain. That's where you wanna put your arrow, bullet, sword, knife, rebar, ice pick, or whatever the hell you've found lying around to use as a weapon. Once you traumatize the brain, they're dead. That includes the red-eyed females.

I hope this has helped bring you up to speed. Now I'll pick this thing up where it seems most logical.

When Dave, Serena and Dave's uncle got back.

Along with some other interesting folks.

*****

Chapter One

Early September, 2013

Rocky Mountain Way by Joe Walsh was blasting from the speakers at the house, and we could see Charlie sitting on the porch from our vantage point, Bunsen and Slider at her feet.

A good breeze had begun to blow the evening before, and distant storm clouds would appear every so often. It had increased by the morning, but it wasn't so bad that we had to put off our work, because so far, no rain had reached us.

We could hear the music floating on this breeze from the field where Gem, Hemp and I worked, putting in perimeter fence posts in preparation for our multi-purpose pasture.

I looked over at Gem now and then, just making sure everything was cool. She'd caught me looking a few times and gave me a wave and a smile, but then her eyes turned right back down to the baby carrier where our son, little Flex Sheridan Jr., was kickin' it while his mama, daddy and Uncle Hemp worked on the fence.

Just a glance, then back to her post hole digger.

Impressive, she was. Hands together, jamming that digger down into the soil, spreading it apart, lifting, turning and making a pile of dirt.

We initially considered using a gas-powered auger, but because of Hemp's suspicion that the red-eyes had regained significant audible senses, we were only willing to take chances with Joe Walsh.

I could see Gem's glistening muscles from two post holes away, wet with sweat, working hard beneath a blazing sun that was busily heating Whitmire, South Carolina to a toasty 85 degrees, despite the wind.

We were setting the posts about 18" deep, using concrete that Hemp was busily mixing small batches of and rolling over in a wheelbarrow. When he got there, Gem would have the post down in the hole, and he'd dump the appropriate amount of concrete in and pull a level from his belt to make it straight and true.

Then on to the next one.

Occasionally, our progress was interrupted by a walker or two, but they'd been stragglers mostly. No sustained, horde-like onslaughts, and we hadn't even seen a regular rat, much less one of the ratz with a "z" for months. Hemp was right. They were dying off, and we just weren't certain why. Hemp confirmed the gas was still bubbling up like Jed Clampett's Texas Tea, so how their metabolisms varied from the human zombies was anybody's guess.

Charlie was enjoying the music, but for the most part she stayed at the house being pregnant, and she didn't like it one bit. Every once in a while she'd ride over on a golf cart and bring everyone water and iced tea, but Hemp ordered her back in the house because of the heat and the fact that she was ready to pop any day.

What we were building was to be an urushiol-coated fence. Wood posts set in concrete, six-and-a-half feet tall and strung with thick baling wire every nine inches. We'd found a good stock of 8' long 4"x4" lumber, so Hemp thought it would be a good idea.

We were working on the last main section, on the north side of the property. We'd already posted and wired up the top three cables on the rest of it, and when all was said and done, it was exactly what we'd intended.

Before it was all done, we'd need a total of about 290 posts and almost 14,000 feet of wire, but we like it here a lot, and we plan to stay as long as the fates allow. It's going to be our home for the foreseeable future.

We planned to create a four-acre space that we could cross-fence inside to keep livestock, using the rest of it for planting whatever else we needed. It was our intention to become self-sufficient, and everybody was on board. We'd only begun to lay out the plans for it when Nelson disappeared, but I'm pretty sure that if he'd have known what we had in mind, the dude would have stuck around to help.

But who knows. Nelson seemed to like an adventure, and since I'm telling this story after the fact, you know by now that he went to California with Dave and Serena. Woulda been nice if he'd have shared that with us. I had the distinct feeling he was gonna need that Subdudo of his when he got back, 'cause Gem and Charlie were bound to kick the shit out of him for disappearing like he did.

Once the fence was completed, we planned to brush coat every strand of that baling wire with a nice amount of urushiol. The sticky oil wouldn't rinse off in water, and even old residue will fuck with a zombie's complexion real good.

While winters were mild in South Carolina, we wanted to have everything ready for spring. We wanted a fresh start with lots of reason for hope, and that included a full vegetable garden and some fruit trees.

The town of Whitmire, which was mostly zombies, only had a few over 1400 people to start with. That meant roughly 140 uninfected folks initially had to figure out what was going on and try to defend themselves against their 1260 zombie neighbors. From what we'd seen in town, it hadn't been pretty. We determined that around 57% of the residents of Whitmire had been women. That puts their number at around 800. Now apply the 3.13% of all women being

14

pregnant, and we have around 25 pregnant Whitmire women at the time of the apocalypse.

Now for the disturbing calculation, which shows that even in a small town like this, there could be big trouble: 22 of the 25 women are likely zombies. Not just any zombies. Red-eyes.

After settling in to Whitmire, we immediately identified the locations of the cemeteries and put signs up to warn others away who were perhaps headed in that direction. These were old cemeteries, though, so many of the occupants weren't quite up to reanimating. Still, people died here more recently, and we just hoped like hell that most of them had been embalmed. They can't come back when their organs – particularly their brains – are gone.

Hemp always wonders how many are still suspended in mid-dig, though. There are bound to still be some. It can't be an easy trek, even for the ones who never sleep.

Anyway, like I said, we intend this little remote town to be our permanent, *start over* point. We're birthing babies and settling in, and we'll protect our homestead like a country should protect its borders.

No more running to find another place, and no more attempts at community building. We'd have to start with our core group – build ourselves a safe, self-sustaining home and work our way outward, expanding as needed. We'd broadcast on the ham and tell everyone who picked it up how to extract urushiol, how to make WAT-5, and anything else that might help . We'd begun filling those super-soaker water pistols with the stuff, and the moment Taylor suggested it, we felt stupid. Of course. Water guns. The simple crap that sometimes escapes an adult's mind.

Getting back to the spring planting season that we looked forward to. Hemp and Charlie would be parents by then, and that would sure as hell go a long way towards providing all of us more of that hope we needed so much.

I've never had kids of my own before, but seeing little Flexy's smile makes my day. Gem swears it's gas, but I think the little guy is smiling at his old man.

Why wouldn't he?

"Got it?" asked Hemp, ready to tilt the wheelbarrow.

"Hold on," I said, moving the level off a bump on the post and adjusting it just a bit. "Okay," I said. "Pour it."

Hemp poured until the hole was full of concrete, and I jammed a stick down beside the post and moved it in and out, trying to work the concrete into the air gaps.

I let go of the post, checked it once more, and found it to be straight. "Good job, buddy. I say we take a break."

Gem carried Flexy's seat over to me and I took it from her, giving her a quick kiss.

"We're sure getting there," she said. "It actually went faster than I thought it would."

"It really did," I said. "Once they're all in, we can work on the rest of the eye screws for these posts, then get the baling wire strung across the north end. For a while we can let the cows and horses run in the big pen."

"We can cross-fence it using just lumber," said Hemp. "But I think the urushiol-coated wire will be a better deterrent. Five strands of wire, five opportunities to get it on their skin."

"How often you think we'll have to re-coat it?" I asked..

"It's an oil, and it's a sticky one," said Hemp. "Maybe monthly, just to be sure. I plan to plant poison ivy all around the outside as well, remember. And with the gas pushing them along, they should grow large and do it quickly. This could be the safest place in America when we're done."

The rotor sounds made us all look into the sky at the same time. We looked all around, then saw a helicopter approaching from the west. I wasn't any expert, but it appeared to be jostling around pretty good in the wind, which gusted occasionally, surprising everyone with its force.

Gem got her weapon and raised it, and I put Flexy's carrier on the ground and stood between it and the chopper. We all had our guns out now. After what had happened to Hemp, we weren't taking any chances. While we knew that Dave and Serena were supposed to be in a helicopter, that didn't mean it was *this* helicopter.

Then something changed. The rotor sound sputtered and died, falling silent.

I think confusion washed over all our faces, at least for a moment. As we watched, the helicopter's nose dipped sharply as it headed straight for our open pasture.

I heard Bunsen bark and looked over. Charlie stood and moved away from the covered porch, her almost 9-month pregnant belly leading the way. Bunsen and Slider were on her heels. She got into the open and held her hand above her eyes to shield the bright sunlight as she looked at what had drawn all of our attention.

I turned back to watch its flight. The helicopter was still moving toward us, but even I could tell it was struggling to stay airborne.

"What the hell's going on?" I asked, as Hemp stared at the now quiet bird.

"Out of fuel is my guess," said Hemp, almost in a whisper, as though not wishing to distract the pilot, who must have been singularly focused at that moment. "It's going into autorotation now," he said. "Hope the pilot is good enough to bring it down safely."

We collectively held our breath as the helicopter came in too fast, its nose now dipping impossibly low, but fighting to regain a more level flying position as the whirlybird dropped from just a hundred feet up.

Another gust of wind, probably not under thirty miles an hour, hit the field. The chopper lifted slightly, then dropped suddenly to the ground, its nose angled more sharply now. When it hit, I cringed as the dirt flew up around it. The nose bounced off the ground and back up, causing the helicopter to hit hard on the skids before bouncing yet again and angling sharply, tilting so far as to bury one of the rotor blades into the grass. The dug-in blade made the chopper's tail swing hard left, the rotor blade pulling out of the soil, now bent to a near 45 degree angle. The rotor had prevented the bird from flipping onto its side, however, and it returned again to an upright position where it finally came to its final point-of-rest.

I heard all of us release our breath at once. The machine was now still, sitting upright about forty yards away from us, almost in the dead center of our field.

A few tense moments passed before the side door opened, and a person with long, blonde hair, wearing a helmet, stepped outside. The helmet came off, and we saw it was Nelson.

He waved at us frantically, dropped to his knees and kissed the ground before turning back to the cabin of the flying machine. He helped a blonde girl out, then others emerged behind her.

We gave a loud whoop and smiles spread across our faces as I scooped up little Flexy's carrier and we all ran toward Nelson and the chopper.

Our friends were home. It might have been a very close call, but they had made it safely back to us.

*****

"Wow, that was freaky!" shouted Nelson. It was quiet now, so there was no reason to yell, but after being surrounded by noise for hours, it was hard to get used to speaking at a normal level, so we said nothing.

"Damned thing ran out of gas!" said Nelson, reaching us. "I can't believe she put it down, but I had Buddha, God, and every other powerful dude occupied for a least a minute or so there."

"It's just good to have you back, buddy," I said, hugging him and squeezing his shoulders. "Why didn't you guys fill it up one last time?" I asked.

Nelson didn't hear. He busily made the rounds, hugging everyone. We saw some others stepping out, including Dave Gammon and Serena Casteneda. My heart settled, knowing all of them had made it safely home.

What appeared to be a child got out of the pilot's door, and I stared in disbelief. The person wasn't looking at us, and stopped to stare up at the tweaked rotor blade.

A shake of the head. Then she took off her helmet and turned toward us, meeting our eyes for the first time. It was a woman. Not a girl, not a child of any kind. I didn't think she could be taller than 4'10" or 4'11".

Gem, Hemp and I went to her.

"I wasn't a hugger before I met these folks," said Hemp, approaching the petite woman. "But I assume you're Rachel, and I'm impressed and so happy to meet you I can't express it any other way."

He hugged Rachel, who stood on her tip-toes to return the embrace. He pulled away smiling, then looked at the helicopter. "A Euro-Copter," he said. "A very good machine, and you did an excellent job of the emergency landing. I have to ask if you've done that before."

Before she could answer, Gem reached and scooped her into a hug. "I'm Gem, Rachel," she said. "And the big, good-looking guy here is Flex. The little cutie in the carrier is our son, Flex Jr."

"An honest-to-goodness family," she said. "That's nice to see." We could see she was still a bit shaken up. She swiped the bangs from her forehead.

"I *am* Rachel Reed, and I can tell by your accent that you're Hemp," she said, looking at him. Her short, brown hair framed her small face, and pronounced freckles adorned her nose and cheeks. Deep dimples formed when she smiled nervously. "And to answer your question, I've only performed that maneuver in a simulator. Never had the need otherwise."

"Well," said Hemp, smiling, "you must have nailed it in training. Good job."

Rachel shrugged, waving her hand toward the bent blade. "It's not even a functioning machine now," she said. "We'd been having some scary fill-ups with Isis aboard, and I underestimated the fuel we had left. Thought we could get here with a gallon or two to spare."

"At least we know you have the skills necessary to fly a helicopter," said Hemp. "Perhaps soon we can locate a solid replacement in working order."

"Yeah, engine-wise it's sound," said Rachel, "but I wouldn't be comfortable trying to straighten that rotor blade."

"I might have the capability," said Hemp. "Depends on how easily we can find a replacement. Meanwhile, we'll have to figure out how to remove it from our pasture."

"Sorry about that," said Rachel, with an embarrassed smile.

Charlie reached the group and gave out her hugs and hellos while the dogs welcomed everyone to the neighborhood with barks and front leg bows, and some smiles that might be scary if you didn't know them. Nobody appeared alarmed.

Gem had her arms around Dave, and she squeezed the life out of him, saying, "That about freaked us out. I can't even tell you how much we missed you guys."

"*You* were freaked out?" asked Dave, a nervous smile on his face. "When I heard the engine stop, I almost pissed myself."

"Oh, don't worry," she said. "It was the same for us watching it," Then: "Oh, my God." Her voice was a whisper.

I followed her eyes and saw a man with long, wavy hair like Dave's emerge from the helicopter, holding a little girl. Behind him, another woman stepped out and immediately dropped to her knees and kissed the grass.

She stood again, dusting off her pants and looking a little embarrassed. Her blonde hair was down to the middle of her back, and she currently had it in a braid. It looked to me like it was close to Hemp's hair color, maybe a bit more on the platinum side.

Gem let go of Dave and we both walked over to where they stood.

"You must be Bug," said Gem, smiling, her eyes moving between the baby and the man, who stood about Dave's height of around six feet tall.

"I am," he said. "I take it you're Flex and Gem?"

"You got it," I said, holding out my hand. He secured the baby girl in the crook of his left arm and shook my hand.

"I can't even believe we're here," he said. "All this shit has happened so fast."

"Extremely fast," said Isis, with perfect clarity.

Gem stared at her in disbelief. "I heard about her eating and sleeping habits, but not so much her language skills."

"She's rampin' up," said Bug. "Kinda freakin' me out a bit."

"So no sleep at all, she only eats meat, and now she's a big talker?" I asked.

"Check, check and I guess another check," said Bug.

21

Gem, leaned forward to put a hand to the child's cheek, kissing her opposite one. "She's a cutie-pie," said Gem, then kissed Bug on the cheek and gave him a half-hug.

"And I take it you're Lola," I said to the blonde girl. "Good to meet you. I'm Flex and this is Gem."

The girl smiled, revealing straight, white teeth. Her eyes were red, but we'd been prepared for that in advance, and had seen our share of the condition before. We'd get the whole story later, especially how it affected her.

"I have *so* been waiting to meet you guys," Lola said. "Dave talks about you like you're comic book superheroes."

"Looks like Dave's the superhero here," said Gem, hugging Lola. I moved in when she let go and gave Lola a bear hug that she returned with enthusiasm.

We glanced over to see that Charlie stood with Dave and Serena, her arms around both of them. They hugged her back, and she stepped away from them, her hands on her stomach. "You're going to be here for the birth!" she said. "I'm so happy about that. God, you're here safe. And you got your uncle, Dave!"

"I did," he said. "If not for Lola and Rachel, not to mention Isis there, we wouldn't be here now. We might still be on our way *to* California."

"Rachel's the pilot?" asked Charlie.

"Yeah, and a hell of a pilot. You should hear what she and Nel did in Dunsmuir, not to mention what she did just now. Anyway, there'll be time for that later. So good to see you guys. God, Charlie, you look good."

"You do," said Serena, hugging her tight. "Beautiful. The proverbial glowing. She leaned forward and whispered something in Charlie's ear that I did not hear.

Charlie's face lit up. "Shut up!" she said.

Serena smiled back at her, and now I couldn't help but smile myself. "What the hell's goin' on?" I asked.

"Yeah, what the hell's going on?" seconded Gem.

"You gonna say it or am I?" asked Charlie.

Now Hemp put his hellos on hold and looked in anticipation.

"I'm pregnant," she said.

"Oh, my God!" said Gem excitedly. "Talk about a baby boom. We're going to have a regular nursery!"

Gem's expression changed suddenly. "You are staying, right? Here?"

Dave shrugged. "That kind of depends on how much Hemp learns about Isis, and what the decision of the group is," said Dave. "I'm going where my Uncle Bug goes. I want him to stay around here, but that little girl does bring with her some interesting problems. I'd understand if the consensus went against … well, what we want."

"Family's family," said Gem. "You'd have to be a serial killer to have blood ties with any of us and be exiled."

Everyone else offered their congratulations and all of the new arrivals, including Lolita Lane and Rachel Reed were well-hugged and welcomed to the family.

"We're going to have to get back out here for more fence detail later on," said Hemp, "but for now, we're done with the mixed concrete. Let's go inside and catch up. Isis can meet the girls and the dogs."

As we all began to walk toward the house, something caught my eye off to the west. It was a tattered rotter, his face fixed on our moving group, and one arm dangling as though broken, the other missing altogether.

"I'll get this one," I said. "Go on inside."

I removed my Glock from my drop holster and walked slowly toward the creature. If I could kill it far enough from our property, we could take our time retrieving the carcass. We had created a burning pile in a pit, and it was working out well. The zombie was very near it.

I picked up my pace. When I reached it, the thing stopped and looked at my hand, holding the gun. One eye was gone, and the other was half out of the socket. His lips were entirely deteriorated, and his former comb over was now draped down to his shoulder on one side, almost non-existent on the other. His rotted teeth gnashed side to side as he emitted the low growl that sounded much like a reverberation of his vocal cords.

As I raised my gun to fire, his one arm moved up, as though to block the bullet, and a piss-poor amount of pink mist sprayed from his tear ducts. He was too slow in movement and too malnourished to generate enough vapor. Besides all that, his hand, even if it had been quick enough, would have been a poor bullet shield anyway. My hollow-point round pierced his forehead and destroyed his brain, sending it out the back of his fragile skull and onto the foliage behind him.

He slumped to the ground, more than a year after the infection that robbed him of everyone, everything and everyplace he knew, and was finally at peace.

I'd move him to the pit later. For the moment, I went into the house to talk to our new friends and family.

*****

Hemp had initially remained quiet, but his eyes never left the little girl called Isis.

Brett Gammon was indeed an older version of Dave, and I liked him right away. He was sort of wild-eyed and a pretty good storyteller, and we all quickly learned everything he'd told the rest of them back in his bunker in California.

"How long after this all began was she exposed?" asked Hemp. "Your wife, I mean. What was her name? Angela?"

"Yeah," said Bug. "I called her Angie."

Hemp looked at us. "This is very interesting, because I was fairly certain that the red vapor was a result of some sort of evolution over time."

Serena spoke up. "We talked about that, Hemp. We thought that maybe the telepathy and other stuff came about over time. The ability to control the zombie masses. We might not have noticed the red vapor versus the pink, especially in groups of them."

"Yes," said Hemp. "But the red eyes. I suppose they could have evolved, too. Doesn't matter anyway. They have the abilities now, don't they?"

"Sure as hell do," I said. "So she's like what? A siren?"

"I want to hear it!" shouted Trina, who had been standing next to Hemp and smiling at the baby, who seemed as taken with her.

"Not that kind of siren," said Bug, smiling and rubbing Trina's hair. Trina pulled back and tried to straighten her blonde locks with her hand while she looked at Bug with curiosity, and I guessed a little uncertainty.

Bug then reached into a pack and withdrew a bag of beef jerky. Isis watched him closely, and her red eyes grew wide, and she smiled, holding her hands.

"Jerky!" she said. "I want a piece, daddy!"

We all stared in amazement.

"How old did you say she is?" asked Hemp.

"Like I told these guys, she was born a bit over a week after this stuff happened," said Bug.

"She just put together a five-word sentence," said Hemp. "That is what gifted children are capable of, and only on rare occasions. Uncanny."

Bug gave her reaching fingers the beef jerky, and she immediately snatched it, said, "Thank you," and started devouring it.

"We got used to this on the trip home," said Dave. "Caught us off guard at first, too."

In mere moments, the jerky was gone and she was looking for the bag. Bug gave her another and she started work again.

"Well, let's show Lola where she's sleeping," said Charlie. "I know you don't have much in the way of luggage, so that part should be easy."

Nelson said, "Dude, I'll set Rachel up with me." He hesitated and shot her a quick glance. "I mean, if that's alright with you, Rach," he added.

"It's fine, Nel," she said, a slightly embarrassed smile on her face. "I'm comfortable with you."

Gem stood and went to Nelson. "Stand up," she ordered.

Nelson did, and opened his arms. He knew what was coming. She hugged him tightly, and he pulled her even tighter. "You gonna kick my ass now?" he asked, his voice muffled in her shoulder.

"There's plenty of time for that," she said. "But I'll need to brush up on my Subdudo if I want to take you down. Right now I'm just glad you're home. We were worried, kid."

"I found Lola here," he said. "She's a siren, too."

"Yeah she is, and she saved us all," said Bug. "If it weren't for her drawin' all those bitches and their dummies away from my door, we'd still be trapped in there."

"When I tell you it was nothing," said Lola, her face flushed red, "I mean it came naturally."

"It wore her out," said Dave. "She kept it up for hours."

Hemp looked at Lola and she shrugged. "I won't lie," she said. "It did tire me out, but thinking about one thing for that long, no matter what the situation, would do the same thing."

26

Hemp's eyes narrowed as he studied her, and I could see his mind working. "Lola," he said, "can you tell me what's involved in calling them? What exactly do you do?"

Lola shook her head. "I don't do anything more than think, come to me, come to me, come to me. Just over and over."

Hemp rubbed his chin. "It must be translated into some command they can understand," he said. "More like a signal than actual words. If that's not the case, then they may have some language skills that we were not aware of."

Lola shrugged. "The first time I did it, I didn't know I was doing it. After I realized I could call them, the simplest command I could think of seemed to work."

"Can you consciously turn it off? The call?" asked Hemp, and the scientist was front and center. He snapped his fingers loudly and said, "Wait! Lola, can you *repel* them?" asked Hemp, staring at her.

She smiled at Hemp's excitement, and I shook my head. She addressed his question: "I think the normal state is off," she said. "I mean, I don't *want* them coming to me as a rule. As for repelling them, I tried once while we were out there," she said. "When they got too close to me and Russell. Nothing happened. That's when I fell. I was worried they were getting on top of us and I tried, but then I remember slipping off that rock. After that, I don't remember anything until I woke up."

"I wonder if the words you're thinking are translated into sort of an impression or a abstract command," said Hemp, obviously thinking aloud. "If I believed in such things, it would be something like a person with telekinesis making an inanimate object move. The object doesn't have to understand what you want it to do, it just moves by the will of the mind."

"You mean after the dead started walking you still have a hard time believing some things?" asked Gem, almost

27

laughing. "Anyway, we've got time to work that stuff out later. For now, I know you guys had a long trip, so if you want to hit the hay for a while, we're all good with that."

"That actually sounds really good," said Rachel.

Lola nodded, too. "I could use some sleep."

"I thought so. We've got extra clothes," said Gem. "My stuff won't fit you, Rachel. Don't take this wrong, but I think Taylor's clothes will.

Rachel smiled. "Don't worry about that," she said. "I'm not offended in the slightest. It won't be the first time I've worn girl's sizes."

"I'll share," said Taylor. Her red hair had gotten long, and Charlie had trimmed it nicely a couple of days before, so she looked cute as a button, her perfect bangs hanging just to her eyebrows.

"C'mon, Rachel," Taylor said. "I'll show you my closet."

"Mine or Charlie's pre-maternity clothes should fit you, Lola." Said Gem. "We'll go on a raid and get you more after you get settled in. Follow them."

Rachel smiled at us and waved as Taylor took Rachel's hand and led her away with Trina and Lola right behind. I figured with Rachel's under five-foot frame, kids took to her. She had a sweet smile, too, and I saw her give Nelson a wink as she left the room.

"She your girl, Nel?" I asked, nudging him.

Nelson returned a shy smirk. "I'm taking it sorta slow, dude," he said. "She's still grieving over her husband."

"Good call," I said. "It's good to have you back. Glad you're okay."

"I was always coming back," said Nelson. "This is home." He pulled a baggie from his shirt pocket and said, "I'll be right back."

He went onto the back porch and faced away from us. I knew he was settling in with a bowl of pot. Things had returned to normal. Plus a little extra.

"Does Isis produce any of the mist?" asked Hemp.

Bug shook his head. His hair was pulled back in a ponytail, and crow's feet formed at his eyes when he squinted. "Nope. Not yet, anyway."

Bug held her on his knee and Hemp asked, "Do you mind if I hold her?"

"Not at all," said Bug. "She's good with everyone. You heard what she put up with back home, right?"

"I did," said Hemp, reaching for her. "A little acrobat, this one."

We'd all heard the Cliff's Notes version. It was the first thing Dave told us when they got in touch via a portable Ham radio that Bug had in his vast array of supplies. They were still on their return trip then.

Hemp lifted Isis and I smiled as he put her on his knee. She stared at him, swallowing her last chunk of beef jerky.

"Little preview of what kind of daddy you're going to make," said Gem.

"I can't wait," said Hemp. "Right, Isis?"

"Right," she said.

Hemp shook his head and smiled as he leaned down to look into her eyes. She did not break the contact, and it almost seemed as though she were analyzing him right back.

Suddenly, she leaned forward and kissed him, a little peck on the lips. Hemp laughed.

"You are a friendly one, aren't you?' he said, and the smile wouldn't leave his lips.

After another second or two of close inspection, he said, "It does appear to be a layer of mist, just like with the more mature red-eyes ... uh, females." He looked at the baby's father. "Sorry about that."

Bug waved his hand in the air. "It is what it is," he said. "She is a little red-eye … only a hell of a lot cuter and a shitload friendlier."

"Aside from her high intelligence and her unique idiosyncrasies, she appears perfectly normal," said Hemp, putting the palm of his hand on her forehead. He then felt her pulse. He looked briefly troubled.

"What's wrong, partner?" asked Bug, obviously catching Hemp's look.

"She's almost cool to the touch, and that's just for starters," he said. "And her pulse seems off."

"What about it?" asked Bug.

"Does she tire easily?" asked Hemp.

Bug shook his head. "No way. She's like a fuckin' Energizer Bunny. Why?"

Hemp took her wrist again and looked at his watch for a long time. "Twenty-one beats in thirty seconds," he said. "Forty two."

"That's really low, right?" I said. "Is that dangerous for a baby?"

Hemp's eyes showed concern, and he again looked into Isis' red ones. "Are you alright, little one?" he asked.

"Perfect," said Isis.

Hemp laughed. "She's cocky, I'll give her that," he said. "Normal heart rate for a 1-2 year old is between 80 and 130. She's at a third of the maximum. It's very low."

"Her color looks fine," said Gem. "I might be on my first kid, but I've seen lots of babies. Flex, you were around Trina and Jesse when they were babies. About the same?"

I shrugged. "I defer to Hemp, but she looks fine to me."

"Yes," said Hemp, biting his lower lip. "She seems to be a healthy little girl, but I'll be looking forward to taking her temperature."

Bug shifted in his seat and seemed uncomfortable for a moment. I saw Dave look at him, and I immediately knew why. Bug didn't make us wait to hear what was on his mind.

"I was worried about comin' here," he said. "After I figured out what was drawin' all the deadheads to my place. I think she's bound to do it wherever she goes. Is that gonna be a problem for you guys?"

Hemp shook his head and looked at me, and I said, "Hell no. You, Gem?"

"Are you kidding?" asked Gem. "She can no more control her abilities than we can control how those things out there react to them."

Nelson came back in and everyone turned. He stopped. "What?"

"I was just saying that we don't have a problem with Isis or her abilities. We'll make do and use all of it to make us stronger."

"Right on, dude," said Nelson. "I never thought anything different."

"Have you got a place I can catch some sleep?" asked Bug, standing as he hoisted Isis on one arm.

"Catch a nap here, Unk," said Dave. "I guess Serena and I weren't too convinced we'd find you and talk you into coming back with us. But, it was always our plan to set you up in the guest house at our place. Or in the main house if you want. Anyway, it's a decent place. Might have been for workers, but it just needs a little sweeping and some bedding. We'll head home and it'll be ready for you by the time you nod out for a while."

Bug nodded. "Thanks, kid, and no rush. I'm good here for a while. You take Serena and head over and don't worry about cleanin' that place up for me just yet. You need some shuteye, too."

He looked around the room and his expression turned melancholy. "I'm real glad you found me, Davey. It's good to be with family and friends for a change. Talk about goin' stir crazy."

Gem walked up and hugged the elder Gammon as he held the baby. She nuzzled Isis's nose with hers before pulling away, then kissed Bug on the cheek. "God, she's cute," she said, smiling. "And you look like some fuckin' Berkley professor."

"Far from it," said Bug. "I was plannin' to vote for Romney when all this shit hit the fan. Absentee ballot, of course."

Gem winked at him. He winked back, but I'm certain that whatever message was sent back and forth was lost to both of them. I was guessing that Gem didn't believe him, and that he didn't believe she didn't believe him.

"Did I tell you she's cute as hell?" asked Gem.

"You're cute!" said Isis, smiling big.

Gem's eyes went wide and her smile disappeared. "She's got … like adult teeth."

"Part of her charm," said Bug. "She seems to let people fall in love with her before she shows them. I think it's her intuition."

"Wow," said Gem, shaking her head. "Anyway, there are lots of couches and lots of bedding. It looks like everyone else nodded out, so you might as well, too. Go down that hallway and turn into the second door on the right. Our room. Nice 7' couch in there. Close the door and we'll leave you for a few hours."

Bug ran his fingers through his hair. "I see why Dave likes you guys so much," he said. "This one here will just hang out with me. I think it recharges her to be around people who are sleeping, even if she doesn't."

"I still can't believe that," said Hemp. "I'm going to want to spend quite a bit of time with her if you don't mind," he added.

"If you can learn from her, go for it," said Bug. "She'll let you know when she's done with you."

Flex Jr. slept soundly in his crib. Gem got up and leaned over him, touching her finger to his lips. He gave a tiny snort and stayed out cold.

"Love this kid," she said. "It's like he has strings attached directly to my heart."

"I'm gonna head down the street and get some sleep," said Nelson. "Feels good to be home. I'll have the radio on if you guys need anything."

"Sounds good, Nel," I said. "Any ideas where we can set these folks up?"

Nelson shrugged. "There's still those two places just off Shelton," he said. "Remember? We cleared them when we got here."

I did remember. "Yeah, tin roof on one of them, right? Maybe Rachel and Lola wouldn't mind sharing."

"Dude, remember?" Nelson said. "Rach is coming with me."

"Your memory sucks," said Gem, teasing me.

"That's cool," I said. "I've got you, and you're always right. I've come to rely on you."

"Smart ass," said Gem. "But we've got Dave's uncle and Isis, too. Maybe they can settle in the other. Be good to have him close to Lola."

"Lola's about as close to a red-eye as you can get without being a zombie," said Nelson. "I'm thinking she doesn't need anyone for protection, but they do know one another. Plus, he has a shitload of guns he brought from his bunker."

"You'll have to tell me about that place one of these days," I said.

"Over a joint, brother," said Nelson. "Photographic memory. I won't leave anything out."

Nelson left.

33

There was a knock on the door.

No. Allow me to correct that statement. There was a sudden pounding on the door, followed by the sound of a woman's screams.

We jumped up and ran to see what the hell was going on.

*****

Chapter Two

By the time we opened the door, the woman who had pounded on it had begun to run away, pulling what appeared to be a young girl with her. She was screaming, and looking behind her, so we followed her terrified gaze.

Three creatures now angled toward her, staggering determinedly after them, but still thirty yards away.

I leaned down to grab my Daewoo, which was in its standard location by the door, and hurried onto the porch and down the steps.

"Stop!" I called after the pair, but Gem had already passed me, saying, "You get the rotters, babe. I'll go after them."

I chambered a round and raised the weapon, walking briskly toward the oncoming mini-horde. I stopped. I didn't want to fire the gun and awaken everyone in the house, but it couldn't be helped. It's not my instinct to grab urushiol or a baseball bat.

I turned and saw that Gem had reached the woman and girl, and was now guiding them toward the front door. I waited.

Once they were inside, I advanced on the flesh-hungry creatures, who were now advancing on me. When they were ten feet away and saw the weapon in my hands, they hesitated, as I had grown used to. Once again, without the red-eyes to guide them, they had nothing more up their blood-soaked, tattered sleeves than the ability to recognize danger. In other words, they had no plan B.

I was glad. I fired, holding down the trigger in full auto mode. With a side-to-side sweep, I blew their faces into a spray of the now familiar red-black, chunky mist, each of the ghouls collapsing in their own unique, walking dead way.

I made a mental note to add their cleanup to our list of immediate tasks, and went back inside.

I was concerned, though. No doubt about that. This was four of them in under three hours. We hadn't seen those kinds of numbers in that short a timeframe in quite a long time. I wondered if this was Isis at work as I mounted the steps and went back inside the house.

The girl was sick. I could see it in her musculature, her eyes and her complexion. She breathed with difficulty and had bouts of sneezing.

After ten minutes, Hemp said, "Take little Flexy into the other room, would you?"

Gem, her eyes filled with worry, said, "Hemp? What's wrong? What is it?"

"I'm not certain," he said. "I'll need to speak with … what is your name, ma'am?"

"Raylene Hackett," she said, still out of breath from her narrow escape. "That's my daughter, Gina."

Gem hurried out of the room, our son clutched in her arms.

"How old is Gina, Mrs. Hackett?" asked Hemp, concern in his eyes. He lifted the child's eyelids and peered into each of them.

I didn't like the look on his face one bit.

The woman looked confused. "I … I don't know what month it is," she said, crying. "She's either four or five, depending on that. Her birthday's September 21st."

"Then she's still four," said Hemp. "Flex, can you get Doc Scofield on the radio?"

Scofield had decided to stay locally, and lived in a house about an eighth of a mile from us. He had a moped that he used to get back and forth, so could be here in a few minutes.

"I'll get on it," I said. I went into the kitchen and pulled the handheld out of the drawer. We kept them on because they didn't draw a heck of a lot of power when they weren't transmitting or receiving, and these had essentially become our telephones.

Scofield answered in thirty seconds and I told him to hightail it over as fast as he could.

I went back into the living room, and Hemp was still kneeling down by the sick girl. "Hemp, can I talk to you for a sec?"

Hemp nodded, touched the girl's cheek, and stood. "Mrs. Hackett, take her over to the couch and let her lie down. We'll be right back in."

She was following our instructions as we rounded the corner into the laundry room, now equipped with not only the electric washer and dryer, but also a wash tub and an old-fashioned washboard. We still used the electric utilities, but only when there were large amounts of laundry to do. When it was one or two pieces, we hand washed to save the generator fuel. We had yet to install the solar panels we intended to pilfer from somewhere.

"What are you thinking?" I asked. "Girl's pretty sick, huh?"

"It could be a flu," said Hemp. "I don't like the look of it at all. What did Doc Scofield say?"

"He'll be right over," I answered. "He's leaving now."

When we returned to the living room, Bug was there with Isis, who stood in front of Gina and gnawed on a piece of beef jerky. Gina sneezed.

"Bug," said Hemp, an edge in his voice. "Please take Isis back to your room. I'll explain later."

37

"Sorry, man. Heard what sounded like gunshots and laid there for a while, but Isis wanted to roam."

"It's not a problem," said Hemp. "The girl's sick, and we don't want it to spread to anyone else."

Bug eyed her for a moment, said, "Nice to meet you guys," and scooped up Isis. He nodded to us and left the room. Isis called, "Bye bye, little girl!"

Gina did not laugh or even smile, and hadn't said a word since she'd come into the house. She was out of it, miserable and obviously very ill.

Hemp sat on the chair across from them and I took another one. "Ma'am," he said. "I have an important question for you."

"What is it?" asked Raylene. Her hair was a tangled mess, and bits of grass and leaves were caught in it. Her eyes were an interesting, almost royal blue, and their intensity fell in sharp contrast to her dirty, gaunt face. "What's wrong with my baby?"

Hemp shook his head. "The doctor, a man named Jim Scofield, is on the way now. I'd prefer to consult with him before I reach a conclusion that may be incorrect."

She nodded her understanding.

"Raylene," I said, "Where did you come from? Before you got here?"

She swiped at her tears, which seemed to be leaking from her eyes constantly. She wasn't sobbing, but I guessed she was so damned glad to be indoors in a safe place that she was an emotional wreck.

"I don't know how far I come," she said. "I was with my daddy up until about three nights ago – that's how I figure the days, because nights are so scary – but he got turned."

Hemp shot me a quick glance, and I acknowledged it and ignored it at the same time.

"What do you mean by *turned*?" asked Hemp, his voice soothing and non-threatening.

I figured he knew the answer to that question, but I didn't blame him for asking.

"An old man, a neighbor from down the street, came by the house the other day. He was sneezing and sick, like my Gina. We knew him since I was a little girl. His name was Roy Dickens, and I guess he was about the oldest man I've ever known."

"Did he pass away?" asked Hemp. "From the sickness?"

She shook her head. "Didn't get a chance. He was all bundled up when he got there, sayin' he was cold and not feelin' good. He scared us when he first showed up because he had a machete in his hand, and we thought he was crazy."

I looked at her, and she met my eyes with hers. "What do you mean he didn't get the chance?" I asked.

"We told him he could stay on the couch that night, but he'd have to go find another place in the mornin'," she said. "We didn't have a hotel – at least that's what daddy said – and we had to take care of our own. He was nice enough about it, but he started complainin' about a bad headache along with everything else that seemed wrong with him. When he took off his jacket, I saw bite marks on his arms."

"Did your father see them?" Hemp asked, glancing at me again.

She shook her head. "No, and I didn't say anything. He was leavin' in the mornin' and I didn't want to be cruel. I thought daddy might kick him out."

I shook my head. "I'm guessing he changed in the night?" I asked.

She looked at Gina, who now lay back on the sofa, her eyes open only to narrow slits. Looking at her sick daughter, I had no illusions that Gina could hear or comprehend anything we said just then.

Raylene's tears came in a torrent. "I heard this terrible screamin' in the middle of the night, and I grabbed Gina. She wasn't sick then, she was just fine. She was half asleep, and I'm glad of it. I ran to my daddy's bedroom, and Mr. Dickens was on top of daddy, growlin' like a dog."

She stopped speaking for a bit and stroked her child's hair, but Gina didn't notice as far as I could tell. After a pause to cry some quiet tears, she continued, her voice shaking.

"It was pretty dark, but with the moonlight comin' through the window I could see my daddy on his back on the bed with Mr. Dickens on top of him, bitin' him. Daddy had his shotgun in his hand, but he couldn't do nothin' with it. It fell on the ground and he was screamin' and screamin'. I stood there screamin', too, but then Mr. Dickens turned to look at me. His eyes were red, and there was this smoke puffin' out of them, and I just ran with Gina and I never looked back."

"It was the best thing to do for you and your daughter," said Hemp, reassuringly. "I'm sure you know by now that once you're bitten, if untreated, a transformation takes place."

"He wasn't bitin' him," she whispered. "Mr. Dickens was eatin' him."

Her tears became shudders and I realized that Hemp had never asked the question he wanted to ask. A knock came on the door. I got up and walked to it, checked the peephole, and let Doc Scofield in.

He nodded to me and said, "Hey, Flex. Good to see you." I shook his hand and looked over toward the girl. "Thanks for comin', Doc. She's over there. Name's Gina."

Scofield hurried over and struggled to kneel down in front of the couch. Gina's head was resting in her mother's lap. Scofield used his stethoscope and listened to her heart and her breathing, and we just sat there, letting him finish in silence.

"I'm Jim Scofield, ma'am," he said. "Sorry about your girl. How long has she been like this?" he asked.

Jim's kind eyes met hers, and I was sure they set her at ease. He was good at that.

"I'm Raylene Hackett," she said. "Gina took a turn about a day after I left our house. I guess it's been about three days now."

"Has it gotten progressively worse?" he asked.

"Progressively?"

"I'm sorry," said Scofield. "I mean to ask if it keeps getting worse from the day before. She hasn't seemed any better one day to the next?"

Raylene shook her head. "We haven't had much food since we run, so we're both pretty weak. This is the worst she's been. I'm worried about her. I had to pull her along all day today, 'cause I don't have the strength to carry her anymore."

Scofield reached inside of his bag to get something, and the girl sneezed. Her mother had seen it coming and put her hand over the child's mouth. When she pulled it away, there was a fine, red mist on her skin.

"Is she bleeding?" I asked.

Gina moaned and her eyes flittered open, but remained unfocused. She yawned, and this provided Scofield the opportunity to use the item he'd removed from his bag. He turned on the penlight and shone it into her open mouth.

Hemp leaned forward and put a gentle hand on her jaw, keeping her mouth open a little longer as he looked inside.

There was a change in Hemp then. Right then. I saw it as clearly as I saw those three rotters comin' toward me outside. He then slid his hands onto her neck, feeling her glands. "Swollen," he said, looking at Scofield and me.

Scofield shifted in his seat. I saw a change in him, too.

"Is it a flu or something?" Raylene asked.

Fuck. I wished it was the flu. But my instincts had already told me something dangerous had entered our home.

41

"Raylene," said Hemp, his voice low and steady. "Did you have Gina immunized as a baby?"

"Shots, you mean?"

"Exactly," said Hemp.

She shook her head. "No, because everybody was sayin' that there's so much autism around that it's from all those vaccinations and stuff they're pumpin' into the kids. She was born at home and I didn't have any of that stuff done and she's always been fine."

I stood up and paced the room. I thought about Gem, and I thought about my son.

Hemp's expression remained as neutral as he could muster, but I knew the man. The next thing he said confirmed my fears.

"Jim, do you have a surgical mask or something similar in that bag?"

"I do," said Jim, pulling one out. He tore open the plastic and gave it to Hemp.

Hemp took it and put it over the girl's nose and mouth.

"What's wrong?" asked Raylene. "Is my baby gonna be alright?"

"Just a few more questions, first," said Hemp. "How old was the neighbor who came over that night? The Dickens fellow."

Scofield looked confused. "This must've been stuff you talked about before I got here," he said. "What neighbor?"

Hemp nodded and said, "A neighbor of theirs came over the night she ran from her house," he said. "She said he was sick."

"I'm pretty sure he was in his eighties," said Raylene. "Pretty spry before, though."

"Did he exhibit similar symptoms to Gina?"

She thought for a moment. "Sneezin', temperature, high-pitched breathin'. Yeah, now that you mention it. I thought she probably got it from bein' around him."

"What do you know about his family?" asked Hemp. "Did they see physicians regularly?

"Heck no," she said. "They were about as bumpkin as you could get. Even worse than us. He was the oldest in their family. They died young, as a rule."

"Raylene, do you know if you were immunized as a child?" asked Scofield.

She shrugged. "I was born at St. Joseph's, so I suppose so."

Scofield and Hemp looked at one another and both stood, Scofield with a good grunt accompanying the movement. He'd had quite a belly on him when we first met, but now his belt was pulled to its last hole, and I could see where he'd even punched two additional ones. His pants bagged on him.

"We'll be right back," said Hemp, nodding to me and Doc Scofield. We followed him into the other room and slid the pocket door closed.

"What are you thinking?" I asked.

"What I'm thinking is not good, Flex," said Hemp. He turned toward Doc Scofield. "Jim, have you ever seen a case of Diphtheria?"

Scofield snapped his fingers. "That's right, Hemp. That black, fiber-like coating in her throat. I knew I'd seen it somewhere before, but it was only in pictures from when I studied it. And that was a *long* time ago."

"That's what convinced me," said Hemp. "Not to mention the bloody sneeze."

"I don't wanna be cruel, but we have to get her out of my house, fucking pronto," I said.

"Can't we just set her up in the basement?" asked Scofield. "It's big enough, and I didn't see any mold or anything down there."

Hemp shook his head. "She appears to be in the midst of the most contagious phase of the disease, which is pretty much the entire duration," he said. "Flex is right. She needs to be out of this house as soon as possible."

I realized I was pissed, but I couldn't blame anyone for it. Instead of blaming, I asked the obvious question. "Wasn't this shit wiped out a long time ago?"

Hemp shook his head. "Diphtheria and other diseases can be contained, but not necessarily eradicated. Regular vaccinations, plus antitoxin, dealt with the problem when it did appear."

"How can something like this fire up again, Hemp?" I asked. "It's not like we don't have enough to worry about these days."

"When there is a breakdown of society and immunizations aren't performed, these are the things that can rear their ugly heads again," said Hemp. "I knew the answer to the question of her daughter's vaccine status before I even asked. While Diphtheria has been controlled for many years, it has cropped back up a number of times since then."

"Do we still get shots for that?" I asked.

"Yep," said Scofield. "Diphtheria is part of the normal childhood boosters. I read about a case in Alaska – in the 1920s I think – where dog sleds were used to run the antitoxin from somewhere across the state to Nome. Whole communities were in danger of infection, which could've killed thousands. Not just Nome, but neighboring towns, too."

"Jim's right," said Hemp. "They transported the serum over 600 miles via dog sled. In fact, the Iditarod is in commemoration of what was then called The Great Race of Mercy."

I could feel the hairs on the back of my neck standing on end. "Hemp, Doc," I said, looking at the men, and looking scared, I knew. "How does it spread?"

Hemp looked grim. "Through the respiratory system, I'm afraid," he said. "It can also be transferred in food, or by touch."

"And exactly how contagious is it?" I asked, my muscles tense. I could only picture Flexy sitting in his playpen when Gina let out her bloody sneezes. Isis had been in there with her for a moment, too.

Hemp put a hand on my shoulder. "It is extremely contagious. And yes, I know what you're thinking, and I'm thinking the same thing. We need antitoxin for little Flex and Isis. And it can't hurt us all to have a booster, too. But Flex," he said, his voice grim. "We need it quickly."

I immediately thought of Gem. She would freak out and there would be no calming her. My mind worked over the ways this could be hidden from her, but it just wasn't possible to do that and keep our son safe, too. The sick girl and her mother needed to be out of the house immediately – before one more sneeze spread more of the disease – and I needed to get to where the antitoxin was.

Scofield said, "First order of business is to find a place for those two and to keep them both away from everyone else. Just to be safe. I'm guessing everybody's had the proper shots, but we just don't know what their parents did, and they were too young to know. Better safe than sorry."

"What chance is there that you're wrong about the Diphtheria, Hemp?" I asked.

Hemp shook his head. "Very little, I'm afraid. Just be glad she's presenting with symptoms. Sometimes they have none at all. There would have been no warning."

"Then you're making me a list of any and all other vaccines I might need," I said. "I'm leaving today. Tell me where I have to go."

"Flex, we don't know –" started Hemp.

"There's lots we don't know, but what I do know is I don't want my son or Isis to die. That's possible, right? This shit can kill you?"

Hemp nodded. "Whatever the mortality rate, it needs treatment."

"What is the rate?" I asked.

Hemp shook his head. "Anywhere from 5% to 20%. Dependent upon age."

"Younger's worse, right?" I asked.

Hemp knew better than to paint shit with pastels with me, and said, "Let's just say we'll need to remove the infected girl and her mother from the house right away as Jim suggested and set them up somewhere else."

"What about my guest house?" asked Jim. "Nobody's in there, plus it's clean. I didn't have anything to do so I got it ready for company."

I didn't wait. I slid the door open and went into the living room. I felt every muscle in my body as tight as a drum, and none of them would unwind until I got on the road to find what we needed to protect my son.

"Raylene, we have a situation here, so do me a big favor and save any questions," I began. "Let's go ahead and get Gina up, and you're gonna go with Doc Scofield here."

"What's wrong?" she asked, violating my first mandate.

Hemp came in and knelt down beside the girl. She was stirring, and Hemp ran his hands gently up and down her legs until she winced. He looked at me briefly, then turned his attention back to the child, sliding up the pant leg on the leg that caused her pain.

I looked in horror as an oozing sore appeared beneath her clothing. It looked like a bloody crater made of raw flesh.

"This settles it," said Hemp, nodding to me and Doc Scofield.

"Oh, my God!" screamed Raylene at the sight of the dripping, pus-coated lesion. Her cry was all it took for Gem to come charging into the room.

"What the hell's going on?" asked Gem.

Hemp looked at Gem but said nothing. He had already pulled the girl's pant leg back down, so she hadn't gotten a glimpse of the horror that, left untreated, could come to our son.

Still on my feet, I staggered backward, steadying myself on a table. "Hurry, Hemp," I gulped.

Hemp nodded and scooped up the little girl. He said nothing to Gem, just carried her out the front door with Raylene on his heels, crying. Doc Scofield followed them outside.

I heard gunshots almost instantly.

"What the fuck!" I shouted as I ran to the porch. Scofield had dispatched a male rotter who had been just outside the porch. Another one.

"Everybody needs to get on the fuckin' WAT-5," I yelled. "Jesus!"

It seemed every piece of shit for miles around had hit the fan today. Our friends and family had come home, the zombies started traipsing in like goddamned homing pigeons and a kid with Diphtheria had now infected our house.

"Flex, tell me what the hell is going on, please," said Gem, her brown eyes piercing and stern. She wasn't asking. The *please* was just a courtesy because she loved me.

"I *know*, Gem, and I will tell you," I said, sweat pouring down my face. "First help me drag this goddamned couch out of here," I said, running to the back door and sliding it open all the way.

"Why?" she asked. "Just *tell* me, Flex!"

I struggled to pull the couch myself, and felt myself spiraling out of control. I wanted to spare Gem the horrible knowledge of what might be as long as I could.

47

"Gemina, if you want to know what's going on, just *help* me!" I screamed. "Where's Flexy?"

Now her near-angry expression turned to fear. She knew me better than I knew myself. I never raised my voice to her unless we were in grave danger.

Her voice responded in a whisper. "In the nursery, sleeping."

"Is he okay?" I asked, looking her in the eyes.

"What the hell do you mean, *is he okay*? He's fine, Flex. What the hell? You're scaring me to death!"

"Couch first," I said, lifting one end. She got behind it and pushed, and I pulled it effortlessly to the door. When I got it onto the wood deck outside, I lifted it over the rail, ran around to the back side, and flipped it over, where it fell four feet to the sloped ground below, rolling away from the house.

"There," I said. "We'll burn the motherfucker later."

"Flex!" said Gem. "Enough of this shit, and tell me what the hell is going on!" Her eyes now burned into me like open flames, and I went to her and pulled her into my arms. I felt her rigid body, none of the tension leaving her, despite the forced embrace.

I let go of her, walked to the table and sat down. She followed, her instincts telling her I was ready to share what I knew.

With one hand, I pulled out a chair for her, but as she reluctantly moved to sit down, I stopped her.

"Hold on. This involves Bug and Isis, too," I said, "I'll figure out how to put this, and you go get Charlie and Bug. Tell him to leave Isis with Trina and Taylor for now."

"Is this you stalling?" asked Gem.

"No, this is me bein' short and sweet. Once I'm done, I'm leaving."

"Flex?" she said, sounding helpless. "What is it?"

"Get 'em, babe," I said. "Hurry."

*****

Hemp had gotten Scofield, Raylene and Gina on their way, and had come back inside the house. He sat beside me, and Bug, Charlie and Gem sat across from us. Just as I opened my mouth to speak, Hemp glanced toward the vacant space that the couch once occupied.

"Good," he said. "I was going to suggest we do exactly that."

"Hemp," I said, "You think you can tell these guys what's going on without freaking them out? 'Cause I don't think I'm gonna be too good at it."

Hemp nodded and looked at the others. His expression was serious, but not as grim as what I figured mine looked like.

"I take it you've all heard of the disease called Diphtheria," he said, looking at the others.

"Diphtheria?" said Gem, incredulous. "Wasn't that eradicated? Like Polio?"

Hemp shook his head. "Controlled through immunizations, like Polio. One of the standard childhood boosters."

"Isis hasn't had any shots," said Bug, his brows furrowed together as he rubbed his beard in a very familiar, Dave-like way.

"I suspected as much," said Hemp.

"Is everyone susceptible?" asked Gem, her stare intense, her brown eyes open wide.

Hemp shrugged, and immediately held up his hands. "I'm sorry to shrug. I am confident that if you had your course of vaccinations as a child, you are protected, but as you know, as Bug said, we have some new members of the world here with us."

Charlie sat there listening, her hands resting on her stomach, as round as a beach ball and so ready to pop you

49

could bounce a quarter off it. It wasn't like her not to ask questions, so I knew she was scared shitless.

"Jesus fuckin' Christ," said Bug, jumping out of his seat and pacing back and forth. He stopped and turned back toward us. "I leave my damned bunker, surrounded by hundreds of zombies and shit, and walk into this? My girl's at risk now?"

"Bug," said Hemp, his voice soft and even, "I understand how you feel. Out of the frying pan and into the flames, so to speak. We've become a close group, and that includes Dave. You and Isis mean a lot to him, therefore, you automatically mean a lot to everyone here."

"Okay, I get that," said Bug. "But how does that change what happened and what we do about it?"

Hemp sighed and put his elbows on the table, resting his chin on his clasped hands as he looked at all of us. "Only by letting you know that Isis is as important to all of us as Flex and Gem's son and our future child. Believe that. And know that I'm not without ideas here, so let me get through this, and we'll formulate a plan."

Bug nodded and glanced toward the hallway where I knew Isis played in a room with the other kids.

Hemp turned to Gem. "Gem, try to remember that this is nobody's fault. If blame must be assigned, you should look right here, at me."

"I'm not trying to blame anyone," she said. "I'm worried as shit, that's all. And why would you take the blame anyway?"

"Shit happens," said Charlie, breaking her silence. "And I'm not sure why I need to say that, considering what's been hunting us for over a year now. Nobody's to blame, least of all my husband."

"I know that, sweetie," said Gem. "Sorry."

Charlie nodded.

Hemp continued. "The reason I say to blame me is because we're such an isolated group I hadn't considered that we needed the immunization supply in advance of our children's births. You can't vaccinate newborns anyway, and I thought we could wait until Charlie gave birth."

"And I realize none of you anticipated my girl," said Bug.

"Little Flexy is just reaching the very minimum age to receive some of his vaccinations," said Hemp. "Isis can have them now, of course."

Gem's expression softened. "First of all, is it an absolute that everyone who isn't vaccinated against Diphtheria will get it?"

"It's highly contagious," said Hemp. "In multiple ways. The girls didn't come out and see Gina, so they may be okay."

Charlie got up and walked toward the hallway. "I'm going to make sure they don't leave that room."

"It doesn't matter now," said Hemp. "Isis was exposed and she's with the girls now. The good news is, both Taylor and Trina are well within ten years of their Diphtheria immunization, so they'll be just fine."

"Isn't it too late to vaccinate once it's been contracted?" asked Gem.

Hemp gave her a weak smile. "Diphtheria is very treatable with antitoxin."

"Which we get where?" asked Gem, her hands clutching one another nervously.

"The CDC mandates stockpiles in strategic areas around the country in the event of an outbreak, so from here, I believe the closest location would be the Hospital of the Carolinas in Charlotte, North Carolina."

"I don't want to be an asshole," I said, "but what if there's not any when I get there?"

Hemp looked at me like he hadn't considered that.

"Yes, good point," he said. "Flex, the next closest stockpile would be the Beaufort Naval Hospital, but I'd guess it's over 200 miles from here."

"I'm going to the closest place first," I said. "How far's Beaufort from that Carolinas hospital?"

"We'll map it all out before you leave," said Hemp. "With alternate routes, too, in the event of road blockages."

"Vaccines and shit need refrigeration, right?" asked Bug. "Gotta stay cold? Doesn't that mean most of that crap went bad right after the power went out?"

Gem's eyes turned to steel. "Hemp?" she said, staring at the professor.

"Yes to most vaccines, no to the antitoxin," said Hemp. "The Diphtheria antitoxin is freeze dried," he said. "It's kept in vials and is activated with saline."

"Can it go bad?" asked Gem.

"Yes, but it has a long shelf life, and I'm certain all the supply in Charlotte wouldn't be on the cusp of going bad."

"Hemp," said Gem, worry in her voice. "What about the other vaccines our kids will need? You said *yes and no*. Will *they* be viable? Can we get them at the same time?"

"I can't tell you how relieved I am to be able to give this answer," said Hemp. "And a couple of years ago, I would not have had good news."

"Spit it out, buddy," I said, fidgeting.

"Dr. Scott Cooper, whose lab is within the hospital facility in Charlotte, North Carolina, has been working on a breakthrough that has been long deemed crucial in societal collapse situations such as this. His goal was to develop extremely stabilized strains of all available vaccines that can withstand heat or freezing. In the past, refrigeration was required to maintain the viability of all vaccines. If the temperature of the vaccine fell below freezing or heated beyond a certain level, they became ineffective."

"Did he do it?" asked Bug, optimism in his voice.

"It is my understanding that he was successful, using the same process across the board," said Hemp. "I am not familiar with the details, as I wasn't directly involved, but the FDA was reviewing his work and I understand they were close to approving it for mass distribution."

"And I assume this is significant because he had his residency at the hospital I'm heading to?" I asked.

"Cooper has a lab at the Hospital of the Carolinas," said Hemp. "And an office. I would guess he also has a supply of the vaccines we need."

"That is wonderful news, Hemp," said Gem. "But let's get back to the Diphtheria, since that's what's scaring the shit out of me now. How long does it take to show symptoms after you're exposed?" Gem asked.

"Gem, sometimes there are no symptoms," said Hemp. "I don't want anyone getting a false sense of security."

"Oh," said Gem, "I don't think anyone's all too secure about anything these days, so don't worry about that. But with or without symptoms, what are we talking about?"

"Anywhere from one to four days," said Hemp. "and I'm glad you got rid of the couch. "The germ can live outside of the body for a time. Not long, but long enough, so I want a bleach wipe-down out here, and any loose blankets –"

"Burned," interrupted Gem. "Fire is what we do with any loose fucking blankets."

"Okay, besides you, who's going to get the antitoxin?" asked Hemp.

"Me," I said. "*Just me*. I don't want anyone slowin' me down, and I'm goddamned motivated. I go alone."

Gem stared at me. "Flex, that's bullshit."

"I think it's obvious that you're staying here with our son," I said. "I'll take a truck with a winch. We got that Land Cruiser that Hemp tricked out with the cow catcher, a heavy duty winch and the AK-47. I'll be fine."

"Take my Crown Vic," said Gem. "Nothing can get in there."

"Too low to the ground, Gem," I said. "I need something with a higher suspension and four-wheel drive."

Hemp had perfected the original design of the Crown Victoria and my first Suburban, and he'd fabricated some magazines with enormous capacity. The winch on the Toyota was bigger than any we'd used before, and it had a nice cow catcher, too. It was the vehicle to take and I had no doubt of that.

"You have to take someone," said Charlie, standing in the hall. We hadn't noticed she'd returned from the bedroom until she spoke.

"How are the girls?" asked Gem.

"They're fine," said Charlie. "Flex, you need someone to watch your back. Buddy system, remember."

"Well, I'm not taking Hemp, because he needs to be here with you, Charlie. I'm not taking Dave or Nelson or any of the new crew because they just got home. I can do this, Gem. I can."

A knock came on the door, only it wasn't so much a knock as a frantic pounding.

I ran over and grabbed my gun again, then checked the peephole.

I pulled the door open. Tony Mallette's big, white teeth met me, but there was a look of alarm on his face, not a smile.

"You see all these fuckin' zombies out here, Flex?" he asked.

I leaned outside. Two were dead just on the edge of the property line. I saw another two moving in the distance, on their way.

"I didn't hear you shoot 'em," I said.

Tony held up a silenced handgun. "I didn't wanna bother anyone," he said. "Used my suppressor."

"And yet you're here, botherin' us."

Tony's eyes flashed, and his expression turned from pleasant to angry. I pulled the door open wide.

"You fall for my shit every time, Mallette," I said, forcing a smile. "Get in here. We got some bad news."

"It's been a while since we seen numbers like this, Flexy," said Tony, stepping inside.

"I'll explain that later," I said. "You up for a road trip, Tony?"

"With you?"

I nodded. "Yeah. It's important."

"Who else?" asked Tony. His short-sleeved shirt was buttoned from just below his solar plexus, down. He'd removed most of his gold chains, but still wore two or three rope chains, and a serpentine with a dangling, Italian *cornicello*, an amulet designed to ward off the evil eye.

I shook my head. "Nobody. Just you and me. We could have a big storm to deal with and we need speed over numbers."

"When do we leave, brother?" asked Tony, the smile now spreading over his bright, white caps. "I like road trips."

"As soon as you grab your shit. We should be back in a day at most, but bring enough for two or three."

"What are we takin'?" he asked.

"The Land Cruiser."

"I'll be back in half an hour," he said. He spun on his heel and jogged his leather work boots back to his Harley, threw his leg over, fired the engine and spun gravel as he left the yard.

I watched as he withdrew his gun again and rode along the dirt and rock road, close to where the straggler rotters were advancing. He braked, put his feet down, and took each of them out with well-placed shots to their brains. The red-black mist pluming from their shattered skulls was visible from my vantage point at the door.

"He's a good guy, but he's a trip," said Gem over my shoulder. "He'll be great to have along."

"Feel better?" I said, turning to put my arms around her and close the door with my boot.

"Not until you're both back," she said. "With that antitoxin shit."

"I know how important it is, babe. I'll be careful and I'll get what we need. I won't come back without it."

"It's my biggest fear," she said in my ear, her voice a whisper.

"It can't match my biggest fears, Gem," I said. "Don't worry. I'll be back."

*****

Chapter Three

Hemp had pulled out some of the CDC maps he'd gotten from Max Romero, and while they were excellent and told me where we'd run into hills and various other terrain, they weren't tight enough for us to determine where to navigate around any road blockages.

As a backup, we'd nabbed a 2012 Rand McNally road atlas that I didn't figure had changed much since the zombie apocalypse. Not yet, anyway. I'm pretty damned sure that as the years pass, some of the bridges on a lot of these maps will just crumble and fall. They sure don't build shit like they used to.

Thought I'd never peruse a road atlas again after the advent of the automobile GPS. Easy come, easy go. What'd we get to use it for, anyway? Like twelve years?

"You'll drive along this road here out of town," he said.

"I can get that far, Hemp," I said. "I've left town before, you know."

Hemp laughed. "Sorry, Flex. Just being my usual thorough self." He ran his finger along the main road out of Whitmire and I saw then that he had a yellow highlighter in his hand. He found every place where multiple roads would lead us to the same place and highlighted the alternate routes.

"Good job," I said. "Should get me around any problems we run into."

There was a knock on the door, and it opened. Tony came in wearing a leather jacket and leather pants.

"Hey, buddy, we're not takin' bikes," I said. "We're takin' the Land Cruiser like I said."

"Too hot?" he asked, the heavy crow's feet on the sides of his eyes scrunching. "Repels bites. I'm wearing regular pants underneath. These are oversized." He pulled at the loose leather.

I shrugged. "It's up to you, dude, but your balls are gonna be one sweaty mess."

Tony looked doubtful for a moment. "You're right," he said. "I'll take 'em off, but can I leave 'em here? I don't wanna go all the way back home."

"You ride your bike?"

"Yeah. The wind is really picking up out there, Flex."

"I know. Makes me wish we still had satellite. Either way, we gotta go. Pull the bike back into the garage and just change in there. Come here first."

Tony walked over to the table with the maps spread out. He looked into the living room where Bug was on his hands and knees, scrubbing the floor. Tony looked at us and tipped his head to the stranger. "Who's that? Hired help?"

"That's right," I said. "You haven't met the new arrivals yet."

Bug looked up. "Hey, man. Name's Bug."

"Like a bug you squash?" asked Tony, smiling. He walked over pulling off his gloves and held out his hand. "Tony Mallette."

Bug waved him off. "Bleach, buddy. We got a little germ problem, which is why you're going with Flex."

"Okay, we'll shake later," said Tony. He looked around nervously and I noticed him pull his gloves back on.

Tony was a germaphobe. His expression was dead serious as he turned back toward us. When Tony got a serious expression, it always looked like he was on the verge of whipping out a firearm and threatening everyone in the room, but not actually shooting them.

"What's goin' on, guys. You can tell me."

Hemp laughed as he stared back at Tony. I liked it when Hemp laughed, especially when the mood was tense.

I knew Hemp, who had basically been a child prodigy with mechanics and could master anything he set his mind to, was often mesmerized by Tony because of his gravelly voice, his Long Island accent and his need to be told something five times before it really sank in.

It's not that Tony's a dense guy, because he's not. When he sets his mind to something – learning something, that is – he'll dedicate himself to mastering the task, and he won't stop until he's better than anyone else – or at least until he thinks he's better.

I think he just has a bad case of Attention Deficit Disorder. He'll ask you a question and instantly let his mind wander while you give him the answer.

Yep. Tony sees shiny things that draw his attention away. A lot. Worse still, he laughs about it.

But holy shit, if Tony thinks he knows something and you fuck up doing that thing in front of him, hold on to your ass. He'll tell you that you rushed it, or you didn't try, or that you need to slow down, or some crap.

Good thing is, he's okay with being told to shut the fuck up, just so long as he likes you. And he likes me, so he'll work out fine as a partner on this trip. Great, in fact.

"Of course we'll tell you," said Hemp. "You're going with Flex to retrieve what we need."

Gem walked in from the hallway with Charlie behind her.

"You know how when you were a kid and your mom tied a balloon to your belt loop so you didn't lose it?" asked Gem.

Tony gave her a quick hug. "Hey, Gem."

"Hey, Tony," she said, squeezing him back.

"Yeah?" I asked. "What's a balloon tied to your pants got to do with anything?"

"It's what I feel like when Charlie's walking too close behind me."

We all shook our heads, and Charlie, who didn't look very jovial, couldn't help a smile. She swatted at Gem, who swatted her back.

"I can see you're worried," said Gem. "I'm trying to lighten the mood."

Hemp left the map and turned to put his hands on her shoulders. "Charlie, what are you concerned about?"

Charlie folded her arms across her chest. "I don't know," she said. "Everything. I've got questions, but I don't want to ask them because I don't want to know the answer."

"Ask," said Hemp. "Otherwise you'll never learn the answers. You might like them."

"Okay," said Charlie, her hair now shoulder-length and curling more than ever. "The baby. Our baby. Can our baby be affected by this stuff? The Diphtheria? Inside me?"

"Charlie, you've been vaccinated, so I'm not worried about you or the baby. But you're due any day, and if he or she is born before we address this, you'll need to go stay with Dave and Serena or something. Or in the lab."

She looked more worried. "Hemp," she said.

"I know. But don't worry. Flex will be back soon, and we'll be okay."

"I'll never get back if we don't get movin'," I said. "Tony, let's put the rack on the back of the car. We're takin' enough fuel to get us as far as we need to go."

"Got it," said Tony.

"Hemp, go ahead and get the maps dialed in, highlighted, whatever," I said. "I'm packin' my stuff and we're getting' the car ready. I wanna be on the road in an hour at most."

"Maps are marked and ready, Flex," said Hemp. "Gem, you can help him if you like. I'll keep an eye on the little one."

"Thanks, Hemp," she said. "Babe, I'll go get some clothes and ammunition for the AK and your Daewoo. Tony, what guns do you have?"

"I have the MP3, like Hemp's."

"Okay. I'll pack ammo for everything, including your handguns."

"Don't forget water," said Tony.

"I won't," said Gem, smiling.

*****

In just over an hour we were ready. We tested the winch and topped off the tank from our large supply. There was more gas in town than we had a right to hope for, and the Piggly Wiggly store had plenty of food stock. Combined with the convenience stores, we wouldn't starve.

We'd killed a good number of walking dead around the town proper, but even then, it was probably less than 300. There were clearly plenty of them shut inside the scattered homes in the rural town.

As for the survivors in Whitmire, as I said when I started this, just under 150 people wouldn't have turned into rotters, but we'd only met a small number. We'd found one group of five living in a house near the gas station, but they mainly wanted to know if we knew what it was like in other places. We let 'em know that they were better off where they were. They had wells and a nearby river for fresh water if the bottled stuff ran out, and restaurants had the large, commercial cans of vegetables and soups, so food was plentiful for now. We recommended they grow their own, as we intended to do.

They didn't ask if they could join us. I'm glad of that. We have too hard a time sayin' no, and our family seemed to be growing fast enough under its own power. We did give them one of our radios and told them where they could find us if they needed to. So far they hadn't called.

As we were buttoning down the car, Hemp looked at the sky. "I'm worried about this weather, Flex," he said.

"Just a storm, right?"

"The gusts are strong. I'd say forty miles per hour, now," he said. "This is a state on the east coast, Flex. This could be a hurricane blowing in."

"Shit," I said. "I don't know why I didn't think of that."

"Be careful, friend," he said. "If you get hit with heavy, driving rain, it could be the outer bands of a large storm. There haven't been any in a while. We may be due."

"Nothin' to be done about it, buddy," I said. "I need that elixir, and I'm gonna go get it. Got that list?"

"It's in the car with the map. I've written down everything that might be on the label, so just read it carefully. All the immunizations necessary are listed, as well as the antitoxin."

"So how far from my first stop to my last resort at Beaufort Naval Hospital?"

"It's just under 80 miles to the North Carolina hospital, which should have what we need. If that fails, you've got a 233 mile drive on your hands."

I looked in the back of the Land Cruiser. "Looks like Gem packed enough shit for a month. We'll be good," I said.

"Ready?" asked Tony.

"Yep. Go on," I said.

Tony got in the car and rolled down the window.

Gem walked up to me and wrapped her arms around my waist, resting her head on my chest. I held her and said,

"Don't worry, babe. If everything goes as planned, we'll be back in six or seven hours."

Gem looked up at me. "Nothing ever goes as planned, and you know it."

"Have faith, Gem. I've never been more determined."

"I'd feel better if I were sitting where Tony is."

"Our boy needs you."

"He needs you, too."

I smiled and squeezed her again. "Gem, he'll have me. Just as soon as I get that juice."

We kissed, and she reluctantly let me go. "Hurry home."

I shook Hemp's hand and threw Bug a wave. He sat on the porch with Isis in his lap, and he waved back, nodding his head. I knew he was counting on us, too.

We pulled away. I could feel the wind buffeting the SUV even as we reached the one mile mark.

*****

I hung a right on Dogwalla Road and pressed the gas down. Tony had his window down and fired well-placed rounds into the heads of several walkers who, without variation, were moving toward our tiny outpost.

"Tony, get on the radio and just let 'em know they're going to have more company," I said. "I'd say if they can set up some sort of urushiol fence barrier, even if it's not that great, they should do it. At least around the entrances to the house."

"Yeah, even a 2-wire fence coated with urushiol will be better than nothing," said Tony. "Like chest height."

We were still close enough to our home base for the simple handheld radios to work, and Hemp was on the handheld and updated within two minutes. Tony put the radio back down, leaving it powered on.

63

"I'm gonna AK some of these bastards," said Tony. He quickly grabbed for the map and followed the highlight. "Turn right here, Flex. It looks like it changes names once or twice, but it's the one we take all the way to Highway 72."

"Tyger River Road it is," I said, turning the wheel, then swerved around an overturned semi truck that was now just a black lump of charred, melted metal, plastic and rubber. Several crashed cars around it were blackened as well, and despite the destruction, I wondered how many hungry things that we simultaneously hated and feared had walked or crawled away from the devastation.

"Hey, Tony," I said. "How about a granola bar, buddy?" I asked him.

"I got some of Isis' beef jerky," said Tony, smiling. "Want some?"

"Does sound better," I said. "Sure."

Tony dug around in his pocket and withdrew a bag. "Here you go, man."

I took the jerky and took a bite, even as I steered the Toyota around two cars that were parked cattycorner in the street, front bumper to front bumper, with the hoods up and all the doors wide open. I didn't know what had happened, but whatever it was hadn't been good. There were still jumper cables running between the batteries, but nobody was in sight. Perhaps the good Samaritan had eaten the driver in distress, but it could have been the other way around.

Either way, both parties had become extremely distracted from the task that had started out so everyday and mundane.

"Shit. "Better stop, Flexy."

A bridge lay ahead, just spanning a narrow ravine with a fast-moving but small river, about twelve feet below. I guessed this was the Tyger River from which the road took its name.

We'd gotten five or six feet over the chasm when the vehicle blockage was complete. It was like a mechanical puzzle, and we sat inside for a few moments, talking about which cars would have to be winched out of the way in order to clear a path.

"How the fuck did they bottleneck this bad in an area where there's no goddamned people?" asked Tony.

"Good question," I answered. "The way it's done ... I don't know. They look like they were placed here."

"But why?" asked Tony. "And if so, are the people who did it behind us or on the other side of it?"

"Either way we gotta get to the other side," I said, pointing north. "So how's about we work our way in. We pull that yellow Kia Soul out first. I can fit in there, and then we'll winch that silver SUV back a ways and I might be able to use the cow catcher to push it one way or the other."

"That thing's handy," said Tony, opening his door. He got out, reached in and grabbed a long range, plastic squirt gun filled with the urushiol blend, shook it and slid it into a drop holster on his right leg. He then reached in and took the MP5 from inside the Land Cruiser's cockpit.

"Disengage the winch," said Tony, closing the door as he walked toward the Kia.

I watched as he pulled the cable from the front of my Toyota and got on his knees. He located the tow hooks underneath the bumper of the Kia and hooked it on to the one on the left. Tony grunted back to his feet and went to the Kia's driver side door. He dropped into the seat, did something, and got back out. He waved at me, giving me one thumb up.

I engaged the winch, and held my foot hard on the brake as the tread on my larger, heavier SUV gripped the road. The Kia's flat tires slid along the asphalt, but did not roll.

Tony trotted to my door and I rolled down the window. "Parking brake was on, so I took that off. No keys in it, though, and it was an automatic, so I couldn't take it out of gear."

"Most of 'em are bound to have keys," I said. "If you can, just put 'em in neutral. It'll make it easier to move 'em."

"I know that, buddy," said Tony, smiling. I figured he was close to fifty years old, and I guessed that all the teeth in his mouth were caps; possibly even implants. They were as perfect and consistent in size as any teeth that had ever been part of any smile.

Right now, Tony Mallette was smiling a sarcastic smile that said, *I've been taking cars out of gear since you were pissing your diaper, punk.*

That might be true, but sometimes I state the obvious for those to whom I feel the obvious may be a stranger. I've met a few people in my life who did very little reasoning on their own, and while I don't consider Tony to be in that category, my old habits die as hard as zombies do.

After the Kia was out of the way, Tony unhooked the cable and moved up to the SUV. This time he went right to it and looked through the window at the interior.

He looked back at me and threw his hands up. My window was still down, so I heard him yell, "No keys here either!"

I put the car in park and cut the engine. I grabbed my K7 and got out, walking to where Tony stood holding the winch hook in his right hand, his MP3 in his left.

"Weird," I said. I walked to a red PT Cruiser butted up against a yellow VW Beetle. Doors were locked on both cars, and looking through the window revealed no zombies inside and no car keys in the ignition. I walked back to Tony, who had just checked what looked like a 1968 Camaro.

"No keys in there, either," he said.

"These two are the same," I said, pointing at the Bug and Cruiser.

"Which means this is a blockade," said Tony. "Think someone's watching us now?"

"I'm guessin' so," I said. I raised my hands, still holding my gun, and turned all around, staring into the thin, tall trees around us. Something caught my eye just west of the bridge, and I lowered my arms and went to the edge to peer down at the water.

Tony came up beside me. "Caution. Zombie Xing," he whispered. "Wonder if there's a sign down there."

As we watched, a line of creatures moved from a muddy trail on the northwest bank into the water. The river was not fast-flowing and the flesh-hungry, former humans staggered in, almost in a single-file line, without hesitation.

It was obviously not very deep, as even when they reached the center of the perhaps 80' wide waterway, they were still visible from the waist up. Still, they fought the current that did exist, and it was enough to direct them underneath the bridge as they made their trek across, making their final exit point the southeast bank on the opposite side of the bridge.

It was then that I spotted her.

A red-eye.

As my eyes met hers, she was already staring up at me. I could see their bright, red glow from the 75' or so distance, and before raising my weapon I poked Tony.

I said nothing. I was afraid to look away for fear she would disappear. With Isis and Lola at our home, I would not leave her alive.

"On three, Tony. Empty your magazine and take her down."

"Got it, Flex," he whispered.

"One. Two. Three." We both raised our weapons quickly and aimed true.

67

Eric A. Shelman

As the rounds reached her and pierced her head and body, she jerked like a wind-up toy at double speed; it was as though her head and shoulders exploded from the rest of her as each round was directed toward her relatively small kill zone. She was literally split in two, the trunk portion almost intact as it dropped and sank into the soft mud.

The moment she went down, the zombies in the river ceased their forward trek. They milled around as though unsure where to go, no longer on a mission, but wandering again. Just wandering. Looking for something to draw them toward it.

"Flex, we gotta take these guys out, man," said Tony. "All of 'em. If we don't, they might head toward your place."

Tony was right. "I agree," I said. "I'll go to the north end and start there. You go to the south side and clear 'em. We'll meet back up here when we've got them all."

We had plenty of urushiol, and Tony had his super soaker at ready. I decided to preserve the ammunition, too.

There were a lot of children in this group – something that always tore me up inside. Just kids living their lives, coloring in coloring books, playin' video games, jumpin' rope. I sprayed each one of 'em and turned away as they deteriorated mid-shamble, melting into the brown water and drifting away with their adult counterparts. The residue from their bodies would wash up on the banks of this river until entirely disbursed, and then they would be nothing.

From men, women and children, to forever hungry, mindless predators, to a sticky, smelly film on the banks of a river. Then nothing.

What a fucked up way to leave lives, that in most cases, were nowhere near finished.

By the time we were done, there was no more zombie caravan. Not on that road, anyway.

*****

68

We were self-conscious as we moved the remaining seven cars necessary to clear the bridge. Someone had put the cars there, and based on the direction of the zombie traffic, which had clearly circumvented the roadblock by walking through the water, it seemed most likely that the responsible party lived on the south side of the bridge.

Tony asked a good question about a mile past the bridge, now back on the road.

"Flex, I'm not so sure that whoever blocked that bridge was on the south side."

"Why?" I asked.

"Well, first off the red-eye was there, so we don't really know if Isis and Lola had anything to do with drawing them this time. Might have just been her."

"Good point, Tony," I said. "But Bug told us the red-eyes are drawn to both Lola and the baby. Lola, for the most part, because she can call 'em, and Isis just because."

"So, that means there's still a possibility that whoever blocked that bridge is ahead," said Tony. "That's all I was really getting at."

I turned to look at Tony and had turned to look back just a second later, and I felt my face flush hot. A line of people with guns stepped into the road about 100 yards ahead of us. Apparently my facial expression changed dramatically, because Tony turned his head to follow my gaze. I slowed the SUV to a crawl.

"Holy fuck, buddy," he said, reaching up for the AK firing handle. "Want me to take 'em out?"

I shook my head quickly. "They're not zombies, brother. They're alive," I said. "They deserve a conversation first, I think. So I'm gonna explain us past this, if you don't mind. They're not shootin' and they see our firepower, I assume, so maybe they're reasonable."

"Okay, Flex, but it's not like we can just spray them with urushiol if they try some shit."

"I know," I said. "Just turn the AK off to the side for now so they know we're not threatening. But keep your eye on 'em. If I suddenly dive to the ground, spin that gun around and go at it."

Tony said, "Okay, Flex," and took a deep breath. "It's kind of a relief I don't need a head shot to take 'em down."

I'd never killed a living person, so Tony's words really hit me. I'd just said it myself, but they were *living people*.

I continued to ease the car forward so I could better see their individual faces to gauge their intensity. I idled the car to a stop ten feet back from the line of what looked like eight women and six men. There were lots of overalls and jeans involved. Some boots, too. Off to the left, I saw several horses.

I put the Land Cruiser in park. Tony kept one hand on the pull trigger and remained in his seat while I got out of the car.

I opened my door and swung a leg out, standing up. I stepped away from the car, my Daewoo held tightly, but raised over my head in one hand. The barrel was pointed away from them.

A woman stepped from behind the line to the front where I could see her clearly. "Put the gun down," she said, as I approached.

I stopped, turned to look at Tony. With a hand motion, I told him everything was okay, and to relax. He nodded back.

I put my K7 on the ground as I prepared to tell them why I didn't have time to have a conversation or stay for coffee.

I hoped the woman would understand the importance of my mission. She had good reason to.

She was pregnant.

70

*****

"When are you due?" I asked, walking slowly forward and stopping about three feet away from her.

The woman studied me. She held what appeared to be an Uzi similar to Gem's, but slightly older. She had pure, red hair in a pony tail, and she stood at least six feet tall. Her face was red from sunburn, and her eyes were green and alert. She wore a white tank top and jeans. Her arms and all other exposed skin was tattoo-free. She appeared to be in her late twenties.

"Why'd you fuck with our bridge?" she asked.

"Why do you think?" I asked, waving my arm at the car. "We needed to get across."

"You could've walked around. Through the river."

"That's what the things you're tryin' to block are doin', so what good is your barricade?" I asked.

"It slows them down," she said.

"They're not coming toward you," I said.

"Why is that?" she asked.

"May I ask your name?" I said. "I'm Flex Sheridan. The guy in the car is Tony Mallette."

"I'm Cara Blake," she said. "Three of the guys you see here are my brothers, and two are my sisters."

"You guys are just like the fuckin' Brady Bunch."

Despite her obvious apprehension, she smiled. "Three and three. Just like mama wanted, but I'm no Marsha and I sure as hell ain't Jan."

I nodded toward her stomach. "Lookin' at your condition, I'd say *someone* isn't your brother," I said. It was my turn to smile.

"You're very observant," said Cara. "I'm seven months, or thereabouts. Haven't seen a doctor, but I'm pretty sure."

71

"You notice any pink farts or belches?" I asked.

"What?"

"I know it sounds like a crazy question, but I said what it sounded like, Cara. Pink belches and farts are bad news. Any of that? Real bad cramps or anything?"

She shook her head. "We know the pink vapor. The eye stuff."

I nodded. "Knockout stuff. Let me warn you right now. If you see one of the female walkers with red eyes – they're much brighter when they've eaten recently – stay clear of their vapor."

"Why? Is it different?"

"It is," I said. "We've seen the effects of a pregnant female getting sprayed, even if she carries a healthy baby."

"And what are the effects?"

"The mother rants a lot and the baby becomes a beacon, once born."

Cara lowered her weapon and looked back at me in confusion. "What do you mean by a beacon?"

"I mean when she's born, the red-eyes will be drawn to her. That means they'll be drawn to you. Your group."

The girl looked at her tribe mates and then back at me. "Where are you coming from?"

I didn't want to say. My family was in Whitmire, and I didn't know these people. "About a two day drive from here," I lied.

"Where are you headed?"

"Somewhere to get something that will help you," I said. "Something you need desperately."

Her expression grew confused. "And what is that?" she asked.

"Childhood immunizations," I said. "And something you need even more. An antitoxin."

Her face grew concerned now. "An antitoxin for what? Snakebite?"

"Why? Have you been bitten by a snake?" I asked.

"No, no," she said. "You said antitoxin, that's the first thing I think of."

"I think you mean anti-venom," yelled Tony from behind me. I realized he had his window open.

"The antitoxin is for Diphtheria," I said.

"What's that?" she asked.

I was taken aback. "Let's just say it can kill your kid and anyone else who hasn't been immunized," I said. "If you've already been exposed, the antitoxin will get rid of it."

"You got any kids that were exposed?"

I nodded. "Yeah, I do. My son Flex Jr. Our friends' baby, Isis, and another woman in our group, Charlie, is pregnant."

"A girl named Charlie?"

"A helluva girl named Charlie," I said. "Cara, I'm so sorry about your bridge, but we have to go. I have somewhere between one to four days, and I don't know where it falls. My boy's just around two months old now, and I have to get the antitoxin for him."

"They wanted me to make you fix the bridge," said Cara.

"Of course they did," I said. "But again, I don't think it's a good idea to block off roadways. What if there's a huge flood and you're attacked from the other direction?"

"Who's going to attack?" she asked. So far, nobody else had said a word. "We know our enemy and where they are. We've got stuff set up around our camp to take care of the rest."

"Cara, you seem like a nice person," I said. "But my son has been exposed to Diphtheria and I have an unknown amount of time and an unknown distance to travel. If they don't have what I need at the Carolinas Memorial Hospital, I have to drive back down to the Beaufort Naval Hospital, so I can't stay here and explain everything to you right now."

73

"You said I need this stuff, too." Her eyes no longer showed any aggression. I guess it's hard to be angry at someone who offers help.

"Your baby needs it, Cara," I said. "Maybe the Diphtheria can't affect you, but your baby needs it very soon after it's born, and I'll bring you some. I'll be comin' back this way, and you've got sentries, right?"

"Every half mile," she said.

"Okay, so you'll know when I get back. Come find me and I'll give you what you need."

She looked around and caught the eyes of several standing around her. I saw some of them nod. Almost imperceptible. Then she turned back to me. "Okay, but we're blocking the bridge again."

I needed that bridge open in case I found what I needed in North Carolina. "Cara," I said. "You've noticed an increase in the things, haven't you? Just today?"

"Hell yeah, we have," said a young man who appeared to be in his early twenties, wearing overalls and work boots. "We didn't have shit for numbers until this morning. Now it's like a goddamned parade. Why."

He didn't say it like a question. He wanted to know, and I understood.

"They're drawn to us," I said. "I can't explain why right now, but I'll tell you there's nothing we can do about it and they're heading toward us. What's the next town up this way?" I asked, pointing north.

"Buckfield," said Cara. "Just about five miles. Population of about three thousand or so. We did some damage there while we could, but there's still a bunch of deaders scattered around the town."

I nodded. "Yeah, you started with around 2,700 of 'em if the usual percentages apply, and I don't see why they wouldn't. What about survivors?"

"There's a few clusters of them, too," said the young man. He, too, had red hair, and his eyes looked almost identical to Cara's. He was one of her brothers, to be sure.

"What's your name, buddy?" I asked.

He laughed and said, "Buddy, actually. Bradley, but everyone calls me Buddy."

"Lucky guess," I said. "Buddy, I'd suggest you post some defenders at a northern point, anywhere you see the things coming in. We're gonna give you a bottle of something that can help a lot. It's got an oil in it called urushiol. If you spray it on 'em, they melt like shrink wrap under a heat gun. It just takes a little, so use it sparingly."

"What's it made of?" asked Cara. "Maybe we have some around."

"Not likely," I said. "If you can find poison ivy or poison oak, pick as much as you can carry and bring it back to your place. Where do you guys live?"

"My daddy's place," said Buddy, pointing behind him. "Just about a five minute walk through them trees. But we don't want that shit on us. The poison ivy. The kids might get into it."

"Trust me when I tell you that you're all immune to it," I said. "If you think back to times in your life someone pointed out that you were standing in poison ivy, you'll remember that nothing happened. It's a fact. It's part of why you're not one of them."

"I think we need to know more about this," said Cara.

"Look," I said. "I gotta get back on the road, like now. Quick question. How are you all staying at one house?"

"It's more of what you might call a compound," said Cara, smiling for the first time. "We got a big family. I guess you can see."

"Yeah," I said, returning her smile. "I'll give you the spray, but if you insist on blocking that bridge again, can you at least wait until we get back? We'll need to cross it to get back home, and the zombies just cross the river anyway."

"Not for long," said one of the men who had not yet spoken. He had a full beard and mustache, a plaid shirt over a tee-shirt, and overalls over those. "If this storm blows in, we're gonna have a good flood here. Been threatenin' for two days now."

"You think it's a hurricane?" I asked.

"It is the season," he said. "So in other words, yeah."

"We have to go," I reiterated. "I promise we'll be back. If they have what we need at our first stop, we'll be back before dark."

Cara nodded and waved. "Get back to your car and get us that oil spray stuff," she said. "Then get outta here and go get what you need," she said. "And please, come back. We've got other pregnant women. Two of them."

I nodded. "Thank you, Cara. I don't make promises I don't plan to keep. We'll catch you on the way back. After I get back home and take care of my son, we'll come back and teach you how to make the juice."

"That'll be good," said Buddy. "Thanks."

"No problem," I said. "I have another question. Why were you guys patrolling just now, when you found us?"

"One of our boys heard you draggin' the cars around," said Buddy. "Thought you might be from Buckfield."

"You got problems with some folks up there?"

Cara nodded. "Yeah. We take care of ourselves. Got good fishin' in that river there, and good huntin' in these woods. Couple of their guys shot Roland. He's not here, but he's okay. Lame now, but okay."

"So it was an accident, right?" I asked.

"Started out that way, I think," said another girl. This one was shorter than Cara, but as with all of the brothers and sisters, the hair was red, her face was freckled, and she had eyes that might have been interchangeable with the others. Her voice was softer.

"I heard the shot and somebody cryin' afterward. I'm quiet, and I moved toward the sound. When I got closer, I saw the bastard walkin' toward Roland, pointin' his gun. He was aimin' it. I shot him. Killed him."

"How're you handling it?" I asked.

"Okay. It was him or Roland. I didn't know him."

"So what?" I asked. "A feud started?"

"Shit sounds so hillbilly, but I guess there's no other word for it," said the girl. "Since then, they've sent regular parties down here with guns. Tryin' to exact their revenge, I guess."

"No explaining?" I asked. "Did you try?"

A big gust of wind hit us, and almost threw me off balance. With it came a general increase in the steady breeze.

"Gonna rain hard soon," said Cara, shaking her head. "Anyway, Krauss and them boys in Buckfield, they're gonna have to die before they leave us alone."

"Krauss?" I asked.

"Yeah," she responded. "He's the leader."

I nodded and said, "Hold on." I walked back to the Land Cruiser. Tony still had the window down.

"I almost came out," he said. "They seem okay."

"They are, Tony. Hand me a bottle of the urushiol, would you?"

Tony smiled and shook his head. "You're generous to a fault, you know that, Flex?"

"No idea," I said. "I just do what's right when I can." I took the bottle from him and walked back to Cara, holding it out. A sound came from behind their group and I tipped my chin toward it.

"Here's your chance to try it out," I said.

Everyone's gun swung around, and I called, "No, no! Try the oil. Just a tiny spray, right in the face."

Cara turned and the group parted. "Keep your guns on it," she said, walking toward the zombie. Its skin hung down in tatters from its face. A large gouge was missing from its left calf and only a thumb remained on its right hand.

Cara stepped to within two feet and sprayed once into its face. It wasn't quite on stream or spray, but somewhere between the two. What resulted was a strong, wide spray pattern that wet the deader's entire face, to use their own terminology.

The gray-green skin bubbled instantly, then sank into itself. It peeled away from the skull, momentarily making the thing appear like a Halloween store decoration, but it did not stop there. The skin continued to peel down its chest. It staggered forward, but still the group holding their rifles did not fire.

"Holy motherfucker," said Buddy. "Cara, you seein' this?"

"Oh, yeah," she said, looking at the bottle. "It's like acid to them."

"Yeah," I said. "The bad kind." I watched as the destruction continued as I'd seen so many times before. The head fell away, dropping to the ground as it sizzled and popped while the body toppled sideways and continued to dissolve.

"Saves on burnin' 'em," said Buddy. "No cleanup."

"Long as you're not on a marble floor," I said. "but now I really gotta go. Get yourselves the plants I told you about. Poison sumac, too. Any one of 'em will work."

"Thanks, Mr. Sheridan," said Cara.

"Flex, please," I said. "He was a good guy and a better electrician than me, but *Mr. Sheridan* was my dad."

Cara nodded. I got back in the car and they parted, allowing us to pass. Tony and I both gave them a wave.

"I'd give my left nut to hear the conversation that happens now," I said.

"Really?" said Tony, looking skeptical. "You really think it's worth a nut?"

I laughed. "It's an expression, Tony."

"I know, but I can't stand the thought of losin' a nut. Hey, I'm hungry. Want some jerky?"

We both ate jerky in silence. After I was done with my first piece, I said, "Tony, do me a favor. Look at that map and see if there's a way around Buckfield."

*****

Chapter Four

I looked at the sky, standing alongside Hemp and Charlie. Dave had radioed from his house, having had a decent nap by then, to tell us he was on his way. When I told him what happened, he was pissed that Flex had left with Tony.

But the weather felt ominous, and at present, another strong, mini-storm blasted the house and the porch where we stood. The clouds swirled at varying altitudes, and I swore I could see the counter-clockwise motion confirming my worst fears.

Flex was out there with Tony. Driving in a hurricane was just fucking crazy.

"It's an outer band, guys," I said. "I've seen enough to know."

I had experienced my share in Miami. My Aunt Ana and Uncle Rogelio always refused to evacuate, so I was tasked with going to their house to make sure their hurricane shutters were up and tight. My uncle would help, but in my heart, I would rather have piled them in my car and gotten them the hell out of there.

The outer bands, far from the most powerful part of the storm, could reach for literally hundreds of miles as they swirled around the enormous formation of spinning air, some of the bands containing heavy rain, wind and lightning, and others just wind and rain. This was the former, and the lightning was intense, and it was close.

"We didn't get much of this shit back home," said Charlie, holding her hair in one fist to keep it from whipping her in the face. "And you say this is nothing?"

"Oh, it's something," I said. "It's only nothing compared to the actual storm."

"We need to batten down the hatches," yelled Hemp, over the cacophony of sound. "I don't need any more convincing."

Bug came out behind them. "Jesus Christ," he said. "Didn't have this crap in Cali." His hair was in a ponytail, so did not pose the problem Charlie's did.

"Judging from these precursors," said Hemp, "It is more than a tropical storm. It's impossible to say how large or how strong until it's on top of us."

"I saw a barometer on the wall in that garage, didn't I?" asked Charlie.

"Broken," said Hemp. "I've been meaning to make one, but I haven't gotten around to it. I don't have a baseline, so at this point it would only tell me what's become obvious already."

"We'll need to wait for this band to pass before we get on it," I said. "And unceremonious is fine. We just need to get the boards up there, esthetics be damned."

"And what are we battening with?" asked Charlie.

Hemp looked at Charlie, a crooked smile on his face. "You, my love, are not battening at all. We've got Dave and Serena on the way."

"Serena's pregnant, too," said Charlie.

"Not as much as you, pumpkin," I said. "And I mean that in the literal sense. Keep your ass inside and let us who can stand close to walls put up the boards."

"Okay," said Charlie, sarcastic. "So what are *you* battening with?"

"The stack of boards on the side of the house should work fine," said Hemp. "One or two nailed over the exterior windows in a cross pattern, just to keep the major debris from breaking them."

"Hey, look," said Bug, pointing.

We all looked. A one-armed girl in a ragged dress walked toward us. Behind her was a woman. I was glad we were all on WAT-5.

Bug removed his .45 caliber Colt Python from his side holster and stepped down off the porch.

"Hold on," I called. "They're … well. Let me, Bug. If you don't mind."

He looked at me. "Because they're female?"

"Maybe," I said. "It's nothing personal at all."

"Sure, Gem," he said. "No offense taken. I'm gonna go in and check on Isis. I'm worried about that little girl."

"Your gun?" I asked. Mine was inside.

He gave it to me. "All the cylinders are full," he said.

I tucked the gun into the front of my pants and stepped off the porch.

"Be careful, Gem," said Charlie.

I nodded, but kept walking and didn't answer. Some days I let this all get to me more than others. The red-eyes and I had something in common now. They were pregnant when they turned, through no fault of their own. Now they have extraordinary hunting abilities and the damned telepathy.

Neither of these were red-eyes. Red-eyes had nice hair, and these two looked like they subscribed to the egg beater beauty techniques with the little remaining hair they had left.

They would have walked right into me had I not reached out to take them each by an arm. The girl by the only one remaining, her left, and the woman by her right.

It was impossible now to determine the age of the older one; she had been ravaged over the past year plus, and believe it or not, I sometimes felt guilty about being the one to end their journeys after such a successful run at the afterlife.

They were like ants in an endless train of other ants. Their work was never finished. Not a moment of self-reflection and peace for them. Just endless hunger and walking, forever walking.

The woman, who still had some wisps of grey hair on her head, indicating she was likely out of her mid-thirties when she was taken, wore only dark-stained blue jeans. By the pattern on the pocket, I knew they were Levis.

One of her eye sockets was dark, the appendage missing. The other darted back and forth and past me, never stopping to focus in my direction long.

Thank you WAT-5.

The little girl was just that; a little girl. Her height told me she was no more than seven, and her tattered dress told me she had been at church – or perhaps in a casket – the Sunday this all began back in 2011. More of her hair remained, and I saw that it crawled with vermin of some kind, though what they chose to occupy their attention with in the sparse tresses was beyond me.

She did not belong to the woman. Judging from their clothing, they had been doing different things at the time.

I walked forward and led them both to the edge of the road. I then stepped off the road into the grass, and led them over the rougher terrain. The trail I walked on turned left, and I walked them another thirty yards – not pushing them, mind you. Just easing them along.

We reached the pit. There were already six or seven bodies in there from our encounters earlier in the day, and some still remained in our partially fenced field that still needed hauling here, to our burning pit.

I heard Hemp call from the porch, but the wind effectively buffeted his words out of existence as far as I was concerned.

I positioned the two on the edge of the hole and released them. The entire walk had only been to save labor later, so don't think I was on some kind of sensitivity mission. I learned my lesson once, and had a half a thumb to show for it.

I held out my gun and fired into the forehead of the woman, whose one remaining eye had briefly changed before the back of her skull blew out. A gust of wind blew her horrid innards squarely back into my face and into my eyes.

"Gem!" came the voice behind me, but I could not see. I wiped my eyes on my shoulder, trying to clear away the muck as I felt something grab hold of my right leg.

I staggered and fell backward, landing hard. The wind rushed from my lungs and I tried to suck it back in, but no part of my respiratory system was ready to allow it.

Then I saw what Hemp had been screaming about. The little girl snarled and growled, clawing at my leg with her one remaining hand, her teeth biting into the thick fabric of my jeans as she pinched me but good through the thick material. My eyes still stung and she was a blur of movement, so I jerked my legs and desperately swiped at my eyes to clear my vision.

Unable to discourage the child zombie and still seeing blurry, ghost-like figures everywhere I looked, I pulled my left leg back and kicked the shit out of her head, but it only served to throw her momentarily onto her back and fuel her drive to get back to me. This time, she used her thrashed knees to push up toward my arms, her mouth stretched open wide to reveal, broken, jagged teeth that would, if clamped down in the right spot, be through my skin in a split-second.

I sucked in my first breath as I saw Hemp rush by me out of the corner of my eye. Mid-stride he kicked the girl squarely in the head. With a wild grunt he dropped down and planted a hard knee in the middle of her chest, grabbed the pre-adolescent rotter with his bare hands and physically lifted her and threw her into the pit. When she landed, he swung his MP5 around and unloaded round after round into her face.

I knew then – I think for the first time – that Hemp saw all of these monsters, old and young, for what they were now. He didn't dwell on the fact that the zombie girl was once a little Trina. He only recognized that she had to die. Permanently.

Breath finally flowing into my lungs, I scrambled back to my feet and wiped the last bit of muck from the older female from my eyes with the back of my hand. I put a hand on Hemp's gun just as it fell silent, pushing the barrel downward. He didn't stop firing because of me; it was only because he ran out of ammo.

I looked at the child in the pit, atop the other decomposing bodies. Nothing had ever been deader than she was at that moment. If that makes any sense at all.

"C'mon, Hemp," I said. "She didn't get through my pant leg."

The wind eased almost at once, and I glanced to our rear and saw the storm clouds moving away. For the moment.

"You need to stay on top of your WAT-5," Gem," said Hemp. "Flex hasn't been gone two hours and you're nearly killed. I'm not certain if I was more afraid of losing you or facing him."

"At least you're honest," I said. "But I vote for the first one. You'd miss the fuck out of me."

Hemp shook his head and I hooked my arm around his as we walked back to the house. We mounted the steps to the porch.

"You fuckup,' said Charlie, smiling. "You okay?"

"Stupid, but okay," I said. "I kind of hoped you didn't see any of that."

"Oh, I saw it all right," said Charlie. "You're just lucky Hemp figured out you were ready to expire on the WAT-5. He was running before you got in trouble."

"And you?"

"He told me to sit the fuck down."

"He's really come a long way, hasn't he?" I said, smiling.

"Don't talk about me like I'm not here," said Hemp, pulling me into the house.

Charlie followed.

*****

Tony was looking at me like the world had come to an end. "Buddy, there's no way around Buckfield," he said. "No side roads, detours. Hell, there's not even a hiking trail."

I'd been driving around 25 miles per hour while Tony figured things out. "I get the picture," I said. "We might just have to talk our way through again."

"If we can, buddy. If we can."

"Maybe we just pour on the steam, no slowin' down," I suggested.

"Roadblocks, man," said Tony. "Bet your ass they'll have 'em."

"Yeah," I said. I knew it before Tony said it, but a guy could dream, right? I wondered how many there were, what their armory situation was, and if they knew everyone in Cara and Buddy's group. If they did, then they'd know we weren't in it, and that could be a good thing.

"I think the smartest move would be just ease in and walk softly," I said. "But as they say, we'll carry a big stick."

"We shoulda brought more urushiol for bribing the natives," said Tony.

I looked at him. "Tony. You might have hit on something."

Tony looked suddenly proud, but even more confused. "Like what?"

"Well," I said, "we have a shitload of WAT-5. More than we'll likely need. We can do a little trade. Passage for invisibility."

Tony shook his head, his brows furrowed. "Aw, I don't know, Flex. Nothin' matches the value of WAT-5."

"Diphtheria antitoxin does," I said. "To me."

"I know, I know," said Tony. "I love that kid. I want him to be okay. But think of what you got there, Flex."

"He *will* be okay," I said. "We'll just have to go back to killin' zombies the old-fashioned way if we run out."

"Did you hear what I said?" asked Tony.

I did, and I thought I knew what he would be getting to, but I didn't want to think about it. I answered him anyway. "I know what we got, and I know people would kill for it."

"Exactly," said Tony, patting me on my shoulder. "They find out we have this stuff that makes you invisible to zombies, they decide they're too lazy to make their own. Now we got a huge freakin' target on our backs."

"It wouldn't do much good to steal it from us," I said. "If we refuse to make more, they're screwed. They'd be better off learning how to produce it using the base mixture we have."

"Well," said Tony. "In case you haven't looked around in the last few years, people ain't getting' any smarter. It's a risk, Flex. That's all I'm sayin." He looked at the road ahead, his brow furrowed in worry. "How far?"

"Another mile or so we'll be there," I said.

"I'll do the talkin' this time," said Tony.

"You sure?"

"Yeah. See this face?"

I looked at this salt and pepper, spiky hair and full beard and mustache, his gold chains and his shirt unbuttoned down to his naval.

"Hey," said Tony, his two fingers pointing to his eyes. "My eyes are up here." He laughed.

"I'm takin' in the whole Tony, my friend," I said.

"Well," he said, "this face can sink a thousand ships."

"Do you even know what that means?" I asked, laughing.

"Not a fuckin' clue," he laughed. "But it's a nice face, right?" His teeth blinded me.

"Not bad, Tony. Okay, go ahead. You give it a shot. Remember to mention Diphtheria and women and kids. And don't tell them where the hell we are. Just say a day's drive, in the middle of nowhere."

"Got it."

We passed a sign that read "Welcome To Buckfield." Someone had written at the bottom of it, "Now suck my dick!" in black spray paint.

"Nice place," said Tony.

"You wanted to handle this one," I said. "Hope you don't have to suck anyone's dick."

"Oh, now," said Tony, shaking his head. "Now you're an asshole."

*****

I drove slowly. While the border of the town of Buckfield, South Carolina was marked with the sign, the town square didn't appear for another mile.

We saw the odd walker, but let them be for now. They were the problem of the inhabitants of Buckfield, and we didn't want to draw attention by blasting either the AK on the roof or our other weapons.

Main Street, a small town standard, had been marked through, and the words *Zombie Road* were written in white in the same crude writing as the *suck my dick* comment on the welcome sign.

"Nice fuckin' place," I said, increasing my pressure on the accelerator. "I'd like to –"

"I think I know what you were gonna say," interrupted Tony. "Ain't gonna happen."

Ahead of us was a barricade. The standard, white sawhorse style with red striped lines. Again, in the same spray painted scrawl, it said, "*Stop, Asshole!*"

It wasn't necessary. This asshole and the one in the passenger seat fully intended to stop.

Three men stood up from the other side of the blockade and walked around to the front. All were armed, and nobody had baked goods. This wasn't a welcoming party.

I had begun to wish we'd brought the Crown Vic. The ballistic exterior of it would have been a real benefit right about then.

I slowed the Land Cruiser and stopped. Déjà vu all over again. I looked at Tony. "Go on, buddy," I said. "Got your pistol in your pants?"

"Yeah," he said. "Under my shirt."

"I'd carry your MP5 out, then lay it on the ground like you're putting down your weapons."

"Good," said Tony. "No worries, Flex. I'll handle it."

Tony stepped out of the car and waved a hand at them. I had my window down to hear what was exchanged.

"Hey, guys," said Tony, walking toward them his MP5 raised. He did what I had done. He stooped down and put the gun on the ground, then held up both open palms toward them.

"Close enough," said one of the guards.

Three men. One, a thin young man with a close, blonde crew-cut, couldn't have been out of his twenties. He wore jeans and a tank-style, white tee shirt. I used to call them wife beater tee shirts.

He was holding onto the barricade to keep it from blowing over, because the wind was now gusting so hard I could feel it against the Toyota even while we were sitting still. What looked like a pump-action, Mossberg tactical shotgun was strapped over his right shoulder, and he aimed it directly at me. If you're wondering how I'd know a fuckin' Mossberg from a Winchester, it's because over a year had passed since humans became dinner, and I'd pretty much had an opportunity to own any weapon out there that you could carry without assistance.

It was kind of funny anyway. If the guy would've fired it holding it that way, it would dislocate his shoulder and knock him on his ass. He'd have to let go of the barrier first, I was pretty sure.

"We're headed to the hospital in Charlotte," said Tony. "Gotta get medication for my friend's little boy. We came from the recreation area down by that big river."

"Nobody's going through this way," said the man in the middle. He was a black man with biceps as big as sewer drain pipes. I imagined him as a zombie and decided he would scare the hell out of me. He was 300 pounds if he was an ounce, and each hand looked like it could curl into a cantaloupe-sized fist.

His cantaloupes were currently wrapped around what I recognized as a Parker Tornado. The crossbow was just like Charlie's pride and joy. A clip held several additional bolts. In drop holsters on his thighs were two more handguns of some kind – I couldn't tell what, but they were either .357s or .45s, from the size of the grips protruding from the sheathes.

Big hands, big guns.

"I understand security," said Tony. "We've had our issues, too. But we're cool with humans, bro. We only kill the zombies, man."

The behemoth black man spoke again, this time his voice so low his words were indecipherable from where I sat. Tony actually took three more steps toward him, cupping his hand against his ear. "Sorry, man," he said. "I didn't hear you."

Now the man forced the words out so loudly that even I could hear them. "Tell the asshole in the car to put his hands where we can see them and get out. Now. Three seconds." He raised the crossbow and pointed it right at Tony's head.

"Ricky," he said to the skinny one. "Get ready."

I heard that. My first thought was, *Get ready for what?*

The third man, who stood taller than the others and had a thick, but muscular build, had a similar haircut to the younger one, but his hair was red and his jaw and neck were covered with rough stubble. He never raised his weapon, instead holding it pointed toward the ground, his eyes not on me, but on the other two.

"Look," said Tony, his hands still raised. "We got stuff to trade you to let us go through. Stuff you don't have and you'll never get without us." Tony smiled big. He liked to use his smile. He'd paid a lot for it, I guessed.

What happened next transpired as if in slow motion. I hadn't seen it coming, and neither had Tony. At first, I wasn't even sure it wasn't an accident, it came so far out of the fuckin' blue.

From my seat in the Toyota, I heard the big man scream, "I said three fuckin' seconds!" The crossbow bolt flew from the weapon and in under a half second had pierced and exited Tony Mallette's head.

It was a point-blank shot.

As I watched in horror, Tony's body teetered there for a moment, and he turned toward me, his eyes filled with what

91

I can only describe as confusion. He pressed his upper teeth against his lower lip as if to say "Flex," but the word never materialized – or if it did, I didn't hear it.

Tony was someone who helped others. He wasn't aggressive or angry. He genuinely cared about people, and he would take any part of his day and give it to you. It's who Tony … *was*.

Because he *was* no more. His body crumpled to the ground.

The man on the right acted next. He was fast, and if he had directed his aggression toward me, I wouldn't be alive to tell you this story.

Instead, as my hand reached for the trigger rope of the AK-47 on the roof of the Land Cruiser, he raised what looked like a shotgun with a drum magazine, blasting the giant with the crossbow in the face as the prick stood smiling, watching with utter pleasure as Tony Mallette lay sprawled the ground, the rain washing away his pooling blood.

Like instant karma, the fat man's facial features disintegrated before my eyes and what almost looked like a headless body dropped like the enormous sack of shit that he was.

The sadistic brute must've thought one of his other pals would take me out, and the skinny guy on the left, still holding onto the wobbly barrier, did fire his shotgun in my direction. Fortunately for me, with only one hand on the pistol grip the barrel flew sharply upward, completely missing me and the Toyota. Hell, the kick might have broken his thumb, but that was about to be the least of his problems.

He lost his balance, smacking into the barrier behind him before bouncing off of it and falling flat on his face.

Pretty sure the third guy wasn't going for me next, I corrected the AK's position and fired on the skinny one scrambling to get back to his feet. I riddled his body with rounds as he twitched and jerked, red blood and flesh explosions shredding his body and turning his wife-beater tee shirt into a tattered, crimson mess.

The other man lowered his weapon, but did not put it down. He raised his hands as he ran over to where Tony lay, motionless. He bent down and felt Tony for a pulse.

I figure it was purely academic. Even I knew Tony was dead. I threw open the door, jumped out of the car and ran over to my friend's body and pushed the man away from him. I lifted Tony's head.

Of course he was gone. His eyes were still open, the confused expression still fixed there. The wind blew harder, the new smattering of rain peppering us.

"We gotta move," said the third, and now only man. "I'm sorry about your friend, partner. I had no idea Clarence was gonna do that. No idea at all."

I couldn't speak. I looked at Tony's lifeless body and tears leaked from my eyes. "Open that rear hatch," I said.

The man didn't argue. He ran to the back of the Toyota as I scooped Tony up. Adrenaline pumped through me, so I didn't feel his weight at all as I lifted him and jogged him to the Land Cruiser. I crawled up inside and rested his body on his back, bent his knees up and closed the hatch.

I knew I didn't need to use any additional assurances that Tony would not reanimate, because the arrow that had killed him pierced his brain. It was news that Tony himself would welcome; he would not be coming back as one of the creatures he not only feared, but despised.

"Take me with you, buddy," said the stranger. "I'm not like them. I was as much a prisoner as you guys might have been."

"Why'd they give you a gun?" I asked.

"Because I'm also a good actor. You learn stuff like that when you're a captive in Afghanistan. Friend, we have to go. The gunfire's gonna bring others. Now."

I made a snap judgment and nodded. "Get in," I said. Another gust of wind blasted us and blew the barrier down flat as we jumped back inside the car.

I fired the engine and dropped the truck into drive, cranking the wheels around the 300 pound speed bump in the middle of the road. I floored it and we started to put some distance between us and Buckfield, South Carolina.

"I'm Frank Magee," he said. "Folks call me Punch."

"Flex Sheridan," I said. "And pardon me, but I don't feel like talkin' right now, if you don't mind. I wanna find a place to bury my friend."

"I'd suggest you drive a few clicks first," said Punch. "They'll be coming after us. When they see me missing, they'll think I planned it all along."

I felt a tremendous weight on my shoulders. With the firepower I had available at my fingertips, I'd let Tony get murdered right in front of me. I didn't respond to what Punch had said. He knew the occupants of Buckfield, and I had no doubt that he was right.

I mourned Tony Mallette immediately. I had made fun of him. Sometimes I'd just barely tolerated him. But he saved our asses in Concord and I respected him. He may have stumbled into the rescue with no idea how dire our situation was, but he didn't hightail it for the hills; he charged in like the fuckin' cavalry and he did what had to be done.

There weren't a lot of men who operated on passion and instinct but he was one of them. I owed him more than what he'd just gotten.

Every once in a while I felt a tear hit my thigh, only then realizing I was crying. Not just a little, but salty water running down my face in rivers.

I wanted to see those bright, white teeth smiling at me again. I felt something happening at that thought.

My sadness was already turning, changing.

Into anger.

The person who ordered such murderous action in Buckfield would pay. Anyone who supported it would pay.

I had a feeling Punch would help if asked.

He stared straight ahead as I drove. He gave me time. I needed it.

*****

Thunder and lightning lit up the black, swirling sky, darkened by yet another of the powerful outer bands of what appeared to be a hell of a hurricane. Hemp did have a wind gauge, and it had already measured gusts upwards of 50 miles per hour.

These precursors to the main event didn't mean the hurricane would be a killer, though. There had been plenty of hurricane seasons in Miami where we'd experienced intense outer bands that exceeded the power of the actual storm, having been ripped apart by wind shear in the Atlantic, miles before it reached land as nothing more than a Category 1 or a strong tropical storm.

I'd spent many a night calming my Aunt Ana, even when I was scared shitless, too. I'm not sure she ever believed my bullshit anyway, but I guess it made me feel better.

"Gem, how are you coming on the boards?" yelled Hemp over the wind's din, he and Dave Gammon hauling more boards over to what had to be one of the last windows. He and Dave were getting them into position and tacking them in place, and I was following behind with Bug, holding them stable while he used self-tapping screws to secure them to the siding.

"We're almost there," I said, my hair a stringy, wet mess and my clothing soaked through to my skin. "Ready, Bug."

He screwed in eight more screws and nodded. "Got it," he said. "Good thing. The charge on this driver drill's dying."

"Okay, let's get the last window done and put this crap away and get inside," I said. "Next time we get a break we'll see what kinds of rotters we have to deal with and we'll gather up anything else that could turn into projectiles."

"You let me, Dave and Hemp handle that," Bug said. His hair was nearly as wet and tangled as mine, and I was certain Dave's was in similar condition.

I heard two distant blasts over the wind and jerked my head around in time to see two rotters toppling over as Serena threw her arm through the strap of her shotgun – her new weapon of choice. As wet as the rest of us, she jogged toward us from the field where we were innocently sinking our fence posts earlier in the day.

"I wanted to haul the posts you guys didn't plant to the burning pit," she said. "But that was more involved than I thought through."

"We can get them later," I said. "Thanks, Serena, but I recall someone – I think it was you – telling us you were pregnant, so you're done."

"I think they're okay," she said, pointing to the field. "I laid out the baling wire and bundled them together. They should be heavy enough to be stable now."

Hemp walked up with Dave. Dave's white tee shirt was see-through now.

"Nice," I said. "Davey, you look like the loser in a wet tee shirt contest."

Gammon laughed. "This calls for an awkward moment joke, but I'm too fucking tired to come up with one." He looked at Serena. "What are you doing out here, babe?"

"Helping," she said. "I'm not that far along, so don't give me any crap, okay?"

"Wasn't going to," said Dave. "But we got it now. Go get dried off."

Hemp stared toward the field. "Serena, the bundles are an excellent idea, but when we get another break between bands, Dave and I will see if we can use the golf cart to push them together. That will ensure they don't blow apart."

Serena pointed beyond the bundled posts. "More goddamned zombies," she said. "Those look like diggers."

Bug shook his head. "We're becomin' a big problem for you guys."

"The storm might help us in that regard," said Hemp. "They're not all that heavy. If they take enough of a beating, they'll be far easier to dispatch, lying on the ground."

"Give us a sec," I said, nudging Bug. He followed, and we put another eight screws in the final window boards.

By the time we got back to the front door, everyone else was inside. I pulled off my top and wrung out the water, and Bug gawked at me.

"Jesus, woman," he said. "You do understand I've been living in a concrete bunker for a year, right?"

I laughed. "Oh shit, Bug," I said. "I'm just an old married lady with kids now. You can do better."

"I'll be sure not to tell Flex that," he said, stepping in the house behind me. "Wonder how he's doin' out there anyway."

I didn't answer immediately. I didn't want to think about it, yet it was all I could think about. I knew they didn't want me out there working on shoring up the windows either, but I had to do something to occupy my mind.

Our timing sucked. I was glad as hell that Dave and Serena were back, and I welcomed all of our new friends and family. But with our fence unfinished, a baby named Isis drawing rotters from what was apparently miles around, and now this fucking hurricane, the last thing we needed was Diphtheria on top of it all.

We knew how to kill the walking dead; how to terminate their dead hunger. We could barricade ourselves away during a storm, too. And I suppose on a normal day, a few-hour run to a hospital in North Carolina wouldn't be the end of the world, either.

Oh, shit. That kind of already happened, didn't it?

Anyway, all this shit at one time, and it suddenly posed what we might just call a problem.

******

Everybody got into dry clothes. Dave had a bag with him, so Bug wore some of his stuff.

The band passed in another twenty minutes, but not before some lightning struck some very nearby trees. Hemp warned us that fire wasn't out of the question, either. Especially with the wind factor.

"Is Doc Scofield at his place?" asked Charlie. "Maybe someone should check on them."

By them she meant Raylene and her very ill daughter, Gina.

"I'll radio him," said Hemp, walking to the table and retrieving the radio. He pushed the button. "Jim, do you read? It's Hemp."

The doctor wasn't decrepit, but he didn't move like we did, either. Hemp gave him some time. Sure enough, in another ten seconds we heard, "Yeah, this is Scofield. Hemp?"

"Yes, it's me," he said. "How are Raylene and Gina making out in your guest house?"

"I got 'em settled in there good. I lit a few of the hurricane lanterns, so they've got light, and I gave them a thermos with fresh water."

"Good," said Hemp. "And how are you, my friend?"

"Not used to this shit is how I am," he said. "What kinda storm are we talkin' about, Professor?"

"I'm 99% certain it's a hurricane of some size," said Hemp. "With no radar, we'll have no idea until it's on top of us."

"What the hell next?" asked Scofield. "If this is God's work, we must've really screwed up at some point, eh?"

"Let's just call her Mother Nature for now, Jim," said Hemp. "No sense in assuming damnation first."

"Gotcha," said Scofield. "I'm gonna stay here. This place has those old timey window shutters, so they're all closed. So does the guest house, to match. Any prediction of when this sucker's due to arrive?"

"No way to tell," said Hemp. "These storms can be hundreds of miles wide, and the outer bands can extend hundreds more. We may be talking sometime tomorrow evening. Even the day after."

"Well, I'm gonna have to take a shit before that," said Jim. "It's not all that easy for me anymore, but when I gotta go, I'm damned well not putting that off for anything. Even this."

"To each his own," said Hemp, smiling. "That's what the kids call … what is it, Charlie?"

"TMI," said Charlie, smiling. "Too much fucking information."

"I had the button pushed, Jim. I assume you heard."

"Nah," said Jim. "Another of the benefits of gettin' old. You miss half the insults."

"They love you, old man," said Hemp. "Okay. Run over and check on our guests now and then, okay?"

"If I'm not takin' a crap, absolutely."

"Roger, out," said Hemp, putting down the radio.

Through the X boards on the front window, we saw a figure pass. Then another. When the wind died down, we heard the shuffle of feet on the porch.

My heart leapt for a moment. I immediately thought it might be Flex.

But it had just been three and a half hours since he left. It was over two hours each way, and that would be with ideal conditions.

There wasn't anything ideal about these conditions.

"Bug," I said. "I know we just met, but would you mind killing the zombies on the porch?"

Bug sighed and stood, then stretched. "Sure," he said. "It's the least I can do for the peep show you gave me earlier."

"Fuck you," I said. "You're just like Dave."

"Nah," said Bug. "He's always been a very respectful twerp."

"First off, what peep show?" asked Dave. "Plus, if you weren't so old, I'd get up and kick your ancient ass."

Dave didn't move, so it was pretty clear he was okay with leaving the zombie killing to his uncle, as well as his ancient ass unkicked. Dave did hold out one of his Walthers, which Bug took. He plodded to the door in bare feet, checked the peephole, and eased it open.

"Here, zombie, zombie, zombie," he said. He took two steps out, turned left and held out his hand. A shot sounded. Then another, followed by a thud. We saw him turn to his right, and he fired again. Another thud.

Then he stood, his back directly against the door and fired a fourth time. This one was apparently not on the porch yet, for we did not hear the sound of a body collapsing against treated decking.

He came back in, wiped his feet on the mat, and closed the door. "Missed the first shot."

"Walther's tricky," said Dave.

"Yeah, I was gonna blame the gun, too," said Bug. "Like uncle, like nephew."

We all settled in and I thought of Flex. I wondered if he was thinking about me.

*****

Chapter Five

Because it seemed to have been the first hurricane to make landfall in the contiguous United States since the zombies arrived, Tony and I had begun to call it Hurricane George, in honor of the Godfather of zombies himself, George Romero.

I missed Tony again. And I wondered if ol' George had become a zombie.

I didn't have time to wonder shit for very long. Punch was talking but I wasn't listening, even though he might have been touching on some important information. As it turns out, the first words I did hear were these:

"We got company, Flex." I guess he'd figured out I wasn't listening before, because he also smacked me on my arm as he said it.

I looked in the rear view and said "Jesus fuck!" I didn't have time for this. It was like catching every light while you were driving your pregnant wife to the hospital.

We were only twenty minutes outside of the barricade we'd broken through. The vehicle behind us was a Jeep, so its off-road capabilities would match or exceed those of my Land Cruiser if it came to that. But there was still one thing they didn't have that I did ... the roof-mounted AK-47, courtesy of Hemp Chatsworth.

"Spin that gun around Punch," I said, popping the *B* button on the GPS screen. "Up there. Just grab the grip and watch the GPS. When they're lined up, pull that rope and fire away."

"You gonna try to lose them first?" asked Punch.

"Fuck no," I said. "I'm haulin' my dead buddy in the back. I'm a little short on compassion right now."

The rear window of the Land Cruiser shattered and a hole appeared cleanly through the front windshield.

"You got a fuckin' hearing problem, buddy?" I yelled, cranking the wheel side to side. "Take 'em out!"

The Jeep suddenly cut off to the left, bouncing through the tall grass on the side of the road.

"Spin the gun toward him!" I shouted, cranking hard left to avoid a staggering rotter that came out of nowhere. I wasn't able to; the front edge of my cowcatcher tore the digger's right leg off and he spun wildly in the road like a demonic ballet dancer, his rotted left arm severing from his body, taken by the powerful wind as he twirled.

"There's another goddamned truck behind us!" shouted Punch.

I heard him that time, but fuck if I could do anything about it, and he had yet to fire a shot. "Then take it out!" I shouted. "Goddamnit, Punch, fire that fucking weapon!"

Two more zombies staggered in front of the Toyota, perhaps six car lengths ahead. Their movement, while as jerky and seemingly aimless as most of the zombies I'd ever seen before, was more ominous somehow; they were, without variation, moving in the same direction. While I hoped it was Buckfield that drew them, I had the distinct fear that it was an unwitting Isis who called to them, as inconceivable as it still was to me.

I was able to crank the steering wheel hard left, clipping the ankles of a bone-thin male, his deteriorated face not registering even the slightest surprise. I then spun the wheel to the extreme right in time for the cow catcher to lift and throw a twenty-something female rotter up over the hood of the SUV, her gray-black, jawless face smacking the lower portion of the windshield before spinning off the Land Cruiser and falling behind us.

With all my crazy turns it was no wonder Punch couldn't line up a reliable shot at our pursuers.

I increased my speed, seeing open road beyond the abnormals I'd just taken out.

"Smooth sailin', brother," I said. "Now!"

Punch yanked the handle, and the AK rattled to life, the ejected shells dropping into the catch bag, saving us the tiny burns of hot brass against our skin. It stopped after what I guessed was about six seconds.

"Got 'em!" he said. "They flipped that bastard!"

Through the shattered rear window I saw the pursuit vehicle falling behind us as it tumbled side-over-side and slid to a stop.

I smashed my foot on the gas pedal again, catching the bouncing Jeep off to my left, almost even with us after my last maneuver, which slowed us significantly. I reached around forty-five miles an hour, but caution was necessary; here and there, more rotters in various stages of decomposition staggered in front of us, assisted by the buffeting wind of Hurricane George.

At my increased speed, relying on the cow catcher wouldn't be very wise. Oh, they'd fly all right, but their mass might bend the shit out of the Land Cruiser's frame, something that Hemp told me when he'd put it on. It was great for pushing them out of the way at around fifteen or twenty miles an hour, but I wasn't willing to risk it at over forty miles an hour.

I heard a machine gun sound and felt rounds whizzing inches from my nose. Then I heard our AK-47 rattle again, and watched as the head of the asshole in the Jeep's passenger seat exploded like a watermelon. As the Jeep fell back and I saw I had open road, Punch continued firing.

I glanced left to see the windshield turn red and the Jeep crank hard across the road behind me, smashing into a thick copse of pine trees.

I put my attention back on the road. Punch turned in his seat and looked out the destroyed rear window.

"Anyone else back there?" I asked.

Punch didn't answer right away. He stared behind us for a while, then turned back in his seat, facing forward.

"We're good for now," he said.

"For now?" I asked. "How determined you think those guys are?"

"There's not many of 'em, Flex, but there's a pretty uneven number of women to men, which ain't good. Only six women in the bunch, and a shitload of testosterone competing for them. They like to show off, to say the least. Taking you out would be some good bragging rights."

I looked at him and snatched my Glock from my drop holster, pointing it at him. "You said *taking you out*," I said. "Don't you mean *taking us out*?"

Punch pressed himself against the passenger side door, his hands up, palms out. "Flex, it was force of habit. I'm with you, man."

"You're sure about that?" I asked.

"I told you I was bullshitting my way through that group until I found a way out. Nobody leaves. That's their rule. They have sentries at night, and even when I was one, there are never fewer than three, so I was fucked."

"You said you were in Afghanistan," I said. "You're savvy enough to take 'em." I put my gun back in the holster. I believed him, but at the same time, I wanted to hear more.

He relaxed again. "Food was under guard. So was water. Vehicles locked down. I don't know if I've made it clear enough, but I wasn't from around there, and I didn't have pull."

"Did they know you were ex-military?" I asked.

Eric A. Shelman

"Another reason they didn't like me," he said. "These guys are punks. Any sense of order or authority and they try to put you in your place fast. I was a threat to their perceived manhood. Particularly in front of the few women available."

I got what he was saying, and I believed him. I didn't say anything, just nodded.

"We cool?" he asked.

"I put my Glock away, didn't I?"

"Yeah."

"Then we're cool," I said.

We drove in silence for another half hour. Silence was only applicable to the two of us, because outside, a storm was again raging. The tall trees that lined the road beyond the wide, uneven gravel shoulder were nearly bent in half, and the wipers of the Land Cruiser could barely keep up with the torrential rain.

There were several cars on the road, interspersed with rotters that we took down here and there. My first goal was to lay Tony to rest, and after that, reaching the hospital and grabbing as much of the antitoxin and other inoculation medication was paramount. In order to achieve those objectives, I had to introduce Punch to WAT-5 and ensure that neither of us was a zombie magnet along the way.

I pulled the Toyota over, set the parking brake and put it in neutral, cutting the engine. "Okay, we've got something to do."

"What?"

I reached into my shirt pocket and withdrew a baggie. I opened it up, took out the wafer and handed it to him.

"Eat this," I said.

He tentatively took it from me. "What's this? Some kind of protein wafer?"

I looked up the road at the dead creatures zigzagging their ways toward us through the dead cars.

"You'll see," I said.

"I'd like to know what I'm taking before I take it."

"You *are* military, aren't you?"

"Yep," he said.

"It's called WAT-5," I said. "If you take it, it's your best friend in Zombieland. Just trust me on that. Life has to hold some surprises, doesn't it?"

"Fuck it," he said, popping the wafer in his mouth. His face scrunched. "Tastes like shit."

He barely got the words out before his eyelids crashed down and he slumped in his seat.

"I'm used to the flavor," I said to the unconscious man as I popped another wafer in my mouth and chewed it up. I'd taken one at the house less than five hours earlier, so I was in no danger of a snooze.

I awakened him a minute later. "We're not sure why it does that," I said.

"What ...does *what*?" he asked, still groggy.

"Never mind. Anyway, let's get out. You can leave your gun."

"What?" His face said he thought I was crazy. His eyes moved from me to the rotters coming toward us in the street.

Then I silently wondered if they were moving toward us or forging their way toward Isis. Being on the WAT-5 I'd never know. Not that they wouldn't stop for a meal if presented with one, so the whole mental exercise was a waste of my limited brainpower.

"Just follow me," I said.

"Flex, there are biters *right there*, man," said Punch. "What's the harm in being armed?" His voice was respectful, but his expression said he thought I was batshit crazy.

"What kinda gun is that, anyway?" I asked.

"It's a Saiga 12 shotgun with a 30-round drum mag."

"Great zombie gun," I said.

"It is. I'm taking it," he said.

"It's up to you," I said. "Just so you know, I wouldn't have left my weapon either. Not based on the word of a stranger."

That said, I left my Daewoo inside the Toyota and got out. I'm not a complete idiot, and still had my Glocks. If any more Buckfield folks came up on us, WAT-5 wouldn't help.

Eyeing me once more, he got out and came around the Land Cruiser to stand beside me.

"What now?"

"We wait," I said.

"For what?"

"You'll see," I said.

There were five zombies within view.

Two were within ten feet of us, and he lifted the barrel of the shotgun.

"Just wait," I said.

"Sorry, man," he said. "I can't."

I grabbed the barrel and pushed it toward the ground, and his large hand jetted out and snatched my forearm. I stared at him, but didn't let go. His grip was strong and his eyes jerked between me and the dead things, now five feet away.

"I got this," I said, my voice calm. I pushed his hand off of my arm and he let go. Before he could raise his weapon again, I stepped between him and the zombies and kept walking. I reached the first one, its filthy, bloody clothing hanging over its frame like a shroud, and took it by the arm. Its lips had long ago deteriorated, exposing its gnashing teeth, but it made no effort to attack, as I had known would be the case. One eye was missing, and in the dark cavern that once held it, I could see what appeared to be a black spider clinging to a well-spun web.

I didn't look any longer than necessary, but I pulled it toward the other one. My current charge was of an indeterminate age, its rotting so advanced, but the other one

108

had clearly been a quite virile young man. He had no shirt on, and I could see the remnants of what might have been some very well-inked tattoos. I thought I made out a dragon on its left arm that ran from elbow to wrist.

Which is where his arm ended. The bones jutted out from the nub, and a family of some sort of small, black bugs had made this place their home.

"You're fucking crazy," said Punch.

"Not as much as you think," I said, now standing behind them with one on my left and one on my right. We stood there facing Punch. I backed up one step, placed a hand on the sides of each of my zombie slaves' heads, and smashed them together with all my might.

Closing my eyes at impact, their fragile heads crushed into one another, and whatever brains remained in their noggins pulverized as sharp-edged, shattered skull slivers pierced and destroyed them.

I took another step back as the formerly reanimated corpses collapsed to the ground for the final time.

"Flex!" shouted Punch, his shotgun barrel quickly in position. I spun around and saw two rotters within five feet of me.

They continued to advance, but not as though they didn't know what I was; not like that at all. Their arms reached out, their pale, bloodied fingers clawing. The walkers gnashed and snarled and advanced as though they knew damned well that I was living human flesh chocked full of delicious meat and blood.

I staggered backward, confused. *The WAT-5 wasn't working.*

"Drop!" shouted Punch, and I did.

He fired twice in rapid succession and in the time it took to clap your hands, the attacking creatures became headless cadavers sprawled on the asphalt.

Something farther behind them caught my eye. Fast movement. Deliberate. Too deliberate for a typical rotter. It disappeared behind a dilapidated Ford Ranger with four flat tires.

It could only mean one thing.

I yanked my Glocks from the drop holsters and ran toward the pickup where I'd last seen it.

In an instant, it was in the air and on top of the Ranger, staring down at me, its bright red eyes – even in the light of day – boring into my own.

It registered in my subconscious that I could see the roiling bump in her stomach where her zombie baby lived, now and forever. I raised both Glocks and fired, but she was already gone. My eyes searched.

Somehow she reappeared on the hood of the Ranger, then she dropped down and was gone yet again.

A split-second later I heard a swishing-scraping sound, and as I looked down, she was right in front of me, on her stomach and crawling forward fast. I fired downward, blowing two holes in her back, but her claw-like hands had wrapped around my ankles and gripped tight.

I fell backward, dropping the handguns to keep from smacking my head when I landed. As my hands hit the pavement, followed by my back, I saw Punch knee the creature in the head and knock her away.

Her clutched claws did not release my ankles. She was determined, and I was dragged the two feet her momentum carried her. Punch raised the shotgun again, put the barrel against her face and pulled the trigger.

The black-red blood and skull flew from her prone form as her body stopped moving.

Still her hands clutched my ankles, even in death. I jerked my legs and her fingers fell away. I grunted back to my feet and took stock of my condition.

The jeans had kept her from scratching my ankles. I had some road rash on my back from the fall and the slide, but other than that, I'd live.

Punch stared at her, at the other rotters moving toward us up the street, and back at me.

"I thought you said they wouldn't bother us," he said. "So much for that theory."

I tried to catch my breath and shook my head. "They won't, normally. I can explain."

"You're lucky I didn't listen to you," he said. "Brought this." He held up his Saiga.

I nodded. "Yep," I said. "You got a knife on you?"

He shook his head. "Nope. Buckfield management controlled all the knives. Said people could kill quietly and get away."

"And you would have, right?"

"Damned straight," said Punch.

"Roll her over and pull up her top," I said. "I have a knife in the truck."

"Is that necessary?" he asked.

"It is," I said.

I went to the truck and opened the back hatch, pushing the shattered glass off Tony's body and our supplies. I found the knife.

It was a Bowie knife with a ten inch blade, a solid wood handle and a brass guard that Hemp had sharpened to a fillet-worthy edge. I carried it over to the red-eye, who was now in a supine position.

Punch stared at her bulbous stomach, his eyes displaying the horror of her condition. Every few moments the impression of a hand or foot would appear from beneath the skin and disappear again.

"She's why the others came after us," I said.

"*She's* why the *others* came after us?" said Punch.

I looked at her, then at Punch. "There's lots you don't know."

"I guess," he said.

I knelt down, cringing at the pain of my shirt rubbing over my skinned back, and jabbed the knife just below her sternum. I cut to one side, then removed the knife and cut to the other. Then I cut downward on both sides. I wasn't a doctor, but fuck if I didn't play one on TV.

I poked the knife blade in and pulled down the flap.

The placenta was intact. I saw the sack moving like a bag full of kittens, and I poked through that and gave it one big slice.

The rotter baby came sliding out of the black-green muck inside, its fingers clawing, its little, disgusting mouth gnashing.

"See this abomination?" I said, looking at Punch.

He nodded, then turned quickly and gave up the last meal he'd eaten. I waited. It was hard the first time. Maybe every time. I thought of Jennifer on that pool table in Concord, and not for the first or last time.

"Okay," I said. "That's enough." I jammed the knife into the fetus' skull and gave it one twist. I withdrew the blade, wiped it on the nasty clothes of the red-eye, and stood.

"One more thing to take notice of, Punch."

Punch wiped his mouth on his sleeve. "What's that?" he asked, his voice shaky.

"Her hair," I said. "Besides the crimson eyes, look for the hair. It'll look almost nice. Like it was shampooed recently. Not sure why."

"You need to explain this, Flex," he said. "But let's drive a bit more and find a place to lay your friend to rest."

I nodded. "Yeah." Another wave of sadness hit me. I'd lost track of the miles we'd driven and how far we had yet to go.

I thought of my son and Gem. No more fucking distractions and no more delays. If anyone tried to stop me again I'd shoot first and never bother to ask questions.

I had only stopped to kill the road walkers because of where I suspected they were headed. It was lucky we took out the red-eye, because she would only broadcast out to others. From here on out, if a gunshot or the roof-mounted AK weren't sufficient, they would have to walk on. If they made it all the way to Whitmire, well, my people would take 'em out there.

They were and are good, capable defenders.

And I needed the antitoxin.

*****

Bug stood at the window. The wind and pounding rain had died down again, but even when it gusted past 40 miles an hour, it hadn't seemed to slow the advancing rotters much, if at all. He turned back toward us.

"Ever since I got on that helicopter, this shit is what I worried about," said Bug. "I didn't want to bring this shitstorm down on your heads."

Hemp got up and walked to the window, Isis in his arms. She had taken to him, which I didn't find strange. Hemp was funny with children and babies, and he seemed to drop right down to their levels, baby talk and all. He looked through the window with Bug.

"I've got some ideas," he said, bouncing Isis in his arms. She laughed, all of her adult-sized teeth showing, and brought her face to his. I think she playfully kissed him on the mouth. Hemp nuzzled her with his nose, and at that moment, I couldn't wait for their child to be born.

I don't know if I ever explained fully about Isis. If you read Dave Gammon's chronicle, then you already know this. I was fascinated as I read just exactly how this child figured into the rescue of everyone, but I had to give credit where it was due, and that meant to everyone. They had done some insane shit that I can't say I'd have ever agreed to.

Anyway, back to Isis. Her mother, who died in childbirth, was eight months pregnant when she was exposed to the eye vapor of a pregnant, female zombie – in other words, a red-eye.

As a result – and I mentioned it earlier – Isis doesn't sleep. Not ever. She'll sit or lie down, almost in a meditative trance, but she doesn't close her eyes.

Her eyes are red, just like the eyes of the red-eyes themselves, but she's not a zombie. Not even close.

Isis refuses to eat anything other than meat. If given a spoonful of food containing vegetables and meat, she'll use her adult-sized teeth as some sort of straining mechanism, and spit out all but the meat.

She talks. She doesn't babble or coo. She provides input to the subject at hand or says hello. No goo goo shit for her. She is perhaps 13 months old, and can construct full sentences.

Since I learned of this ability, I'd been waiting for her to say something that freaked me out.

Last, but definitely not least, she is what we've been referring to as a siren. She is a siren to the zombies, and her mere presence calls them; beckons them to where she is. Hemp, because of information provided by Dave and Serena from their trip, believes there's way more to this than we know right now. Hemp thinks that Isis may have defenses that she hasn't even figured out yet.

Hemp also believes that Isis carries with her almost supernatural intelligence and he suspects that every ability she has is by some alternative design.

I believe him. He's the damned scientist, after all. The thing that's kind of put me on edge is Hemp's belief that Isis will either say or do something that changes our lives forever, and he's fairly certain that she will instinctively know when to share this.

This is a bit strange coming from a man of science. I suppose the whole corpse reanimation thing has given him reason to re-think the puzzle pieces of life and how they all fit together.

Hemp and Bug kept looking out of the window, and now Isis was, too. I got up and went over to see for myself.

"We've got a break, huh?" I said, squeezing between them and putting my hand on the back of Isis' head.

She smiled at me. "Hi, Gemina," she said.

"Hi, Isis," I said, ice running down by spine.

There were two reasons for the ice, but since I'll get into the next one in a moment, let me explain the first reason now.

Isis' voice is baby-like, but not baby-ish. Imagine – and if you've never met her, then I realize it's impossible – a baby speaking in its own high-pitched voice, but clearly annunciating, as she had just said my name. Now imagine that she can not only speak, but she can listen and understand not only the words you speak in return, but tones, undertones, sarcasm, emotion, and the rest. The whole gamut. Once you can swallow all that, then you can begin to understand how eerily uncanny it is to have a conversation with an infant that you're not certain isn't smarter than you.

I learned a lot over those next few moments.

Hemp turned a half-turn and looked at Isis, then me. "This is the first day you've met this little one," he said. "I never heard anyone say your actual name."

"It's why I have chills right now," I said. "I never did. Nobody calls me that, and for good reason."

"Isis Gammon," said the child, smiling. She turned to look out the window and her little finger jutted out, pointing. "The mothers are here for me," she said, matter-of-factly, holding out her arms to me in the universal baby language for *Take me!*

I say that knowing that Isis could simply have said the words. Hemp nodded and gave her over. I looked at her. "How did you know my name, Isis?" I asked.

"Gemina Cardoza," she said, with perfect pronunciation. It is how I would have said it in my head.

"I need to sit down," I said. I carried Isis to the couch and sat beside Charlie.

"This is weird," said Charlie.

Bug was staring. "She's never talked this much," he said. "And only once or twice about stuff she shouldn't have known."

"Weirder than weird," said Dave. "Isis, you do know stuff, don't you?" he said, smiling.

"I just do," she said, putting her hands out like, "Oh, well!" Her big-toothed smile was infectious, and we all caught it, smiling ourselves.

"I'm afraid to ask her how Tony and Flex are doing," I said. "Afraid of –"

"Anthony is gone," said Isis, cutting me off. "I'm sorry."

All of our smiles, including Isis', disappeared.

Hemp and Bug turned from the window and both walked quickly back to where we sat.

"Isis!" said Bug. "You don't say stuff like that!"

"It's real, daddy," she said. "Anthony is dead. Not by the mothers or the hungerers."

Tears welled up in my eyes, and now Serena was wide awake. I suppose she had just been resting her eyelids. When Charlie and Dave found her, she had been living in ZFZ-4, or Zombie-Free-Zone #4 in Shelburne, Vermont, where Tony Mallette ran the shelter.

Serena got out of the recliner and moved quickly to where I sat with Isis on my lap. "Isis," Serena said, kneeling in front of me and taking the child gently by the arms. Isis returned Serena's concerned gaze with an expression that spoke of compassion and understanding that should have been no part of her emotional depth at such a young age.

"Arrow," she said. "He died quickly. You worry about suffering." She reached up and took one of Serena's hands and squeezed it in her tiny ones. "He never knew pain," she said.

"I can't do this," I said. I couldn't sit and listen to a child speak of things she couldn't know. She might see it all in her little mind, but I was without the ability to put all the little pieces together and determine whether what she said was either good or bad news.

Clearly what she'd said about Tony was horrible news. "I think I need to go outside and clear my head in between these storms," I said.

Isis turned suddenly to me and said, "Wait, Gem."

I cried harder. I believed her. I couldn't stop my next words. "Isis," I sobbed. "Is Flex alright? Is he alive?"

Isis' mouth turned upward into a smile, but she did not part her lips and expose her teeth. She nodded. "Flex is with Punch," she said. "Safe. Killed one mother who almost hurt Flex. Killed hungerers."

"Hungerers," said Hemp. "Isis, is that what you call them? The ones outside?"

"The hungerers," she said. "They follow."

"Then the mothers can only be what we call the red-eyes," said Hemp.

"What's a punch," I asked. "Isis, what is punch?"

"A man," she answered.

"A good man?" I asked.

"Like Flex," said Isis.

I let out a sigh and let my eyes close. I didn't know what to believe. I remembered what we've all said a thousand times. *Kids say the darndest things.*

117

Isis turned away from Serena and clutched my shirt as she moved her mouth up to my ear to say, "It is real."

Her voice was a whisper, and each word that left her lips and drifted into my consciousness felt true and undeniable. "Flex and Punch will bury Anthony," she said. "But the angry follow."

The angry. I didn't want to ask Isis to whom she referred as the angry.

Isis wrapped her little arms tightly around my neck and squeezed me. She spoke once more, her tiny voice innocent, but clear and unwavering. The infant, red-eyed Isis was as convincing as any psychic who delivered her prognostications with such resolve that you dared not disbelieve them.

"No more telling now," she whispered. "Flex is safe. Punch is a good man. Sadness only for Anthony."

I broke down then. When I did, we all did. We had no doubt that what Isis had shared with us was true.

And we all knew what Tony Mallette had done for us.

Dave held Serena, whose tears came in a flood.

Our hearts weighed like stones.

*****

We had the small, collapsible military shovels in the Land Cruiser that were handy for snuffing out campfires and performing other tasks. They could be useful for occasionally severing the gnashing heads of zombies, though I'd never used them for that yet. Together, using this equipment, Punch and I dug a three foot deep grave for my friend.

We'd found a spot down a gravel side road that was easy to miss. In fact, we'd missed it at first and had to turn around. Punch thought it would be unlikely the Buckfield people would head that way if they were still in pursuit, which he was fairly certain they were.

"That's good enough," I said, looking at the three-foot deep hole near the bank of a small, clear-running creek. There were no trees there, so we encountered no roots. I had a blanket in back of the Land Cruiser, so Punch and I wrapped him in it.

The rain was still falling but it was much lighter, dripping off the highest branches of the trees and falling in large, crystalline drops.

Tony's body lay on the wet ground beside what would be his final resting place. I looked at the cylindrical bundle, my fingers playing over the gold cornicello he had worn. He once told me it was to ward off the evil eye, believed by Italians to harm nursing mothers and their babies, bearing fruit trees, milking animals, and the sperm of men – the forces of generation.

I had initially chosen a gold medallion that Tony always wore with the likeness of St. Christopher molded into it, accompanied by the words, *St. Christopher, Protect Us.*

I changed my mind just as we prepared to wrap him in the blanket. Instead, I took the cornicello.

St. Christopher had failed Tony Mallette, just as I had. The good saint and I had screwed the pooch on that task.

But we still had Charlie and Hemp and their forthcoming baby to think of, not to mention our infant son and the other children yet to be conceived. If we were going to put any stock in superstition or religion after what had happened to Tony, I figured I'd just as soon put all my chips on the power of a gold, horn-shaped talisman and its ability to ward off the evil that would most likely affect the thing that all of us would soon care about the most: The crucial repopulation of this planet.

I closed my eyes. I don't know what Punch intended by it, but I heard him step away from me as I spoke. After

119

all, he didn't know me and maybe he was just giving me privacy he thought I'd appreciate.

"Tony, you were a good man," I began. "A real good man. You were a strange motherfucker, I'll grant you that. You freely helped my friends and me in Vermont, and you never made us feel like it was an inconvenience for you – not even a small one. In Concord, you came along when we needed you most and least expected you, and you helped whenever anyone asked. Almost like St. Christopher sent you himself. Who knows? Maybe he did."

I paused a moment. Another strong breeze worried the higher branches of the soaring trees, and shook a thousand gathering raindrops on our heads. Before long, the wind picked up enough to swirl even the wet leaves at our feet. I closed my eyes again and went on.

"When I knew I was coming on this trip, I didn't want anybody else along. I didn't want anyone holdin' me back by draggin' ass. You didn't. You wanted to do your share, and it got you killed. And while this might not be in accordance with your apparent Catholicism, I will see your death, my friend, and raise it as many as necessary to protect the rest of your family. Us. All of us were your family, Tony."

I was finished. I didn't say Amen because I wasn't talking to God. I was giving thanks and talking directly to Tony Mallette. If what he believed was true, he caught every word.

I turned and nodded to Punch, who leaned down and lifted one end of the bundle that was Tony Mallette's body. I took the other end, and we laid him gently in the hole.

Punch grabbed the shovels, gave one to me, and started filling in the grave. After two scoops, he said, "Nice, Flex. I'm sure he knew what a good friend you were."

I didn't answer right away. I waited until Tony's body was beneath a full layer of dirt, then said, "I could've been a better friend. Just a little more effort and I'd have been the kind of friend he needed. He'd still be alive."

Even as I said it, I knew that if Punch had been in Afghanistan, he'd seen his own share of Hell long before it became widespread.

We finished the burial in another fifteen minutes and kicked leaves around the hole to hide the obvious, freshly-disturbed soil. I'm not sure why; I just didn't want anyone rooting around, no matter what it was they sought.

We got back to the Land Cruiser and checked the map. Based on the small, unnamed road, and the proximity to the creek, we figured out that we were less than an hour's drive from my destination.

I geared up for it, mentally.

*****

Rachel and Lola had slept through the worst of the on-again-off-again storms, showing us all just how tired they were. Nelson had ridden his scooter over, and he was now fully equipped with a Daewoo like Flex's.

"Holy shit there's a lot of rotters around," he said, toeing his kickstand down. He'd found the scooter in a shed at his new digs, and there was no convincing him to leave it there. It was like he was home again. This one even had double pegs so he could tote Rachel on the back, who admittedly, wouldn't add much weight. Once there, he peeked in on Rachel and Lola before coming outside to help us.

We rechecked the windows, and despite the fact that we hadn't had much over forty mile per hour gusts, we were still relieved to see they held so far.

Hemp came back from the field in the golf cart with Bug. "We pushed the bundled fencing together and doubled the baling wire," he said. "Even went around several of them. I think they're safe enough."

Bug stood beside him, drenched to the bone again. "Took out another six rotters, too," he said, shaking his head. "Be honest. What kind of numbers were you lookin' at before we got here?"

I decided to oblige him. "Four a day was a lot."

"It's like they were following us in the chopper," said Nelson. He shrugged. "Maybe they were."

"We adapt," said Hemp. "Isis may yet have some abilities we're unaware of. It seems likely that even she doesn't fully know what she'll be able to do."

"You gonna train my kid like a puppy?" asked Bug. He wore a wry smile.

"It's actually an excellent analogy," said Hemp. "She, like a puppy, may very well have abilities she's not aware of. She's certainly smart enough that if we suggest something, she could put it to test. If she understands and tries, she can tell us her thoughts."

"She makes my Subdue-do look like amateur-time," said Nelson.

"You're memory is your true talent," I said. "I'd give anything for that."

"That's a good point," said Hemp. "Nelson, when I work with Isis, I'd like you there whenever you can manage it."

"Why?" he asked.

"Because. As we accumulate information on her abilities, nothing will slip your mind. You may put puzzle pieces together the rest of us miss."

"The pothead?" asked Bug, nudging Nelson.

"Dude, you know better than to touch me," said Nelson. He held up his hands. "Come on."

"I don't feel like gettin' muddy right now," said Bug smiling.

Dave walked around the corner of the house and we all looked toward him. It was by force of habit. The abnormals had a way of just moseying up, even when we were all on WAT-5. Right now, none of us were. We were on full alert and armed, so it would have been a waste, mostly.

Dave gave us all a wave as he came closer. "I put all the chairs and junk from the back porch inside," he said. "No projectiles back there."

"Cool," I said. "Thanks, Davey."

I looked at my watch. I only wore it when I was worried about someone out on a run, and I wasn't even sure it was right anymore. It didn't matter, because it told me what I needed to know.

"They've been gone four hours," I said. "They could be back any time," I added, then caught myself. "Flex should be back," I corrected. I was glad that Serena hadn't been outside when I screwed up. She was having a hard time with Isis' news of Tony's death, as we all were.

"Give him time, Gem," said Hemp. "He's got the weather, the situation with Tony, a new companion. It's going to slow him down."

"I get that," I said. "But doesn't he have a portable Ham in that damned truck?"

"He does, but so might others," said Hemp. "I recall a certain infant saying something about *the angry*. I don't know who that might be, but she clearly named the others, so I don't believe she was referring to abnormals."

"They might have a radio," I said.

"Exactly," said Hemp.

"We done out here for now?" asked Nelson. "Wait. We're not done yet." He unstrapped his Daewoo and jumped off the porch, skirting by his scooter. To his left were two apparent diggers, moving rickety-slow toward the front porch. He raised his weapon and with two single shots, detached the skull caps from their heads.

Nelson then swung the barrel right. With a single shot, he knocked out the third. He turned toward us. "Where the hell are you putting all these?"

Hemp pointed. "Golf cart. We're dumping them in the pit. Hold off for now, Nel. Let's go have a rest."

"You guys have been working," said Nelson. "They look deteriorated enough. I'll take care of them and be back inside in a few."

"Dude, I'm not letting you do it by yourself," said Dave. He turned to us. "You guys go inside. We'll be there in ten."

We obeyed. The two longhairs did the heavy lifting. We went inside, took off our wet, muddy clothes and boots and collapsed for the moment.

I checked my watch again … and every five minutes for what soon became longer than I was built to stand.

*****

Chapter Six

As he had since I'd encountered him and his friends, Punch looked behind us every few minutes, and it made me nervous. I couldn't take any more delays. I needed to get to the goddamned hospital, get the stuff and get back.

Punch was on the gun and he'd used it a shitload already. The rotters were on parade, and the blasting wind and driving rain, while slowing them down substantially, was not dampening their spirits.

Maybe because the fuckers had no spirits.

"Here," said Punch, pointing to a sign ahead. The sturdy wind buffeted the sign, causing it to twist in place as if it were silently screaming, "No!"

"Take the 77 north," said Punch. "Just after this bridge make a left."

I saw the onramp. It was wide open, and I got on it and hit the gas. I knew it was only around 40 miles from this junction, and I was ready to get there.

"Shit!" I cursed, reaching the top of the ramp and slamming on the Land Cruiser's brakes. "Fuckin' jammed."

The traffic on both sides of the 77 was, at one time anyway, heading south. Nobody was trying to get to Charlotte, which told me one thing; it was ZombieWorld – the worst fuckin' theme park ever invented by man or planet Earth.

The rain had stopped again, but the dark, swirling clouds remained. The rain that had fallen in bucketfuls from the sky was not enough to clean away the filth that had accumulated on the many vehicles over the last thirteen or so months.

Yeah, I was in a hurry. So why did I sit there, looking at the line of cars that stretched away from the Land Cruiser's bumper as far as any creature's eye could see? Because it was like every apocalyptic movie I'd ever seen, only this was real. That made it way more frightening and far beyond any suspension of disbelief I'd ever engaged in before.

I was fucking waxing philosophical or something. I was waxing some shit to be sure.

"Flex?"

I guess I heard Punch's voice, but I didn't do anything about it but continue to stare. I think Tony's death had freaked me out more than I knew at the time. I looked at the cars, lined up in a jagged row, once chock full of wanna-be refugee survivors. Some of the men, women and children in these cars might have tried to escape the traffic jam, but if they tried, it means they got out and hoofed it, no doubt hauling all the survival possessions they owned on their backs. Without proper weapons, they would've been chew toys for the stinking dead before very long.

I could see by looking at the cars that the drivers had been of varying types; there were the cars that were arrow straight in their lanes. These were the determined drivers who had snatched their little spot on the highway and were goddamned happy to move that foot or so every half hour. They turned off their engines to save fuel, waiting patiently for the next inches of highway to slide beneath their cars.

These drivers had been countered by those who angled toward the lane either to the left or right of their own; the ones never content to stay where they were, always looking for that foot or two of open highway beside them, sure that lane was moving faster. Once they saw daylight, they jammed on the accelerator just enough to squeeze ahead of the car beside them.

The opaque windshields, thankfully, were so obscured by muddy filth that we were spared the horrid sight of the hundreds of squirming, flesh-hungry carcasses that no doubt remained captive atop leather, cloth and vinyl seats for more than a year now.

"Flex, man," came Punch's voice again. This time I turned toward him and raised my eyebrows.

"Yeah?" I said.

"I can't look at that shit anymore, bud. Saw enough of it in the middle east."

At first I didn't know what he meant. I turned back and lowered my eyes to the ground around the cars.

Skeletons. Everywhere. Scraps of clothing caught under flat car tires. Some doors were open on the cars and bodies draped out of them, their mouths forever opened in silent screams.

I hadn't seen the decaying trees for the rusting, steel forest.

I shook my head. "Shit," I said, putting the gearshift in reverse. "Sorry, man. It's a lot." I turned my head and started backing down the onramp.

I drove east on the road we'd come in on. "Check that map, Punch. See if you can find another way to the city."

"You got some balls on you, man," said Punch, serious. "All those cars jamming out of the city and you're still going in? They were running from something."

"And we know what they were runnin' from, but I don't have a choice, Punch. My son needs the antitoxin for sure, but he also needs any other vaccines I can grab. Kid's wide open. Polio, the fuckin' Diphtheria that's already showed up, smallpox, all sorts of shit just waitin' to kill him."

"You never think of that crap, do you?" asked Punch. "Civilization, man. We take a lot of things for granted." He shook his head. "Right here, Flex. Turn left on Edgeland."

"This road will get us there?"

"It looks like we'll be going around Robin Hood's barn to do it," said Punch, "but yeah, I'm pretty sure. It's clear, anyway."

"You're using the term loosely," I said.

"Clear means we can get through or winch our way."

I drove on. Whenever Punch saw a walker, he blew him off the road unless the pilot was in position to sweep them aside, breaking their legs. I figured even the most industrious abnormal couldn't get all the way to Whitmire with a pair of broken sticks to walk on.

The ride was bumpy and parts of the road required full 4-wheel drive to get through. The Land Cruiser had been the perfect vehicle, though. Before we knew it we'd knocked out twenty miles.

I checked my watch. It was almost six o'clock in the evening, and the sun was working its way down. I hadn't wanted to get into the city at night, but choices weren't plentiful now.

"Buddy, can you reach back there and see if you can grab that big, green duffle?"

"Sure," he said. He crawled back over the seat and extended his long arm, snatching the bag and dragging it into the back seat.

"What do you need?" he asked.

"There's a portable Ham radio in there," I said. "It's a Yaesu."

"Good radio," he said. "Familiar with them."

"Then get on a frequency and start broadcasting. Just say Flex Sheridan over and over. Our guys scan, so if they hear you, they'll answer."

Punch kept it up for so long that I got sick of hearing my own name.

"Give it up for now," I said. "Thanks."

"No problem."

At some point, Edgeland Road had changed to Mt. Holly Road.

"Shit," I said. "That sign said I-77's up ahead. It's gonna dump us back on there."

Punch scanned the map. "No, Flex. Just stay on here. It's the 31, and it looks like you can snake your way to the hospital from here on side roads."

"You sure?"

"Looks like it," said Punch.

The area was getting more populated, and we were seeing a lot more abnormals, both diggers and other varieties, staggering in the streets. The good news was that they weren't all working their way south, toward Isis.

Or, for that matter, my wife, my son and a ton of other people I love.

A sign said I was now on the 31. "I want to stop and have a bite to eat before we head into the big, bad city," I said. "I got a funny feeling we're gonna need our strength."

"Hey," said Punch. "There's a convenience store up there. Maybe they got some beef jerky. Nice protein."

"I could use a break," I said. "Got plenty of food, but Tony only snagged a couple of pieces of jerky. Got a baby back home that hoards the stuff."

"A baby?" asked Punch, a smile on his face. "Eating jerky?"

"Long story," I said. "Help me do this, and I'll take you back with us. That might not seem like such a great offer right now, but once you meet everyone, you'll change your mind."

"Any place is better than Buckfield, Flex," he said. "Thanks."

*****

We all sat in the living room looking like zombies ourselves. Ordinarily we might have been on the front porch, but things had changed in a hurry. More walking dead; storms that could blow your pants off; rain that blew sideways so hard it sounded like someone was outside sandblasting the siding.

If the rotters could push their way through that shit to get to little Isis, we could very well be in a world of hurt.

None of us heard him coming because of the melee outside, but suddenly the door flew open and Jim Scofield came in, slamming it behind him.

"Another storm band's coming through," he said, wiping the rain from his hair and face. He shrugged out of the raincoat he wore and dropped it by the front door. "Other than that, I have worse news."

I would have thrown out a snarky "No shit, Sherlock!" at his comment about another band coming through, but his last statement overrode my normal sarcasm.

"What is it?" asked Hemp, beating me to the punch. Hemp looked like he really needed a nap himself. I checked my watch yet again. It was now almost 7:30 PM and the sun had disappeared. The sky, already shadowed by the storm clouds, lingered between the light and the darkness.

I hoped like hell that Flex and the man named Punch had reached the hospital, gotten what we needed, and were on the way back. I also hoped Isis was wrong about Tony. I held onto that hope.

"Gina's taken a turn for the worse," Scofield said. "She's having a lot of trouble getting even a small breath."

Serena, who had plopped down on the couch half an hour earlier and fallen asleep in under thirty seconds, sat up, rubbing her eyes. "Oh, my God," she said, fighting a yawn. "Is she going to be okay?"

"Not without help," said Hemp. "That means it's advanced. The other symptoms, while unpleasant, won't necessarily kill you, but she needs a respirator, and I have one in the lab."

He went to the door and looked out. It was pouring rain, and visibility was almost nil.

"Can this kill her?" I asked. "That fast?" While I thought of Gina first, my mind went to Raylene a split-second later. A mother's worst nightmare had to be watching her child suffer and being helpless to stop it.

"We can't know for certain how long she's had the disease," said Hemp. "But the advanced symptoms of Diphtheria can paralyze the muscles that control respiration.

She may not have much time at all without assistance breathing."

Doc Scofield was at the door, grabbing his coat and throwing it on. "C'mon, Hemp. You know where the stuff is."

"It's in the mobile lab," said Hemp. He didn't bother with a coat. He was out the door and on the porch. Before Jim closed the door, Hemp said, "It's very bad out here, Gem. Start the small generator on the back porch and get that Ham radio on. Flex might try to reach us."

I kicked myself for not thinking of it earlier. There I was, worried as hell about Flex, and he didn't even have a way to get in touch with us.

Hemp wasn't finished. "I might need to get hold of you when we're at Jim's, too, so keep the other walkies on."

"Go!" I said, and ran to the back door.

"Need help, Gem?" asked Dave, following.

We went to the back porch and I lifted the panel and hit the start button. The little generator fired up instantly.

"I'm good," I said, and ran past him back inside. I powered up the Ham and saw Hemp's MP5 leaning against the wall.

"Shit!" I shouted. "Hemp didn't take his weapon!"

"Is he on WAT-5?" asked Charlie.

"No," I said. "Damnit!"

Charlie ran to the kitchen drawer and pulled out a baggie. She took out four wafers and ran them to Dave. "Take these, Dave. They're probably still in the lab. Hurry!"

Dave took them, grabbed Hemp's gun, and ran to the door.

"One of them is for you," said Charlie.

"I can't eat it now," he said. "I'll pass out."

"Shit," said Charlie.

I grabbed two pistols from the counter and hurried to the door as Charlie pulled it open, the roar of the storm filling the stillness of the room. She gave him the wafers and he stuffed them in his pockets.

I gave him the guns. "No time for holsters, buddy," I said. "Just tuck these in your pants and go. Careful, they're ready to fire."

Dave took the guns, following my suggestion, sticking them in his pants for the moment.

"Okay," said Charlie. "Be fucking careful!"

"Got it," he said, opening the door and hitting the porch full stride.

I saw the taillights of Scofield's car, already too far away to hear him, even if Dave screamed.

I ran back into the kitchen and unhooked the keys to the Crown Vic from the rack on the wall. I ran back to the door and threw them to Dave. "Take the Ford and go, Dave."

Dave was halfway to the Crown Vic in seconds. He reached it, got in and fired the engine and we watched him spin the tires in the wet mud and gravel as he pulled out of the drive and hit the pavement.

Charlie and I watched as one of our rotting nemeses staggered toward the house, fell, struggled back to its feet, and continued.

"Come on, Charlie," I said. "I want everyone on WAT-5 tonight. Go get the girls, would you?"

Bug was in our room with Isis again. A thought crossed my mind. "Will it work on her I wonder?" I said.

"What, Gem?" asked Charlie.

"She's talking about Isis and WAT-5," said Serena.

"She only eats meat," said Charlie. "I wonder if she'd even try it."

"Meat eater or not," I said. "It's medicine, and you take that shit whether you want it or not. That's the rules of childhood, and they're not negotiable."

"Good luck with that," said Charlie.

After the boarding up of the house was completed and there was another break in the storm, Nelson had taken Rachel on his scooter back to his place. I suppose I should say *their* place. Lola was in with Trina and Taylor, who were playing with an old Spirograph game that I hadn't seen since I was a little girl, and thank goodness the directions were still there. Right after they'd started playing with it, every once in a while Trina would run in and show me what an amazing new picture she'd drawn with it. She knew I liked to draw, too.

"I'm going to tell Lola what's happening and bring them their wafers," I said. I liked Lola. She reminded me a little of me and a little of Charlie.

"We'll dose," said Charlie. "Wake us up when you come back."

"Gotcha," I said, walking down the hallway.

The door was cracked, so I pushed it open. All three of them were sprawled on the beds dead asleep, the old drawing game abandoned for now.

I sat on the edge of the bed and gently shook them awake. "Hey, girls," I said.

Lola's eyes opened and she tried to focus. It was still her first day here, and I could see that her sleep was thick and deep. The last thing she wanted was to be awake, and I knew after flying across the country in a helicopter, she probably cherished the relative silence of the house, even with the howling wind and rain outside.

"We're passing out WAT-5," I said. "I guess you have experience with it from your trip with Dave and Serena?"

Lola smiled. "Oh, yeah. So what you're saying is, if I want to continue my little nap, this is a perfect opportunity to do it."

"How do you feel?" I asked.

133

Lola's eyebrows went up and she nodded her head. "Pretty good, actually. I might like to take the WAT-5 and mess around with my siren abilities a bit."

I looked at her. "What do you mean?"

"Well, they asked me if I could repel the red-eyes, and the fact is, I only tried once. Might be one of those things that takes practice."

I thought about it. Just because one piece of a particular talent came easily, didn't mean they all would. Like a diver who can swan dive as though he's been doing it since birth, but a reverse dive with a triple twist takes him a while to master.

"Once you're on the wafer, it's up to you how you burn the time," I said. "We're only doing this because in spite of this weather, Isis seems to be getting them here."

Lola stood. The girls were still sleeping soundly. "Where is Isis?"

"In with Bug," I answered. "I guess you guys are still pretty wiped, huh?"

Lola nodded her head and smiled. "Yeah, but relieved. I don't know how long I'll stay, but I'm just glad to spend time with other people for now."

I know I was mushy, but I already liked this girl, and didn't want to see her go. "Lola, where would you go?"

"Texas, for starters," she said.

"Texas?" I asked.

"I love Texas. I like shit kicking music, boots, cowboy hats. Not to mention western holsters and sidearms."

"Using the zombie apocalypse to fulfill some fantasy?" I asked, smiling.

"Maybe," said Lola. "I don't know. Maybe some time here with you guys will change my mind, but Texas is definitely on my radar."

I shrugged. "Not positive Texas really applies anymore."

"There will always be a Texas," said Lola, smiling. "With or without a United States of America."

I had to ask. "Lola, have you ever been to Texas?"

She nodded. "Once. I was driving through with my mom, and we went through Kerrville. Everyone who passed by waved at us – mostly pickups – and we saw deer on the side of the road with beautiful, tree-covered hills behind them. Not what I pictured about Texas before that."

"I just envisioned a cabin in the middle of that," I said.

"I'm sure I can find one if I go there," she said. "I might want to find a partner to enjoy it with, though."

"Stick around," I said. "Maybe this Punch guy will push your buttons."

"If he's a halfway decent guy, I'd rather he flip my switch," said Lola, smiling. "He doesn't want to push my buttons."

"Okay," I said. "You've got Taylor, I'll get Trina." I leaned forward and put my nose in Trina's ear, puffing air in and out. In a moment, her hand moved up to her ear, trying to push me away. I then resorted to kisses on her neck.

"Mommy," Trina groaned, rolling onto her back, her eyes cracking open. I lowered my face and nuzzled my nose into her cheek.

"C'mon," I said. "Time for WAT-5."

"Yuck," she grumbled.

Trina sat up and saw Lola tickling Taylor behind her ear with a very light touch of her fingers. Taylor involuntarily arched her back and pushed her head back, but Lola just moved to a different spot.

Lola leaned down, her lips very near Taylor's ear. "You guys get very tired drawing pictures with a fifty-year-old toy," she whispered.

"It's fun," said Taylor, her eyes opening now. "Did you see what I did?"

"Yeah, it's how I learned, silly," said Lola. "Yours look better than mine."

"Okay, up now girls," I said. "Come out front and we'll give you the stuff. I want to tell you what's going on. Who wants to go wake up Bug and Isis?"

"Isis won't be sleeping," said Trina. "Right, mommy?"

"Right," I said. "She apparently doesn't do that."

"C'mon, Tay," said Trina. "Let's go get them. Mommy, Bug doesn't sleep in the buff, does he?"

I laughed out loud and shook my head. "The fucking buff? Where did you hear that?"

"Nelson."

"In what context?"

Trina cocked her head. "Huh?"

"How did he use it in a sentence?" I asked, smiling.

"He said 'I sleep in the buff. Pajamas make me feel like I'm tied up.'"

"Sounds like Nelson," I said.

"I think so too, and I've only known him a week or so," said Lola.

Lola and I went into the living room where Serena and Charlie sat slumped against one another, both apparently having taken their wafers at the same time.

I heard noises on the porch. I thought of Hemp, Doc Scofield and Dave out there. I shook the two girls, who began to stir, then I went to the window to peer between the boards and the window frame.

There were at least twenty rotters out there. As I stared out, Lola came up behind me and looked through another gap.

"Shit," she said. "Isis?"

"Wasn't like this yesterday," I said. "Hasn't been like this since we settled in."

"She's going to be a challenge," said Bug, walking in behind Trina and Taylor, Isis in his arms. "One you may or may not want to deal with."

I turned away from the window and smiled at him. "The world's full of challenges, Bug. That beautiful baby deserves protection until she's old enough to figure out what she's got built in."

"Thank you, Gemina," said Isis, smiling with a full mouth of visible teeth.

"You're welcome, sweetie," I said.

"May I?" asked Lola, walking toward Bug and holding out her arms.

"If it's okay with Isis, it's okay with me," said Bug. "But she can pretty much answer for herself."

"Let's play," said Isis, holding out her hands.

Lola took her, and I couldn't help but smile as I watched the pair. Lola bounced her, and Isis seemed to enjoy it, but she kept looking at the couch, pointing. "Sit!" she said.

"You want to sit down?" asked Lola.

"Yes," she said. "We'll think to each other," said Isis.

Lola carried her to the couch, and Charlie and Serena, who were still shaking away the cobwebs, slid to either side, allowing Lola and Isis room between them.

Lola balanced Isis on her lap, facing her. Once in position, and being held firmly by Lola, Isis stared into Lola's eyes. Lola, smiling, stared back.

Two crimson-eyed girls, sharing a moment. I was fascinated. So, apparently, were Charlie and Serena. They watched, mesmerized.

"What are they doing?" asked Taylor, leaning on the back of the couch, watching the two.

Then, almost imperceptibly at first, something began to happen. Mist started drifting from each of their eyes as they fixated on one another.

No blinking. Their noses were six inches apart, no more, and they did not speak. It seemed that to them, we had all disappeared, and now we all stared at them as they stared at one another.

The mist was almost laser focused between them. It was the deep red, not the pink of the typical rotter on the porch. It was like that of the red-eyes themselves, and now the mist from Lola's eyes blended with that of the infant, Isis.

"What is happening?" whispered Charlie.

Serena slid closer to them and looked closely at Lola. "Her pupils are enormous," she said. "and the mist is swirling."

"Careful," I said.

"I've never seen Isis put out any vapor before," said Bug. He had moved around beside the couch on Serena's side, and was staring, open-mouthed. "What the hell are they doing?"

Serena turned her attention to Isis. "Hers, too. Big eyes."

It went on and on. Ten minutes passed. Suddenly, it was as if the molecules of which the vapor consisted just vanished. The vapor drifted upward slightly, then it was gone.

Lola's expression changed, and her eyes refocused. She turned toward Serena, then Charlie. "Wow," she breathed.

"What just happened, Lola?" asked Bug.

"You might ask your daughter," said Lola, a slight smile spreading over her lips. "She did it."

Bug moved around to the front of the couch and lifted Isis from Lola's lap. Lola's hands fell away and he hoisted her up.

"Hi, Daddy," she said.

"Hi, baby girl," he said. "What were you doin' just then?"

"Learning of her past," she said. "I wanted to know how she became like me."

"But she's not like you, sweetheart," said Bug. "She sleeps, she eats things other than meat."

"She has moving thoughts, daddy."

He looked at all of us. "Moving thoughts?" he asked. "How do you mean?"

"Thoughts that carry on the wind," she said.

"How the hell do you even know what wind is?" asked Bug. "You're just a baby." He hugged her to him. When he pulled back, she looked at him again. She smiled, her full-sized teeth gleaming.

"Because you know, daddy. You've taught me much."

"But Isis," said Bug, with almost what I'd call fear in his eyes. "We've never talked about things like that. About wind and weather and stuff."

Isis reached out and placed an open palm on the side of her father's head. "I hear from here," she said. "When you sleep, and when you sit quietly. I learn from you, daddy. I know you're sad about mama. You see her when you sleep."

Bug turned around and dropped down hard between Serena and Lola. Serena pressed herself into the arm of the couch to give Bug room.

"How do you know, baby?" he asked. "That daddy's sad?"

"You cry with your eyes closed," she said. "I listen to your thoughts. You always dream of mama. Every night."

Bug started to cry. Isis just stared.

"I don't remember my dreams," he said.

"That's okay," said Isis. "You remember mama. The pictures in your head let me see her, too. She is beautiful."

"Give me my goddamned wafer," said Bug. "Only thing's gonna keep me from bawlin' like an idiot is to pass out."

Lola stared at Isis. "It went both ways," she said. "Isis shared with me, too."

"What could she know to share?" I asked.

"Dave got to the house," said Lola. "But there is death there."

I looked at my Uzi by the door. It was instinctive. The handheld clicked. "Gem? Gem? You read?"

It was on the table. Charlie flew off the couch and snatched it up. "Hemp, we read! What's going on? Is everyone all right?"

"No, I'm afraid not," he said. "We've lost the girl."

"What do you mean we've lost her?" asked Charlie, staring at us as she spoke.

"Her mother's dead," came Hemp's sad voice. "Her … who's listening, Charlie?"

Charlie looked at us, checked the back patio, and walked to the door. She slid it open and went outside.

We didn't hear the rest of the conversation. None of us talked.

"Raylene is in transition," said Isis with perfect annunciation. "Gina is one of the hungerers."

I understood. I walked quickly to the slider and pushed it open. I closed it behind me after I stepped onto the porch.

"Charlie," I said.

She held up her hand, listening to Hemp on the other end of the radio. I held out my hand and she passed it to me.

"Hemp," I said.

"Gem?"

"Yeah, Hemp. It's me. Isis says Raylene is in transition. Take her outside and shoot her in the head."

"Her daughter got a good head start on that, Gem. But the information you received is correct. She didn't destroy Raylene's brain."

"Shoot her now."

There was a pause on the line.

140

"Dave just took her outside. She's unconscious."

"Good," I said. "No sense in her being frightened."

"Gem?" said Hemp.

"Yeah?"

"How did she know?"

"Isis?" I asked.

"Yes," said Hemp.

"Same way she knew about Tony," I said. "She just knows shit."

"Okay. We've taken the WAT-5, so we're good now."

"Not if a red-eye is directing the show," I said. "Hurry back. All of you. And get Nelson and Rachel on your way back. They need to be on WAT-5, too."

"10-4," said Hemp. "Out."

We waited. There didn't seem to be anything else to do. It was now working its way toward 9:00 at night.

Suddenly static sounded on the Ham radio. Then a voice: "Flex Sheridan. Flex Sheridan. Fle-"

It cut off.

Shit! It's on scan!

I ran to it and moved back one frequency, then grabbed the transmitter. "Flex! Are you there? Flex?"

I tried to calm my pounding heart.

"I'm here, Gem," I heard, but it was broken up and I only caught enough to be able to piece together what was said. The storm wasn't making things easier.

"Are you alright, Flex?"

"I am, Gem. I'm right outside of Charlotte, but it's night now, so I'm wonderin' if I shouldn't wait until morning to go."

"See many abnormals?" I asked, my heart settling now, just at the sound of his voice.

"Yeah, they're here," he said. "Gem, I have some terrible news."

"Is it … about Tony?" I asked. "If it is, then you don't have to tell us. We know."

There was silence. I took it as confusion, and understandably so. "Flex? Isis knew," I said.

"The … the baby?" he asked.

"There is only one Isis, Flex. And she knew. She also said you're with someone named Punch."

"My God," said Flex. "I'm fightin' chills right now."

"Is he safe?" I asked. "Is there a Punch?"

"There is a Punch," said Flex. "And he's a good guy, but I need to warn you, Gem. The place where he was, Buckfield, there's a bunch of heartless, desperate motherfuckers. They're not rotters, which means they use weapons and they think."

"Okay, but why do you think they'll come here?"

"Not sayin' they will," said Flex. "But we winched a bunch of cars to clear the bridge, so they might figure out we came from the south. They could just drive until they find out from where."

"Why, Flex? Would they try to kill us?"

"Probably some, yeah," said Flex. "But according to Punch, they're short on women, and you know what that could mean. I want you to be extra careful."

"How far from us?" I asked.

"About forty-five minutes north. I don't know if they'll try anything in this kind of weather, but I have a feeling they might come looking around that way. They could use the storm to mask their approach."

"Are you safe?" I asked.

"For now. How's little Flexy?"

"No symptoms so far," I said. "But Hemp says that's not unusual. The girl just died, Flex. Gina."

"Jesus," he said.

I turned away from the group and held the transmitter close. "After she died, she turned, babe. Then the bitch ate some of her mother."

"I don't want to wait until the mornin', Gem." He said, new determination in his voice. "But if I think it's safer, I'll have to. If it's not too big a risk, I'm gettin' what we need and comin' home. Tonight."

"Don't get killed. Take WAT-5. Promise."

"Don't worry, Gem. I promise I won't be stupid."

"Put Punch on, Flex."

"What?" asked Flex.

"I want to talk to Punch."

"Okay," said Flex. "Go ahead."

I waited a couple of seconds. "Punch?"

"Yeah," he said. "Hi, Gem."

"Don't do anything to hurt my husband."

"I hadn't planned on it," said the man's voice, which sounded gritty, but somehow timeworn and honest. I don't know how I got that out of a few words, but I tended to make snap judgments that usually turn out right.

"I'm giving you the benefit of the doubt, but I'm telling you that if you do, I'll find you and kill you."

Punch didn't hesitate. He said, "I'd do the same thing if I were you, but I can promise you we're working on the same side. So don't worry. I got his back. Can't wait to meet you."

"Okay, then," I said, feeling much better. "You guys get in there, get the shit and get back here."

"Will do. Here's Flex."

I heard a gunshot, then another, over the radio. "Flex?" I said, my heart pumping.

Two seconds later, Flex's voice came back on. "No worries, Gem. Had to take out a couple while you threatened Punch. Don't worry, babe. He's a good guy of the Semper Fi variety."

"Good. I love you, babe," I said. "We'll talk about how you knew I threatened him when you get home. Be careful."

"I will," said Flex. "I'll leave the Ham on this frequency. Radio if anything changes with Flexy or anyone else. And Gem?"

"Yeah, Flex?"

"Give my love to everyone."

"You just did."

It fell to static again, and this time I turned it off.

The door opened and Scofield, Dave and Hemp came in. All three were covered in blood.

*****

Chapter Seven

The new band of rain pounded the highway and our car, and the shattered rear window was allowing the water to soak many of our supplies in back.

Lightning lit up the roadway before us, darkened by a thick blanket of black clouds.

Highway 31 became US 21, and it snaked beneath I-77 over and over until we were very close to the hospital. We weren't comfortable at the small convenience store we'd seen back a few miles, so we had waited. There had been something strange there. Something about how the boards were over the windows and what might have been knotholes in the plywood, but what also might have been gun turrets.

Maybe uninfecteds inside, laying in wait. Both Punch and I had felt the same, so we kept moving. Our instincts might have been nothing more than paranoia, but either way, we were still breathing. Better safe than sorry.

Now we reached Highway 160, and there was an Exxon station on the corner with two roll-up bay doors and a pretty nice store attached. Looked like they had some specialty peach preserves, a small restaurant and western wear for sale, too.

I thought if nobody else had robbed the store of the clothing, that I might be due for a nice cowboy hat. If I found a little one for Flexy, I'd damned sure pick that up, too.

I swung the car in and backed it into a space. We were immediately approached by a group of rotters, so I spun the AK-47 in their direction and promptly turned their heads into a black-red-blood mist explosion, the unimportant, lower part of their bodies falling away. Two were on the store side, and I didn't want to break the front glass, so we just got out. WAT-5 was in effect, so we could handle them as needed.

"Still not too sure about this stuff," said Punch, nervously eyeing a walker three feet away from him. The thing walked up to the Land Cruiser, moving around Punch. It stood there, staring through the windshield.

"Good time as any to shoot it," I said. "You can get a clean shot."

Punch nodded and raised his pistol, which was one of Tony's Smith & Wesson .40 calibers with hollow-point rounds. He kept the weapon 10" or so from the creature's head and fired. It unceremoniously dropped.

"Another one bites the dust," said Punch. "Let's get some food."

We moved toward the entrance. I pulled on the door and it opened, but the broken glass told me it wasn't that way to begin with. Someone had arrived to locked doors and had broken in. They likely unlocked the door from the inside to make their exit.

Inside, it stunk like putrid, rotting vegetables and rotted flesh, but musty, too. That was an indicator of how long ago the fruit and flesh had deteriorated.

"Let's clear it," said Punch, waving me to the left. He went right.

I moved down the aisle and found a body almost immediately. It was nothing more than torn clothing over skeletal remains. The head had been smashed against the ground, and I saw chunks of the skull with hair still attached, scattered around it.

It reminded me of my brother-in-law's body, back on the very day this all began. I'd never forget seeing his ravaged corpse lying on the floor torn open, and the realization that I did not know the condition or whereabouts of my sister, Jamie, or my nieces, Jesse and Trina.

I stepped past it and kept going. I reached the window at the front of the store and saw more of the mindless, hungry things outside. We were okay. The wafers were making us just a part of the furniture, as it were.

"You clear, Flex?" asked Punch.

"Yep," I said. Now I flipped on my headlight and scanned the aisles. There were a bunch of bottles of apple and peach cider and other natural juices in well-sealed bottles. I took one from the rack, looked at the expiration date. Not until 2015. I looked up and saw Punch on the next aisle. "Fresh fruit juice, brother," I said. "A year ago, anyway." I tossed him the bottle and he caught it.

I grabbed another from the rack and shook it. I tore off the seal with my teeth, twisted the cap off, and tipped the bottle to my lips. It tasted just like nectar from Heaven running down my throat. The bottle was 750 milliliters, but I drank the whole goddamned thing. When I lowered the bottle, I saw Punch finishing off the last of his, too.

He wiped his mouth on his sleeve. "Good shit."

"Hell, yes it is," I said. "I want to clear this rack. Flexy'd love this stuff."

"Baskets over there," said Punch. He went and pulled one from a row near the door and rolled it over. He started loading bottles into it.

I found some breads sealed in vacuum-packed cans with pull tabs. I dumped them in the basket, too.

"Anywhere to rest up for the night?" he asked. "Maybe go in the morning?"

"I don't know, Punch. The girl already died, like I said."

"Is your son showing any symptoms?" he asked.

I shook my head. "No, but Hemp says that doesn't mean he hasn't got it."

"Hey, man. I'm cool," said Punch. "I've stayed up for three days straight under some pretty stressful conditions."

"I've only been under stress since this shit started," I said. "And yeah, I'm tired. It has been a long day."

"Sometimes you operate more efficiently if you take the time you need to rest before you start out," said Punch. "I say we stop and do this by the light of day. We can start out at 0500 hours."

I thought about it. He was right of course. I'd be better off if I just approached this like we'd approached everything else; with patience and good preparation. Okay. Maybe *sometimes* with guns blazing and no plan at all, but that was usually when all our other options went out the window.

"Okay," I said. "Looks like there might be an office or something up those stairs. Let me find a hat first, and I want to get back on the radio to let Gem know what we're doing."

"A hat?" asked Punch.

I pointed. "Over there. A Stetson. Hemp always calls me a John Wayne, so I'm gonna give him a reason."

Punch laughed. "Sounds good. Get your hat. I'll see if the office is open."

I nodded, and found a display of several hats. I might be a good guy, but with the blood flying around, I needed something that would hide bloodstains. Or at least let me wipe it off. I looked at some of the nicer, straw models.

A black Stetson fit just right. It settled nicely on my head and didn't touch my ears. I turned to look for a mirror.

"Fuck!" I screamed, staggering backward. A walker was four feet behind me, its arms outstretched, its mouth opened in a silent bite. As my eyes fell on it, it let out a creak that mimicked a rusty door hinge and moved past me, uninterested.

My heart drowned out the distant thunder and I said a quick thanks to God, WAT-5, and Hemp Chatsworth was in there too, just for good measure.

Any motherfucker coming up behind you will scare your ass. Now make him look like the damned crypt keeper and you've got yourself some Fruit of the Looms that are full of shit.

I hadn't heard the rotter come in, and that surprised me. I looked down, and saw the creature had on a tattered pair of Reebok running shoes. He was pretty stealth for a bumbling zombie.

I shot him in the face, and felt the cold blood spatter me, the stink of it reminding me the thing was already dead. I always close my eyes in close combat to avoid the introduction of that shit in my bloodstream.

Take no chances. Shit that smells that bad just had to have legs, even when its host was down.

"You all right down there, Flex?" shouted Punch.

"I'm good," I answered. "Stray rotter down here."

"Okay," he said. "Scared the shit outta me up here."

I grabbed a shirt off the rack beside me and removed my new hat. I wiped it thoroughly with the shirt, turned it inside out and swiped it quickly over my face and put the Stetson back on my head. Tossing the shirt aside, I regained my composure and went to the door, locked it, and spotted a large fixture that I thought I could move. With only one good grunt, I got it sliding on the wood slat floor. With two more caveman growls, it was in front of the broken glass door, providing adequate protection for the night.

Then I turned to see my reflection in the mirror. I pulled off the headlamp – because the fucker was blinding me – and shone it sideways at my image in the mirror. The hat looked good. Damned good. On the other side of how good it looked, my face looked kind of haunted and strange with the leftover, blackish blood smeared on it.

Fucking polyester shirts suck for cleaning windows and bloody skin. It just isn't absorbent enough and I guess I was more worried about the new hat than my mug.

I grabbed another shirt, still smiling at my earlier scare. I gave myself another wipe-down as I headed upstairs and saw that Punch had discovered a pair of couches that would do just fine.

*****

I was awake by 4:00 in the morning. Punch was on the other couch snoring, but I could tell his sleep was fitful at best, as it had been through the night. Storms had rolled through every hour it had seemed, and some powerful enough to make me wonder if the main storm was approaching. When they passed after an hour, I knew I was mistaken.

Nope. Not the most restful night of sleep I'd had. I switched on my headlamp and got up.

I'd seen some chicken wire fencing rolled up in a storage area and had an idea. I liked the Land Cruiser a lot, but with that blown out rear window, it was a break in our defenses that made me nervous. I checked Punch once more, then headed downstairs, trying to be quiet.

"Where you headed, Flex?" he asked, after I'd taken two steps. He sounded sharp; not like a guy who'd been asleep.

I turned, smiling to myself. "I should've known better trying to sneak out of a room occupied by a U.S. Marine," I said. "I need to take care of that rear window, Punch. Go ahead, brother. Catch some more Zs. I left a handheld on that table beside you. If I get into any shit, I'll call."

"I'll be down in a minute," he said. "When I'm up, I'm up."

"Cool." I continued down the steps and went into the main store.

The storage room we'd searched last night was under the stairs, and inside were a lot of displays and other sale supplies. I tugged on the roll of chicken wire, caught behind two melamine signs that said, "Peach Sale!"

"Perfect," I muttered to myself, pulling out the larger of the two signs. Now I needed to find some tools. That wouldn't be too hard, because there was also a service station attached. I pulled my radio.

"Punch, you up?"

"Yeah, brother," came his voice. Not over the radio. He was halfway down the stairs.

Punch wore a pair of camouflage pants that looked like military issue, and the boots definitely were. He still moved like a ghost in them. His shirt was just a standard, white tee.

"Check your watch, Flex," he said. "Time for WAT-5?"

Gem would be pissed if she even knew I cut it that close. We had about twenty minutes left on our five-hour dose. I reached into my pocket and pulled out the bag of wafers. I passed one to Punch and popped another in my mouth.

He ate his down with the grimace I was waiting for.

"You'll get used to it," I said.

"Hey," said Punch. "It beats what those fucks out there want to eat."

"Makes 'em a nuisance for the most part," I said. "But they can still accidentally scratch you, so it's best just to take 'em out if they get too close."

"That board'll make a good rear window, Flex."

"My thoughts exactly," I said. "I had my sights on the chicken wire, but that might come in handy for something else. Let's see if those bay doors will roll up. We can pull the Toyota inside."

Punch walked around the stairwell and I followed. We came to another windowed door marked SERVICE. He wiped at the glass and turned his head from side to side, scanning. "Nothing's moving in there."

"Be my guest," I said.

Punch pushed the door open. Because the shit hit the fan on a Sunday – which had come to be a blessing for a lot of the places we needed to go – the garage had been closed and the mechanics weren't working. We stepped inside, our guns at ready. When the door swung closed behind us, we stopped and listened.

It was quiet inside. We both turned our heads in all directions, shining the light of safety in every dark corner. Just because mechanics weren't servicing cars that day, it doesn't mean some clerk from the store didn't run in here to escape certain death.

"So far, so good," said Punch, moving farther into the 2-bay garage. Parked over the lift nearest to us was a classic Pontiac GTO in what shone back at me as a deep purple. Four nearly flat tires, but the hood was down and it didn't look like it was in the middle of any work.

"Is that a '67 GTO?" I asked.

"Hell yes it is," said Punch, whistling. "Jesus, that's just like my dad's old car. His wasn't purple, but same exact one."

"Buddy, if you want it and it's in one piece," I said, "we'll pump those tires up and swing by here on the way back. A muscle car like that might come in handy at some point."

"Flex, you got more to worry about than getting me a little piece of my past. Let's do this and we'll see how long it takes. We make good enough time, I'll beg you to bring me back."

I walked over to the toolboxes and saw the lids down. I tried one. Locked. I looked at Punch. "Hell no, the mechanics aren't gonna leave their boxes open over the weekend," I said.

"Let's test the strength of Snap-On," said Punch. He looked around, his light illuminating pegs on the wall. Seeing what he wanted, he went to the wall and pulled down two large hearing protectors.

"You'll need these," he said, handing me a pair. I fitted them over my ears and stood back.

Punch knelt down in front of the large, red toolbox and raised the barrel of his shotgun, angling upward at the top hatch's lock.

Punch fired and the lid of the chest flipped backward, folding around the backside of the rolling treasure chest.

I was glad I wore the ear protection. The soundproofing in a garage was for shit. We took them off.

"Good thing they didn't try that in a commercial," he said, smiling.

"Let's see what we have," I said. Once the top was open, the sliding rods released all the other slide-outs. We pulled them all open, starting at the larger, lower drawers. Punch reached in and pulled out a hacksaw.

"Perfect for the melamine," I said, taking it.

Next, he opened a drawer with a tin snip set. Punch took the medium-sized pair.

"Chicken wire killer," he said. "Bay door?"

I went to the door in front of the empty service bay and pulled the spring-loaded chain down and out of its slot. The door sprang up immediately, and I left it for a moment while I dropped the Daewoo into a good ready position.

I pulled the chain, hand over hand, and the door moved easily in its track. I stopped when it was high enough to get the Land Cruiser inside.

"Keys," said Punch, holding out his hands. I tossed them to him.

"Be right back," he said.

He wasn't ten steps out when I heard the boom of his shotgun again. I didn't hear the thud that I was pretty sure followed, but then again, depending on the range of the rotter, he might have been in smaller pieces than I could hear spattering on the ground.

I checked again to make sure it was clear, and went to the GTO. I opened the driver's door and fed my Daewoo inside, sliding into the seat.

The keys were in the ignition. The damned mechanics locked their precious toolboxes up tight, but left the garage door latched with a spring-loaded chain and the keys in a classic ride.

Fuckin' mechanics. I turned the key. A red light shone, so dim it was almost imperceptible. I tried anyway. One click, then dead. Lights out. I reached down and popped the hood as I heard the Toyota's motor roar to life.

I walked around to the front of the Pontiac as the Land Cruiser swung around to the open bay door. Punch executed a quick, three-point turn and backed it into the service bay.

I raised the GTO's hood. Intact. I shone my light around. Not only intact, but pristine. The motor looked brand new, and all the mounts, belts and everything else shone, too.

If Punch helped me, he'd have this car. I'd see to it. Hell, it was right off the highway and an easy get.

Memories of your dad didn't come along everyday. If it helped him through his days, he could use it.

Punch pulled the SUV in all the way, then went around and pulled the door closed again, latching the chain.

"Only one encounter, huh?" I said. "Not bad."

"There were others," he said. "Just not an immediate threat."

"Pontiac's in one piece," I said. "Baby looks brand new. Got a fuckin' 400."

Punch stepped over and looked down at the engine. "Don't make me cry, man," he said.

154

"Don't worry. I have a tentative plan. I say that so we don't break your heart on the way home."

We got to work. I opened the rear hatch door and we knocked away all the remaining chunks of glass.

I got in the Toyota and turned the key on, lowering and raising the window that wasn't there, until we heard the remaining glass pieces fall away.

Afterward, Punch got inside and we closed the hatch again. I handed him a black marker and pushed the melamine board tight against the hole, and Punch marked it from the inside.

After he got back out, we started cutting along Punch's lines, adding about an inch on the very bottom. All in all, it took us about half an hour to cut it and fit it into the slot. Once he had it loose, I got back in the driver's seat and raised it up. It slid right into the slot and it was as tight as the original window.

As long as we didn't try to lower it again.

"Ready to go find some antitoxin?" I asked.

"God, I hope it's there, brother," said Punch. "Something's gotta be easy now and then."

"One more thing first," I said. "Top off."

"Hell yes," said Punch. "That way we can leave the cans here and pick 'em up on the way back. We'll need to fill 'em again, right?"

"They are stinkin' up the car," I said. "Works for me."

We got busy and soon, gas was running down the side of the Land Cruiser. We stacked the empty cans behind the SUV.

"Give us a reason to come back," said Punch, eyeing the GTO.

I pointed to the hand air pump hanging on the back wall. "That's for the tires. Jumper cables are hanging right beside 'em, so you'll have your GTO, brother."

Eric A. Shelman

Punch smiled as he unlatched the chain and rolled the bay door up. "Don't worry about shit like that, Flex. Let's save your boy."

I liked Punch a lot. A whole lot. We left the garage feeling a little – not a lot – safer than before.

*****

I stayed in bed long past waking. I missed Flex and I worried about him. I knew better, but I still couldn't help it. While our situation was far better than most of the world's – I mean, we did have WAT-5 and urushiol – anyone could still be caught by surprise, and that included my husband.

It was of much greater concern considering what we knew about the red-eyes; their intelligence, their speed and strength, and their ability to hear. It was something we still forgot about now and then.

Sure. Most pregnant women couldn't leap over things or drop to the floor and spider-crawl like a ... well, *like a fucking spider*.

With an announced "Fuck it," I got out of bed and went to the window. There hadn't been another band of storms through the night – none that had awakened me, anyway. As I scanned the horizon, I saw the southeastern sky was as black as hell and the trees for as far as I could see were taking a beating from the now strong, steady wind.

It was moving in for the kill now.

I padded to the closet and pulled one of Flex's shirts from a hanger. It was a long-sleeved, faded blue, chambray shirt with worn elbows that looked like something a real man would wear, like Timothy Olyphant or Sam Elliot.

It screamed, *Flex Sheridan: Badass Son-of-a-motherfucker*.

I thought about that and smiled. It was true, right? We were all the sons or daughters of motherfuckers.

156

I shook off the morning mind-wandering and pulled on some jean shorts. I buttoned them, zipped the fly, and realized they could nearly slip off over my hips.

I'd lost weight since having Flexy. More than just the baby weight, too. The zombie apocalypse was the best diet known to mankind.

Coffee. It was all I needed. And a donut, but I hadn't had one of them in so long, I can't tell you. I slid my feet into some Dearfoams and went into the kitchen.

This was a big house, and I was damned glad of it. It was also one of the newer homes in close cluster that we had chosen to live in, so Hemp and I had agreed last night that if the storm hadn't hit by the morning, everybody should grab what was important to them and get their asses to our place.

"It's close now," said Hemp. I hadn't seen him standing by the sliding glass door. We hadn't boarded that one, because it was already hurricane glass. We assumed the owners of the home hadn't wanted to be left completely in the dark in the event they needed to board up.

"Coffee, Hemp?"

"Sure," he said. "I'm off the tea. Really starting to enjoy coffee."

"Puts hair on your chest," I said. "Wanna see?"

Hemp laughed and walked to the kitchen. He sat on the stool and folded his arms on the granite counter. "I'll pass, Gem. It'll ruin my fantasy."

"What fucking fantasy is that?" came Charlie's voice. We turned, and she was smiling as she walked into the room. "And I better be in it," she added.

"Not this time, girl. I offered to show Hemp my chest."

Charlie stood stock still, her hands down by her sides. "One nip slip and I will kill you."

I undid my top button and looked from Hemp to Charlie. Then another. The shirt began to fall open as I undid the next to last button.

Nobody said a word. I pulled open my shirt and curled my fingers beneath my bra.

Up it went and out came the girls.

"For fuck's sake, Gem!" said Hemp, and I thought he was going to fall off his chair. He turned quickly away and started laughing so hard I thought he'd have a heart attack.

Charlie was doubled over, laughing with him and I quickly lowered my bra and buttoned up again.

"I told myself that if the coffee was done before I finished unbuttoning that I wouldn't go through with it," I said. "Okay, Charlie. Go ahead and kill me."

"I can't," she said. "Not while I'm laughing."

"I'll never respect you again," I said.

"Well," said Charlie, still laughing, "you've got my fucking respect, I can tell you that. Plus, it wasn't even what you did. I hope you were looking at my husband's face!"

"I know," I said. "It's still red."

Hemp said, "Is it safe to turn around?"

"Yeah," I said. "Thought we could use some laughs this morning."

"Just so you know I wasn't laughing at you," said Hemp. "I was laughing with you."

"Hell yes, you were," I said. "I'm the best prop comedian for miles around."

"The props being your tits," said Charlie.

"I travel light … sort of," I said.

"Got enough in that pot for me?" asked Charlie.

The wind hit the house hard, and we heard an exterior wall somewhere audibly groan.

"I need to go out and see what we're looking at," said Hemp. "After a cup. For now, let's radio everyone and tell them to get over here. I'm fairly certain today is the day."

I poured his coffee black and slid it over to him. He opened up the sugar bowl and put four spoonfuls in, stirring it.

"Yeah. You *love* coffee," I said.

"I like it a certain way," said Hemp, smugly. He took a sip. "Ah, excellent."

"We've got fresh eggs, but someone's going to have to go out and get them," said Charlie.

"Not anymore," I said. "Dave moved the coop onto the porch last night. With the top on the coop, the chickens are safe from rotters but hurricane force winds would whirl them around in there like a Mixmaster."

"I'll go harvest them," said Hemp. "I need to walk off this erection anyway."

Charlie leaned over and pinched his arm hard, and he laughed through his grimace. She really got him.

He opened the slider and went out.

"This your first hurricane?" I asked, pouring her cup and sliding it in front of her. I slid the Coffee Mate and sugar over, too.

She shook her head as she doctored her brew. "Nope. I was in one years ago when I was visiting New Orleans. Nothing like Katrina, though."

"I'm an old hand at them," I said. "Spent my entire life in Florida. This is the most I've seen of the rest of the country since I was born."

"Traveling is overrated," said Charlie. "All you gotta remember is that square states are boring. Stick to the edges as far as the USA goes. Way more fun stuff happens at the edges, at least according to TMZ."

"I'll keep that in mind," I said.

"Let's radio everyone and make Hemp scramble the eggs," said Charlie. "We'll let the girls sleep for now."

"Perfect," I said.

There was no need to awaken anyone, though. Everyone was up and concern about the storm was high on everyone's list. They had all agreed to drive in their heaviest vehicles and even Nelson decided to leave the scooter in his garage.

We brought chairs in the living room from all over. The house was warm because we had the doors and windows all closed, but Hemp had filled the multiple generators the night before, so we had juice to run the ceiling fans, which helped.

Nelson and Rachel sat beside one another on the couch, and Dave and Serena had taken two chairs across from them. We'd brought a playpen out for Flexy, and Isis asked to be put inside, so in she went.

And when I say she asked, that is exactly what she did. So weird. Hard to get used to.

"Lots of rotters out there," said Nelson. "Dudes are funny, though. They were all blown up against stuff. Having a hard time maneuvering in fifty mile per hour winds."

"Anyone done a porch sweep in a while?" asked Scofield.

Doc Jim Scofield did not kill a lot of zombies. He was proficient with a gun, but the prescription for his glasses was outdated before the zombie apocalypse struck, and he said they were almost worthless. They had to be close range, and he preferred to leave the gun-toting to those with better vision.

"You guys all came in the back, right?" asked Gem.

Everyone nodded.

"Then it's been all night," I said. "Dave? Serena?"

"I'm good," said Dave. "But Gem?"

I turned. "Yeah, Dave?"

"What we talked about last night. Being quieter. Where are the machetes?"

"Right outside the door on the right. We cut slots in the decking to slide the blades into, so just the handles are sticking up."

"I'll come," said Nelson. "I'll use some stars. It's been a while."

Dave, Serena and Nelson got up. Nelson got his pack and pulled out a handful of throwing stars.

"Gem, you got a little bucket in here somewhere?"

"What for?"

"Rinse bucket for my stars," he said. "I plan to re-use them, and I'll need to swish 'em around."

I gave him one and dumped some of my cleaning water in it. Not potable. That was precious.

Bug sat at the other end of the loveseat, and hadn't said a word that morning. His eyes moved from one of us to the other, but he just observed. I thought about his time alone, just him and Isis, for almost a year.

I suppose it would still be better than Tom Hanks' situation in the movie Castaway, and way better than solitary confinement at a prison.

Still, I was sure it affected Bug.

"You hungry, Bug?" I asked. "Hemp's getting eggs."

As if on cue, Hemp came in with the basket brimming with eggs. "There's a good amount this morning," said Hemp. "All this wind must be forcing their production."

"If they were fucking smart, they'd keep them inside for the extra weight," I said.

Nelson, Dave and Serena were at the door, ready to open it. "Wait!" I shouted.

They all turned. "What's up, dude?" said Nelson.

"Photographic memory aside, *dude*," I said, "you better remember to take the WAT-5 before you go out there. No chances, guys."

"Gem, you're so far behind," said Nelson. "We already did the old *take and wake*, right over there on the couch. Serena woke us up. We're dialed in, mamasita!"

"Hey!" I said.

Nelson stopped again. "Yeah?"

"You know that's Latin-American slang for *hottie*, right?"

"Of course," said Nelson, smiling and poking a finger at his temple. "Photographic memory, remember?"

They went outside. They were murderously quiet, and came back inside half an hour later.

They had taken out twenty-six of them.

It was more walkers than we'd seen since we moved to Whitmire, South Carolina.

I wished Flex was back as the wind outside howled like a ghostly, distant wolf pack.

*****

Chapter Eight

The ghouls were everywhere. Punch's eyes darted from side-to-side, just like mine.

The creatures fought the wind but they were ill-equipped for such tactics, their body weight too low and their coordination and brainpower too long gone to figure out how to lean into a strong wind like the one that dominated them.

The wind buffeted the Land Cruiser and large drops of rain began to fall then, pelting the vehicle. I turned on the windshield wipers, but even at full speed the rain was winning the battle.

"Flex, you need to go right, but fuck if I can tell if it's clear. Damned rain!"

He was right. I could see maybe five feet out of the passenger side window, and not much more through the windshield.

"This shit is exactly why we've tried to avoid big cities," I said.

"Hell yes," he said. "More people, more of *them*."

"It's always been my philosophy," I said. "No choice this time. Damn, I'm glad we fixed the window."

"I'm glad we got rid of the gas cans," said Punch. "Now I can breathe."

I backed up and saw what looked like an opening between a fire hydrant and a motorcycle lying on its side.

"Should be enough room to skirt through," I said, and turned the steering wheel left. I drove slowly and tried to run over the curb, but the damned cowcatcher was too low to the ground. "Shit," I said.

"Try more of an angle, Flex," said Punch.

"Right," I said. I backed up, hit something that I was pretty sure was an unlucky rotter that had been blown to the wrong place at the exact wrong time, and threw it back into drive. I cranked the wheel hard, increasing the angle of my tires to the curb. This time, the pointed front of the pilot moved alongside the curb, allowing my front left tire to roll up. Once I achieved that, I was able to squeeze through the two fixed objects.

"I'm tryin' to avoid having to get out and winch," I said. "We'll be soaked to the bone."

Fifteen to twenty of the staggering dead had obviously seen the movement of our vehicle and were now doing their best to work their way toward the big Toyota, but I plowed right through the most industrious of them. I was moving slowly enough that the cow catcher worked as intended. The roar of the storm outside spared us the squishy impact sounds as the angled, steel appendage snapped their brittle ankles, threw their knees into the grid, then easily flipped their battered bodies to the side and out of our path.

We'd likely have to remove some arms and legs from the angled grid work before we headed back. Yeah, it was the optimist in me; I planned to get back home and I didn't want to arrive there with rancid body parts dangling off the front of the SUV.

"Thing works like a charm, Flex," said Punch. "Your buddy Hemp's idea?"

I smiled, mostly because the thing did work great, and the truth was, I'd forgotten who thought of it.

"Let's just assume it was Hemp, 'cause I don't really recall," I said. "But it sure *works* like somethin' he came up with."

We drove slowly out of necessity, making our way up Kenilworth Avenue. The wind slammed us again and the rain sheeted sideways, rendering the wipers pointless for a few, brief seconds.

I hit the brakes hard and stopped the truck. It was better to wait than to run headlong into something bigger than us. A tank, maybe. We hadn't seen any signs of military since this shit started, but we hadn't been in the most likely places they would focus.

I looked at Punch. "We wait, I guess," I said. "Until we can see *somethin'*."

We waited, staring at the sheeting water. The wind shifted suddenly and then it seemed to be blowing the rain forward, away from our windshield.

We could see again. What we saw wasn't encouraging.

The roadway heading left was a mess of crashed cars that looked like someone had set them aflame. Doors hung open and the paint was burned away on six or seven vehicles. No way through.

"Can't go straight, either," said Punch, pointing. "Wow. That must've happened a while ago."

In the middle of Kenilworth, just past Harding Place, the fuselage of a Medevac helicopter lay in chunks and pieces, all as burned as the car. Around it, several destroyed cars, including a police cruiser, sat forever idle as though in a graveyard of devastation.

Weeds had begun to spring up from cracks in the street, and it just felt to me like we were both starring in some end of the world flick where a director would scream, "Cut!" and praise the special effects team's talents.

I stared, frustrated, then remembered something. I was tense. I was tired. I flipped down the sun visor and a pack of Marlboro reds dropped into my lap. "Right the fuck now I can use one of these," I said.

"Shit," said Punch. "I don't think I've had a smoke in six months. Pony up."

I gave him one. "There's a lighter in the glove box," I said.

Punch opened the glove box, shifted around several boxes of 9mm rounds and found the Bic. He struck it and lit his, then gave the lighter to me. I lit mine, stared out at the melee through the downpour and inhaled deeply.

"We needed to turn left here, on Harding Place" said Punch, wiping again at the condensation collecting on the inside of the window.

"Any other way around?" I asked.

Punch held the map up, and ran his finger along it. "Yeah, yeah. Just turn right here. Up a block and we can try to get around this mess."

Out of nowhere a bolt of lightning struck so close to us we both covered our heads and ducked. Seconds later, a crack sounded, loud enough to be heard over the downpour. We both looked over to see a huge oak tree aflame, twenty feet to our right, on the corner of Harding Place and Kenilworth. The leaping flames fought the rain even as they were fueled by wind, and I saw the ancient tree was almost split clear down the middle.

The weight of the upper boughs strained the intact trunk of the tree, and it remained upright for the moment, even as we smelled the sharp odor of ozone leak in through the Land Cruiser's air vents.

As we watched, the massive tree trunk began to split in two as the behemoth oak started its slow fall in two directions.

"Flex, go!" shouted Punch. "That tree's gonna block Harding. Now!"

I could still see well enough to follow his instructions, and I laid my foot on the gas, simultaneously spinning the steering wheel hard to the right. The tires lost traction, then gripped, jettisoning us onto Harding and directly into another wasted biter, who rolled up the cowcatcher and onto the hood before being thrown off to the side as the Land Cruiser fishtailed. We were still beside the falling tree and needed a few more crucial feet before we'd be in the clear.

"Stop fuckin' slidin'!" I shouted, letting off the gas for a moment, even as the tree angled more sharply toward us, the accompanying cracking of wood announcing our coming, crushing demise. The tires caught again and I cranked the wheel around an abandoned taxi that appeared right in front of us. More forward momentum and two more sharp turns and I felt the vibration of the tree's final impact behind us. With the shuddering earth came the ear-piercing sounds of crinkling metal and exploding glass as the taxi we'd just passed became an unrecognizable mass of crumpled, yellow steel wreckage beneath the weight of the old oak.

What a difference a split-second makes. Had we been just a tad unluckier, that would've been us.

The road ahead was clear. I stopped the SUV and looked at Punch. I dragged off the smoke again and smiled at him. "Thanks, pal," I said. "If I'd have waited another second before making that turn, we'd have been blocked or crushed."

"Thank me when we're on the way back, man," he said. "But to be honest with you, this is the most fun I've had in a year … you know, without being naked."

I laughed, rolled down my window, and flicked the cigarette butt out. Punch did the same.

I wondered what surprises lay ahead for us.

I didn't have to wonder for very long.

*****

Hemp stood at the window, peering out between the boards. Charlie stood beside him, her left arm around his waist and her right hand touching her stomach.

"Is she kicking?" I asked, walking to stand beside them.

"Oh, yeah," said Charlie. "Why do you say she?"

"Just a feeling," I said. "Isis might know."

"She might, huh?" said Charlie. "Strange. She's so damned cute, but talking to her is still freaky." She kept her voice low, despite the fact that Bug and Isis were still in the guest bedroom.

"What are you thinking, Hemp?" I asked. "That's a thousand mile stare if I've ever seen one."

He pointed out the window. "Not actually," he said. "It's only about forty yards."

I moved forward and looked. "Where?"

"There," he said. "To the right of our trail to the burning pit. A red-eye."

I looked out and saw her. She stood, bracing herself against the mailbox post, staring at the house as though nothing could pry her attention away from the draw of our little resident siren.

The wind, which must have been a steady sixty miles per hour at that point, blew her hair over her face, but when it whipped it away periodically, her red eyes became brief pinpoints, staring directly at us.

"That shit is eerie," I said, shuddering.

"What's up with her?" asked Charlie.

"I haven't had one to work with in a while," said Hemp. "But now that we have Isis, I have to figure out what this connection is and what they want with her."

Charlie looked at Hemp, then at me. "Do you think there's something they want, or is it just instinctual?"

"Nothing in nature is drawn to anything else without a purpose," said Hemp. "The clown fish is drawn to a sea anemone because the anemone provides protection and food for the clown fish from its meal scraps."

"Sounds like a one-way deal to me," I said. "What does the anemone get out of it?"

"The sea anemone picks up nutrients from the excrement of the fish," said Hemp. "Not only that, the nitrogen excreted from the clown fish increases the algae incorporated into the tissue of their host. That aids the anemone in tissue growth and regeneration."

"So now you're a fucking marine biologist?" asked Charlie.

Hemp laughed. "Just found it interesting," he said. "So I studied it."

"So which is Isis?" I asked. "The anemone or the clown fish?"

"If it's a symbiotic relationship, I'm not certain it matters," said Hemp. "There is a chance – and it's not necessarily a good thing – that they can *both* gain from the interaction." Hemp looked at the red-eye again and shook his head. "There's some connection between them and I need to investigate it further."

"Have you talked to Bug about it?"

"About what?" asked Bug from behind us. We turned to see him carrying Isis in from the bedroom.

"Did you sleep alright?" I said. "Nothing could've kept me awake. I was zoned out."

"Isis kept wanting me to take her to the window," said Bug. "I can sleep through anything, but she was persistent."

Hemp looked at her. "What did she do when you took her?"

"Pointed. Kept saying 'mother' over and over."

Hemp stared at him. "Was she pointing over to the right? Where our trail begins?"

169

"I couldn't see anything out there. The wind was crankin' and I just indulged her as long as I could, then tried to get her to settle down."

"Did she?" asked Charlie.

"Not much," said Bug. "I'm still wiped, but I guess I don't have any plans today anyway. At least until this thing blows through."

Hemp's stare told me he was onto something.

"Bug, have you ever checked her night vision?" he asked.

Bug looked confused. Isis tugged on his beard and smiled, then turned to us as she gave it another tug. Her big teeth appeared and she laughed. "Fuzzy!" she said.

We all smiled. Except Hemp, who walked up to Isis and stroked her hair. "Hi, Hemp," she said.

"Hello, little one," he said. "Isis, can you see in the dark?"

"What is dark?" she asked, with perfect annunciation.

"Nighttime," said Hemp. "When the sun is gone."

She put her hands out and gave us a very cute shrug. "I don't know!"

"Well, let's go into an interior room and see, shall we?" asked Hemp. "May I?" He held out his arms.

Bug gave Isis over to him. "Sure," he said. "She likes you."

"Don't make him feel special," I said. "Isis likes everyone."

"But I'm her favorite," said Hemp, bouncing her in his arms. "Okay, Bug. What of hers did you bring with you from your California bunker?"

"What, like toys and books and stuff?" asked Bug.

"Exactly," said Hemp.

"She loves Dr. Seuss," said Bug. "I brought some of those for her."

"Good," said Hemp. "Go and get two or three of the books and come to the walk-in pantry. There are no windows in there."

Hemp carried Isis toward the kitchen and Bug went to his bag, reached in and pulled out a handful of books.

"Keep them behind your back for now," said Hemp.

"I'm coming," I said. "I love this shit. I should've married you, Hemp."

"We can always have a duel," said Charlie. "I choose the weapons."

I smiled over my shoulder and went into the pantry behind Hemp. Bug came in last and closed the door behind him.

It was pitch black in there. All that was visible were Isis' red eyes, pinpoints in the darkness.

"Okay, Isis, are you okay?"

"I'm okay!" said Isis.

"God, she's cute," I said.

"Okay, Bug," said Hemp. "Just randomly hold up a book."

"Okay," he said. "I'm holding one up."

"What book is that, Isis?" asked Hemp.

"Cat in the hat!" shouted Isis. "Read it to me!"

"In a little bit baby, just hang on a bit," he said. He cracked the pantry door open, letting the ambient light filter in. He held it up. It was Cat In The Hat.

"Okay," said Hemp. "Close it again and show another book."

When the door closed, it was impossible to see my hand directly in front of my face. Pure dark.

"One fish, two fish!" shouted Isis, unprompted.

"Holy shit," said Bug. "She has night vision?"

"Which likely means the red-eyes have it as well," said Hemp. "I'd suspected, but never confirmed it."

171

"We need to teach this one how to shoot," I said. "She'll be the ultimate hunter."

"Okay," said Hemp. "I've seen enough. Now, storm or not, we need to capture a red-eye."

As if in direct response, a huge gust of wind pummeled the house. Something slammed against the front wall and we heard another thud immediately afterward.

We all rushed out of the pantry and Charlie was already at the front door, looking out the peephole.

She turned toward us. "One of the diggers. Blew right into the door. Wind is picking up big time out there."

"We're not in the thick of it yet, I don't believe," said Hemp.

"You're going to have to wait, Hemp," said Bug. "You can't go out there, man."

"It goes against my grain to wait, Bug," he said. "But you're right." He went back to the window and peered out. "She's gone anyway. Damn."

"There will be others," I said. "Let this storm pass and let Flex get back home. We'll have plenty of time after that."

Hemp nodded. "Is the radio on?"

Charlie said, "The Ham?"

"It's on," I said. "I was up until around 1:00 this morning, sitting there beside it."

Rachel came in carrying Flexy, who was rubbing his eyes. She had taken him that morning and offered to give him a bath, which was awesome of her.

When he saw me, his eyes went wide and he babbled and cooed. My smile was automatic and I went to him and lifted him from her arms.

"The moment I diapered him, he let loose," Rachel said, smiling. "I got that taken care of but now I think he wants to refill."

I touched my tender breasts and winced. "Of course he does," I said. "Like father, like son. Thanks, Rachel."

"No problem at all," the petite, freckled woman said. "The smell of a clean little baby is like air freshener in this rotten world of ours."

"I know, right?" I said. "If I could dangle this little booger from the rear view mirror of my Crown Vic, in this stinking world I'd start a craze."

"You're weird," said Charlie. "Which is exactly why I love you so much."

*****

The scattered debris from the medevac chopper, along with all the burned and wrecked cars in the roadway had screwed us up good. We ended up on Berkley, taking that residential street to Belgrave, and working our way to Romany, where we took a left. Luckily, by the time we got back to Kenilworth, we were past the wreckage.

Punch looked up from the map again. "Turn right on Scott and make a quick left on Blythe," he said, and in two quick turns we were there. The buildings all around us blocked much of the wind, but when it gusted, it whipped through the buildings like a wind tunnel. The rain continued to pour down in a deluge.

"All these buildings look like they're connected?" I asked, Punch.

He looked around, craning his neck. "Looks like it, Flex. We got walkers in front and by the doors, though."

"Okay," I said. "We're on the WAT-5 and I have more. We'll need to take more in two hours at best. You got a digital watch?"

"I do," he said. "I'll set the alarm for 9:00 AM." It was just past 7:00 in the morning, and much of our time had been whittled away as we figured out how to get through the storm and the age-old congestion of cars and drivers long stalled and most likely, long dead.

173

Eric A. Shelman

"Okay," I said. "Checklist. Let's take WAT-5, more urushiol, lots of rounds and your gun of choice."

"That's gonna be this baby," said Punch, raising his Saiga.

"It is a can't miss tool," I said. "Ready?"

"As ready as I'm gonna get," said Punch.

"You understand I have no idea where the hell to find this antitoxin, right?"

Punch nodded. "We'll conduct a logical search. You got another of those headlights?"

"Yeah, in that same glove box under those same boxes of ammo. You probably pushed it aside to find the Bic earlier."

Punch found it and pulled it out. "Okay," he said, strapping it over his cap. "Let's do it."

"Hold on, bud," I said. I whipped the steering wheel hard right and punched it over the curb and onto the grass. A sidewalk led to a glass door, and I rolled to within five feet of the door and parked the Toyota.

"Now if we can find this door again when we leave," I said, "We should be able to make a quick exit."

"The best laid plans," said Punch.

"Hold on," I said. "I don't want to fuck around too much when we get inside." I ran back to the Land Cruiser and keyed open the rear door. I pulled out two baseball bats and a crowbar.

I held it up. "Can you manage this, too?" I asked. He held out his hand and I tossed it the ten feet to him. He caught it and hefted it.

"I'm all about saving ammo," he said.

"Good," I said, returning to the door beside him. I pulled on the handle. Locked.

"Pretty much what I figured," I said, jamming the chisel edge of the crowbar into the jamb. The aluminum door frame bent, but not enough to pop the lock. I turned the bar around and put the other side in, with the sharp bend.

This time, with a strong push, the door popped open and an shrill alarm sounded.

We both jumped. "What the hell?" shouted Punch. He looked up at the gray box mounted over the door. "Battery powered?"

"Must be," I said. "Fuck it. Let's go."

The door had swung closed, but would no longer latch because of the damage. We switched on our headlights and moved down the hall. Punch had his Saiga at ready, and my Daewoo was leading the way. I had also strapped a headlight around it, and I turned that on, too.

"Let's find a reception desk," said Punch. "They might have directory information behind the counter."

"Good idea," I said, and we moved through some double glass doors that were once likely automatic, but that now took some effort to push open. That hallway led into a wider one, and we eventually saw a sign that said "LOBBY."

I nodded to punch, and went through the door.

"Watch out, Flex!" shouted Punch, and I saw his bat swing in the corner of my eye. I pushed forward and heard the splat of hardwood meeting skull and brains. I turned to see the creature down in a sticky pool of black liquid.

"Thanks, buddy," I said, spinning around to find another one – this one a former nurse, complete with her sensible, white shoes still on her black, vein-riddled feet, staggering through the opposite doors, which someone had shattered at some point.

I fired my Daewoo, now in single-shot mode, into her face, sending her back against a heavy, glass wall. She slid down, and her pink eyes went black.

"Let's clear first," I said. "You check those halls."

He pushed through another pair of glass doors and moved away from me. I walked about twenty feet down

175

another hallway and saw nobody. As I came back, an office door was closed on my right. I looked behind me again and put my ear to it.

Yes, there were sounds coming from somewhere beyond the door. If they were human, they would have yelled something or come out. They didn't know how to come out. That was the fact.

And it was just fine with me. I left them there and returned to the reception rotunda.

I lifted the counter hatch and went behind it. There was a skeleton on the floor with the same kind of shoes on as the former nurse who had come at me moments ago, only this had clearly been one of the unlucky uninfecteds, her pain long over.

I heard a booming shot, and recognized the power of the Saiga shotgun. I imagined some wall or other was just redecorated with some new biological décor.

Very green, indeed. Wholly natural. Nelson would be proud.

Punch came back in and leaned against the counter, his eyes still searching the perimeter. "They can be anywhere," he said.

"The red-eyes sit sometimes, too," I said. "That can really surprise you, so look for it. No urushiol, either. Bullet in the brain."

"Got it," said Punch. "Find anything?"

I shook my head. "Not yet. Here. You go through this." I tossed a blue book on the counter and Punch flipped it around. I took out another one that was next to the multi-line reception phone.

"This one has departments on it," said Punch.

"Pharmacy, I guess, right?" I said.

"Can you call your buddy?"

"Let's check it out first," I said. "It's spotty with the Ham radio, especially in this weather."

"Says it's on the first floor," said Punch. "But it's in Building 2. Where are we?"

I looked around, then went out the door directly across from the desk. The doors here were unlocked but still required my crowbar, as they were automatic, sliding doors. I pried them open, and when they spread an inch, they slid easily. I left them open and ran outside, nearly getting blown over by a strong gust of wind that had to be clocking almost sixty miles per hour.

I looked up. On the side of the building was CMC, BLDG ONE. I ran back inside and pulled the doors closed behind me. As I went to run through the interior doors, I saw a sign that hadn't been visible to us before, on the wall by the door. It said BLDG 2, and had an arrow pointing to the left.

I ran through and pulled the second set of doors closed behind me, too. "Punch, c'mon. Follow me."

"Bringin' up the rear, buddy."

We moved down the connecting hallway and reached another closed door. I pulled it open and the stench that hit us was too sharp and pungent to be over a year old. I stopped in my tracks and fought to keep from gagging. "Massive decay," I choked.

"Shit," said Punch, wincing. I clearly didn't need to announce it. Punch pulled a bandana out of one of his cargo pockets and rested his gun against his leg as he tied it over his nose and mouth.

I didn't have one, so I just scrunched my face up in disgust as we moved further into the mysterious bowels of the dilapidated hospital.

*****

"Punch, be on the alert," I said. "If you see glowing red eyes in the distance, just fire at 'em on full auto."

I walked ahead of Punch, the crowbar dangling from my belt loop where I'd slid it through. I walked the baseball bat like a cane in my left hand, and my Daewoo was in fire position in my right. Last, a super soaker water gun dangled from a thin bungee cord, attached directly to my belt. That was filled with urushiol.

Punch's setup was similar.

"The red-eyes are that serious, huh?" he asked, his voice a low whisper, following my lead.

"Dead serious," I said, turning so he could hear me.

I came to several vinyl nameplates on the wall, and one said PHARMACY. The sign specified the pharmacy was in room 2100 and that it was down the next hallway.

We reached it, and I motioned to Punch to stop. I leaned around and saw something strange.

The hallway was solid with zombies, but not for about twenty feet. I stared, and Punch looked from behind me.

"What's the deal?" he asked.

"Not sure why they're not coming," I said. "They're just standing there."

Punch reached into his pocket and pulled something out. He put it to his eye and looked past me.

"What is that?" I asked.

"Monocular," he said. "Smaller, and it fits in my pockets easier. There's a glass door down there, Flex."

I held out my hand and he put the device in it. I held it up to my eye and saw what he was talking about.

The creatures were trapped behind a single glass door midway down the hall, set into a glass wall that closed off a hallway beyond. We could get closer to them, but they apparently couldn't advance on us.

"Good," I said. "At least we can study the situation before we try to thread that needle."

"Thread the needle?" asked Punch.

I didn't want to scare him off, so said nothing.

He tucked the tool away and we scanned in all directions as we moved down the hallway. The walls on both sides were a light color of some kind, and most doors were glass, except those leading into what I assumed were offices, because this was clearly more of an administrative section of the hospital.

We were now within five feet of the wall of zombies. I turned to Punch. "Turn off your headlight, Punch."

He didn't ask why; he just did it. I flipped mine off as well and said, "Look for red eyes. Ignore the pink. Crimson is all you're looking for."

Together, we scanned the group. Before turning off the light, I'd noticed the long hallway between the doors where they were trapped was about fifty feet long and about six feet wide. The rotting walkers were packed inside, with some, but not much room to mill around.

"Nothin' so far," he said.

After another three minutes of searching and seeing no red-eyes, I turned my light back on. Punch followed suit.

"What are the fuckin' odds of that?" I asked.

"Of what?" asked Punch.

I thought for a moment before answering. Hemp had figured out that all of the red-eyes were women who were pregnant when they turned. That didn't necessarily mean that all of the pregnant females became red-eyes. This fucked with my brain for a moment or two, and I came up with a possibility, but could have been full of shit.

I suppose I could've been stalling our inevitable trip through the zombie gauntlet, but either way, I filled Punch in.

"The red-eyes were all pregnant women when they turned, according to Hemp," I said. "With pregnancy comes massive production of estrogen. The very purpose of the increased estrogen is to assist the neurotransmitters in their brains so they can still function. So, when zombiefied, the unexpected consequence of all that estrogen was a huge increase in mental capacity."

"Man," said Punch, looking at the crowd beyond the glass. "Sounds like you've heard your scientist friend tell that story plenty of times."

"That is true," I said, impressed with my own ability to automatically spew the information. "And it's not like they're just smart, Punch. They're fucking psychic. You saw that bitch on the way here, right? She seemed to know what I was about to do and countered every move before I made it."

His light swung from side to side as he shook his head. "I know you explained some of this on the way here, but buddy … I had no idea."

"It's good shit to know," I said. "Give me a sec. I gotta count."

Using an unreliable method of trying to remember rotted faces, shredded clothes and even particular shoes, I quickly figured there were around 285 infecteds shuffling around inside the area. At their feet was a good amount of what appeared to be sticky, blackish goo, and stuck in the muck, I could see the clothing fragments and bones of at least three people who no longer existed.

There was what looked like a piece of curved aluminum on the floor, too, but I couldn't tell what it was.

"So," I said, "assuming my numbers are right – and I'd guess I'm close – there should be around five pregnant females in there, if it's a 50/50 split between men and women."

"They've been in there a long time," said Punch. "No food. Does that make a difference?"

"It does with the regular vapor. The pink stuff," I said. "But I have another idea that just hit me, so because Hemp didn't come up with it, you can't take to the bank."

"What's that?"

I sighed, knowing for sure that I was stalling now. I should have been through that door and talking while we walked. I still didn't move.

"In every red-eye case that Hemp knows about ,there was a little zombie fetus inside, too. Turned, just like mom."

"Fuck," said Punch. "Sad."

"I know," I said. "Sad and gross. I've seen one, so I'll add fucking haunting to that. Anyway, maybe if the baby didn't turn, they didn't become red-eyes. Maybe only if the baby also changed."

"Is that possible?"

I shrugged. "No clue, and it doesn't matter anyway. We've dicked around long enough, so just have your gun or your bat ready, just in case."

I reached for the door, but saw that it had no handle. There were two holes where a handle had likely been, but it was missing. Someone had removed it.

Punch put a hand on my arm. His grip was firm. "Wait, Flex. How'd they all get in there?"

I looked the group over again, even as their blank eyes, stared back. "They're not patients," I said. "They're all either in suits, scrubs or lab coats, save for a couple of 'em," I said. "And those are probably salesmen or something."

"But how did they all get into this one hallway? And was it before or after they turned?"

"No way to know. Why?" I asked.

"I'm wondering if someone put them in there on purpose. Like a moat filled with alligators or something."

"Protecting something?" I asked.

Punch shrugged. "Maybe a buffer for something," he said.

My eyes fell to the curved metal on the floor, and it hit me what it was. It was aluminum tubing and it was U-shaped. It was a damned door handle.

"The handles were removed on purpose," I said, pointing at the floor and shining my light on the aluminum piece that lay in the black goo.

"Someone could be beyond that far door, then," said Punch. "We need to be quiet."

I looked at the door to my right. It was number 2040. I shone my light to a door within the hallway. It read 2044. The numbers were going up, and we needed the pharmacy, which was 2100. The pack of rotters definitely lay between where we were and where we needed to be.

"Maybe someone was tryin' to keep folks on this side or the other," I said. "No way to know, but anyone not wanting to die would avoid this path."

"They must've baited them in here, then closed the door," said Punch.

I looked at them again. They were pushing against the glass door and it wasn't budging. "It's a pull," I said. "Zombies have a bitch of a time with pull doors. They're prone to push."

"So," said Punch, his voice tentative. "Are *we* goin' around?"

I looked at him, smiled and shook my head. "Not a chance, partner," I said.

"WAT-5?" asked Punch.

"WAT-5, exactly," I answered.

I tried the door. As I suspected, for us it was a push, and it was unlocked. I was validated once more in front of my new friend. I smiled at him. "I'm guessin' the other door is a pull from the inside, too."

Punch turned around suddenly. "You hear something?"

I listened. "No. Maybe you're getting spooked. Sooner we get this over with, the better. Believe me, the anticipation's worse than the journey when you're on the magic wafers."

I pushed through the door and gently elbowed the rotters to either side of me. Two were persistent, their rotted faces getting too close to me. I reached slowly down for my super soaker and raised it up, giving each of them a little shot of the zombie juice, right in their skanky, lipless kissers.

Sizzle, pop, hiss, and down.

"Jesus," said Punch. "Works like a charm, huh?"

"Close that door fast," I said.

"Fuck it stinks," said Punch. "I've been around some rotted shit – whole buildings full of drone-struck jihadists – this is like a hundred morgues."

Like logs floating down a river, the abnormals moved toward us as I edged my way deeper inside to allow Punch room behind me.

Punch pushed the creatures away from the opening and struggled to inch the door closed a bit farther as each walking corpse cleared the gap.

He finally got it, and once again, they pressed against it.

"Wait, Punch," I said, an idea striking me. "Why don't we just let 'em out? It'll be easier to come back through."

"I learned somethin' a long time ago," said Punch. "Don't tear down a fence until you know why it was built. We don't know what this particular fence is for yet."

"Good call," I said.

We pushed through, agonizingly slow. We were about one third through, and moving like molasses in winter.

"If you need to take any out," I said, "Use the urushiol super soaker or your bat. If there are any red-eyes around, they're startin' to hear better, too."

"But we gave ourselves away in the lobby," he said.

"Yeah, I tend to reach for my gun first, but that's just because I'm reactionary," I said. "Even if they heard us earlier, they might not know where we are now."

As the words left my lips, a flash from behind us reflected off the glass walls all around.

I turned to see distant flashlights bobbing near the rear hallway behind us.

The ravenous creatures that surrounded us became immediately agitated. Their mouths gnashed and chewed, and black saliva dripped from their destroyed lips as they pushed forward, threatening to crush Punch and me.

I knew why. While we were on WAT-5, the new visitors weren't.

I dropped immediately, snatching Punch's arm and yanking him to the floor with me.

"Move to the other door!" I whispered with urgency, and Punch was down on his hands and knees with me, pushing past the shuffling legs of the rotters. We worked our way through the putrid coating of muck on the floor, scrambling for every inch as we attempted to reach the opposite door.

Suddenly gunfire erupted. The glass door behind us exploded, and the bodies around us began to erupt in showers of black-red rain, with hail-sized chunks of brain and skull mixed in.

Many of the walking dead men and women fell; some scrambled back to their feet, advancing on our uninvited guests.

Punch and I were now ten feet from the opposite door, practically spider crawling, trying to stay low. These attackers were using automatic weapons and their actions were splattering zombie guts, brains and body parts on every surface, including us, and making our forward advancement agonizingly slow.

Because of the sheer number of shuffling bodies between them and the opposite glass door, it had not yet shattered, the bullets finding plenty of rotted flesh in which to embed themselves.

I didn't shout or scream except in my own mind, my worry for my wife, son and my family so heavy on my mind as I scrambled toward safety. I wasn't certain that whoever was firing toward us had determined there were living beings among the horde. It was thinning out toward the other door now. We were running out of time.

I felt Punch right behind me as I hit the opposite door, now completely free from zombies, as they were all pushing toward the people behind us. I got to the door, tucked my fingers beneath it, and pulled it open. I slithered on my belly through the opening, and made sure Punch got out, too.

We both instinctively looked behind us. We still could not see the people who had fired into the crowd, but that meant they wouldn't be able to see us, either.

The door behind us had been splattered with the blood and muck of a hundred zombies, which offered camouflage, but at the moment we got back on our feet, the glass blew into a thousand fragments, pelting us as we ran down the hallway toward our destination.

I hoped their lights weren't trained on us at that moment.

We kept low, crouching below the height of the rotters behind us and reached the door marked 2100 with the plate in the center that said PHARMACY.

I snatched the nameplate off the door and threw it down the hall. Then I grabbed the handle and turned it.

Thankfully, this one was not locked. We pushed inside and looked for a way to barricade the door.

*****

Chapter Nine

"This storm has definitely made landfall," said Hemp, nervously watching out the back sliding door. "Those winds have to be exceeding seventy-five miles per hour now."

"I haven't seen rain and wind like that since Hurricane Andrew," I said, holding a sleeping Flexy in my arms. "And that was scary as shit." I looked at all of them to make sure they saw the serious expression on my face. "We didn't have the benefit of a basement in south Florida," I said, "but we have it here, and we need to get into the damned thing."

"The problem is, we've got no clue where the storm is yet," said Hemp. "We've got no satellite radar telling us when we should start to worry. Gem's right, though. If this is just the outer edge, we could be in for a minimum Category 4 storm."

"I agree with both of you," said Dave Gammon. "We're better off if we get to the worrying part sooner than later. Might save our lives."

We'd gone into the bedroom to speak privately for a few moments, and everyone was so bored and distracted they didn't even notice. Bunsen and Slider saw us, though, and they came, too. They both sat there, staring at us, panting as though they didn't like this shit one bit, either.

"Settled then," said Hemp. "Let's go back in there and round up the troops. Gem, Charlie, why don't you set everyone about securing as much food and water as they can collect, and then we should be tucked in that basement in a half an hour at most."

"I need to radio Flex," I said.

"We'll take the radio down with us, Gem," said Hemp. "The antenna wire can reach, and we'll try him once we get settled. I've got to wonder what he's doing now, with this storm raging."

"It's all I can think about," I said. "And this little guy." I held the back of my son's head and put his face against my neck, rocking him.

Hemp started the process of moving the Ham radio, and we got everyone started, gathering lighting, food, batteries, water and every other provision we could think of. Like a CSX freight train, it moved from person to person down the concrete steps and into the spacious basement.

The wind grew even stronger outside. Not just stronger. It started to roar, gaining in volume and intensity.

Hemp held a bag of headlamps and AAA batteries in his hand and stared out the rear slider.

"Oh, my God!" he shouted, frantic. "Run, everybody, run into the basement now! Now!"

"What the hell is it, Hemp?" I screamed over the noise that had grown a hundred times louder than just a minute before.

"It's a tornado!" he shouted over the din. "Everybody, go!"

I saw Trina and Taylor run down the steps, and felt my heart racing. I had Flexy in my arms still, but his playpen was already in the basement. I chanced a look back as I moved to the basement steps, and saw the monster twister bearing down. It was perhaps a half mile away, but I saw trees being torn and flung like toothpicks, which was enough for me.

As I looked, a tree, a very old and large one, slammed into the back porch, and the decking and railing exploded into enormous splinters.

I didn't wait to see any more. I descended the steps and heard Charlie on my heels. I reached the bottom and turned to look up at the others coming in. Hemp and Lola came behind me, followed by Bug with Isis cradled in his arms, but nobody else followed.

"Where are Dave and Serena?" I shouted, frantic. Hemp was trying to close the door, and felt a hand on my shoulder, and heard a voice. Dave's voice.

"Gem, we're all here," said Dave. "We're here, babe."

I spun around and saw him, Doc Scofield, Rachel, Nelson and Serena all standing behind me.

Hemp had the door closed now and he ran down the steps.

"Mommy!" shouted Trina. "Mommy, Bunsen and Slider are out there!"

I whirled around and grabbed a flashlight from Dave. I shone it in every part of the basement. Trina was right. The dogs weren't here.

Trina was crying. Hysterical. Taylor joined her in her agonizing over the missing dogs.

I ran over and rested Flexy inside the crib and charged to the steps. Hemp grabbed me as I tried to push past him, and I elbowed him hard to the face, felt the solid impact, and charged away, now free.

As I took the steps two at a time, I screamed, "After all this shit, I'm not leaving them out there!"

"Gem!" shouted Charlie, but I didn't slow. I fumbled with the lock for a second, flung the door outward and flew out of the basement, slamming the door behind me, drowning out Trina and Taylor's cries with the sounds of the terrible, storm of the apocalypse.

Just as the door closed, I glanced toward the sliding door again, but it wasn't necessary. The rear, left corner of the house began to crack, and I saw the wall moving, just in the breakfast nook off the kitchen.

It seemed to sway back and forth for a moment, and I didn't stay to see more. I ran into the rear hallway and charged into the bedroom. I immediately saw Bunsen, our canine matriarch, with not-so-little Slider tucked beside her, both their faces looking – if it's at all possible – relieved that I was there.

"Come here! Come on, guys!" I ran into the hallway, which was the age old, universal signal for *Chase me, let's play!*

I charged into the living room and saw that the kitchen wall was beginning to suffer the same fate as the now ruptured missing nook wall. Relieved to hear barking behind me, I risked a turn of the head to see both pups on my heels. I ran to the door and flung it open, but it whipped out of my hands, throwing me to the side, where I hit the arm of a wooden chair and went tumbling, my back screaming with pain.

I recovered enough to lift my head and see Bunsen and Slider charge through the basement door, and I have to admit I was relieved to see Dave Gammon standing outside the door, one hand holding it, and the other reaching out for me. I extended my hand to take it, but at that moment, the entire back wall disintegrated.

The roof began to collapse. I put my hands down on the floor for leverage, screamed, "Get back inside, Dave!" and kicked at the door, pushing him back through and possibly down the steps, the door slamming hard in its frame.

A huge timber fell from the ceiling and landed against the basement door. I cried then, thinking of my girls and my baby and my best friends down there.

I was sure I was going to die. I'm not one to give up; that's not me. But in that very moment, as debris flew all around me; so much that I couldn't open my eyes for fear of having tiny pieces of wood and metal jammed into them, I didn't see that anyone could survive what had to be coming next.

Thinking of the ones I loved, I slid beneath the timber and felt around. Nothing. Something hit me about ten seconds later, and I grabbed it. It was one of the cushions from the loveseat. I wiggled my way completely beneath the timber now and stuffed the cushion over the top of my head and chest.

Then I cried with joy and fear, as my mind danced crazily over a hundred different thoughts that came in rapid fire succession. The joy because I was still alive. The fear was because I didn't know how long I would be able to have that thought.

Of my thoughts, these were some: I didn't regret saving Bunsen and Slider. They were two lives. I was only one. There was a lot of love down those steps for the girls and my son. Flex would be back to be his father. My mind kept going to Isis. Every other thought. Dave. Isis. Serena, Doc Scofield. Then Isis again.

For some reason, Isis came to me again and again, amidst all these speedster thoughts. I heard her little voice inside my head, drifting to me from everywhere and nowhere at once, even through the raging storm's din; the last words I remembered before everything went black.

You will live, Gemina. Feel our love.

*****

The gunfire behind us had hopefully masked the noise of the door latching. It continued to erupt down the hallway, but the storm outside also added to the racket.

We both put our baseball bats on the floor as we slid down into a seated position with our backs pressed against the steel entry door.

"Could you tell how many there were?" I asked, breathing hard, trying to keep my voice low.

Our headlamps were off and I could not see Punch, just inches away, through the pitch blackness of the room.

"Nah, man. I just saw the light. I'm wonderin' if it's Buckfield guys."

"If it is, they know how to tail 'cause I sure as hell didn't see 'em,' I said. "Punch, turn your headlight to red and see if you can get a make on this room."

"Got it," he said. Seconds later, the room illuminated in the soft glow as Punch faced the wall opposite the door.

There was a counter with sliding glass windows, both closed. A closed door to the left of the window. Behind the glass a face watched us. I wondered how long the abnormal had been doing so. The creature was a near cadaver, its skin nearly peeled from its face, black stains all over the front of the smock that I realized would have had a red-black hue had the color of the light not cancelled it out.

"He won't be a problem," I said. "Try that door, Punch."

Punch slid up the door into a standing position and listened for a moment before removing his weight from it. I planted my boots as best I could and pressed my back against it. I wished I weighed about three hundred more pounds.

"Hurry, man," I said.

Punch moved toward the counter and rapped lightly on the glass. The creature behind it leaned toward him, but it was devoid of gnashing or snarling, because its ravaged brain obviously did not realize what we were.

191

"This is thick, Flex," said Punch.

The gunfire stopped. Punch quickly tried the handle of the door leading to the pharmacy stockroom, but the lever did not pivot downward.

Punch hurried back to the door and pressed his weight beside mine, flipping his light back off. "Fuckin' locked, brother."

We waited. It was all we could do.

I looked at the glow of my watch hands. Five minutes passed. No sounds.

Another five slipped by, and I had to remind myself to breathe.

Finally, I said, "Punch, with all those rotters, they couldn't begin to think anybody was in there with 'em. They'd assume we went another direction."

"But we melted a couple of the fuckers, Flex," he said.

"Yeah, but they don't know about urushiol, and they don't know what it does," I said. "If they even noticed."

"They'll still be lookin' if they saw your truck," said Punch. "Which I'm pretty sure they did, if it's them."

"I'm so fuckin' tired of losing my vehicles," I said. "Anyway, let's give this five more minutes, then we're gettin' through that door there."

No sound came, and after the five minutes, we gave it another three. I flipped on my own red light and looked down at the knob of the door we'd come in through. It was a key lock from the inside, too.

"If I was Hemp, I'd reverse pick this bitch and lock the door," I said. "Anyway, we're gonna have to take a chance. They might not give up the search, but it's a big hospital and that horde of zombies had to tell 'em we didn't come this way."

"We need to see if there's a door out of that room," said Punch. "An emergency exit, anything."

"We gotta get the fuck in there first," I said. "Any ideas?"

Punch knelt down in front of the door. "Flex, the deadbolt's not flipped, so we only have to get by the knob lock." He took off his headlamp and shone the red light between the jamb and the door slab. There was no guard plate in front of it. Punch looked back at me. "Cross your fingers, man."

Believe it or not, I did.

Punch pulled a knife from his pocket. It was a Swiss Army Knife of the type I and every other boy between nine and twelve years old dreamed of owning.

"Fuckin' MacGyver?" I asked. "Thought you guys weren't allowed to have knives in Buckfield."

"This one was a secret, and as you can see, not too effective to kill a man with. And as to whether I'm a MacGyver, no more than this Hemp friend of yours, I'm assuming," he said. "Have you got a knife, Flex?"

"I do," I said, and extended my leg, reaching into my pocket. "It's not fancy, but it does in a pinch." I gave it to him.

He put the light back on his head and said, "I know it's quiet, but see if you can lay down and block that crack beneath the door. I'm gonna need full light to see what I'm doin'."

I remained in a sitting position, but slid to the side of the door and extended my left leg, pressing it against the 36" wide gap. It would have to do. I bent my right leg, steadying myself, and raised my Daewoo toward the door, prepared to blow the fuck out of any unlucky prick who decided to search that particular room.

"I'm ready, buddy," I said. "Go."

Punch turned on the light to bright white and opened the longest blade on both of the knives.

I couldn't see what he was trying to do. We were vulnerable as I sat there, my back no longer pressing against the slab. Should anyone try the door now, I would kill them. I knew I could handle that. The rest depended on how many would come behind our first unlucky visitor.

Through all of it, I had never forgotten the only goal was to get the Diphtheria antitoxin. Everything else could wait if necessary. I needed to save my son's life and worry about protecting him from other stuff when I could.

I heard a click and the door pushed inward. Punch turned to me and smiled. "I saved the lock, too. We can stick this rotter in the waiting room and lock the door behind us, buddy."

"Get your light, Punch," I said. He turned it off and I grunted myself to my feet and followed him inside.

"You wanna do it?" I asked Punch.

"Do what?"

"Lead this boy out the door."

"Punch shrugged. "Why not."

The creature stared at us, but he had likely been so hungry for so long that even without the WAT-5, he would not have been able to create any vapor. He did not even gnash. He looked at us like he was willing to go with whatever flow we set.

Punch was not as gentle as me. He reached out and grabbed the thing by the arm and yanked the abnormal hard toward him.

Only the thing did not *move* forward. Instead, the arm ripped easily from its socket with a sickening, squishy, sucking sound and Punch stood there holding it briefly, the tendrils hanging down from the black-dripping wound, before dropping it in horror.

I laughed aloud, then choked it down. "Dude," I said. "I'm sure that never happened in Afghanistan."

"You coulda said something," said Punch, disgust on his face."

I smiled. "Easy, brother. Just guide him. He'll move."

"Fuck that," said Punch. He got behind the walker and pushed him hard. The thing staggered forward. I held the door and my new friend gave him another hard shove square in his back, ejecting him into the pharmacy lobby. Then he turned around, looked down and gave the severed arm several kicks until it was through the door, too.

He then closed it with more care than I knew he wanted to, just to be quiet. His expression was not one of joviality.

"Ever take anger management courses?" I asked, still smiling. The one-armed monster milled back and forth in the outer lobby.

"I'd just as soon take out my anger on them," he said, nodding his head toward the thing.

"Time to go shopping," I said. "Hemp said there would be inventory sheets somewhere, and the drugs should be in alphabetical order."

"Pull out your list," said Punch. "I'd give my left nut to be on our way back."

"Well," I said, "I don't know who the fuck would make that trade, but that fucker in the lobby might take you up on it."

We worked our way between the aisles and found a computer set up on a rear desk. Beside it was a long binder. I picked it up and looked over the pages.

"Bingo," I said. I flipped through until I was in the D section. I ran my eyes down the list until I saw what I wanted: *Diphtheria Antitoxin.* I slid my finger along the page and saw a number. It said 42. I hoped that was how many doses they had on hand.

"Punch," I said, "Check out the shelves. How are they organized?"

Punch slid down an aisle and shone his light around. "Looks to be alphabetical," he said.

"Perfect. Find the D section," I said.

Punch moved to the second aisle and I walked up beside him. A cardboard bin was marked with *DIPHTHERIA ANTITOXIN*. I slid it out.

There was no antitoxin inside. My heart nearly stopped. All this way, and the bin was empty.

"Fucknuts!" I exclaimed, trying to suppress my anger and keep my voice low. I let the empty bin drop to the floor and something fluttered out of it, landing on the floor a foot away.

"Fucknuts?" asked Punch. "What's wrong? Nothin' in there?"

Shaking my head, I leaned down and picked up the item and held it in the beam of my headlight. It was a business card.

"Just this," I said. "Dr. John Perry."

"Just a card?"

"Yep," I said. "Maybe it's a message."

"Anything on the back?"

"I turned it over. There was handwriting there.

Antitoxins and vaccines are safe.
4301 Yancy Road. J.P., M.D.

I looked at Punch. "Sounds like Doc Perry's taken the stuff we need for safe keeping," I said, relieved. "He didn't list a city, so I assume that's still Charlotte?"

"I'm not from around here, but we'll check the map," said Punch. "His house, maybe?"

"No clue," I said. "He must be keepin' the drugs under the right conditions."

"If he's still alive," said Punch. "Never know."

"Yeah," I said. "Who knows when he wrote this."

"Most likely when the drugs were viable," said Punch.

"We'll know when we get there," I said, pulling out the list Hemp had given me. I ran my eyes down the scrawled drug names, and saw several that I recognized as antibiotics and pain meds. He had a separate heading called *ESTROGEN BLOCKERS*, and a list of medications under that. I knew why, and I was excited that if we could deliver them, Hemp could start work on a new defensive weapon he'd been hoping to come up with. It was to defend against the red-eyes, and the idea was based on his final experiments in the Concord lab.

I carefully tore the list in half and handed a piece to Punch. "See what you can find here," I said. "I'll get the other half, then we'll see if we can get out of here undetected and hit Yancy Road."

"Good enough," said Punch, turning immediately to conduct his search.

I found a pair of canvas bags with handles and tossed one to Punch. He dropped what he'd already collected inside, and moved on down the aisle. It took us twenty minutes to fill Hemp's prescription.

Now it was time to get back to my truck and blow this popsicle stand.

*****

The pelting rain had awakened me, and as I opened my eyes into narrow slits, the huge droplets peppered my already blurry vision, making it even worse. I tried to lift my head and was able to do so, if only slightly. I looked to my right, only because it was less painful than turning left.

The door was intact. The wall it was mounted in was intact.

197

There was no longer a ceiling attached to the wall, though. Nor was there one over my head. I struggled to take in more.

Above me, only sky. I wondered if Heaven still existed beyond the dark, swirling clouds, or if it ever had.

I heard their voices somewhere around me then, and my heart and soul soared with joy. The sounds were muffled and almost inaudible, but they told me my family was alive! They were alive!

I distinctively heard Hemp and Dave calling, and even Trina's little voice came to me. I tried to draw in a large enough breath to call out, but even that hurt. I let it back out slowly, realizing I'd be lucky to emit a whimper, much less a shout. I moved my right hand and found it was free and mobile.

I balled my hand into a fist and rapped on the floor with my knuckles. Once. Twice. A third time.

A cheer erupted from below me, and I realized they had heard me and were celebrating. I tapped three more times, which was rewarded by three taps that vibrated on the hardwood beneath my back.

I smiled and lay there, my eyes gaining focus, my neck beginning to loosen. I turned my head to the left.

An enormous tree trunk lay over what was once a sliding door with impenetrable hurricane glass, extending over the now missing deck and into the forest beyond for perhaps a hundred feet or more. The tree had possibly existed longer than the United States of America herself.

The roots faced me, a massive jumble of once subterranean vines whose ball extended from the floor all the way to where the ceiling had once been. The rain poured down atop it and the dirt ran in rivers from the twisted system of roots, flowing to the floor, only to be pounded aside by the rain from the hurricane.

I was soaking wet, but I wasn't cold. The wind howled outside and while it was nowhere near the speed of the tornado that had ripped the house apart, it seemed to be blowing stronger than before our home became more debris than safe haven.

Either way, the sky overhead still appeared angry and occasionally an enormous crack and a flash of lightning would occur almost simultaneously, indicating the hurricane was either right on top of us or close to it.

I prayed for Flex. With only a vague idea where he was and no idea of his well-being, I worried. He should have been there with me. Flex Sheridan would do anything for me, and he was the only man in the world to whom I would give up control, knowing he would protect me at all costs. Sure, I put on a show; I acted as though I were self-reliant and strong and I suppose I was, but since I met him, I'd never felt safer than I did in his presence.

He was out there. We should have just taken our son and gone together, and at least then I would know I still had him.

But on the other side, words spoken by Charlie back in that Concord bar retuned to my ears. It was when he was at the men's prison with some other guys, zombies and ratz were on the move, and fire burned out of control. Flex had been gone for three hours or so when Charlie reminded me by saying, "Nothing brings out Super Flex better than him having somebody to watch out for."

She was right, of course. Talk about resolve. My husband had that. I put my worry away and thought about my current situation instead.

My back hurt. My neck hurt. I had pain in my left leg and as I tried to move it, I found I couldn't. The wind gusted again and I heard something out of my line of sight crash to the floor.

This was bad enough. Tornados on top of everything else was just insult added to injury. The events that occurred just prior to everything going black as I cowered beneath that sofa cushion flooded back.

The ravaging, swirling twister splintering the corner of the house first, then attacking the roof. I recalled the massive, stormy sky that had appeared overhead as the sound of destruction filled my ears and the roof started to peel away. I remembered hearing the sound of timbers squealing, nails pulling out of wood, followed by the enormous beam coming down against the basement door.

The beam that I now rested beneath.

A dog barked from somewhere below me. I smiled again. The dogs! Bunsen and Slider had made it in. That was the story here. I was alive. The dogs were alive. My family was alive.

I didn't give a shit who else thought so, because I knew I was a hero right then, at least to Trina and Taylor. And maybe to Charlie, who loved Bunsen like no other animal that ever walked the earth.

I would celebrate my heroine status later. For now, as always, there was more work to do. Plus, I had a distinct feeling Flex would not approve of my heroic actions one little bit. Much as he loved those dogs, he would remind me that they were not humans and they were not as important as me.

Because the timber I had crawled beneath was around a 6x10, it had prevented some larger limbs, boards and trusses from landing on me.

But not all of them. With movement, my neck became more flexible and I could now effectively look downward to see what prevented my leg from moving. A 2x4 with a nail protruding from it had fallen on me, and I could see that all but perhaps a half inch of the nail had plunged through my left ankle.

What was worse, the nail appeared to have embedded itself in the hardwood floor, essentially nailing my leg down. I could not tell by looking how deep it had entered the floor, but I guessed it could not have been much. I looked around. Nothing else pinned my body, but I would need some ingenuity to free myself.

I lay there on my back, craning my head forward enough to see the culprit nail. With all my strength – which I'll admit wasn't quite up to snuff at that moment – I tried to jerk my left leg up and off the nail.

A bolt of pain ripped from my foot all the way up to my waist. I felt dizzy, as though I might pass out.

Breathe. Just breathe a moment.

I looked again, my vision, momentarily having gone to black spots from the pain, now cleared. Nothing had changed. No progress. I was stuck.

My eyes darted around and I searched for anything that would help me.

A huge gust of wind came then, followed by a sustained current of air that moved at least twenty miles per hour faster than previously. Debris whipped around and smacked into everything in its path, and I knew that my time would soon be gone. I could not simply lie here in a supine position, waiting to be crushed by a flying tree or a falling wall.

There was another 2x4 to my left that appeared to be around five feet long. I strained as I reached, stretching my left arm toward it until I was able to throw my upper torso outward and curl my fingers around the tip of the board. I snatched it and pulled it in.

Looking at it, I could see it had once been connected to the other one that had nailed me to the floor like Jesus on the cross, only in this case I was the sinner, not the savior.

Now the tricky part.

The radio on my belt clicked. *"Gem, can you read? Gem, do you read us?"*

It was Charlie's voice. Unfortunately, I couldn't see the radio, and wasn't sure exactly where it was. Hearing her voice gave me renewed resolve, however, so I pulled back on the 2x4, dragged the base of it along the debris-riddled, rain-soaked hardwood and jammed it beneath the piece of wood through which the nail protruded into my ankle.

Sort of a fulcrum, but using just me, the floor and the board. I used both hands to push upward with leverage.

I felt the nail withdraw from my leg and I screamed at the unexpected pain, but I could not sustain it. Prior to that, I had not been able to feel anything. Until the board moved, I had believed my leg was numb. Wishful thinking. It felt as though someone had heated the nail in my ankle up to 1,000 degrees.

Breathing hard, I kept my arms raised and my shaking hands on the 2x4, waiting for the pain to subside. I took ten deep breaths and resolved to try again – just one more hard lift.

I squeezed my eyes closed and tried again, ignoring the tears that came as I forced my weakening arms all the way up. I again felt the galvanized steel nail slide against raw meat.

My raw meat.

A different sound met my ears and I bristled. I turned my head to my left and saw her standing there, beside that massive tree, ten feet away from me. Her red eyes glared and a hand steadied herself against the rough bark of the tree that lay atop the downed sliding glass door. The tatters of her dress whipped behind her, and as I watched with dread and amazement, I saw her fighting the wind that buffeted her slight frame.

She was the blaring alarm clock. She was the bank of speakers mounted to that high pole that blares sirens when the nuclear facility has suffered a catastrophic meltdown.

This red-eye was my motivation, and I can tell you that nothing bolsters Gemina Cardoza's survival instinct more than the prospect of being eaten alive or gassed into subservience at the cost of my family.

I pushed again on the board in my hands, but I had reached the top of my range-of-motion. I could not lift the board any higher without repositioning, and that meant only one thing.

I looked back at the creature. She had moved another foot toward me, finding another handhold on the large, downed tree.

Looking down at my drop holster, I realized it was pinned beneath me. Again I looked at the red-eye. I was on WAT-5 but we knew that was spotty at best, and she wasn't there for shelter, that much I knew.

She senses your strength, Gemina. She wants to consume you.

The words had entered my mind, and from the small voice and eerie confidence with which they were transmitted, I knew they must be true.

Isis had spoken them.

Did the strange child see what was happening? How could she know?

The creature took another step toward me. Again I tried to push up another fraction of an inch, but gained nothing. No choice. I braced myself for the pain.

I released my arms and the nail plunged back through my ankle. I cried out, and my show of weakness only emboldened the red-eye, for she let go in the gusting wind and gained yet another step toward me.

With no time to allow myself time to recover, I slid the 2x4 in my hands further beneath the board holding the nail.

At least it was out of the floor now, but I had to get it out of me.

With a grunt and one eye on the advancing, intelligent rotter, I pushed both arms outward like double pistons. The board lifted and the nail pulled free, and I immediately pulled my left ankle toward my body and allowed the board to fall.

Then I slid out the 2x4 and drew back my arm, throwing it at the creature whose face had changed. She stared at me, her dead expression now somehow angry, no longer patient and calculating.

I had pissed her off. I felt precious, warm blood running from the hole left behind and wondered if she sensed it, even with the WAT-5's influence.

Red-eyes took another step toward me, but this time she did not pause. She released the tree trunk and staggered a second step, then a third.

Panicked, I tried rocking myself onto my left side to free up my drop holster, pinned beneath my right thigh.

She was four feet away from me now. I hooked my left arm over the beam just above my head. Twisting my body, I felt my right leg flat against the floor and my holster free.

I reached down with my right hand and pulled the Glock from the holster. A round was always chambered.

Suddenly, I couldn't breathe as the intelligent zombie curled her fingers around my throat, her mouth opened in a gory display of black gums, brown teeth and putrid breath.

I raised the weapon and jammed it against her skull so hard I heard bone crack. Just as a bright red vapor began to pour from the creature's red eyes, I forced all the air from my lungs and pulled the trigger.

Her brains exploded from the right side of her head and she collapsed atop me, but not before the recoil sent the semi-automatic flying from my hand, landing with a thud somewhere on the floor to my right.

But my single round had been effective. Seconds after firing the weapon, I heard screams from below.

She no longer squeezed, but her nasty fingers still lay curled around my neck, and I threw her hand off of me and pushed her body aside. She flipped over and lay on her back, her black lifeblood leaking from her wasted body.

I started the painful process of sliding out from beneath the beam. I moved into a sitting position and put a little weight on my ankle. It was already clotting, telling me my body was functioning well. I leaned forward, adding a bit more weight to the leg.

After another five minutes, and lots of searching the room for threats, I pushed myself to my feet and stood there wobbling. Next move: let go of the wall.

Finally I stood on my own two feet again. I tore off a piece of the red-eye's gauzy dress and tied it over the wound on my ankle. It was wet, but the pressure felt better than nothing at all. I hoped infection wouldn't set in.

Once up and stable enough to continue, I found the dropped gun and checked my surroundings again. No more rotters had emerged. I holstered the Glock and looked for my Uzi. It was not in clear sight, but nothing in the room was where it had been before the twister. Stuff was either moved, hidden by debris or completely gone with the wind.

I worked my way around the room in the pouring rain, grateful the Ham radio was now in the basement with my family of fortunate survivors. I spotted my gun. Just the tip stuck out from beneath what was once the nook dining table.

I worked my way there and wiggled the Uzi from side-to-side until it came free, careful to stay out of its line of fire just in case something out of sight pressed against the trigger. The gun finally did come free, and I was happy to see it looked intact.

Clipped to the shoulder strap were four full magazines, too.

I had an idea. It was all I had, so I hoped it would work.

I needed to get my family out of their prison below. If anything happened to me, they would be trapped down there forever.

*****

Chapter Ten

I pulled open drawer after drawer while Punch looked on. "What the hell are you lookin' for, Flex?" He asked.

"Syringes," I said. "Hemp said to find them and bring as many as we could."

Punch did not respond. Instead, he went to the front counter and started yanking drawers open beneath until he said, "Got it."

I turned, and sure enough, in his hands were cardboard dispenser boxes with syringes. Two unopened, and one open. Both contained 100 syringes.

"This outta do it for bit, you think?" he asked.

"Take 'em all," I said. "Give me one. Your bag's looking a bit full."

He did, and I crushed the box as much as I could before stuffing it in my canvas bag. Then I undid my belt, slid it through the handles of the bag, and re-fastened it. My supplies now dangled, eliminating the need for me to hold onto the bag. I reached for a stapler on the desk and stapled the top of my bag closed. I never knew when I'd be sliding along the floor or jumping out of windows, and I didn't need to be losing any of what we'd risked life and limb to obtain.

"Good idea," said Punch. He followed suit, freeing up his hands for battle. One held his baseball bat, the other held his crazy shotgun.

"Okay," I said. "I sure wish we had WAT-5 that would keep uninfecteds from seeing us, but one way or another we gotta get the hell out of here and get to this Yancy Road address."

"How we set on WAT-5 anyway?" asked Punch.

I didn't answer. I just tucked the baseball bat between my legs and reached into my shirt pocket, withdrawing the baggie. I gave him a wafer and I took one myself and chewed it up.

"Time flies in zombieland," I said. "Better overly cautious than gourmet food for the undead."

Punch opened the door to the lobby again and the one-armed zombie shuffled over to us. Punch casually raised his super soaker on its bungee cord and gave him a little shot in the middle of his face.

I turned away this time, but heard the sounds of zombie skin and flesh dissolving into mushy badness. I heard and smelled what was happening as the monster's body collapsed to the floor with a swish rather than a thump, and became clothing sunken in goo.

"Shit works," said Punch. "You guys are geniuses."

"Little genius, little luck. Lots of Hemp," I said. "You'll meet him when we get back."

"I'll hold you to that," he said. "Time to go for it?"

I nodded. We had our headlamps off as he opened the door. We wanted to check the corridor for light and sound first. We both leaned out into the hallway. I looked left and he looked right.

"Nothin'," I said.

"Same here," he said. "Hear anything?"

I listened to the whistling and low vibration. "Just the wind," I said. "Sounds crazy out there, considering the size of this building. We shouldn't be able to hear anything."

"What did you call this? Hurricane George?"

"Yep," I said.

"George is a mother fucker," he said. "I say we go back the way we came in. See if they found your truck."

"I'll let you lead with your big gun," I said. "If you hit any trouble, feel free to deal with it as you see fit."

"Will do," said Punch.

He moved down the hallway, me directly behind him, watching the rear. We were forced to walk on top of some of the bodies in between the glass doors, both now shattered, but doing that, as disgusting as it felt beneath us, minimized the noise of crunching over chunks of tempered glass.

We passed the pair of zombies I had sprayed with urushiol, and I was relieved to see they were beneath other bodies and were likely not noticed by the unknown visitors.

Once clear of the segmented portion of the hallway, bodies were strewn all over. Bullet holes riddled the walls, along with blood spatter. The reek had to have been as bad or worse than any other enclosed space with similar death and decay, but to be perfectly honest, I just didn't notice much anymore.

I had once done an electrical job at a factory that produced a polyurethane glue. The process created a sharp, pungent odor that was very strong in the factory proper, but still permeated the air within the offices. I remembered asking them how they stood the smell for an entire work day.

Their response was unanimous. "What smell?"

Goes to show you ... you can get used to anything.

Punch stopped up as we reached the door leading back into the main hallway that connected building two with building one.

"I don't know where they went, Flex, but we look to be in the clear so far."

"Could be lucky, or they could be stakin' out my truck."

"It's a big building, Flex," said Punch. "If they're searching for us, it's gonna take 'em a while."

I didn't see that we had much choice. Hiding wasn't an option, and if we did come across them, we'd play it by ear from there.

I nodded toward the main lobby. "Go on, brother. Side-by-side from here on out."

We moved along, his tactical shotgun in his hand, my Daewoo in mine. Nobody accosted us as we moved around the circular partition in the reception area, and through the doors leading back to the hall where we entered the building.

"I gotta take a leak," said Punch. "Like now."

"Go ahead," I said. "I'll go on to the door and see if anyone's scoping it out."

Punch rested his bat against the wall and prepared to do his business. I moved down the hallway to the end. Once there, I put my ear to the door and listened.

The wind raged, and the rain pounded. Above the howling wind and showers, I heard voices, yelling. Two men.

"How long they been in there?" said one.

Another, younger voice answered, screaming at what must have been the top of his lungs in order to be heard. "I ain't got a watch," he said. "You know that."

"Yeah," said the other voice again, lower-toned, deeper and stronger. "Still don't get why he made us wait outside instead of just inside that door."

"He said in case someone tries to take this truck. He really wants it."

I was done listening. I pulled a Glock from my drop holster, and flung the door open hard. The wind caught it and did the rest. I heard it impact something solid, and I guessed it was one of the sentries.

I stood in the open doorway and spun around to snatch a rifle from the unprepared hands of a very shocked kid of perhaps nineteen years. I put the Glock to his head, glancing toward the heavy door that flapped in the breeze behind me.

"Inside and on the floor, spread eagle!" I ordered, with more forcefulness than I liked to use, what with being a lover rather than a fighter and all. "Move!"

Apparently it worked, because the skinny kid practically dove into the hallway and lay on his stomach, his arms stretched out in front of him.

To be honest I felt kind of bad, but not for long.

A round pierced the metal door and I felt my pant leg ripple, and not just from the breeze.

"Punch!" I screamed. "Watch this guy!"

"Where the hell did he come from?" asked Punch, zipping and running at the same time.

I didn't answer him. I was already in mid jump to avoid any more low rounds. Once clear of the door, I curled my fingers around it and pulled it hard against the crazy, buffeting wind until it reached the point that the force of the wind slammed it shut. Behind it was another young man – this one slightly older than the other one. He was on the ground, his forehead emblazoned with an angry, red welt, no doubt from where the flying door had smacked him moments earlier.

I dropped a knee onto his chest and ripped the rifle from his grip. I was lucky the son of a bitch hadn't connected with his blind shot, or I'd be lame, the bones in my ankle shattered beyond repair.

I tossed the gun beneath my truck and grabbed the kid by the coat. Adrenaline drove me, but that wasn't all. There were four zombies moving along the wall – sliding toward me sideways along the exterior painted concrete, occasionally being caught by the wind, but always managing to suck up to the solid surface again and gain one more step toward us.

I knew it wasn't me that drew them; it was this guy and what had to be his brother, from their similar features. I was on WAT-5, but these mugs were about as fragrant as the walking dead could hope for.

Once I had him in position in front of the door, I pulled it open and planted my foot behind it to avoid the full tilt slam against the wall. "Crawl your ass inside!" I shouted over the roar of pounding rain, the water running down my face, the wind pelting my eyes with rain so that I was far less a threat than either of the strangers knew. I was operating on instinct and hoping for luck.

The young man crawled like he was playing a game of speed Twister. Right hand to red, left hand to yellow, right knee to green, left knee to blue.

In the end, he fell on top of the other guy, rolled onto his back and stared up at me in horror as I closed the door and turned my Glock on both of them again.

It wasn't necessary. Punch was already training his shotgun on them, and they weren't moving a muscle.

"These boys from Buckfield?" I asked Punch.

Punch shook his head. "Nope," he said. "Never seen 'em before, plus they're too young. Buckfield guys are all thirty plus."

I looked up the hall and saw two men approaching. Both were armed with rifles of some sort, and neither appeared to have seen us yet.

Making eye contact with Punch, I raised my chin slightly, moving my eyebrows. Universal sign for *Some motherfucker's behind you.*

Punch swung his tactical shotgun with the huge drum of shells around and held his fire. The men stopped, their guns raised. Neither fired.

"We don't want to hurt 'em," I called. "Was that you who shot up the hall full of infecteds?"

The men, just silhouettes from where we stood, backlit from the gloomy daylight of the reception area, didn't

212

respond to my question. They turned toward one another and said something that we couldn't hear.

Then one of the men said, "Those are my boys there. They okay?"

"Answer my question first," I said. "Did you kill the zombies in the hall?"

"Yeah, that was us."

"Lower your weapons," said Punch.

"Not gonna happen," said the one on the left.

If we were in a goddamned movie, I'd have pointed the Glock at either one of the boys and said something extraordinarily threatening. That ain't me. I always try to get things done with convincing rather than threats, but after what happened in Buckfield, I wasn't about to take any chances that my mistake would leave my son and Trina fatherless.

"I can understand that," I said. "It's a tough world out there. We're just here for medicine. That's my truck out there."

"Not anymore," said the guy on the right.

"You're gonna get on his bad side if you start getting' possessive over his truck," said Punch. "Just a warning."

"Fuck these guys, Todd!" shouted the second man, raising his rifle barrel.

Now if I were called on to list the top ten stupidest moves I've ever seen anyone make, that guy would've made the top three. Possibly right between freshman Joey Evans copping a feel on Angie Murray on the bus, who happened to be the girlfriend of the senior star tackle at my high school, and those dumbfuck predators I saw on that news show who show up at the homes of minor girls with six packs of beer, only to try to explain it to the show's host.

I don't know whether Punch and I fired at the same time or not, but I do know the fuckwad at the other end of the twenty-five yard long hallway never got a shot off before his feet lifted off the ground and he flew backward through the air.

My Daewoo was up and the trigger pulled while that prick was still swinging his barrel around. It was only then that I realized that it was still on single shot mode, and I suppose, in retrospect, it was a good thing. Still, I'm pretty sure I got that round off before Punch fired two blasts from his shotgun, causing the guy named Todd to flop to the linoleum floor like a rag doll. As for his buddy, he ejected into the reception area. the glass behind him shattering with ear-splitting efficiency, clearing his flight path.

I didn't fire again. I looked down to see both boys' frightened faces staring the length of the long corridor toward their father. He had been the man standing on the left. Todd.

"Punch, go check on 'em," I said. "I got these guys."

Punch walked toward me, leaned in and whispered, "Just birdshot, buddy. I didn't want to kill them." He turned and started down, his shotgun held out in front of him, and I looked down at the kids.

I wasn't sure how to feel. I was pretty sure that I'd hit Todd's friend square in the chest with the round from the K7.

I knelt down and said, "This isn't what we do. Your dad was bein' reasonable, as far as I can tell. Who's the other guy?"

"He's our uncle," said the older of the two young men.

"You two can stand up," I said.

They slowly got to their feet.

I watched them. "Any more weapons on you?" I asked.

Both guys shook their heads.

"Dad says we suck with pistols," said the thin, dark-haired one. He could not have been more than nineteen years old. He wore a hat with the Bose insignia on it, his jet black hair sticking out from underneath. He was about 5'-10" tall and wore a blue jean jacket over a black tee shirt, with Levis. His tee-shirt also had the word *Bose* printed in the center. Kid must have been an audiophile back in the days when music became a young adult's entire focus.

"You suck," said the taller, thicker one. "He won't let me have a pistol because he thinks you'd be upset."

He was clearly older than the other kid by at least two years. Other than that, they looked almost the same, but the older guy looked more road-worn. His hair was down past his shoulders and he had a good sized bruise on his right cheek and what looked like a bullet graze scar on his neck. Could've been anything, I suppose, but I tend to imagine the worst.

"Your daddy's right," I said. "Handguns take a lot of practice. How many of you were inside?"

"Just my daddy and uncle," said the young man.

"They're both breathing," said Punch.

"Come with me," I said, standing aside and motioning them down the hall toward Punch and the two downed men. They walked ahead, and as they got closer, they walked faster. As they approached the two men, one of them struggled to sit up, leaning against the wall.

"Joey, Benny," he managed, his voice strained.

"Dad!" the boys shouted at once,

"I knew that vest would come in handy, dad!" said the younger of the two.

My light hit the man's face, and I saw the red rash all over it.

"Birdshot's not lethal from that distance, but it can sure put a good rash on you, and fuck your vision," said Punch. "I like a bit of scatter in between kill rounds." He looked down at the man and said, "What's your name, man?"

"Todd Chambers," he said, blinking his eyes.

"Todd, can you see?" asked Punch.

"Lucky I closed my eyes just before you fired," he said.

Eric A. Shelman

"You're lucky I fired both shots high on purpose," said Punch. "I'm only into killin' what's already dead these days. Your brother here blew it."

"Brother-in-law," he said. "Hey, Cole," he said, slapping the other man on the arm. Cole didn't respond. Todd's expression changed and he leaned over and shook the man, but he still didn't move.

Punch lifted the man's head and listened. "Shit, Flex," he said. "He's not breathing." He put his fingers to the unconscious stranger's neck. "No pulse."

Punch quickly slid his gun out of the reach of Joey and Benny, rolled the man onto his back and ripped open his light jacket.

"He's got on a ballistic vest, too," said Punch, reaching down. He dug at something with his fingers, then tossed me the piece of lead. "Dead center. Nice shootin' for a machine gun."

"I've had some practice," I said.

"Is he okay?" shouted the younger son.

Punch didn't answer. He straddled him and began performing CPR. He pumped his chest several times, listened for breathing, and pumped some more.

I was starting to lose hope. Punch was approaching one minute of CPR when the man suddenly gasped and his eyes went wide.

"Uncle Cole!" shouted Joey, a smile spreading over his face. "Uncle Cole, you're okay!"

The man hyperventilated, but Punch got him into a sitting position and supported him there. "How you doin', Cole?"

He looked at us. "I didn't mean …"

"Doesn't matter," I said. "We do a lot of shit we don't mean out here."

The man nodded and breathed in and out, taking shallow gulps of air.

"What did you come here for?" I asked.

"Looking for the pharmacy," said Todd.

"Did you find it?" I asked.

Todd shook his head. "Nah. Storm started sounding worse, and we figured we had the wrong building anyway. Plus, when we saw that ton of zombies, we kinda lost our resolve. Figured we'd come back with more guys later."

"Who's sick?" asked Punch.

"Nobody we know," he said. "Doctor Perry said people were bound to get hurt in the storm, and he needed more antibiotics and pain meds. There are closer pharmacies, but he cleaned them out already. He's been here, but just to save what he thought was critical."

That explained to me why he'd taken the antitoxin and other vaccines. I owed the guy a debt – if he was willing to share it as needed. I didn't see any other reason he'd take it, and it all might be an exercise in futility anyway, depending on how long this went on. With new babies being born and no vaccinations being administered to them, our world could revert back to the days of the black plague, I imagined.

"Why not wait until after the storm passes?" asked Punch.

"We were going stir crazy," said Todd. "Been afraid to go anywhere for the last day waiting for this damned storm or hurricane or whatever it is."

As if on queue, the door at the end of the hall slammed twice hard, then flew all the way open.

"It's getting worse by the minute," I said. "Let's get Cole on his feet. We need to get where Perry is. He's got what we came here for."

"What's that?" asked Todd.

"I'd rather hold that info until we see him," I said. "Don't worry, we won't take it all."

"I don't want to take these guys there," said Cole, still trying to catch his breath. "I don't trust them."

"Not your call," I said. "We've got his address and we'll take your weapons if you get shitty."

"Uncle Cole, shut up!" shouted Joey. "We won't make it back without our guns!"

"They're not taking our guns and we're taking them to Perry," said Todd. "Cole, it's time to quit being an asshole and try getting along. Jesus, man. How many lessons are you going to have to learn?"

"Can you get up?" asked Punch, holding Cole's shoulder.

Cole did his best to jerk his shoulder from Punch's grasp and grimaced as he got to his feet with some difficulty. I imagined he was going to be nursing a hell of a bruise underneath that vest by the next day.

"We're not your enemy," I said.

Just then, the door that had been slamming against the wall over and over stopped. The wind still howled, and the light from the open door still illuminated the hallway. I turned to see what had changed.

We all turned.

A red-eyed female stood in the center of the doorway, my truck and blowing debris visible behind her. She clung to both sides of the frame, stilling the door, her hair whipping upward. Her red eyes did not waver from us; sizing us up.

I swung my Daewoo toward her but the moment I began to move, she released the door frame and was gone. I got a chill.

I turned back to our new acquaintance. "Did you see that, Cole?" I emphasized my next words with jabs of my finger toward the now empty space. "That thing with the red eyes?"

He nodded slowly, his eyes darting between me and where I pointed.

"If you want to be around for your nephews here," I said, "you better remember your enemy's out there, buddy.

Me and Punch here just might be the best friends you meet all day."

*****

I was completely drenched, and I might have been crying. I don't remember. Occasionally, I screamed, "I'm okay! I'm okay! Hold on!"

I did it for everyone in the basement and for me in equal parts. Knowing they were down there, just yards away, gave me comfort. I also recognized that if they knew I was alive, it would give them the same peace that I so desperately needed.

As I formulated my plan, I talked to Flex. I knew he couldn't hear me, but that made me feel better, too.

Quick scans of the room. Glock unsnapped and ready. I'd need all the rounds in my Uzi to execute the task at hand.

The beam had fallen against the entrance to the basement and slid down to within two feet of the base of the door. Had it not been twenty or more feet long, I might have attempted to move it myself, but looking at the amount of crap stacked on top of it, it would be more wasted effort.

I pounded on the door and put my ear to it. The wind and rain was so loud, it was nearly impossible to hear anything from below, but if someone came up the stairs, I might be able to be heard.

I heard a double slap on the door, and a muffled, "Gem?"

"Yes!" I called. "I'm going to be firing my gun! Don't worry, okay? I'm okay!"

"Okay," the voice came, and I knew it was Hemp. I wanted to hug that scientist and only let go when I heard Flex call my name.

I looked at the ceiling beam again. I didn't know if the fucker was hardwood, softwood, Douglas fir or some kind of pine. I knew it was blocking the door that would lead me not only to safety, but to my family, and that was enough.

I raised my Uzi and pointed it at the lower corner of the beam, about two feet away from where it pressed against the door. If I was successful, I needed room to swing it open.

I fired a three-round burst, my eyes closed. I knew that wouldn't prevent a ricochet from blowing a hole in my face, but it made me feel better, just like my periodic shout outs to my friends in the dungeon.

I opened my eyes and saw severe chunks blown out of the wood. This was it. Aim carefully, chip away.

I saw it once on the TV show, *Myth Busters*. It's actually how I thought of it. They used a Gatling Gun on the show, but this was a smaller beam than the tree they cut in half with their gun.

I put the Uzi on full auto and eyed my pattern. I would just move inward slowly and see what I had. I could always adjust, and could probably find more ammo if necessary.

I fired, holding down the trigger until the gun fell silent. I opened my eyes, and let out a "Woo hoo!"

I was a quarter of the way through. I was so encouraged, I ejected the empty magazine and slammed in the new one. This time I wanted to see.

I chambered the first round and took aim. I stood back a foot and a half more and let the rounds fly, this time watching where the devastation was taking place. With that spent magazine, I was nearing the halfway point.

I stood back and kicked at the timber, once. Twice.

Okay. My foot hurt, and I felt stupid. Did I really think I could kick the equivalent of an oversized 2X4 in half?

I heard the sound of brass clicking against brass behind me. At the same time, I heard a tiny, mature voice in my head say, "A mother is here."

I reached for my Glock and spun around, and there she was, another red-eye, just three feet behind me.

I fired two into her right leg as I lifted the weapon, and by the time she started to crumple, her head came down to meet my line of fire. I blasted her almost right between the eyes and watched her body flop harmlessly away, coming to rest on top of the now useless flat screen television that had blown off its wall mounts.

I scanned the room again, thinking, "Thank you, Isis."

I heard nothing in return, but I felt her there, as though she nodded. I'd hate to play that Simon memory game with that kid. Her *or* Nelson. Fuck, even Hemp. All too smart for me.

Well, I had my little genius, telepathic baby alarm, and I had spent brass all around my feet, so I felt generally comfortable continuing with the blasting. I reloaded the Uzi again and continued chewing up wood.

When I had spent all five magazines, there might have only been a half inch of wood left to break. A smile came across my face and I must have looked like a real idiot there, brass and sawdust at my feet and hair that had to look like a string mop.

My ankle hurt like hell, because I'd obviously forgotten about it when I'd tried to break the board earlier. But staring at the piece of wood in front of me, I knew I wouldn't need a goddamned Anthony Robbins personal fucking power course to snap it.

I stepped up onto the board and gripped the knob of the basement door. I jumped.

It broke.

My tears erupted the moment it gave way, and I was a blubbering idiot as I dropped my Uzi and bent down to lift the small piece of wood away to clear the path for the door.

I stood there for a moment, exhilarated and exhausted at the same time. I turned the knob and flung the door open, almost falling down the steps as I tried to hurry down them.

Charlie and Dave charged up the stairs and met me at the halfway mark, and I only remember falling into their arms and letting them carry me the rest of the way down.

Once inside, I didn't even notice Hemp rush up the steps to retrieve my Uzi and pull the door closed again, because I was tackled by Bunsen, Slider, Trina, Taylor, Serena, Nelson and all of my family that I loved so much.

Even Lola and Rachel waited their turn and moved in for hugs. Doc Scofield was next, and his hug was firm. I saw tears in his eyes, too. None of them seemed to notice or care that I was sopping wet.

I don't know when I quit crying. I didn't want to stop. It felt good, so good to be crying tears of happiness rather than tears of fear and sadness. I wanted the salty stuff to flow forever.

I went to little Flexy then, my baby boy. He lay in his crib, his eyes bright and alert. His little mouth turned up in a smile when he saw me, and I knew he probably never even realized I wasn't in the room. Had I not been so wet already, I would have noticed the milk leaking from my nipples at the very sight of him.

I moved over to a sink mounted to the wall and wrung the water from my hair as best I could, then went back to his playpen and leaned down to put my lips to his warm cheek and wet his soft skin with my tears.

My clothes were still dripping and I didn't want to soak him, too, so I was content for the moment just smelling and kissing him.

"Somebody's been waitin' for you," said Bug. I looked at him and saw that he held Isis in his arms. She smiled at me and said, "I missed you, Gemina."

She held out her arms. I went to Bug and kissed him on the cheek. He nodded to me and looked at his daughter, whose eyes never left me.

I put both of my hands on the sides of her face and kissed her cheek, too. Her little red eyes stared, her mouth turned up in a smile, and I was again reminded by her unsuitable teeth that she was not an ordinary child.

"I heard you, Isis," I said.

"You were supposed to," she said, her smile still in place.

"You saved me from her," I said.

"The mother," she whispered. She actually whispered.

"I have other names for them," I said.

"I know," she said. "It's not their fault, Gemina, but they must die."

I stared at her, so grateful inside that she felt that way, even with the strange kinship she seemed to have with them.

"Will we ... will we make it, Isis?" I asked.

Isis did not answer my question immediately. She looked at me, seeming to study every line and wrinkle, then she reached out her tiny hand and touched my face.

"I do not see ahead," said Isis. "I see only now, near and far. Now you are alive. Now, Flex and Punch are alive. They are with others."

Isis turned and looked at her father. "Jerky!" she shouted. "Please, papa!"

"Isis," I said, my voice pleading.

She turned to me again and nodded. "He is not in danger now," she said. "He thinks of you, and of us. But mostly of you and your son."

The horror of just a few minutes earlier faded and it struck me how important this infant's abilities were to all of us. I guessed that much of what she was to become wouldn't be known until she grew older.

I felt a tugging at my wet blouse and looked down to see Trina smiling up at me. She put her hand next to her mouth as though she wanted to whisper to me, so I knelt

223

down and put my arm around her. She put her lips to my ear and said, "Mommy, that is a really smart baby."

I laughed – which felt like the equivalent of an orgasm after so much tension – and pulled her closer, squeezing her. I forgot that I was wet and she came away, I'm sure, with mixed feelings about her now moist clothes.

"Gem," said Hemp, standing beside me. I quickly kissed Trina again and stood.

"Hi," I said.

"Good to have you back," he said, smiling. "Now sit in that chair over there and let me and Doc Scofield look at your ankle. It's bleeding."

******

The foursome we had met at the hospital drove a Ford F350 Crew Cab that looked brand new. It stood up to the wind well, but it was blowing harder than at any time previously, and sheet metal, roof shingles and branches were smacking into the sides of both our vehicles the entire way, which was about four miles.

The rotters had all but disappeared, and their mere absence made me nervous. My people knew how the red-eyes hid, and from what Dave reported from his trip to California, we also knew they could control the dumb walkers, too. Get 'em all something that Dylan had sung about; Shelter From The Storm.

Whether or not they had the mental resources to think along those lines, I didn't know. I never had reason to think about any such situation.

I gripped the wheel hard, fighting the wind and running over debris that I hoped wouldn't flatten one of my tires, and followed behind the Ford. We had turned our gun to the rear to make them feel more comfortable.

When we arrived at 4301 Yancy, we discovered it was not a residential address.

"What is this place?" I asked.

Punch pointed to a sign that I hadn't seen through the rapidly swiping wipers. "Piedmont Natural Gas," he read.

"It's got a fence around it," I said. "Built out of brick, too. Not a bad place to hole up."

The Ford stopped outside the gates and I could only see the silhouettes of the four men. I picked up my radio on the seat beside me and flipped the switch around until I heard, "-here, Doctor Perry. Got some guys with us."

We'd only caught the last part, but now that we knew 15 was the right channel, I stayed there and listened.

"Who's with you?" asked a voice that I assumed was Perry.

"Ran into them at the hospital." It was Todd. I was glad, because I was certain Cole would not spin us quite as fairly, and we really needed to get in to see the man.

"Friendly?" asked Perry.

I pushed the button. "We are, doctor. We're from Whitmire, South Carolina, and we've got what we believe is a Diphtheria outbreak. Small right now, but we need antitoxin."

Silence on the line.

Punch looked at me. "Buddy, we're goin' in either way. You know that, right?"

I nodded. "I was hopin' you knew."

He nodded.

"I'll be right out," the man at the other end of the radio said.

A few moments later, a bald man came out. He was dressed in a yellow rain slicker and he leaned into the wind as he approached the gate. He used a key to unlock a padlock, and lifted the metal latch, swinging the gate inward on its single, rolling wheel.

The Ford rolled in, and we followed.

They stopped and waited until we cleared the fence, and the man, whom I still assumed was Doctor Perry, closed and locked the gate again, then ran to the truck and jumped in the back seat with the boys.

They started rolling again and we followed them up to a parking area beside the doors. I checked to see what kind of trees were around to blow over and smash our precious truck, but we were in the clear.

Punch and I grabbed our guns and threw them over our shoulders. I made sure my baggie of wafers was safely tucked in dry storage in my pocket, and I kept the super-soaker attached to my belt. I saw Punch had his with him, too.

We were pretty scary aside from our colorful squirt guns. Hell, maybe it would disarm them a bit, and I mean that in the attitude sense.

The wind was to our backs and pushed us toward the building. We half-ran, and reached the door where the other men were just going inside. We followed. Once inside, we hung our guns from their straps and tried to find a dry spot on our clothes to dry our hands.

"Come on in," said Perry. "I've got towels."

"Clean towels?" asked Punch.

"Washer, dryer, gravity water feed," he said. "Everything here runs on natural gas," added the doctor. "And I have enough to last for years."

I now realized the reason for coming here. This was a large, natural gas processing plant, and there were tanks of the stuff, ready to go, onsite.

Punch held out his hand to the doctor. "I'm Frank Magee," he said. The doctor took his hand and shook it. "Friends call me Punch."

"Well, Punch, I'm John Perry. Feel free to call me John."

I introduced myself. "Just Flex," I said. "I've got a son just over eight weeks old and he's been exposed to Diphtheria. He's had none of his boosters."

"He's just about at the age where he can begin to get them, so you're not late," said Perry. "But the Diphtheria outbreak makes it all the more crucial."

"How'd you pinpoint this place as your home base, doc?" asked Punch.

Perry began walking further inside and we followed. Where we'd come in was a side, employee entrance, so there was a check-in window on the left, but it quickly opened up into a place where you could store jackets, etc. There was a bank of lockers on the right side with combination locks. The flooring was linoleum, and there were low, wooden benches bolted to the floor, perhaps for people removing muddy shoes or other articles of clothing.

Todd, Joey and Benny all plopped down on a bench near the entry, looking on. Cole stood by the door, leaning against the wall.

Perry looked around, smiling. "Piedmont Gas was a big employer here," Perry said. "They required staff here at all hours, obviously. They have sleeping quarters, break rooms and a laundry facility. They even had their own employee restaurant. When I got here there were a ton of the converts around and lots of dead bodies, too, but I methodically took them out and cleaned as I went. I've been pretty much ruling the roost since then."

I watched the doctor as he led the way. He was soft spoken, stood about 5'5" tall, and wore black, plastic-rimmed glasses. He was not imposing, and would probably have made a good pediatrician.

"Perfect shelter, really," said Todd. "Plus, we have an in-house doctor in John here."

"Well, I assume you saw my note and you know I took all the Diphtheria antitoxin?" asked Perry.

"Yeah, we know," I said. "We got into the pharmacy and found your note."

"Glad I put them in the boxes I emptied," he said. "I only wish I'd have emptied more. When I set out the first time, I was by myself and I just couldn't carry any more."

Punch looked at me. "Doc, did you trap all those zombies in that hallway?"

"Call me John, please," he said. "And yes, on my only run to the hospital – and I'm familiar with the layout, of course – I went into Building 2, which is purely administrative."

I interrupted him. "Were you armed?"

The doctor reached beneath his rain slicker, which he still wore, and withdrew a long-barreled revolver. But not just any revolver.

"Elvis Presley?" I asked. "May I?" I held out my hand. Perry gave it to me.

"This a .44?" I asked, looking it over.

"It is. My dad was a huge Elvis fan. He bought this on limited release a few years back."

The metal was bright gold, and the barrel was at least 8" long. The grip looked like Walnut, and on the sides of the cylinder were two images of Presley – one, a close-up of his face, and the other side an image of him playing the guitar. Along the barrel was Presley's printed signature.

"So that's what you used to corral all those walkers?" asked Punch.

"Like I said, I know the hospital layout. The hallway runs around the entire building. The glass walls in the hallway were installed because there's a good-sized conference room centered there. During meeting breaks, people would go into the halls to stretch their legs, and people complained about the noise. So they put up the two glass walls with doors."

"Convenient," I said.

"Very," he said. "When I first got there, I saw that huge horde coming at me, so I ran to the near door and just pulled it closed. I'd already figured out that they weren't that bright, and the far door was still open, so I just stood there like human bait, letting them file in."

"How'd you get the far door closed?" asked Punch.

"That's when I needed that," he said, pointing to the Elvis .44 in Punch's hand. "I went to run around to come up behind them. There were still lots of stragglers around in the back hallway, so I took out maybe seven or eight on the way. The ones you saw trapped in the hallway couldn't get past another door in the rear. It also swung inward and it latched."

"Then you closed the other door?"

"I did, but it wasn't that easy."

"What do you mean?" I asked.

"Eventually they were all in and seemingly very engaged with me. I made sure they were pressed against the wall where I was, and then I ran as fast as I could around the back hall and into the corridor behind them. Problem was, every time I opened the door to look, I found that some had drifted back, and had to figure something out."

"What'd you do?" asked Punch, curious.

Perry lifted his sleeve to reveal a 10" scar that looked to be long healed. "I cut myself good and dripped blood all over the glass and the floor."

"Painful, but a good plan," I said.

"But why put them in there?" asked Punch. "Lots of work."

"Two reasons, but mainly because I couldn't kill them all with my Elvis .44," Perry said, holding his hand out. Punch gave him the gold revolver, and he ran his fingers over the smooth, gleaming metal as he spoke. "The other benefit was protecting the pharmacy. I let one zombie inside there before I left, and since the entry was right beyond where I'd trapped the rest, I was pretty sure people would give up rather than try to get around them. I also knocked down some big shelving units to block the back hallway, just to give the illusion that it was impassable. Obviously it wasn't."

It was all becoming clear now. "I kinda thought that horde looked like it was left there for a reason," I said.

"You should've told your guys that I guess," said Punch. "You know they killed them all."

Perry looked at Cole and Todd, his eyes suddenly icy. "Is that true?"

Todd pointed a finger at Cole, but he did not appear nervous in the slightest. "I told Cole that before we went in. You told us it might be kind of a shock at first, but not to worry because they were trapped."

"I didn't fucking hear him saying that," said Cole. "So shoot me."

"Well," said Todd. "He said it more than once. Anyway, on his first couple of shots he shattered the glass wall and they were coming at us. It was all we could do to alternate reloads and kill them all before they killed us. We just tried to get what you sent us for."

"But you didn't get it, did you?" asked Perry. "Is all that true, Cole?"

I heard a change in Dr. John Perry's voice then. It went from conversational to steely cold.

Cole shrugged. "They need to all be dead, doc," he said.

"What did I tell you when you came here two weeks ago?" asked Perry.

"I know what you said," the man barked, "but I'm no fucking robot. I've got ideas, too."

Perry noticeably bristled. His eyes never left the other man's, as though everyone else in the room had departed and they were alone. "Cole, I appreciate that you're interested in being a contributing member of this team, but there's one problem."

"What's that?" Cole asked, his expression dour.

"You're not smart enough or you don't care enough to follow simple, sensible instructions and sooner or later, you're going to get people killed." Perry opened the chamber on his Elvis gun and I looked down to see it was full. He snapped it closed again, looking once more at Cole.

"Nobody fucking died today," said Cole. "And maybe you're the odd man out here," he added.

"What do you mean by that?" asked Perry. "Think very hard before you answer."

"Maybe it's time for you to move on, doc," he said. "Group could maybe use a new leader, since you can't seem to keep people in line." He smirked this time, nudging Todd with his elbow.

"Do *you* feel this way Todd?" asked Perry.

Todd quickly shook his head. "It's just Cole being Cole," he said. "He's kidding."

"Well," said Perry. "I'm not so sure he is joking. Are you joking, Cole?"

"I don't need this shit," said Cole. "Like I said, nobody died and it's over. You don't need to fucking micromanage my ass."

"Yes, Cole," said Perry. "Someone did die." He raised the gold-plated revolver and fired a single round into Cole's forehead. Blood sprayed into the entry hall behind the man as his eyes stared for a moment at his killer. Two seconds later, they rolled back, his legs gave way beneath him, and he collapsed like a Jenga game at its conclusion.

I ripped the gun from Perry's hands and tackled him to the floor. Once down, Punch was there, searching Perry's pockets for other weapons. He removed a 10" Buck knife from a sheathe on his left calf.

I got off Perry and stood up, just staring at him.

Both Joey and Benny were in terror, staring at their dead uncle on the floor, and they staggered backward, pressing themselves against a far wall.

Todd, his eyes glued to Perry, said nothing. He moved to stand in front of his sons, like a shield.

Punch had his shotgun aimed at Perry's face.

Perry's expression didn't change. He slowly stood again, his eyes alternately on me and Punch. He said, "Todd, would you have your boys put his body outside?" He then looked at me and Punch. "And we should talk about what you came here for."

"How many others are here with you?" I asked. "What's more, how many others have you killed?"

"Gentlemen," said Perry. "There are exactly twenty-six of us … now, anyway. And to answer your question, I've only found it necessary to kill this man, and one other. The other was a woman, and while appearing to be human, she had reddish eyes and would suddenly start saying and doing things that put our group in danger."

I looked at the cowering kids and said, "Todd, get them out of here, would you?"

Todd nodded and moved the two boys further down a first floor hallway, disappearing into a room off the corridor.

A few moments later, Todd came back in and stood in silence, listening.

"This red-eyed girl you're talkin' about," he said. "What kinda stuff would she do?"

"She would open doors and windows, mostly," said Perry. "But she would do it in the middle of the night, so if we didn't have sentries, we might not be alive now."

"You could've just locked Marlene up," said Todd, his eyes still on his brother-in-law's body.

"That would have been more cruel, I'm afraid, Todd. She was perfectly aware and normal most of the time. But

232

all of that was offset by how reckless the things she did were. I didn't see that I had a choice."

"How has he treated you since you got here?" I asked Todd.

Todd looked at Perry, who nodded at him. "Go ahead," said the doctor. "Speak freely. I'm unarmed."

"I know this sounds crazy compared to what you just saw, but he's been good," said Todd. "So much so that I *never* saw that coming just now. He's a good organizer, and a good doctor. He laid out a set of rules and conditions when we moved in here, just like he did with everyone else. I don't think he really stressed the consequences clearly enough, though." He shook his head and looked again at Cole's body. "That might just be the understatement of the year."

"Cole had his good moments, but everyone here knows he was a loose cannon," said Perry. "Being your brother-in-law, I expect you've known him a decent amount of time, Todd. Perhaps you know a different side, but he's been nothing but confrontational since I've known him."

"Nope," said Todd. "There was pretty much only one side to Cole. He's pretty big on the 'my way or the highway' philosophy."

"And he knew I was, too," said Perry.

"Where's the rest of your people?" asked Punch. "I'd like to check on 'em."

"They're fine," said Perry. "Upstairs."

"Might be a good idea to get Cole's body outside before anyone sees it," I said. "You made this mess, Dr. Perry. I'll help you get him moved."

"I'd like my gun back now if we're going outside," he said.

"All due respect," I said, "I think you'll understand if I hold onto it for a few. You got strong fences and we need to talk."

Perry shook his head, staring at me. "Friend, if you think this was Cole's first strike, you're wrong," said Perry. "He's put us at risk at least four times I can think of in the time he's been here."

I sized Perry up to be a man who did what he felt was necessary, whether it was easy or difficult. It was a trait I respected, but on the other side of that coin, I feared his willingness to act without fear of consequences, and no matter who looked on, meant he was more instinctual and reactionary than thoughtful; perhaps more cruel than kind.

"Let's just get this done," I said. "We can chat outside."

"You good?" asked Punch.

I nodded. "Yeah. And maybe before you go upstairs you can have Todd here help you find something to clean up this blood." I glanced at Perry. "The good doctor here may not be all that concerned about the psychological effect it could have on the others, but I am."

Punch nodded, and Todd led him out of the room.

"You're misjudging me," said Perry, looking frustrated.

"Maybe," I said. "If that's the case, I'm sorry. Like I said, we'll chat while we work."

I tucked Perry's Elvis revolver in the back of my pants.

I lifted Cole's feet and made the doctor lift him from the shoulders. The man was stronger than I thought, and he lifted his half of our burden easily. I made him walk backwards.

I followed him out the door we came in through, hefting the dead weight of the man that I hadn't liked very much – in fact, the man who would've been dead an hour before had he not been wearing a ballistic vest.

When we got outside, Perry led us behind a wall that ran the length of the front of the building. It was solid block, and served as an excellent wind and sound barrier. We lowered the body to the ground about twenty feet from the entrance.

I said, "I want to speak with the others here before we get down to business."

"I'll remind you this isn't your home," he said, his breathing labored.

"Acknowledged," I said. "But I've found that cruelty isn't just limited to the occasional killing. I want to see how you interact with your guests."

"I think of us as a group of survivors, working together," said Perry.

I believed he did feel that way, but the enforcement of his *rules and conditions* seemed to be a little harsh and perhaps a bit erratic.

"Maybe so, but when they fuck up, you have another option," I said. "You can kick 'em the hell out rather than kill 'em."

"Been there, done that," said Perry. "I booted one guy early on, and he hooked up with some other tough guys. They tried some Molotov cocktails on the building and I'm just lucky I was able to take them out before they were successful. It's not worth risking the revenge factor."

"We'll talk to your people just the same," I said.

"So you want to talk to everyone else to see if I'm mistreating them or holding them hostage?"

"Wouldn't you?" I asked. "Or are you not that curious?"

Perry shrugged. "I'm confident enough in what they'll tell you, but you need to know something. I was here all by myself for six months. I didn't have to ask anyone permission for anything. If I needed to shoot something – or someone – I did it. And believe me, there were some pretty bad sorts that came here in the beginning. They weren't interested in cohabitating – they wanted me dead or gone and that was that. I did what I had to do to prevail. I take no chances anymore."

"You sound rational."

"I think so," said Perry. "I don't like killing. We need numbers, but not at *any* cost. I don't expect my shelter to consist only of beautiful, cooperative people with magnetic personalities, but at least for now, I don't want people here who are going to get us killed."

I stared at him for a few moments and said, "How about this. We're gonna tell everyone what you did, and that means that very clearly, we're going to let them know that you shot and killed Cole in front of his nephews and brother-in-law. We'll ask them who wants to leave, and anyone that wants to will be able to do so immediately."

"Fair enough," said Perry. "Nobody's a prisoner here."

*****

Chapter Eleven

No fewer than thirty candles lit the basement, which had become more and more damp as leaks formed through the now exposed floor in the main house above. The walls stood, but the ceiling had either blown away or collapsed, and rain poured down.

Several battery-powered camping lanterns also lit the space. We'd filled a cooler with all the ice in the refrigerator, another large bag we had in a chest freezer in the garage, and since much of the dry goods were stored down in the basement anyway, there were plenty of supplies.

There was no bathroom, however. I tried not to think of it. Hemp had put up black, plastic sheeting, suspended from a clothesline, in the farthest corner of the room, along with a plastic, 5-gallon bucket. They had found an old toilet seat and lid, but it was just placed precariously on top of the bucket, and I wasn't sure I wouldn't topple off it if I attempted to sit down.

So far only Trina and Nelson had used it. The area could not have been farther away from where we gathered, but no matter its location, I imagined I could smell human feces, which just made me want to gag.

"We've no choice than to stay here until the storm passes, I'm afraid," said Hemp. "Particularly since there is now no roof on the house."

"What if the rest collapses and we're stuck in here?" I asked. "Another tree could fall, the wall with that door in it could blow down. Hemp, it happened once. We can't take that chance."

Hemp chewed his lower lip and became lost in thought. "Hold on," he said.

He went up the steps and pushed open the door. I could see that it wasn't easy, as something else had clearly fallen in front of it, proving my earlier point.

Hemp threw his shoulder into it and got it open another foot. The noise of the raging wind, rain and flying debris, which was already loud as hell, grew exponentially louder with the door open. I was certain that had the door not been partially blocked, it would have flown from his hand and slammed against the wall, possibly ripping from its hinges.

Hemp surveyed the scene above for only a brief moment before slamming the door shut again.

He came back down the stairs, his face and hair wet from the brief look. "I would have to put this at a Category 5 hurricane," he said. "Wind such as I've never experienced, and debris is collecting everywhere. Also, it's … infested up there," he said.

"With … *them*?" asked Charlie.

Hemp looked truly disturbed. "Yes," he said. "I spotted eleven of them in that brief look, and I wasn't even able to see behind the door. Oddly enough, they're lying flat, as though aware they could be caught by the wind. Males and females alike."

"Mothers and hungerers," said Isis, standing in the playpen with little Flexy, who was asleep. "The mothers guide the hungerers."

I got my usual, rippling chill at the sound of the one-year-old's voice speaking with intelligence, and said, "I wonder how many mothers there are compared to the others."

238

"They won't stop comin'," said Bug. "Isis draws 'em and they're not goin' anywhere until she does."

"So how do we stay down here and keep safe, *and* prevent ourselves from getting trapped?" asked Lola.

Hemp went to Isis and pulled up a chair beside the playpen. He sat and looked at her.

"Hemp," she said, smiling.

"Isis," he said. "I don't know if this question has any merit, because I'm not sure of all that you're capable of yet."

"Knowledge comes with inquiry," said Isis.

"Jesus, kid," I said. "You've gotten to where you're using bigger words than me. I'm getting an inferiority complex."

"Not likely," said Dave. Maybe in a room full of rocket scientists and superheroes."

I looked at him and gave him a snide look.

Hemp touched Isis on the arm and she touched his arm with her other hand. "Yes, Hemp?"

"Isis, do you have a sense of foreboding about the future?"

She looked at him. She was no longer smiling and her teeth weren't visible, so she could have been any child at that moment. Still, we expected an answer that we all realized we could not get from anyone but her.

"I do not see ahead," she said, as she had indicated to me before. "They want *here*. They want *me*."

"Why?" asked Hemp. "Do you know?"

Isis nodded. "Maternal pull," she said. "Each of them has a child," she said. "Dead inside them."

I had a thought, and Hemp articulated it as though we were connected. "Isis," he said. "Can they understand the thoughts of the fetus within them?"

"No thoughts," said Isis. "The children within them are dead but not dead. No thoughts. They are hungerers."

"So the adult hungerers have no thoughts either, right?" It was Lola who asked the question.

"No, but they can be commanded," she said. "Water and beef jerky, daddy?"

Bug walked up and lifted her from the playpen. As he propped her on his arm, she scooted her bottom until she was comfortable and looked at him.

"Baby girl, you have to eat somethin' besides jerky."

"Hungry," she said, and my heart almost broke as tears squirted from her eyes. Now she looked just like any little girl that wanted food, except as she opened her mouth to cry, her full-sized teeth told a different story.

"She's got those teeth for a reason, right?" said Dave. "Maybe she knows best that she's supposed to be on a pure protein diet. And what she said about the zombies being commanded, we know that from California. They moved the hordes at will."

"Until Lola pulled them away," said Serena. "Hey, Lola, do you think you can do the same thing, but in reverse? Like … tell them to go?"

Lola shook her head. "Guys, I've never tried it, but you're talking a truck pull with a monster truck pulling on one side – that would be Isis here – and a goddamned Yugo on the other. That would be me."

"You might underestimate yourself," said Rachel. "What you did in California was amazing. And it shows you can make them leave somewhere, even with this kid's magnetic attraction."

Bug had reached into his pocket and pulled out a stick of beef jerky, and Isis was now busily munching on it, tearing at it with her sharp teeth, and chewing with her little mouth wide open.

It was cute, really.

"Isis," asked Hemp, "why do they want you? Do you know what they want with you?"

240

"There is a longing," she said, in between chews. "Each believes that I am their child, even while their unborn hungerers remain within their bodies."

"The language is astounding," said Hemp. "It's as though she gleans it from all of us. Perhaps subconsciously. She's learning at an amazing rate."

"Keep in mind, she hasn't been around this many people for any sustained period until now," said Bug. "I guess everything she picked up in my bunker was learned from me."

"And now, surrounded by all of us," added Hemp, "she's absorbing not only our spoken vocabulary, but clearly, our unspoken words, too."

By now, Dave, Serena, Nelson, Lola, and Rachel were all listening intently. Nelson, joined in, saying "Whoa, dude. Let's go back to what you said before."

Nelson paused, looked at Rachel and said, "I can't believe I'm talkin' to a baby!"

Rachel laughed and Nelson looked back at Isis, his face dead serious. "So all those zombies think you're their baby?"

"Yes," said Isis. "If you are referring to the mothers, then yes. They believe that to be true."

"You say tomato and I say to-mah-to," said Nelson, "but you've never seen a George Romero flick, right? Those dead chicks and dudes are zombies, little talking baby."

The tension in the room dissolved as everyone laughed at Nelson's choice of words. He looked around, shrugged, and said, "I tell it how it is, man."

Lola, who was the only female among us who had been sprayed with the vapor of the red-eyes and had been immediately treated with the red-eye wafers, said, "Isis, what would they do if they … got you?"

Isis looked at Lola and Lola looked at her. I wondered for a moment why Isis didn't answer her, but in another second it became clear.

241

Lola gasped, and her expression changed. She stared at the rest of us, clearly horrified.

"What is it, Lola?" asked Dave. "Did she say something to you?"

Lola slowly nodded. "Yeah," she said. "I didn't like it."

I walked up to her. "Lola, would you mind whispering it to me? I don't want to upset Trina or Taylor."

"Sure," she said.

I leaned toward her. She said, "She says they'll try to kill her if they get to her."

I don't know why I had any reasons to believe otherwise, but somehow, that shocked me. I had clung to the hope that Isis would ultimately have some kind of control over them.

"Did she say why they would kill her?" I whispered to Lola.

"Isis believes the minds of the mothers can't ever be quieted as long as she exists. Her existence speaks to them and calls to them night and day, and to them, she's a lie; she's the promise of their dead babies that can never be fulfilled."

"Wow," I said. "She said all that shit that fast?"

"She's a pretty good communicator for thirteen or fourteen months old," said Lola. "But yeah, that's pretty much what she said."

"We can't do much about that," I said. "I'm worried about getting caught down here. Hemp, can we see about cutting another way out of here if that door gets blocked?"

"When you were stuck outside I found a gas-powered chain saw," said Hemp. "It's low on petrol, but there are several other small, gas-powered devices I can likely rob the fuel from. Just put it all together."

"Better make a shitty plan rather than no plan at all," I said.

"That's what we used to say in the military," said Rachel. We operated under FUBAR rules."

"What's fubar?" asked Trina.

"Okay to tell her?" asked Rachel.

"Sure," I said. I was familiar with the term.

"Fucked up beyond all recognition," said Rachel.

Trina was not quite up on the idea of acronyms. She looked at Rachel and scrunched up her mouth. "How does fubar mean all that? I don't get it."

Trina didn't wait for an answer. "Hey, Taylor!" she called. "Wanna play Fuck Off?"

"Why not?" asked Taylor. "This is boring."

It was boring.

And it was intense as the storm raged and Hemp tried to cut us another way out, just in case it was necessary.

*****

Frank "Punch" Magee stood beside Todd and his sons when Perry and I walked back in.

The room looked like a game room of some kind. There were two pool tables, a ping-pong table, foosball and some pinball machines and other video games that were powered off. From the playing cards fanned out face down on the tables, I assumed some of them had apparently been playing card games, none of which could have been as entertaining to watch as Trina and Taylor in a heated game of *Fuck Off,* their version of Go Fish.

There was some murmuring at the appearance of a stranger – that would be me – and some hopeful looks as their leader once again made an appearance.

I looked at them and ran a head count. The doctor was right on the money, so clearly knew his little community. I noted a large number of women, all with a certain amount of athleticism to their builds. I wondered if they had a fitness center at Piedmont, and decided they probably did.

The men were either on the younger or older side. I wasn't sure why that was, but speed and agility would keep you alive, as would seasoned-citizen street smarts and common sense. None of the men and women appeared harried or sunken-eyed. All appeared healthy and just curious as to our presence.

"How is everyone?" Perry asked.

An older, grey-haired man stood up. He was medium build and had some good biceps on him. Definitely a gym in the building somewhere.

He said, "John, we've been told by Todd, Ben and Joe that you killed Cole. We heard the gunshot from up here. Mind telling us why?"

"I can," said Perry, "but first, allow me to ask all of you a question. The question is this. Any of you who has been afraid of me – even one time – since you arrived here, please raise your hand, but not now. I'm going to turn around first, so that I can't see you. Then I want you to answer honestly. Now's your time to bump me out the door if you have a mind to."

He turned around and Punch and I looked out over the crowd. Benny, Joey and Todd raised their hands. Nobody else did.

"Okay, you can turn around again," I said.

Perry did. "I'm going to guess that Benny, Joey and Todd raised their hands. Don't get me wrong, I'm not saying that I blame them. I did something in front of them that should have been done in private."

Perry walked to the center of the room and said, "Cole put everyone here at risk. You all know from witnessing my previous dealings with him that he was unwilling to cooperate with my direction, which is wholly intended to keep us alive, and he refused to leave."

"So you did it for us," said the man.

"I did," said Perry. "I may have gone about it wrong, so for that I'm sorry. You all know you're free to leave here if you start to feel it's not right for you."

The crowd murmured again. I felt it had been put to rest. I still didn't completely trust the doctor, but he had something we needed, and at the moment, I wasn't sure where it was stored, and I doubted my ability to recognize it if I saw it.

"Doc," I said, looking at my watch. "It's almost 10:00 in the morning. Can we go to where you keep the vaccines and other stuff so we can get back to my family?"

"Absolutely," he said. He turned back to the crowd. "Another half an hour and it'll be time to start preparing lunch, everyone. I think chili is on the menu."

My stomach growled. Chili was one of my favorites.

*****

Perry led us to an upstairs room and opened the door. He turned on the lights, which was almost so alien to me that I felt I'd gone back in time.

"Your generator run all the time?" I asked.

"We limit the power usage so we don't waste the fuel we have on hand, but it's always running."

The room appeared to have formerly been a break room, because there were vending machines lined up on one wall. I was surprised to see they were fully stocked with candy bars, gum and some hard candy, but no pretzels or chips. I assumed they had either been eaten or had gone stale.

"How long you been here, doc?" asked Punch.

"Almost from the start, but I can tell you it was a mess when I got here," Perry answered. "Deadheads were everywhere and the people they'd eaten were scattered throughout this blood-soaked building like racetrack-discarded greyhound carcasses in the desert."

"Who cleaned it up?" I asked.

"If you're referring to the deadheads, I cleared the building myself. I raided local pawn shops and firearm stores," he said. "I'd never fired a gun before all this started, but I sure got to be good from around five feet away. Took me forever to figure out that a 1911 was actually a .45 caliber."

His comment again reminded me of what he'd done to Cole downstairs. "John," I said, "I know we talked about this already, and I don't mean to tell you your business, but nerves are fragile these days. Shootin' that guy down there can only make these folks turn on you down the road. The townspeople might just rise up when you least expect it."

"I was never a violent man," said Perry. "I felt myself getting harder and harder with every one of the things I killed, and when people started showing up here, I staked my territory and told each and every one of them that my rules were *the* rules and if they didn't like it, they could find somewhere else to live."

He walked over to the line of small, apartment sized refrigerators that hummed on the far wall and turned back to face us. He shrugged and said, "I was willing to let almost anyone in who agreed to my conditions, and I even gave the rest of our people first right of refusal. I always agreed to allow newcomers to stay the night and introduce themselves to everyone so they could form a consensus."

"How'd that work?" asked Punch.

"You saw," said Perry. "I can tell you that almost everyone who got the nod is still here."

"What's the arrangement?" asked Punch. I wondered if he were interested in staying here.

"I may make it sound like a dictatorship, which I suppose it is, but everybody has their duties. Cleaning, cooking, washing. We're not a bad community, but as I told you outside, Cole was a loose cannon. He was repeatedly asked to leave and he refused."

"You couldn't just get a group consensus and forcibly remove him?" asked Punch.

"We're over half women and the men here are either on the younger side or the older side. Nobody wanted to ruffle feathers, particularly Cole's. If it turned out he didn't leave, they didn't want to anger him."

"What kinds of things did he do that disrupted the place or put you in danger?" I asked.

"Several times he didn't secure the gates. Other times he got into fights with the others, and I don't mean arguments. I mean fisticuffs. I spoke to him about his anger issues and even offered him some Prozac, which I have in pretty good supply, but he scoffed at that. I'd tell him he was dangling from his last thread and he'd promise to comply, but I knew he said it to placate me. What he pulled at the hospital caused that thread to break. I don't know if he shared it with you Punch, but I told Todd and his boys that if Cole wouldn't leave on his own, I was considering eliminating him."

"Not what they said," said Punch.

"People hear what they want to hear," said Perry. "I think I've told you where I'm coming from. I'm not a bad guy, otherwise I could've given a crap about all the medicines and vaccines. I want the old world back. I'd give my eye teeth for a justice system with cops, attorneys, judges and the works. Military. What I wouldn't give for some military expertise and someone who could clean up the streets."

"There's lots of cleaning and not many of us," I said. "My friend Hemp says it's around 90% conversion, plus the diggers. Subtract everyone that became food for the rotters, and I guess you can see why it's each man for himself, at least when it comes to organizing an army."

"Well," said Perry, "I want society to rebuild. I'm hoping this hurricane helps wipe out a good amount of the rotters, as you call them."

"They are kind of sparse in the streets right now," I said. "But there's a lot you probably don't know about them."

"Like what?" he asked. "I know you have to take out their brains."

"You've seen the red eyes?" asked Punch.

"Yes," said Perry, seeming very interested now. "I've noticed they're faster than the others."

"Man," I said. "I wish I could un-know some of the shit I've learned. I'd sure sleep better at night."

"You indicated you're in a hurry," said Perry. "But are you sure you want to drive back in this storm?"

"I don't have a choice, doc," I said. "My son's been exposed to Diphtheria, and so has another little girl. A woman and her daughter showed up and brought it into our home before we knew what she had."

Perry nodded. "It happens. I hate to change the subject, but I have to ask about your truck. Nice setup."

"Custom built cow catcher and AK-47 courtesy of Professor Hemphill Chatsworth," I said, smiling for the first time since I'd arrived.

"Let's get the stuff you need and get you back on the road then," said Perry. "I hope you're satisfied that everyone here is well taken care of. You're also welcome to return for more meds. I intend to continue to collect them from wherever I can to preserve as much as possible."

I counted along the wall. There were fifteen of the low freezers, all ringing slightly with the rattle-hum-whistle of the compressors.

"These electric?" asked Punch, looking around.

"No," said Perry. They're all running on natural gas."

"Of course," I said. "Where the hell did you get them all?"

"Well, it's been hurricane season, and the big box hardware stores stock up on these things this time of year. Some of them I got myself early on, using a forklift at Home Depot. The others I got later when I had more help from new residents."

I looked at Perry. "John, has all the stuff been kept refrigerated? The important stuff?"

"It all was," he said. "Never a moment, except during transport, that it wasn't. Nothing's gone bad."

"I have a list from Hemp. He's a former CDC guy we ran into in Florida."

"Give me your list," said Perry. "I'll fill the prescription. How many doses do you need?"

"For the regular vaccination boosters, we're gonna need it for at least … let's say, ten infants. Everything they'll need until adulthood, if you've got them. We grabbed quite a lot from the pharmacy, but if you've got an immediate need for anything, you can certainly have it."

"You're not going to need it?" asked Perry.

"The main reason we're here at all is because it's one of the two closest places to Whitmire. They don't keep the Diphtheria antitoxin everywhere. As for pain meds, antibiotics, stuff like that, we've got pharmacies near us where we can get it."

"Ah," said John Perry. "True. I hadn't thought of that. Well, anyway, the antitoxin is freeze-dried and doesn't have to stay cold anyway."

"I know," I said. "But I was afraid all the other vaccines and booster shots would have gone bad. Can't tell you how happy I am that you took 'em."

"Just to further ease your mind about me," said Perry. "Let me tell you a little story. The moment this crap all started, over fourteen months ago now, I started to plan. My wife and daughter changed. Both of them tried to kill me, and I was psychologically comatose myself for two days after having to end their lives."

Perry walked to one of the chest freezers on the south wall of the room and lifted the lid. He reached down to retrieve something.

I saw Punch's gun barrel lift up, the speed almost imperceptible, but the barrel dead on the doctor.

Perry continued speaking as he pulled out a plastic box. Punch lowered his weapon before the doctor noticed.

"I guess I was waiting, but for what, I don't know," said Perry. "Once the power went out and I realized that nobody was going to swoop in and airlift me to a place this wasn't happening, all I thought about was the medicine. I knew they were what allowed humankind eighty-plus years of life in a world where our life expectation was once under 40."

He moved to another freezer and opened the lid. As he reached in, I saw Punch eyeing him and watched his gun barrel raise again.

"A 40-year lifespan doesn't sound like such a bad thing in a world like this one," said Punch, lowering his gun when he saw that Perry only held a plastic rack full of small, glass test tubes.

"I'm an optimist," said Perry. "Aside from what you've seen so far, I am. We'll get back to normal, and until we do, we'll need all of this. I only hope others have taken the same precautions that I have."

"So do I, doc," I said. "How long before we can hit the road? And don't forget to go through my bag," I said. I took the camouflage backpack off and dropped it on a counter, unzipping it. I pulled out the two canvas bags Punch and I had filled.

"I'll get you everything I know I have, and we'll go through yours. And Punch, you don't have to keep pointing your gun at me. I do not keep weapons in my freezers."

"Sorry, doc," said Punch. "I'm former military, so I don't tend to take chances."

"Understood," he said.

After pulling several items from the many freezers, he went through my bags from the pharmacy.

"What's with the estrogen blockers?" he asked.

"Ongoing experiment," I said. "I'll fill you in before we leave. Believe me, it's stuff you want to know."

"Your people have a Ham radio?" he asked.

"They do," I said.

"Let me know if you'd like to talk to them before you start heading back."

"That's a definite yes," I said. "I know their standard frequency."

The doctor removed what I could only describe as a large cold sack from one of the freezers and put all of the medications inside. He got a rubber band from the drawer, rolled the pack into a cylinder, and secured it. Perry turned to me and held it out. "This will keep the pharmaceuticals cold for up to twelve hours. Beyond that, I'm not certain how long the vaccines will last, but try not to push it."

"Thanks, John," I said. "Now put this whole thing back in that freezer there, and I'll tell you what you need to know to kill lots more of them and preserve your ammo rounds."

He agreed, and I shared everything we knew. He rewarded us further by taking us to his Ham radio station.

Nobody answered my repeated calls, and I tried for longer than I should have. I didn't know if it was the storm, or if they were in trouble. Talking to Gem would've gone a long way toward putting me at ease. I worried for my son, too. He needed me more at that moment than he probably ever would again in his life.

Before we left, we wolfed down a bowl and a half of chili each. It was pretty damned good, even without cheese and onion.

*****

The layout of the basement was a bit different than the floor above because several additional walls had been built below. A corridor ran alongside the wall where the sliding glass door was above, and here, the floor was partially collapsed from where another tree had slammed into it.

The massive girth of the tree's midsection now stuck about two feet into the basement and water was running down the bark, flowing fast into our concrete sanctuary.

Hemp stood and looked up at the light streaming in and pointed. "This is not a bad thing, actually," he said, "assuming the storm isn't moving too slowly."

"What's not bad about water pouring into our temporary home?" asked Nelson.

"Well, we've put down buckets to catch it," said Hemp, "so we'll have additional drinking water if necessary. And we've already got a hole started here that I only have to enlarge with the chainsaw in order to free us."

"But I take it you're not going to start that work until we know the door's blocked, right?" I asked.

"Correct," said Hemp.

"Good. The fumes would choke us out," I said.

Doc Scofield came down the hall carrying little Flexy, and at the sight of his little pink face I felt my heart flutter and as always, I missed my husband. "Gem, I need you to see something," he said.

His normally sparkling eyes were not joyful. He added, "Hemp, you need to take a look, too."

"What is it, Jim?" I asked, hurrying to him. Hemp was right behind me.

"His throat," he said. "He looked like he was having trouble swallowing. It's just red now, but what do you think, Hemp?"

Hemp took a penlight that Scofield held out and touched my son on the chin. "Open your mouth, little guy," said Hemp.

It wasn't in response to Hemp that Flexy yawned, but it served its purpose. Hemp shone the light in and said, "Hmm."

"Good *hmm* or bad *hmm*?" I asked.

Hemp switched off the light. "Symptoms for Diphtheria shouldn't begin for a minimum of two days after exposure. Still, I would have to consider the redness in his throat a symptom."

"How fast could it progress from here?" I asked.

Hemp looked at me for a moment before answering. "Gem, it's different in every case. As I said before, sometimes there are no symptoms. This could be unrelated, but since we don't have the antitoxin yet, it's all academic anyway. Nothing can be done until Flex arrives with it."

"Could there be something different about this one that makes it advance more quickly?" asked Scofield. "A new strain?"

"I hope not," said Hemp. "A new strain might take a new antitoxin, and I'm afraid there's not one."

"Where the hell is Flex?" I said, not expecting an answer. "If he's not here in a few more hours, I'm going to go out and find him."

A sudden crash came from over our heads, and as we all involuntarily ducked, Bunsen and Slider went nuts barking.

The noise continued, like splintering wood and collapsing walls.

"It's not above us," said Hemp.

"Sounds like it's near the stairs," I said.

We all ran back toward the main room where Dave stood, his muscles tensed and his eyes darting from the ceiling behind him back to us.

"The ceiling shifted twice," he said. "I don't know what happened up there, but something pretty damned heavy is trying to fall through."

Another sharp splintering began.

"Get to the edges of the room!" shouted Hemp. "Now! Everyone, move!"

Our girls ran to where we stood with Dave and dropped onto their bottoms on the wet, basement floor, tucking their heads against their knees. They did just what we had taught them.

Bug snatched up Isis and he, Rachel, Nelson, Serena and Lola tucked themselves into the opposite corner across from the steps.

"Bunsen! Slider!" shouted Lola. "Here, now!"

They had only known her a few short hours, but already they obeyed her, seating themselves on the floor in front of the humans they would give all of themselves to protect.

I took Flexy from Scofield's arms and covered him with my body as I nudged my way farther into the corner, sliding down against the wall as the girls had. When I looked up, the candles were flickering wildly. The ceiling must have already gone in another part of the basement, for the wind was now ripping through the space, and the floor was covered in a quarter inch of water that soaked through our clothing.

Another crash came from over our heads and as we watched, a massive crack spread across the ceiling from wall to wall, pulling apart as I stared, wondering when it would stop and how much danger this new development posed for all of us. The center of the ceiling began to bulge, pressing down farther and farther until we could see what appeared to be a tire through the opening.

The entire wheel was exposed a moment later, and the tremendous creaking strain grew even louder. I have to admit that while I was a bit stressed that a car appeared to be falling through the ceiling, I was just relieved it wasn't the Crown Vic. I didn't know what was happening to it out there, but at least it wouldn't be stuck in a basement, no good to anyone.

"Be ready to jump out of the way if it rolls when it drops!" shouted Dave. "Hemp, move more to your left, man!"

"Dude, this is insane!" shouted Nelson.

Bunsen and Slider stood side-by-side, barking up at the ceiling, as though telling anything that might be thinking of coming to where we were that they would be eaten by wild dogs.

Very pretty, not-quite-wild dogs, in reality. The two Great Pyrenees would stop barking and look at us occasionally, perhaps for approval. During the last of their pauses, the ceiling finally gave way with a tremendous crack as the floor joists beneath the heavy vehicle split into jagged pieces. The car plummeted to the floor, landed on its flat front tires, and remained angled upward, caught on the severed part of the beam.

Nelson reached into his pocket and pulled out a handful of his precious Ninja stars. He crouched at the ready, saying, "Watch for zombies, guys!"

No sooner had Nelson said the words, a body, its arms windmilling as it fell, dropped through the massive hole, rolling down the top and hood of the car to the concrete basement floor.

As though on cue, Bunsen and Slider were back on their feet, barking like bloodhounds on a scent. Rachel and Lola grabbed their collars just in time. If you didn't know our two canines, you would have thought them deadly attack dogs.

Everyone screamed as the creature bounced off what was the rusted hulk of an old Chevrolet Caprice Classic that had been deteriorating for years on the edge of the woods just behind the house. The tornado must have lifted it up and dropped it somewhere around Trina and Taylor's bedroom above, and I realized with some relief that had it landed just twelve feet farther to the northwest, I would have been crushed by it when I had been caught outside earlier.

On its back and staring upward, this male zombie, his eyes pumping copious amounts of the pink knockout vapor, struggled to get to its feet. Its left arm was snapped horribly, and the bone protruded from it. It had clearly just broken, as the surrounding skin and flesh looked freshly torn, dripping its reddish black lifeblood to the floor, blending with the water that continued to deepen.

"Take him," I said, giving Flexy over to Dave, who received my son automatically, not realizing that I was moving to do what he likely would have done in another split second. I snatched the bottle of urushiol hanging from his belt and ran toward the thing just as it got on its feet and turned toward us.

Its face was greenish-brown, and the eyes searched for the food it seemed to know was there.

"We're all on WAT-5," said Hemp. "Why is it discharging the vapor?"

"There's only one reason, Hempster," said Nelson. "There's a red-eye telling this dude what to do!"

I held out the bottle and pumped once, directly into its face. Before I dropped my hand, a brass star flew through the air and embedded deep into the side of the rotter's head, almost disappearing beneath its flesh.

"Bull's eye!" shouted Nelson.

I shimmied sideways away from the collapsing zombie, which was not only already dead from the trauma Nelson had inflicted to its brain, but was rapidly melting into an urushiol-induced muck as he sank to the basement floor in a bubbling mass of dissolving flesh and bone.

I was often mesmerized by the melting creatures, fascinated that a component they had not been immune to in life could have such a devastating effect on them as they moved about, having cheated death.

They could not cheat it a second time. Urushiol put a stop to them, and Nelson's star put a goddamned exclamation mark on it.

As I turned to say thank you to Nelson, I felt something grab my hair and yank upward, nearly lifting me off my feet. Instinctively, I tried to drop down to free myself, but whatever it was just curled tighter and pulled with even more strength.

Trina and Taylor both shrieked at the top of their lungs; Bunsen and Slider were topping them with ear-piercing barking, and when I reached up to free myself from whatever had ensnared me, my fingers curled around a dry, scaly arm. As I looked at my friends and family, I saw that each of them was wound up, preparing to spring into action, but it seemed that for a brief moment, everyone was waiting to see who would go first. If they had all gone, Keystone Kops shit would have ensued.

I turned my eyes upward to see a ginger-haired rotter lying prone on the sagging floor above, her arm stretched toward me through the wrecked ceiling, her dead fingers twisted and entangled in my hair.

"Drop your arm and let go of her, Gem!" shouted Charlie, now on her feet.

"She needs to let the fuck go of me!" I screamed, then realized what Charlie meant.

I released her, dropping my arm, and was immediately sorry I had. The moment I let go of her, the estrogen-charged female's dead, powerful fingers spread to take an even larger handful of my locks and she yanked me upward so hard I felt my feet leave the floor and my hair ripping from my scalp. I squeezed my eyes closed at the pain, crying out.

"Gem!" screamed Charlie, and I forced my eyes open to see her standing right in front of me, swinging the machete in a wide, high arc toward the arm that held me there dangling, my feet two inches above the floor and increasing.

Black-red liquid, the stagnant lifeblood of these monsters, spattered my face and rained down on me as the dull blade of the old machete sliced through the creature's shriveled skin and brittle bone. I dropped like a stone to the basement floor, landing on my back and ass, barely straining my neck forward enough to avoid slamming my head into the concrete. When I realized I was free, I stared upward and saw her – the crimson-eyed female – glaring down as though she had been cheated.

As I watched her watching me, there was hatred in my heart and horror in my soul. The expression on her face did appear angry somehow, her dry, cracked lips stretched over a black-toothed grimace that bore no resemblance to a smile.

I couldn't look away. Nor did she, but she suddenly skittered backward away from the hole, disappearing from view. Bug gripped Isis, his eyes darting around the ceiling, trying to catch sight of the creature again through the more severely sagging drywall above us.

Trina and Taylor still sat on the floor, their knees pulled up to their chests, their backs against the wall. Taylor cried. Trina did not. My tough little thing who had been through so much kept a watchful eye on the ceiling, but she appeared more prepared than terrified.

A sharp streak of pain shot up my spine as I twisted my body to get on my knees and onto my feet, but I pushed through it. As I got to my knees, preparing to plant one boot on the floor and stand, I heard Lola call out a warning.

"Gem!" she shouted. I looked at her and she was pointing to the ceiling just to my right.

Then everything changed.

The sopping wet, bulging drywall above our heads collapsed inward and three flailing bodies plummeted to the floor nearby.

Charlie, who still held the machete gripped in her hands, rushed toward one of them – this a female, wearing only a filthy, bloodstained flannel nightgown, her skin, where exposed, was gray and cracked. One leg was twisted horribly beneath her from her ungainly landing.

With a primal scream that made my heart sing, Charlie brought the machete down hard upon the creature's head, the blade cutting cleanly to below the one remaining earlobe of the rotter, its head splitting evenly in two pieces, still connected at the chin and jaw line.

A fluid that was decidedly more clotted and viscous than that which had leaked from the red-eye's severed arm, ran down the dying thing's back and chest as Charlie tried to see-saw her blade out of its skull.

She got her blade free with one final yank, and in what we would later remember as kind of comical, she fell onto her ass into the shocked crowd of Rachel, Lola and Dave, behind her.

To his credit, immediately after softening Charlie's landing by catching her beneath the arms, Dave crouch-crawled over to the side of the other fallen zombie – this one a fat male who probably weighed 300 pounds even then.

Dave Gammon pressed his suppressed Walther PPK, against the giant's head, and with a sound no more consequential than a drum stick smacking a pillow, sent a deadly bullet directly in the forehead of the behemoth zombie.

A clean, black hole appeared in its skin, and the bullet exited the backside, black spray exploding outward like a dirt clod through a high-velocity fan. The creature uttered a strange squawk before its pinkish eyes went white and dead, collapsing onto the female who had expired from a splitting headache that was probably far worse than the one she had experienced just prior to her previous metamorphosis into a bloodthirsty, flesh-hungry walker.

I wondered if the now motionless fat boy might have been an integral part of the red-eye's strategy to encourage the weakened floor above to collapse into our formerly safe haven. I didn't want to believe they were capable of such strategy, but I could no longer disregard any possibilities at that point.

They were smart enough for such strategy, I was fairly certain.

All of the above happened in under ten seconds, and the one-armed female rotter was lying so close to me that nobody could take a chance firing on her, lest they risk shooting me as well.

My eyes darted from the red-eye to Rachel, who was the only one in position to fire without hitting someone else. She had seen that, and was already sighting her weapon.

A microsecond before Rachel's finger squeezed the trigger, the red-eye sprang to her feet so quickly that Rachel's bullet ripped harmlessly through the midsection of the incredibly fast abnormal.

Believing she would try to finish what she had started with me, I pushed through my pain and got on my feet. My gun strap had slipped from my shoulder and only then did I realize I didn't have it on.

Shit! I thought, but it didn't matter. The intelligent, hungry creature did not return my gaze. Her attention was drawn elsewhere.

Her eyes were glued to Isis. She gnashed her horrid teeth as black saliva dripped like putrid molasses down her chin.

"You are of the Mothers," said Isis. "I am not of you."

It was at that moment, when nobody was in a position to fire on the monster without killing one of our own, that I hoped upon hope that this special child, our Isis, would show us something – some ability – that we had not yet had cause to see. Perhaps a new power borne of her exposure to the red-eye vapor while in her mother's womb that could allow this toddler who wasn't really a toddler to strategize and save us all.

Suddenly the creature closed the gap of five feet between where she had gained her footing to where Isis sat tucked in her father's arms.

As the red-eye moved quickly toward Bug, he stumbled backward, away from her, his back slamming the wall. Everybody looked on, but still, no one could shoot her for fear of hitting someone else.

That wasn't entirely true, for there was movement in my peripheral vision. I turned in time to see Nelson, his arm already raised, flick one of the razor sharp throwing stars from his fingers. He was tucked in a crowded corner, however, and was unable to draw his arm back as far as he typically would.

While the spinning star found its mark in the back of the rotter's head, it obviously did not embed in her skull deep enough to do anything other than esthetic damage to the creature, for she continued to advance. The red-eye was now just two feet away from Isis and Bug.

Isis held up her hand, her palm facing out.

The zombie stopped dead in its tracks.

"No, mother," Isis said, her voice strangely vibrato. "Your child is within you."

The female stared. Its one remaining hand dropped down to clumsily touch its stomach. The storm roared overhead and rain poured down through the wrecked ceiling. Cracks of lightning destroyed things that we could not see and the potent wind howled above us, throwing debris from any number of sources into other things, ensuring devastating destruction.

Everything happening around us – the storm, Flex's progression toward home and the confrontation between a Mother and a special child – were all as out of our control as they could be. Still, we were fixated on the one thing unfolding just feet away.

None of us spoke then. Something was happening and somehow we all seemed to have this unspoken confidence that a baby girl named Isis would have the ability to protect us.

On the surface, logic like that should have resulted in a room full of dead people. Even then, I did not feel that was a remote possibility.

We all watched Isis and the creature. Similar to the rest of them, this one's red hair hung bodiless and straight, reaching just above her shoulders. The wind that moved through the room whipped it across her ragged mouth and element-ravaged face.

Isis held out her right index finger and pointed directly at the creature's stomach. Then Isis's hand curled into a claw and started to open and close.

As we all looked on, the bulge in the red-eye's stomach, fully exposed because the light cotton blouse had long ago been torn away, churned as if on cue beneath the grey, pocked skin. It was as though the child cocooned within the zombie became agitated, stretching and roiling inside of her. The would-be mother zombie appeared to have become as mesmerized as we all were, looking on.

Perhaps this was the Isis miracle I had been hoping for. The strategy.

The shape of tiny hands appeared on her skin, the little palms and fingers pressing from within her. The zombie stared down, her hand hovering inches away from where her reanimated fetus seemed to push toward freedom.

Isis said, "Your baby." Again, the strange vibrato or vibration accompanied it.

Again, Isis held out her right hand and began a clawing-scratching motion with her tiny fingers. The red-eye continued staring down at her own stomach, only now, her hand pressed against her belly, her fingers clawing at the cracked skin, the jagged fingernails that had continued to lengthen after the creature's death providing sharp tools that could easily shred away the dying skin that entombed her fetus.

Scrape by scrape, the blackish-green dead flesh peeled away. Hemp quickly jumped to his feet and inserted himself between Trina and Taylor, blocking their view of this sickening display.

Isis's eyes maintained direct contact with the red-eyed rotter, her little hand remained held out before her, her fingers mimicking the scraping motion of the zombie's tearing fingers.

Then I knew what was happening. It became as clear to me as all of the other realizations I'd had over the past year and a half.

Isis was not mimicking the motion. *Isis was guiding it.*

Isis's fingers clawed in mid-air as the red-eye's fingers scratched on, finally tearing through her skin, plunging into her womb and through the dry, shriveled placenta. The baby's hands appeared next, wrinkled, half-decayed appendages, followed by its black-smeared head and face.

Upon seeing the dead-but-not-dead child emerge from her shredded belly, the red-eye no longer seemed to be aware of our presence. She lifted her horrid zombie baby by the neck, held it up and dropped it into the crook of her remaining arm with what I could only describe as a jerky kind of tenderness, her eyes transfixed on the thing that would have been her pride and joy in a world where insanity hadn't assfucked humanity.

Maybe it still was a precious baby to her injured mind. I wondered if Isis played any role at all now, or if seeing the baby that had come from within her had erased all attraction to Isis – at least for this red-eye.

"Mother, child," said Isis, a strange vibrato accompanying her voice when she spoke to the rotter. "*She* is from *you*."

And looking on, I could see that the dead, squirming fetus was indeed a female. Isis could not have known from her vantage point, and yet she did know.

When the child strained to turn its head and its puffy, pinkish eyes fell upon Isis, it emitted a strange growl, and its toothless mouth gnashed.

Jealousy?

I almost threw up. The smell that came from it was rancid and rank, as though an eight-year-old boy had found the bloated carcass of a road kill raccoon and had poked it with a stick, releasing decaying gasses into the room.

I hesitated for a moment, watching it all unfold before me. I knew I had to act because I couldn't take what was happening any more.

The red-eyed freak was distracted and I had learned all I needed to know from the macabre act playing out in front of us. I pulled my 9mm from my drop holster and took two quick steps toward her. I turned my shoulder into her and knocked her backward. Her feet caught on the body of the downed 300 pound rotter and she tripped, falling hard onto her back, her head colliding solidly with the concrete floor, giving her extraordinary brain a severe jolt.

Her reanimated rotter baby, still connected to her by a shriveled umbilical cord, slid beneath the basement steps, the cord tearing in two as it slammed against the far wall. A sickening gurgle emitted from its throat.

I had ridden the powerful creature down in free fall, already knowing I would not need the gun. I let it slide away, pushed her remaining arm against the floor and snatched a handful of her hair in a tit for tat gesture.

I took greater advantage of my grip on her than she had earlier, when the roles had been reversed.

"Girls, heads down!" I screamed. I didn't look to be sure. I wasn't taking my eyes off that bitch. Pulling her head up, I slammed it back into the concrete once, twice, and a third time, all of my strength behind it, until I heard a sound that told me her skull fractured and I saw the evidence of her formerly grey matter running black and gooey beneath her.

I released her and stared down at her face. Finally. She was as dead as she should have been well over a year ago.

I heard something and looked up to see Charlie withdrawing the machete from the zombie fetus's head. When our eyes met, Charlie said nothing. She just nodded.

I thanked her with my eyes.

"More mothers," said Isis. "Near."

"We have to leave here," said Hemp. "Everyone, gather your things and we have to go. We're far too exposed now."

Hemp was dead right. We didn't argue. We started gathering necessities.

*****

Chapter Twelve

The streets were flooded now. Far worse than when we had arrived and just figuring out a way to detour around the many puddles of indeterminate depth was a bitch.

"Flex, I don't know, man," said Punch, his eyes on a river of water flowing across the roadway ahead.

"Neither do I, but it's a fuckin' Land Cruiser, so it should be able to handle a foot or two of water."

"I'm just worried about getting swept off the road into deeper stuff," said Punch. "This crap is obviously coming from some river overflowing somewhere."

The rain was torrential and even the heavy 4-wheel drive was feeling every shift in direction the blasting wind took. First the gusts slammed us head on, forcing me to press the gas harder to continue my forward progression, and next thing I knew I was cranking my wheel hard left into the wind to prevent us from being blown off the wet roads. My arms were getting tired from fighting the steering wheel.

"I gotta push through, buddy," I said. "We're gonna need to find an alternate route besides the way we came in, too," I added.

"Yeah, those roads were marginal then," Punch said. "I know I saw other alternate north south corridors on the west side of the interstate. Just stay on this road as long as you can. If we have to get off to get around something, we'll just make sure we get back to it."

I rolled through a puddle that turned into a tiny lake. The river we'd rolled through moments earlier was flowing fast, but was only about a foot and a half deep; something the Land Cruiser could handle with relative ease.

Now the wheels were submerged. We rolled forward more, and I saw the water top the fender wells. Only when it topped the hood did I become concerned about the vehicle's ability to keep water out of the electrical components. Even well-sealed electronics would start to leak if the submersion was prolonged.

A hand appeared in the water ahead, but I could do nothing but continue inching forward toward it. If I stopped, there was a chance that either I would become stuck or the engine would stall. As I gained another two feet, the hand slid onto the hood, followed by the connected arm, shoulder and head. The other arm appeared, and before we knew it, a dead face peered through the windshield at Punch and me, his ravaged, nude body spread-eagle on my hood like Punch and I had been engaged in a macabre zombie hunt where we'd bagged ourselves a buck.

The engine kept running and I did my best to ignore the former floater – now a crawler – who had determined that we were a mobile island refuge. I'd shake him off as soon as the Toyota's big tires found solid purchase on higher ground.

Meanwhile, I rolled forward, paying silent homage to whatever patron saint it was that was in charge of keeping combustion engines running.

We drove on, and each time the engine sputtered or hesitated, I gripped the steering wheel more tightly as though such force could prevent anything bad from happening. Had I driven any faster, the water would have splashed onto the windshield, so I inched along, the clinging, nude dead man riding us onto dry land.

In another thirty feet the water receded and soon, we were again able to see the asphalt beneath us. I revved the engine, trying to dry any components that had begun to get wet, and after a bit, the engine began to smooth.

The storm was knocking us around even as we sat still. Our guest did not vacate the hood, so I thought it was time to use a little bug spray on him. Despite the pounding rain, I rolled down my window, and with my super soaker in one hand, I sprayed him in the face with another shot down his back just for good measure.

Watching what happened next was fascinating. The face shot had begun the process of melting his features, like a wax figure from Madame Tussaud's Museum. His eyes ran down his cheeks and his nose melted to his open, gaping mouth. He gnashed on, appearing to swallow himself.

"Fuckin' A," said Punch. "Wow."

My hands resting on the steering wheel, I watched the shot of urushiol that I'd sent down his exposed back working, and as we looked on with fascination, it dissolved him like sulfuric acid, his body splitting end to end right along his spine. As the zombie-caustic liquid worked its way through his narrow mass of reanimated flesh, the peaked slope of the hood and the weight of the two halves of his body pulled him slowly apart, the connecting tendrils and melted innards stretching away from one another like the inside of a warm, gooey cinnamon roll being torn in two for sharing.

His right side slipped across the hood toward the driver's side of the Land Cruiser, occasionally hindered by the intense wind that rippled it like the surface of a lake. The rotter's left side, in this case assisted by the same wind, slid off toward Punch's side of the vehicle. It was impossible to turn away, even as the already destroyed face that still turned toward us began to tear apart, pulled along by the steady disintegration of the body behind it already underway.

Because the lower trunk of the creature had not been fully effected by the urushiol, eventually, the whole mess slid forward from the hood and out of view. I was more than certain it had come to rest in one form or another on the inside of my cow catcher, slopping onto itself like a massive pile of raw liver.

I was suddenly glad it was raining. If it were hot and sunny, we'd have ourselves some baked on zombie that might permanently damage our winch, which was mounted directly behind the cowcatcher, the cable running through the heavy steel pilot.

The rain peppered away at the hood, and eventually the streaks of gore left behind were rinsed away, leaving no sign that the zombie had ever clung there – at least from inside the SUV.

Punch looked at me. "Holy shit, man. That was something."

"Imagine the first time we saw that juice at work," I said.

"Better go, man. While we've got open road."

*****

As it turned out, the storm was solely responsible for the flooded streets in the city. From the map, Punch didn't see any nearby rivers whose banks could have overflowed enough to cause such flooding. Old Hurricane George was just a massive storm producing torrential rains.

The roads had been high and dry up to the point where we saw the bridge ahead of us. According to the sign, hanging by one mount and dangling upside-down, it spanned the Catawba River. The pilings supporting the bridge beyond the flapping sign had washed out, and the two-lane bridge was angled sharply to the west with the southbound lane completely submerged in water. The river washed over it so fast that I didn't even have to look to Punch for his opinion.

"Shit!" I yelled over the howling wind and sharply angling downpour.

The water sheeting across the bridge met the incredible force of the wind, which whipped it into the air in a ocean-like spray of mist. The finer particles of water were pounded back to the earth by the driving rain in a circular battle that would not end until the storm passed. There would be no winner in the conflict that raged before us, and certainly, with visibility ahead entirely diminished, we were the losers.

"We gotta go around it, Flex!" shouted Punch, quickly unfolding the map enough to see other possible routes we could take to skirt around the damaged overpass.

His finger ran along our current path, and as he leaned toward me to offer his solution, something slammed into my driver's side window.

I turned to see a skeletal female pressed against my door, so short that her head barely reached the top of my mirror. One bony hand clung to the window, and I guessed that she had been blown into the side of the Land Cruiser by Hurricane George.

I threw the vehicle into reverse and punched the gas, catching her head with the rear view mirror, plucking it from her shoulders. It caught there in that steel nook between the door and mirror mount, and I could not take my eyes from it as the body it once utilized for mobility fell away and collapsed on the side of the road. Still intact and undamaged, the head looked at me and began to gnash its few remaining teeth, its black tongue, shriveled and tar-like flitting in and out of view.

I slammed on the brakes and cranked the steering wheel, but the head did not fall away. Once the truck was facing a direction where the sharply angling rain would not pour into my window, I said, "Punch, give me that fuckin' Maglight off the floor there, man, would you?"

He retrieved it and passed it to me, saying, "Your girlfriend's pretty cute, man, and I can see she's kinda attached to your truck. Sure you wanna end it this way?"

"Yeah, fuck off," I said, laughing. I hit the down button on the window, let it click into *Auto* mode and held the heavy flashlight with the handle down. Once the window hit bottom, I pounded on the top of the rotter's cranium, driving it out of its wedged-in position.

No tears and no goodbyes. She popped out and dropped to the pavement below without so much as a grunt. I put the window back up.

"I can go through this shit a thousand times and every time it's different," I said. "I guess I'm just thankful she wasn't a red-eye."

"I'll second that," said Punch. "Buddy, drive about half a mile back this way to Sutton Road and make a left. You're gonna need fuel, too."

I looked at the gas gauge. It was on empty. I tapped it. "That's not right, man. We filled it just before we got into town, remember? We left the cans where your GTO is."

I tried the headlights. Nothing. I realized the dashboard lights were dead, too. I looked at Punch.

"The only thing working is the ignition," I said.

"I thought I smelled something earlier, but I didn't want to jinx us by saying anything," said Punch. "The electrical system might be sizzling away as we speak. Better make time, Flex."

I hit the gas hard and we reached Sutton Road and I turned. I saw the signs for I-77 immediately.

"Shit," I said. "Maybe we can zigzag our way through."

"Other than that we're looking at an old train bridge about half a mile east of here," said Punch.

"Wonder if the bed is wide enough to drive across," I said. "It might actually be our best bet."

"Only a half mile to the 77," he said. "Let's take a look. If it's a no go, we'll just flip it around and take Sutton back to the train tracks."

I drove on, fighting the storm and praying I didn't stall the Toyota. There was no longer any guarantee that a turn of the key would yield any result.

*****

Something else had blocked the upper door since I had returned to the basement. We now stood in two inches of water and Nelson and Dave were at the top of the stairs taking turns kicking the door.

"How's it going, guys?" asked Hemp, who had taken everything from the basement he thought we could use, but we still did not have an idea where we would go or how we'd get there.

"It's open a couple of inches," said Nelson. "Another couple of my Subdudo kicks ought to crack the sucker."

"Be my guest," said Dave, moving three steps down. I saw it wasn't easy coming at the door from below, because there wasn't an upper landing upon which to stand.

"Here goes nothing," said Nelson, standing on the second step below the door. He didn't appear to use much effort, yet the door shook pretty good in its frame and I heard a substantial crack.

"I think I got it," called Nelson, looking down at us. Trina and Taylor had become very reserved. I could tell they were scared and I thought it strange that these two little girls were more frightened of a hurricane than they were of reanimated corpses. Ain't that just the way of the world today.

"One more kick outta do it," said Nelson. "Looks like it might split about two feet up, so we'll have to do a step-over maybe."

"Everybody, come over here," Hemp said, standing in a far corner where the rain wasn't being blown by the savage wind.

Everyone moved toward Hemp. He spoke in a loud voice to be heard over the cacophony of nature's rage.

"I've consolidated a lot of things," he said. "But I need you all to gather every gun, every piece of ammunition and every baseball bat," he said. "I want you to have anything and everything that can kill the abnormals. Knives, urushiol-filled squirt guns, you name it. There may be no opportunity to come back here."

"What about the WAT-5?" I asked. "Hemp, did you get it all?"

He nodded. "We're good for another hour," he said. "When we get to the lab it might be a good idea to take more."

"Oh, my God," said Charlie.

We all looked at her. "What's wrong, Charlie?" I asked, but the way she was holding her stomach was something I'd seen many times – including once with myself. "Oh, my God, Charlie. Did your water break?"

She looked at us and nodded, her eyes terrified. "I'm afraid so," she said.

Hemp rushed to her. "Charlie, are you having any contractions yet?"

Charlie shook her head. "I don't think so," she said. "I was having some pretty good cramps, though. Didn't want to say anything."

"Of course you should have said something," said Hemp. He looked at me. "And Gem, the answer to your question is that I have our entire supply of WAT-5 in my pocket. I've got enough that all of us are good for another twenty-five hours or so."

I was relieved to hear it. If we had to leave, we needed protection, at least from the normal rotters. "Where does that leave us?" I asked. "Do you still have the base mixture on ice somewhere?"

When the eye vapor from a regular zombie and the component coming out of the earth was blended under subfreezing temperatures, it formed a gel-like substance. Once it warmed, the blended components self-multiplied – I don't know the technical term for it, but it keeps growing forever until you halt the process by adding urushiol. Without the urushiol, a quarter-sized amount would fill a cookie sheet in a matter of two or three minutes. We never found out whether it would eventually stop on its own. We would merely make what we needed and re-freeze the remainder so that we wouldn't have to mix the two components again.

Hemp said, "We've been down here for some time now, so I'm assuming our small generator on the lab has run out of fuel, without us there to refill it. If that's the case, I'm assuming the freezer's temperature has risen significantly above 32 degrees at this point. The mixture might be growing exponentially as we speak."

"Hemp," I said, "That's a perfect place for the doc to deliver Charlie's baby."

"It is," said Hemp. "My thoughts exactly."

"Well," said Scofield, taking Charlie gently by the arm and leading her to a chair in one of the driest corners, "until we get you there, I want you to relax."

Charlie went with him but did not sit. Instead, she held onto the back of the chair and kept one hand on her stomach.

"Charlie, you need to get off your feet," said Scofield. He looked up at Dave and Nelson. "How's that door coming, guys? This little lady needs to get somewhere safe and dry."

Charlie gritted her teeth and folded forward, her eyes squinted against the pain. Hemp rushed to her and steadied her.

"Ow, shit," Charlie moaned. She blew out hard, emptying her lungs, then sucked in a deep breath. "Wow. Wow," she said, her eyes moving from Hemp to Doc Scofield.

"Okay, that was a contraction," said Scofield. "Gentlemen, I can deliver the baby here, but I'd prefer that she not be lying in almost three inches of water."

It felt as though we were in some sort of limbo. So many things needed to happen, but it seemed everything that did happen was happening *to* us, not being initiated *by* us.

We were in reaction, rather than action mode. Not good in the times of zombies. I looked up to see Rachel watching Nelson at the top of the stairs and Bug holding onto Isis, his full pack on his back, clearly ready to roll when an exit was established.

Lola sat quietly in the corner watching everything unfold, and Serena stayed with Trina and Taylor, making sure they were calm. The two children looked at Charlie, and I could tell they were worried about her.

All the supplies had been gathered, and nothing else could be done by anyone.

Hemp helped Charlie sit down. She did so reluctantly, but slid down in the chair, extending both her legs. The chair was straight backed and wood, and would only do for a temporary perch. On the next contraction, I knew Charlie would be either on the floor or back on her feet.

Hemp held Charlie's hand and said, in a voice loud enough for Nelson and Dave, who were still on the stairs, to hear: "We'll be out of here in just a moment, Charlie. Then we'll get you into the mobile lab. Jim can deliver our baby there."

Nelson had kicked at the door another six or so times, and I could tell he was tiring. So much for the power of Subdudo on inanimate objects. I ran up the steps and did what I should've done fifteen minutes earlier. I swung the Uzi from my shoulder and called down, "It's gonna be loud, so cover your ears!"

I immediately squeezed my trigger in full auto mode, stitching a nice perforation across the door at approximately the two foot high mark.

I nodded to Nelson. "Okay, Subdudo dude, now give it a goddamned kick," I said, and trotted back down the stairs.

A crack came from the stairway above, and I looked up to see the door had split easily with his single, additional kick.

"Got it, dude!" shouted Nelson. "Good job, Gem. Not sure why I didn't think of it."

"Yeah, I'm a little embarrassed, too," said Dave Gammon, who was indeed a bit red-faced.

Once open, the door was caught by the wind, which slammed it repeatedly against the upper wall.

"Nel, can you safely check the status of the mobile laboratory?" asked Hemp.

"I'll go with him," said Dave, running back down the stairs. "Hemp," he said. "I need more WAT-5. A couple of wafers."

"Are you past due?" he asked.

"No, I don't think so. About four and a half hours now, I'm estimating."

Hemp gave him two wafers. Dave popped one in his mouth right away, looked at Serena who stared back at him, and when he didn't pass out, he smiled. He went to Serena and said, "I'll be careful, babe."

She nodded and he ran back up the stairs and gave Nelson the other wafer. He gulped it down and held onto the wall for a moment until he was sure he wouldn't pass out.

"Let's go, dude!" he said. "Guys," he said to all of us, "we'll be right back inside."

"Hurry," said Hemp. "I only need to know if it's accessible."

Dave and Nelson, guns in hand, ran into the raging storm.

*****

Interstate 77 was jam packed, just as we'd seen it earlier. We were unable to drive up the ramp, so we stopped the Land Cruiser just below the onramp, left the engine running, and climbed up a short embankment to scope out the situation.

As we crested the hill and the line of cars came into view, it appeared to be just as it had been on our way to Charlotte. The only difference was that these dead vehicles were all pointed in the logical direction, away from the city.

We walked along the shoulder to see if there was any room at all to squeeze the Toyota through, but it was a mess.

"Shit!" said Punch, jumping back, quickly raising his shotgun, and discharging it twice. Dark mist sprayed into the air, along with chunks of brain and bone that were immediately helped along by the charging wind.

The dead walker had been crouched near the rear door of a Lexus, and as we moved cautiously forward, we saw several more doing the same thing. It was clear they were trying to avoid the wind that they seemed to know would blow them helplessly away.

"Buddy," I called over the raging wind. "This means red-eyes are around."

"Yeah?"

"Hell yeah," I said. "These guys aren't smart enough for this shit. We call 'em hiders, whether it's just red-eyes or a mix. They take their marching orders from the smart ones."

While I knew very well that they could recognize some dangers, as well as their own deficiencies – something Hemp and I had figured out over a year previous – they took only the most remedial action to avoid injury.

"Say no more," said Punch. "Let's head over to the train bridge. Looks like our only option."

I knew he was right. So long as a train wasn't stalled in the middle of it, there wouldn't be any cars on it. I only hoped it was wide enough for the Toyota's tires.

*****

Dave and Nelson came back in soaked to the skin. The moment they came in, Bunsen and Slider bounded up the stairs, and when they saw the guys weren't going to stay at the top, they both turned tail and trotted down ahead of them.

Nelson came down the stairs right on the dogs' tails, taking them two steps at a time. Dave was right behind Nelson, just a bit more cautious. They had been gone about ten minutes.

"Are they still out there?" asked Hemp.

Dave nodded. "If you mean the rotters, yeah," he said. "They're kind of hard to see because most of them are just lying flat. Some are getting covered with debris. It's like they're making themselves small or something. How are you, Charlie?"

Charlie smiled and shrugged. "Hanging in there, I guess."

"How's the lab?" Hemp asked.

"It's *pretty* good, dude," said Nelson. "Gem, your car's cool, too, which is *really* good. We're gonna need that winch."

"Why, what happened?" I asked.

"The lab like blew over or something," said Nelson. "It's leaning against the house at like a 45 degree angle."

"The tornado must've done that," said Dave. "We're lucky it didn't do more damage, but it looks pretty good. Some debris and crap around it."

"But Gem's car can be positioned to pull it back over with the winch?" asked Hemp.

"I think so. Gem, give me your keys," said Dave.

278

I tossed them to Dave, who caught and pocketed them. I went to Charlie and knelt beside her.

"So this is pretty dramatic, huh?"

"Hell yes," she said. "I had fully intended to be listening to Sex Pistols when this happened."

"It ain't over yet," I said, smiling. I hugged her. "Charlie, it's gonna be okay … you know that, right?"

She opened her mouth to answer, but the words caught in her throat as another contraction hit her and her face creased with pain. I took her hand and squeezed it. "Breathe, Charlie. Now I can say I know what you're going through. No pushing, okay?"

It passed and she released the breath she'd been holding and gave me a brave laugh. "No pushing," she said. "And as far as everything being okay, since I met you guys I've never thought any differently," she said. "Kinda lost my negativity."

I rolled my eyes. "You're delusional, but seriously – this *is* gonna be fine. We'll have you through the rubble and into the lab in no time."

Bug carried Isis across the room and handed her over to Lola. "Take care of her, would you? You seem to have a good connection."

"Absolutely," said Lola, taking the child in her arms. "It's you and me, little one."

"I'm all yours," said Bug. "Let's go do this."

"Excellent, bro," said Nelson. "Someone needs to be inside the car operating the winch, and I think a couple of us need to clear stuff away from the wheels of the lab and hook up the cable."

Dave went to Charlie and said, "Just hold off on delivering that kid a little longer and we'll have you on your back and your feet in stirrups."

"There aren't any stirrups out there," she said, fighting what appeared to be another contraction.

"Then you haven't been out there in a while, kiddo," said Dave. "Hemp's been planning for this."

"I have been," said Hemp, "but it was always my intention to bring the delivery bed inside. We'll improvise."

"Watch for flying debris," said Serena, her eyes on Dave. "We don't need anyone decapitated out there."

"It may be an extreme example, but she's got a point," said Hemp. "Be very aware of flying objects. As soon as you've got the lab accessible, park the Crown Victoria right up alongside it, and come for us."

Nelson, Dave and Bug climbed the stairs, stepped over the split door and disappeared into the crazy wind and rain above.

"I feel as useless as tits on a boar," said Doc Scofield.

"If my kid has anything to say about it, that won't be the case much longer," said Charlie, winking at the doctor.

Hemp sloshed through the water to a work bench on the far side of the room. He pulled open a lower drawer, withdrew a sports glove of some kind and threw it aside. He leaned down and pulled out two helmets and turned around, holding them up.

"They may not be your size, but girls, I want you wearing them when we go outside."

I could now see that they were hockey helmets. Not goalie gear, but both had face shields, so their eyes would be protected.

"Cool!" shouted Trina, walking cautiously through the water and moving well clear of the dead zombies that littered the floor.

What a world we live in, I thought. *Where dead bodies can be relatively ignored by seven and eight-year-old girls.*

After a brief wipe down of the helmets, the girls donned their oversized head protection, ultimately looking like life-sized bobble heads. As for us, we listened to the storm wreaking its devastation above our heads and bided our time, hoping Charlie's baby would do its part by doing the same.

*****

We had moved Flexy's playpen onto four cinderblocks we'd found, well out from under the gaping hole in the ceiling. He now slept like ... well, like a baby.

The dogs had settled again, but they weren't digging the water, particularly Bunsen. Both sat on their haunches, eyeing the many authority figures as though awaiting commands. Whenever a new, louder noise came from above our heads, they both jerked their heads toward the door, and I knew it was because they were looking for Flex.

It took a full half hour, but in that time the roar of the storm grew to its most intense since the tornado that had so taken us by surprise. We heard several distant gunshots from above, which meant that our friends were taking care of business and assuring us a clear path when it was our turn to run the gauntlet.

The wind and rain raged over our heads, the latter running down in rivers through the open ceiling. Looking around, I estimated two more inches of water had accumulated in our little swimming pool habitat. It was still not high enough to affect my sleeping son.

The girls were now resigned to keeping their feet up on their chairs for fear of what might be gliding through the water. That was made even worse because Taylor had shared a story she had once heard about rats swimming in sewers, which, as everyone knows, are similar to basements.

We heard stomping on the steps and looked up to see Bug and Nelson coming back down, both dripping wet, but looking encouraged.

I'm positive that all of us except Charlie got to our feet at once.

"Ready?" I asked.

"Yeah," said Bug. "I say you guys all do a chain, holding hands. It's rough out there."

"Should only take about five minutes if we're careful and watch out for each other," said Nelson."

"Where's David?" asked Serena, her eyes worried.

"Right here," said Dave, bounding down the steps, looking every bit the drowned rat that Bug and Nelson had. "I was prepping the RV. Got the gen started and the A/C on. Humidity in there was killer."

Hemp approached Dave. "Is the table okay?" he asked.

"Great shape," he answered. "Not that it's a surprise. You built that delivery chair like a brick shithouse."

Hemp glanced at Serena. "Because it's going to be used more than once, my friend. Now Dave, do you think you can carry Charlie? You're strong enough, and the only other option is a two-man carry. I don't like the position she'll have to be in for that."

"Understood," said Dave. "Absolutely, Hemp. But you need to be in front with that MP5 of yours. There are red-eyes clinging to fence posts and other places they can hang on to, fighting the wind. Almost looks like they're waiting for something."

He nodded and turned. "Everyone!" shouted Hemp. "If you see a red-eye when we get out there, I want you to call my name and their position on the clock. 10:00, 1:00, you know how it works. I'll take them out. I don't want any of them getting near us."

"I'll take my girl," said Bug. He looked at Isis. "Baby, I know I don't talk to you like you're a big girl much, but you changed a lot in the last couple of days, didn't you?"

"I did not want to scare you, Daddy."

"How did you know it would?"

"By the way you talked to me," said Isis. "Like a baby."

Bug kissed her nose. "That's because you're like 14 months old. I didn't expect to be playing chess with you yet."

"I'll take the lead," said Hemp. "Gem, you get Flexy and wrap him in a dry blanket, and Bug, you do the same with Isis. You'll both be in the middle of our chain."

I searched the room with my eyes and saw the pile. "Dry towels and blankets, over there," I said, pointing.

Rachel went to the pile and took five or six. She gave one each to Trina and Taylor, then gave me and Bug one. We busily wrapped our charges in them.

"Everyone else, keep a hand free for fighting and another to keep you in the chain," said Hemp.

He mounted the steps, followed by Nelson, Dave with Charlie in his arms, Doc Scofield, Serena, Trina, Taylor, the dogs, both on leashes held by the girls, Bug with Isis, Rachel, me with Flexy tucked tightly against me, and Lola behind me. In Lola's left hand was a long-bladed knife, and in the other was a .38 Special that she said she felt very comfortable firing and reloading.

Before we were halfway up the stairway, I think all of us had to steady ourselves to keep from being blown back down.

Dave struggled up, step-by-step, his right arm under Charlie's knees, and his left arm around her shoulder.

"I'm trying to think light," said Charlie. "Is it working?"

Dave was red-faced and focused on nothing but his next step. He offered a smile-grimace combination and pressed on.

He, as we all did, looked determined.

*****

Punch pored over the map while I drove along Fort Mill Parkway, the driving rain coming down at a sharp angle, sheeting across my windshield and putting visibility at a bare minimum.

When I reached an intersection after passing nothing but overgrown fields for a couple of miles, I stopped the SUV, relieved to have a short break from the anxiety of maneuvering through the intense storm.

"How do we get to the tracks?" I asked.

Punch checked his map again and ran his finger along the road we were on until he found what he was searching for.

"Fuckin' street sign's gone I guess," he said. He searched for a few moments and we both saw it at the same time. The brown and white street sign was jammed beneath an old station wagon.

"Brickyard Road," we said together.

"That's the one," said Punch. "Veer left here and it takes a sharp right. There should be a railroad crossing up ahead."

We were in a pretty rural area at the moment, and no rotters had spooked us. We had passed one or two wandering around open fields and clinging to trees or signposts, but had not encountered any serious situations. The storm had its benefits but I was well aware it could be as deadly as the zombies in mere seconds.

The downside was that being killed by the storm didn't necessarily mean that either of us would stay dead. I'd put a bullet in my brain to avoid becoming one of them.

"You ready for this?" I asked. As if in response to my question, the wind-driven rain slammed into the side of the Land Cruiser, challenging every advertisement Toyota had ever run with regard to its toughness and durability. The heavy SUV rocked under its force.

"Depends," said Punch. "Drive on, man. Let's say our prayers and hope that bridge is in good shape."

In less than a quarter of a mile, we hit the railroad crossing and saw the track and surrounding gravel bed running north-south. No stalled trains, and while grass and weeds grew from the middle and sides of the tracks, it was still very clear where we'd have to center our wheels to turn the rail into a temporary highway.

I made the turn and rolled up onto the gravel, my cowcatcher initially hitting the track rail. I backed up as I had done before to mount the curb, took it at a sharper angle, and rolled my front passenger side wheel over the track. When I came down, and I got the rear wheel over the rail, I straightened it out and drove slowly, the cross ties jostling us with every foot we drove.

"Do me a favor and light me a smoke," I said, nodding to the sun visor. Punch reached up and took the pack. He lit two of the stale Marlboros and passed me one.

I put it between my lips, dragging on the cigarette, squinting to see past the sluicing rain that was busily defeating the fast-beating windshield wipers in a head-to-head battle. As the tires clattered across the tracks, it felt like my brain rattled around in my skull.

The weeds had grown so high since the last maintenance crew or screaming locomotive did their part to trim them away, they almost completely obscured the tracks ahead. I took three good hits off the smoke and felt the nicotine start to calm me, putting my senses on alert at the same time.

We reached a small clearing, and the bridge came into view. Something appeared to be stacked on the tracks ahead, and I hoped whatever it was could be run over rather than us having to get out of the Land Cruiser with the now sketchy electrical system to clear the tracks.

I didn't even know if the winch would work if I needed it to, and damned if I wasn't afraid to even try it for fear the surge of power would burn something else up.

Beyond the pile of debris was the raging Catawba. What was likely once an easy-flowing tributary was gone, replaced by a wildly churning river that overflowed its banks, eating away the sandy soil that once provided the ground support and nourishment of the foliage that grew alongside it.

Now, even as we watched, the massive blasts of wind bent the flooded trees in half until they couldn't take another foot-pound of pressure, forcing their root systems to burst from the earth like long hibernating subterranean creatures ready for their time in the light of day.

As we stared upstream, we watched as at least forty trees were uprooted and swallowed by the angry, flowing water. These weren't saplings by any stretch. They were, in some cases, enormous oaks and pines that might have been over a hundred years old.

As I stared for that moment at the devastation caused by the angry waterway, I decided that the Catawba River was the equivalent of a man, once calm and friendly, now transformed into a flesh-eating monster that recognized neither friend nor foe. All things in its path were to be destroyed.

As frightening as it looked, there was good news. The bridge appeared solid, and it was high enough that the river was passing under, rather than over it. There was still a problem, though.

"Holy fuck," I said, stopping the Land Cruiser just before the solid, gravel bed upon which I drove became the actual bridge.

"So we're not the first to get this idea," said Punch.

The bridge, as near as Punch could tell from the scale on the map, was 1,100 feet across. While it looked to be only five feet wide to my cynical eye, it was likely more like 10' or 12'. There weren't any side rails though, so if the gusting wind decided to turn extra nasty – even for a second or two – we could be blown into the churning current below.

If the fall didn't kill us, we'd drown for sure.

At what appeared to be near the center point of the span, an old rusted out Volkswagen Beetle hung precariously off the east side of the tracks, clinging to its present altitude only by the right rear tire. The driver's door hung open, flapping with the breeze and shaking the old VW. Being hooked on the edge of the track bed like it was, I couldn't for the life of me figure out what held it there in the throes of the storm.

"Wonder when they tried to cross," said Punch. "Thing looks like it's been there a while."

"It's gotta be caught good," I said. "Wonder if he tried to drive with his tires right on the rails."

"Wheelbase is about right, but that's fuckin' crazy," said Punch. "Especially if he tried it during this storm."

"With that driver's door open," I said. "I'm bettin' whoever it was dropped into the river. I don't see a way they crawled over the top of the car. That wheel would've slipped right over the rail for sure, gettin' jostled like that."

"Either way, their nightmare's over," said Punch. "As for the car, I'm guessin' we can nudge it off the bridge pretty easily with that cowcatcher of yours."

I looked at Punch and took another hit off my smoke. "Buddy, I was hoping you wouldn't say that. It's gonna be tough enough just drivin' over that sucker in this weather."

"There's no other way, Flex," he said.

"I know that shit," I said. "Doesn't mean I wanna hear it."

"I'll drive if you want," said Punch. "Drove a few Hummers in my day, and if anything is as distracting as this hurricane, it's artillery fire comin' at you from all directions."

I took a deep breath. I trusted the guy and I had no illusions that he'd volunteer for something he didn't feel equipped to do. I turned to him.

"I got two things to tell you, Punch," I said. "Number one, thanks for your service to the United States of America, no matter what it's become since."

"No need to thank me," said Punch. "I did it as much for me and my family as for you and yours. Plus, I made a lot of good friends in the Corps." He slapped my arm. "But thanks anyway. What's the second thing?"

I looked out at the bridge again, then back to Punch. "If you were just bein' nice about drivin', you're screwed, because you're hired," I said. "In a minute."

I put the truck in gear again and eased forward, bouncing over the wooden cross ties as we drew closer to where the bridge span actually began.

"Holy shit," said Punch.

"Holy fuck," I said.

It was hard to tell from inside the cab and through the downpour, but it appeared there were three or four skeletons on the tracks ahead. In the center of the tracks appeared to be something that looked like the handle of a gardening tool.

"Deadheads or live ones when they died?" asked Punch.

"Who knows?" I said. "Dead now. Ain't comin' back."

I sighed and tried to shake off a dizzy spell that washed over me outta nowhere. "Slide on over," I finally said.

If he responded, it was drowned out by the storm as I opened my door and climbed out, maneuvering my way carefully around the front of the SUV. I checked the condition of the pilot and even reached down to jerk it back and forth a few times, just to be sure it wasn't jimmied loose during our earlier escapades.

I was putting off the inevitable, which surprised me. Did I really want to stand outside in the driving rain and wind of a Cat 5 storm rather than address a pile of bones just behind me?

Seemed that way. Somehow, when they were just bones, you didn't know whether they were zombies or the victims thereof.

It was time to say fuck it. I turned around and looked at the almost intact skeletons. The arms on all of them had been broken, as were a couple of the legs. While not completely crushed, dark holes appeared in all the wrong places in all of their skulls, indicating they might have been taken out by the driver of that dangling VW. The bastard's last gift to us.

Not a shred of clothing clung to any of them; I wondered how they had come to be there on the tracks. Clearly, none had been hit by a train, or their bodies would've been kindling.

Four quick gusts that had to have exceeded one hundred miles per hour slammed me, throwing me off balance. I staggered off the tracks briefly, whirled my arms to regain my balance, and ducked into the wind as I pushed back to the tracks where the bodies lay.

I kicked and stomped on the bones until they were out of the way or flat enough to go beneath the truck, making sure nothing sharp lay in the path of the tires. The wind kept up its intensity and I ducked to avoid a flying piece of plastic from somewhere or other.

The bones were cleared. I saw the handle of the tool I'd seen from the cab and pulled it out of the ground.

A skull was stuck on the blade. It was, indeed, a sickle. I tossed it aside, got back in the Toyota and slammed the door. "Go for it McQueen."

"What?" he asked.

"The actor, Steve McQueen? Le Mans? Great driver? Any of this ringing a bell?"

"You seem like a good guy Flex, but I guess it's time to remind you that you've got like fifteen years on me. I'm guessin' this guy's dead?"

"Yeah," I said. "Shut the fuck up and drive."

He drove. I lit another smoke. This shit could be nerve-racking.

*****

Chapter Thirteen

As Hemp hit the top of the steps, he stopped and clung to a fallen roof truss, turning in all directions as his hair whipped across his eyes. After a moment, he stepped over the broken door and leaned against a low wall that still stood, continuing to scan the area for dangers, both of the flying and biting type, I was sure.

He turned back toward us. "All of you, but especially Trina and Taylor – watch for exposed nails and other things that can hurt you. It's very windy up here, so also watch for flying debris, okay?"

The girls both answered him in the affirmative. All of us nodded automatically.

As I watched from near the end of our little chain of humanity, he raised his weapon quickly and fired. He then looked down to his left and fired twice more. After two more scans of the area, he turned toward us and waved us forward. "Come on now. Hurry, but as I said, be watchful, both at ground and eye level."

Even Nelson, who wasn't a fan of guns, had a 9mm in his hand. Hemp may have decided he'd handle anything that got in our way, but several of us were ready to back him up just in case.

"Come on!" Hemp shouted. "Clear for now!"

We all continued our upward trek now, and in probably less than two minutes we were all back on the main floor of the house.

I hadn't expected what we found outside that basement door, even though I'd seen part of the destruction myself prior to making my way to safety. I'm not sure why. I think when you live in Florida you begin to believe that no hurricane can faze you, having seen and experienced so many.

As if by a miracle, the only walls remaining were the one in which the door to the basement had been mounted and the wall connecting to it, which served as the wall to the third bedroom. Everything else was ripped away and in splinters. The rain was now torrential, and being heard over the cacophony was not an easy task.

"Trina! Taylor! Watch where you step!" I shouted ahead, unsure if they could hear me at all. The roar of the wind and the rain as it bounced off a hundred different surfaces of the ripped-apart house created a white noise of sound that kept nerves on end and drowned out one's own thoughts. Still, I called out again: "Make sure you have a solid surface with no nails sticking up to step on *before* you take the step!"

I thought I saw Trina nodding up ahead, but heard no reply.

"Red-eye!" shouted someone. "At 9:00!"

Again, the thunderous wind and the reverberation of debris scraping and rolling over other debris was so loud that the voice could've been either a man or woman, or perhaps two people at once. I could no longer see Hemp, for the human chain had now curved around a pile of downed ceiling joists and flapping insulation that snapped like a giant whip in the wind. I did, however, hear the familiar sound of his Heckler & Koch snap out a three-round burst to accompany the wall of noise that surrounded us.

I hoped he had hit his target. He didn't fire again so I made my assumptions.

Bug and Isis walked ahead of me, and he had the strange little girl tucked so completely into him that I could not see her at all.

But I heard her. The sound chilled me, and her words came before I saw the alarm she meant to send up.

"Mothers, mothers, coming," she said from beneath her cover. Her voice was as clear in my head as though it was a thought from my own mind, and I saw that the moment I heard it, everyone looked around nervously.

Perhaps she had projected it to us all, for I saw Dave, hauling Charlie in his arms, suddenly turn his head from side to side, then look behind him. It had been a warning, we soon learned, for I felt a presence to my left, and just as I turned my head, a blonde-haired red-eye stood just feet away from me, as though she had simply materialized there. In reality, she had probably been lying flat as the boys had said they had been, but she must've popped up like a goddamned jack-in-the-box.

She surged toward me as though the wind had no effect on her; I swore her eyes focused on my son, clutched in my arms, rather than on me, and I had a feeling of protectiveness wash over me that should've told any zombie with even the remotest of telepathic powers that I, Gem Cardoza, was a dangerous weapon to be feared.

With or without my gun.

With her red eyes flashing and her horrid mouth opened in a toothy maw, she advanced. Her guttural groans intensified as she grew to within a foot of me and little Flexy. I raised my right hand, held the 9mm pistol six inches from her face and fired in one motion, blasting her features into fleshy slivers of skin. The black-red blood spatter was immediately pelted down by the rain and washed away in rivulets through the rubble beneath our feet as her body collapsed among the timbers and shingles.

I quickly turned back to see Lola nod at me just before she whirled around to fire on another zombie that appeared seconds later – *after* she turned.

I knew then that Lola not only drew them – perhaps on a lesser scale than did Isis – but she sensed them, too. How similar it all was to Isis, I didn't know. I did get the distinct impression that Lola was an unwitting participant in this ability; that she was as surprised at her telepathic early warning system as any of us would be had we suddenly learned we had the power of X-ray vision.

We had cleared the chimney and followed the path of least rubble scouted by Dave, Nelson and Bug on their run outside, but the storm was at full force and our way forward was fluid and changing. Isis began again.

"Hungerers!" she shouted.

I spun around, holding little Flexy tighter in my arms, and saw three zombies advancing behind Lola. These were not red-eyes, for they were male, but since we were all on WAT-5, I knew they were being guided to us. Where the crimson-eyed, director bitch currently was, I didn't know.

Each of the rotting creatures supported themselves by clinging to some piece of fallen debris or other, but none lost their footing. They gripped their various handholds and drew closer, step by ragged step.

I opened my mouth to warn her of the rotters closing in, but before I could say a word, she either read my eyes or my mind, for she turned and stopped, the long-bladed knife clutched in her left hand.

One was around three feet to her left. The second one was directly in front of her now that she had turned, maybe two feet away, and the last was just off her right shoulder about four feet.

Lola also held the gun, but to my surprise she holstered that weapon and stood there as though waiting.

The one that was closest reached her and Lola's arm shot out like a piston, smacking him in the chest and knocking him back two feet. He staggered, amazingly caught his balance, and was now even with the other two abnormals.

I watched her, this girl I hadn't known for a full two days. She stood there, soaked to the bone like all of us, her hair hanging down in strings, waiting. Her back was to me, but even from my vantage point she looked like a warrior, as though she should have been in the movie 300, fighting to the death alongside King Leonidas.

They were two feet away when Lola, holding the knife as though she were shaking hands, drew her right arm back over her left shoulder, the gleaming, steel blade by her left ear, poised to strike. Again, she waited. I couldn't move – *wouldn't* move – because if anything went wrong, I would hold Flexy with one arm and blow their heads off with my Glock.

It wasn't necessary.

With a smooth strike from left to right, she leaned toward them and drew the blade swiftly across their necks, tearing them open and releasing three simultaneous gushes of fetid gore. Nearly as fast as she had opened their throats, she revised her grip on the knife and brought it down into the skull of the one on the right, the center and the left.

A sudden gust of wind blew the wasted bodies of the now dead creatures into a pile of bloody remains. Lola stood still, only the wind nudging her side to side, watching them. When she was satisfied, she turned and caught my eye. She wasn't even winded. When she reached me, she smiled. I had no words. We moved to catch up with the group, who had seen none of it.

"Mothers," said the toddler in Bug's arms again. While Hemp could not have heard it from where he walked, even he turned at her spoken word.

It became clear to me that there was more to Isis' abilities than an uncanny mastery of speech and a connection with the zombies themselves. She could, if desired, transmit her thoughts to any of us.

Then my mind went to the more important issue for the moment: *Where?* I thought. *Where are the mothers?*

"Mothers! Charlie!" shouted Isis, but it came from within my head as though I were experiencing some virtual reality that could not exist and from which I could not extricate myself.

As before, I *heard* her little voice, but *didn't* hear it. I looked at Charlie, her left arm around Dave's neck, his arms supporting her, and witnessed something happen that would set off a chain of unavoidable events that even our resident clairvoyants were powerless to stop.

Dave Gammon's left foot plunged through a roofing shingle that had nothing beneath it providing support. Ten or so inches of his leg was in a hole of some sort and as he stumbled forward, he threw his right leg forward so that Charlie would not fall on the nail-riddled and razor sharp tin flashing interspersed among the wreckage of the house.

It seemed to happen in slow motion and none of us could do anything to keep them from going down.

Charlie had curled her left arm tighter around his neck and threw her right hand out in an attempt to brace herself for the fall. To his credit, Dave only gripped her more tightly, and the trick with his leg did effectively break her fall, but in the end, Charlie was on her back on top of Dave, whose left leg was bent behind him and his right extended out from beneath Charlie.

Hemp apparently sensed something behind him wasn't right, because he turned to see his wife and friend in a heap among the rubble.

He screamed, "Charlie!" and though he was at the head of the pack, he dropped his weapon to free his hands and ran back toward us.

Something stopped him midway. His right leg flew backward and he fell face down among the debris. He grunted as he landed and did not move immediately, except for his right leg, which he jerked hard, but could not seem to free.

"Something's got my ankle! he screamed, and Nelson took action. "Hang in there, professor!" he yelled, and took three leaps over the piles of shingles, wood and tin to reach him. He looked down.

"It's a zombie hand dude!" he shouted. "Reaching up from under all this shit!" Nelson's eyes darted back and forth, searching the pile. In a moment he found what he was looking for, because he reached down and pulled a long piece of conduit from the mess at his feet, the electrical wires streaming from its end.

He moved around Hemp and jammed the conduit into the pile. He withdrew it and did it again, and again. The last time he drew it up, a dark liquid oozed from it, and was soon rinsed clean from the pouring rain.

Hemp's mind wasn't on Nelson or his predicament. Once his leg was freed, he pushed himself from the ground with some difficulty and resumed his move toward his pregnant wife.

"I'm okay, I'm okay!" screamed Charlie over the sheets of wind that blasted her words away even before they were out of her mouth. I heard her, though. I thanked God.

"Keep going!" she yelled.

Hemp didn't hear. He kept coming.

"Mother," said Isis.

And as if from nowhere, she appeared. Right beside Charlie. Our beautiful, pregnant Charlie.

The creature had platinum blonde hair even when sopping wet. It might have ordinarily hung down to the middle of her back, but was currently being whipped nearly three feet with the wind. This creature had been lying on her back beneath a thin layer of shingle and broken plywood pieces.

What had Hemp named them? *Hiders.*

From this moment, what I'm about to tell you happened in such a lightning sequence that I don't know how to express it so that it will be clear why so many of us could do so little to stop it.

Trina and Taylor's shrill screams filled the air, their eyes on the creature beside Charlie. Rachel and Serena had somehow both made the same split-second decision. They had immediately fallen upon and draped themselves over the girls, using themselves as human shields.

Hemp was in front of Nelson, who had gone to retrieve Hemp's MP5. Hemp was out of his mind; more than I had ever seen him. With a primordial scream, he charged the red-eye with as much speed as his feet could manage over the stacks of junk, and he leapt from a flat section of the collapsed roof toward the walking dead thing, his arms outstretched like an NFL tackle.

Without turning her head, the creature, which had appeared to be fully focused on Charlie, gave Hemp the rotter's version of the Heisman. Her right arm pistoned out, slamming him squarely in the chest. His forward momentum halted like a Smart Car in a crash test, and he was thrown backward, where he hit the advancing Nelson Moore, throwing both men onto their backs amidst the rubble.

Neither rose to their feet immediately. I didn't know why at the time, but my mind was still working to sort out the rapid turn of events.

Unaccosted now, the creature's loose, dead skin rippled in the gusting wind and her eyes glowed red, but worse, she pushed out her strange vapor. It was useless with the gusty wind, and dissipated immediately.

Pulling the blanket more tightly over my son's head, my pistol dropped to the ground, disappearing into a dark crevice at my feet. Unable to assist, I dropped down to my haunches and protected my child, willing someone – anyone – to stop the beast that focused on our Charlie.

Dave's gun was trapped in his drop holster beneath him, but he scrambled to reach it and pull Charlie away from the monster at the same time.

He was not successful. He didn't have enough range of motion, and the thing was already making her move.

The powerful abnormal's hands shot out and pulled Charlie's face toward her. Charlie fought her, but the creature was within three inches of her mouth and nose when she poured out the crimson mist, completely engulfing my friend's face.

The wicked bitch never opened her mouth as if to kill Charlie or eat her. Instead, she seemed content to blast her with the red vapor that had, a little over a year ago, transformed Isis into a new species of human within the womb of her mother.

Lola screamed from behind me, "Gem, move!" and as I turned to see her, she stood with her long knife in her hand, preparing to throw it.

"No!" I shouted, fearing she would hit Charlie, and Lola hesitated, her eyes darting toward me.

We both looked up again at the sound of loose boards clattering ahead of us, and there was Bunsen, all four feet in the air, her wet fur matted and her teeth bared in a horrifying growl that I had no idea she was capable of.

When her feet touched down, her mouth closed on the neck of the red-eye. She then did what came naturally.

Bunsen's powerful jaws twisted and tore at the sinewy veins of the creature's neck, ripping away the muscle, causing the red-eye's head to fall to one side.

Bunsen released her and repositioned to bite even deeper into her collarbone, shaking her like a favorite chew toy. After two or three seconds of jerking her back and forth, Bunsen released the zombie. The once-powerful rotter fell onto her back, revealing a neck that was shredded like Mexican carnitas, but the head that sat upon that neck was far from dead.

Seeing this, Bunsen growled again and advanced. The creature's arm thrust out, snatching her front foreleg and upending Bunsen. When our determined girl fell onto her side, she opened her mouth, plunged her snout forward and chomped down on the monster's face, her massive mouth tearing her cold, gray face open from her right eye socket to her left cheek. Bunsen's jaw muscles worked, almost scissoring side-to-side until her mouth was almost closed, her teeth deeply embedded in the red-eye's flesh. Her wet, matted fur was now crimson and pink with diluted zombie blood.

And then Slider was there, single-minded and as vicious as any junkyard dog protecting his territory and his pack. He focused on the creature's feet and legs, biting and snarling and tearing away at the putrid flesh, occasionally stopping and waiting to see if it was still moving.

Bunsen's last bite must have destroyed some crucial part of the blonde creature's brain, because the dead bitch went limp and fell away, rolling into a gap formed in the destroyed wood, metal and shingles. She didn't move.

Hemp was beside Charlie. "Oh, my God, darling, are you alright?" he asked. "I'm so sorry! I was up there, I couldn't get to you!"

"I don't know," she said. "I'm dizzy ... and like ... confused."

In a burst of what could only have a combination of shock and adrenaline, Dave was back on his feet and scooped up Charlie. This time he didn't wait for any goddamned conga line; he ran over the debris like an urban street performer, reached the edge of the house and dropped out of sight.

Hemp seemed a bit flabbergasted, if you want to know the truth. He shouldn't have been surprised. He'd asked Dave to carry Charlie, and Hemp was no stranger to how much Dave cared for her.

That aside, we all ran then, wanting to be out of the path of the zombies and the shitstorm that rained down upon us relentlessly.

Two minutes later, we all crowded inside the mobile lab, sealing the vents and closing the doors behind us. The generator had been running so it was cool. Dave rested Charlie in the chair that Hemp had built for her, and she lay there, her chest rising and falling fast, her head back and her eyes closed.

Everyone wheezed like their lungs were on fire. Trina and Taylor were still both in tears, and I gave my soundly sleeping boy to Lola and moved to console Trina in my arms. Serena had her arms wrapped around Taylor, who seemed to be settling a bit.

"It's okay, baby," I whispered. "We're all going to be okay." It wasn't the first time I had lied to my daughter.

The wind continued to howl, and debris slammed against the side of the heavy-duty motor home. Haunted eyes took silent inventories, not only of their friends and loved ones, but of their cuts and scratches. Infection was not welcome here. Infection could make you die.

"The storm seems to be moving faster," said Hemp, addressing us. "That's a good thing. It means that in a few hours it may be past us and we'll begin to experience less wind and rain. I'd guess that by late tonight we'll be in the clear."

Everyone nodded. "Hemp, sir?" asked Rachel, using respect so typical of members of our military. "If you don't mind my asking, where are we going from here? I was so happy to see such a warm home and to meet you all. I'm sure you're all devastated."

Hemp looked at Rachel – all 4'11" of her – and said, "This may be a cliché, but it's always something," he said. "We've yet to get someplace and just settle in for any amount of time before something goes wrong."

"Maybe you need to do an analysis of states with the lowest population and the fewest natural disasters," said Lola. "Raise our likelihood of survival."

"Perhaps it would be safer for a while," said Hemp. "But once the red-eyes found us, it would be the same old, same old."

Lola shrugged. "It'd give us time to fortify against them before they showed up. There are a lot of us now. More workers get more done. I'm a good worker."

"I'm sure you are, Lola," said Hemp. "For now, I suggest you all get out of your wet clothing. There are towels in the cabinet on the right, two doors from the rear. Wring your things out and hang them, and they should be good and dry to wear later. Modesty will have to be set aside for the moment, and a towel will cover you just fine until your clothing is wearable again."

Nobody answered. Nobody got up. They just sat there nodding.

Hemp went to Charlie and reached out to stroke her cheek. "Charlie," he said. "Sweetheart, open your eyes."

"I'm afraid," she said.

I walked over, still holding Trina's hand in mine, and took Charlie's with the other.

"Hey, Charlie. It's me and Trina," I said. "Now come on and open your eyes so you can see we're all safe."

"They sting," she said.

"Blink them," said Hemp. "Get some moisture coating them."

She did. I couldn't stop myself from gasping.

Bug walked slowly over, removing the blanket from Isis. When she came into view, her little red eyes were already on Charlie.

"Mother," she said.

Charlie looked at us through her blood red eyes. Then she turned to look at Isis.

"Charlie," said Hemp, tears beginning to run down his cheeks. "Charlie, I would have Jim perform a Caesarian section right this moment if we had the available blood, but we don't. That means I need you to relax and see how fast you can deliver this baby."

"Hemp," she said, her crimson eyes tearing up. "Are my eyes ... red?"

Hemp nodded and squeezed her hand. "You and the baby will be just fine," he said. His eyes lit up and he ran to the work bench and opened the top right cabinet. He withdrew a plastic Tupperware container and popped the lid off.

"Here," he said. "Eat this now. It's one of the red-eye wafers that we gave Kimberly and Rebecca in the lab in Concord."

"Will it work?" asked Charlie.

"You know it does," I said. "At least it won't make you want to do anything."

"Just remember that it prevents you from being under their control, sweetheart. It won't stop you from hearing their commands," said Hemp. "The rest is what it is," he said. "But that's why I need you to relax. The sooner you give birth, the better for our child."

"Isis," said Bug. "Baby girl, you seeing anything?"

I think everyone that was awake turned to look at the pair at once. Bug looked around the room and shrugged.

"She's such a chatterbox these days I thought it couldn't hurt to ask," he said, smiling.

He stood and carried her closer to Charlie, who managed a smile through her tears at the child's small, strange face.

Very slowly, Isis' serious expression changed. Her mouth turned up on the sides. She looked at Charlie's stomach and back at Charlie. Then she pointed to Charlie's stomach, looked at her father with a gleeful expression on her face and said, "Brother!"

She looked up at her father again, her face absolutely glowing and angelic. "Brother, daddy!" she said again.

Charlie passed out.

*****

We were a quarter of the way across the train bridge, and to me, the wind felt as though it would blow us off like a piece of lint at the mercy of a flicking finger.

"Just cruise," I said, my firearms forgotten for the moment. They wouldn't do me any more good in this situation than the death grip I had on the grab bar above my head. "Not that I ain't in a hurry, you understand."

"Looked wider from the road," said Punch. "The pilot's helping me keep nice and centered."

We were still well away from the Volkswagen, but we could see it more clearly now. The color initially appeared to be red, but I could now see it was either primer or just rusted. The car was actually teetering on its final foothold, but refused to fall.

I hoped we could encourage it out of the way.

A blast of wind slammed our right side and Punch responded by holding the wheel tight. His knuckles were white on the steering wheel, which was about as pointless with power steering as my involuntary actions.

He drew to a stop as we rolled to within twenty feet of the VW.

"What's that there?" I asked.

"Where?" asked Punch.

"Behind that one wheel."

He leaned forward and squinted. "Got binoculars in this rig?"

I could've slapped myself. "What the fuck," I said, popping open the glove box. I pulled out the pair of camo Bushnells and put them to my eyes.

"It's the fuckin' rear axle," I said. "Jammed right up against the rail. No wonder that bastard didn't flip off the bridge."

"Is it gonna make nudging it tougher?" asked Punch.

"I'd have to say yes," I said. I looked at my watch. We'd left Piedmont Gas over four hours ago. It was now approaching 3:00. Gem had to be freaking out by now. I only hoped things were boring enough for her to have the time to worry about me.

At least everyone back home already knew about Tony. I still couldn't believe that Isis had known. I wondered then how much she knew. Did she know how he died, or only that he was no longer?

There was so much to learn about that child that I was afraid Hemp's head might explode from the utter volume of data input as the next months and years passed. Of course all that knowledge depended on whether or not we could keep Isis safe.

Hell, if we could keep any of us safe.

I remembered Cara. I promised her I'd drop the antitoxin for her baby, too. Maybe I'd come back after I made sure my family was safe and the storm had passed.

All of this served to take my mind off what I had to face.

"Let's try nudging it," I said. "Maybe that axle's just in the perfect position to keep it up here. We jog the whole car and it might just go."

"We're not gettin' anywhere parked," said Punch. He put it back into drive and eased forward again. Up and down, over the cross-ties we went, until we were five feet from the car.

"Sure we can't skirt around it?" I asked, gauging the distance between the car's rear bumper and the far edge of the tracks.

"You're on the side that goes down first," said Punch. "I can yank open my door and try to leap clear, but you're done for."

"Now I know why you offered to drive."

"Nope," he said. "Didn't see the car."

"You stallin'?"

"A little," he said, smiling nervously.

"Big, bad Marine."

Punch turned away from me, looked out the window, and gassed the Land Cruiser. It jolted forward and my legs pressed hard against the floorboards and my knuckles were white again.

He drew to within a foot of the VW and tapped the brakes lightly, easing up to the contact point. Then he rolled forward a couple of inches, bumping the Bug.

Instead of toppling over the side, the VW slid along the rail and stayed good and caught.

Worse, we were nudged to the right.

"Pilot's angle is pushing us," said Punch. "Maybe a hard jolt?"

"If we're getting pushed right – which you reminded me is certain death for one Flex Sheridan – then be sure to turn into it when you push. Just don't push too hard."

He tried it again, just as a sustained gust that had to be ninety miles per hour or more rocked the Toyota and sent the VW swinging on that axle and wheel.

"Whoa, shit!" I said. "This is nuts!"

Punch gripped the wheel and tried it again. This time we slid a good six inches off to the right and the VW moved perhaps another two along the rail. I swore I felt the right rear tire sink a little bit. I looked out, but saw only air and raging water below.

"It's not gonna work, buddy," said Punch. "Fucker's caught good, and we're gonna throw ourselves off the bridge."

"Fuck!" I said. "I got nothin' inside I can pry it off with, either. Nothing long enough to give me enough leverage."

"There's only one option, man," said Punch.

"I know where you're goin', and it makes sense. Just not suspended fifteen feet over a raging river in a goddamned hurricane."

"We have to winch it," he said, blabbing the very words I didn't want to hear.

"And what happens when the car goes over and we're hooked to it?"

"Geronimo?"

"You know that shit but you don't know who the hell Steve McQueen is?"

"This is you stallin' again," said Punch.

"This is me thinkin'," I said. "We need to figure out a way to use the winch to jostle that car free, and make sure we don't go over with it. I gotta get out and look at how it's caught."

Eric A. Shelman

"I can do it, man," said Punch. "I'm surefooted, like a goat."

"You smell like a goat," I said, forcing a smile. "I got it."

I eased open the door and the rain sprayed my face like a showerhead. I made my first mistake and looked down. There was perhaps a foot and a half of track bed between my door and nothingness. With the rain pelting me head on, I slid out and planted my feet, the wind directing everything right in my face and eyes, but I needed both hands to cling to my perch and just plain had to suck it up. I couldn't have heard anything, even if Punch had tried to talk to me.

I slid off to the side and slammed the door, then grabbed the side mirror to steady myself as I worked my way along the front fender, and finally onto the center of the tracks in front of the SUV. I clung to the cowcatcher's steel grid for a moment or two, getting used to the strength of the wind.

When I felt ready, I crouched down, most of my pressure on my left leg to prevent my body from blowing off the east side of the bridge. Forward movement was as slow as a parade of slugs, but I reached the car and lay flat on the tracks to get a look at how it was wedged.

It wasn't just the axle. It *had* snapped, but the tire was flat and the rim had dented, conforming to the rail with the constant swinging in the wind. I almost got on my knees and tried to rock it, but came to my senses.

I didn't know how long that car had been there, but it wasn't going anywhere on my manpower alone.

I turned and motioned to Punch, pointing at the winch. I gave him a cranking motion with my hand and he understood. A moment later I saw the winch spin forward and the cable loosen.

I remembered how fortunate we were that it still worked at all, what with the Toyota's electrical problems.

I crawl-shuffled the three feet back to the SUV and reached down for the cable. When I had it, I inspected the hook.

Then I had an idea. It would either work or kill one or both of us.

I dropped it again and started alongside the large vehicle again to get to the rear hatch.

I needed a crowbar and I needed a prayer.

I said the prayer while I watched the furious Catawba River eat away its banks, expanding its territory and destroying what once was, as so many things seemed to be doing lately.

Meanwhile, all I wanted was to be back with my wife, my son and my friends, on the solid ground that was now our home.

*****

It was nearly four o'clock in the afternoon. We'd left the dungeon – now likely a swimming pool – around two hours before, and Charlie wasn't in the throes of delivery yet. I hadn't expected it, but Nelson and Dave seemed to think the baby was just going to fall out once the water broke. How do you get that age and not know anything about childbirth? Nelson should've known, what with being the grandson of Doc Scofield, but it was pretty clear he wasn't in on the entire process of birth.

While delivering Flexy hadn't been as hard as some I'd heard about, the process still took almost ten hours after my water broke.

Tired and needing sleep, Nelson and Dave had curled up on the floor inside the Plexiglas walls that once housed Hemp's zombie subjects. Lola seemed exhausted after her encounters with the zombies, and both Bunsen and Slider had needed some major toweling off and clean-up with peroxide once out of the rain. Now they both snored, sprawled out by the entry door, probably awaiting Flex.

We were the only zombies inside right now, and none of us had even bothered to peer out the windows in so long we had no idea what kind of undead population surrounded us now.

Maybe none. Maybe a hundred.

The mobile lab's rocking and rolling with the wind had become the norm, and I suppose we all just came to accept it, like traveling in a ship on the ocean. I'm not certain anyone was particularly frightened it would flip onto its side, because despite the movement, our condition appeared to be at a terrorist alert level of GREEN, or whatever the lowest was.

I then wondered what the hell ever became of that lame system. Either way, we'd always be at the RED level these days. There was a 100% chance of being eaten if you went out unprepared.

For the moment, the fortified lab stayed put alongside my heavy, ballistic steel-sheathed Crown Victoria.

The basement had been relatively quiet in comparison; this was about as sketchy as being in a nylon tent with a family of bears outside. It just didn't feel like enough, but it was where we were for the moment and there weren't any other options.

"Darlin', you just breathe easy and relax," said Scofield, seated between Charlie's legs. He gently withdrew his hand and said, "You're only dilated around five centimeters. It's gonna be a while yet."

"I don't want … my baby to be inside me …" she managed.

Hemp stood on her other side, her left hand clasped in his, looking directly into her red eyes. His face was intense and worried and scared, all at the same time.

I don't see that a lot with a guy like Hemp.

He said, "Charlie, it's out of our control. We can't perform a C-section and this is your first child. It's just going to take as long as it takes."

"But … Isis," she said.

"Our child will be who it will be," said Hemp. "As long as he or she is healthy, nothing else matters but you."

"He *is* my brother," said Isis.

I looked at her, and my heart ached for Charlie. Isis was unique and special and beautiful, but she wasn't normal.

You always want your first baby – no, fuck that. You obviously want *all* of your babies to be healthy and normal. You pray for it every day whether you believe in God or not, and the closer you get to your delivery date, you begin to believe more and more that you did everything the way you were supposed to, the stars aligned, and your baby would be perfect.

Perfect. It's what Flex and I had hoped and prayed for, and it's what we got with our little boy. Charlie had done everything right and this goddamned cursed world got to her anyway. I asked myself every few seconds, why Charlie? Why her?

Why anyone? Because. Just because. It was the shit world in which we lived nowadays. And now a little baby was predicting the sex of an unborn child and we accepted it.

"Isis," asked Rachel, as though reading my mind. "What do you mean when you say he's your brother?"

"Isis isn't alone," she said.

"You were never alone, baby girl," said Bug. "You'll always have me."

"I know, Daddy," she said, and I swore she rolled her eyes. None of this – not the storm and its lightning and wind, not the zombies, not the prospect of Charlie's baby changing within her – seemed to bother the child.

She was either very brave, or she could see the future whether she knew it or not. I suspected it was a whole shitload of both.

Isis had been standing at Bug's knees, watching what was happening intently. The girls had been fidgety and alternately frightened and bored. Frightened when a lightning strike would hit nearby, and bored when it seemed everything was status quo.

I wasn't so sure they didn't actually enjoy being scared more. With Trina and Taylor, anything beat boredom. Whenever a loud thunderclap would shatter our nerves, they would scream and cover their faces, but when they took their hands away, they were always looking at one another and smiling in anticipation of the next.

Isis pursed her lips and Bug bent down to kiss them. She smiled big and turned purposefully to walk toward Charlie. Once there, she said, "Charlie, he's happy."

Charlie turned her head, seeming surprised that Isis was beside her. She had been looking at Hemp, who stared at them now, his eyes grateful. "Is he, Isis?" he asked.

Isis nodded and smiled again, showing every gleaming tooth. Not a spec of beef jerky hung from them.

"I feel him," she said. "He cannot think to me now. He is too much a baby and does not know many words."

"*Many* words?" I asked. "He knows some words *now*?"

"Only those I have thought to him," said Isis. "Not many. He will not be able to speak them for some time." She looked again at Charlie, the strange smile on her lips again.

Charlie managed a smile. "Isis," she said. "Is he … like you?"

Isis nodded her head rapidly, a coy smile on her face. "Yes, but he is male."

"Will he be ... like you? Will he sleep, Isis? Will he eat asparagus and fruit? Will his eyes be red? Will he have ... teeth like yours?" Charlie hesitated on that last question.

"Charlie," I interrupted. "He'll be beautiful."

"He is beautiful," said Isis. She smiled again. "Like me!"

"Come here, you goof," said Bug, who looked like he could use a good pillow beneath his head. I saw him glance over toward where Dave and Nelson slept on the floor every once in a while, longing in his eyes.

"We'll watch Isis," I said. "Why don't you drop down and take an hour or two."

"Oh, I'm not worried about her," he said. "But I think we all need a new dose of WAT-5 before anybody does anything. We're goin' on six hours now."

Hemp checked his watch. "Oh, my God," he said. "I can't believe I let that happen."

"Don't sweat it," said Bug. "All that means is I'll actually get to sleep fast. That's special for an old guy like me."

Hemp reached into his pants pocket and his expression changed. He felt his other pocket, shock on his face.

"It's not here," he said.

"You sure?" I asked. "Hemp, you had them."

"I know, I know," he said, re-checking his pockets again. "but they're gone. Probably during the altercation with the red-eye."

"How many did we have left?" asked Charlie.

"Enough for at least ten more hours of protection," said Hemp. "I'm sorry, everyone."

"I lived without it for the better part of the last year," said Lola. "Guess I'll survive now, too."

"I was hidin' in a cave before, so I had no need for it," said Bug. "Since I came out, it's been the only thing that's really set my mind at ease – especially with this one." He bounced Isis in his arms.

"Well, everyone needs rest," continued Hemp. "We have very limited food, but the water tanks were filled, so we're okay in that department. Let's hope Flex and Tony –"

He stopped. "Sorry, guys. Let's hope Flex gets back soon. We've got the weapons and ammo that we have, but I'm afraid it's not as much as we would choose."

"I don't like the wafers much anyway," said Trina. "They make me want to puke sometimes," she added.

"You never liked them, silly," I said.

"I don't like them either, but mommy says they keep us safe," said Taylor. "Right, mommy?"

"Yes, baby," said Charlie. "And don't worry. We'll have more soon."

"Are you okay, mommy?" asked Taylor. She got up and went to Charlie, leaned against her and hugged her tightly.

"As long as I know you're here with me," said Charlie. "My brave, strong girl."

Dave and Nelson had slept through the bad news, so Hemp went into the room and nudged them awake.

"Hey, dude," said Nelson, yawning. "Is everything okay?

Dave rubbed his eyes. "What's up, Hemp?"

"We've lost the remainder of the WAT-5," he said. "I'm afraid we need to take stock of our weapons and ammo. I'd say we need to check outside to assess the situation, but ultimately, it doesn't matter because we're limited on what we have. When it's gone, it's gone."

Dave lowered his voice and eyed Hemp. "Pretty dire. What happened to the WAT-5?"

Hemp took the hint and knelt down beside them. I had to know what the conversation was, so I went in with them and joined the huddle.

"I lost it when Nelson and I fell, I suppose," said Hemp. "I guess it wasn't stuffed very deeply in my pocket."

"Nobody's fault, Hemp," said Dave. "Do we know what the situation outside is right now?"

"I haven't looked, and I don't recommend you do so either," he said, keeping his voice low. "No sense in alarming anyone else if it's dire."

"True," I said. "Once you look out, someone's gonna ask what it's like out there."

"Exactly," said Hemp. "Look. Flex should be back soon. I know we haven't heard from him in a while, but if we can trust Isis, he's still alive."

"Thank God for her," I said. "She's my only peace of mind where Flex is concerned."

Dave stood up and yawned, looking over at Charlie. Charlie turned her head and smiled back at him, giving him a little wave. He waved back. "Had that kid yet?" he asked.

"Not yet," she said. "I'm thinking maybe some Sex Pistols would help me along." She turned her eyes to Hemp.

"Back to sleep with me," said Dave. "I'm more of a Bob Seger guy."

"I dig The Grateful Dead," said Nelson. "Got any of them?" he asked.

"Not in here, but I know a few record stores we can hit later," said Charlie. "For now, get on that ammo inventory."

"Sure," said Nelson, tucking his hair behind his right ear. "Better to know where we stand. I have like six Ninja stars left."

Bug went into the Plexiglas room with Dave and Nelson, pulled up a spot on the floor with a small stack of towels beneath his head and closed his eyes. "I'm wiped," he said.

Isis had gone over to Rachel, who picked her up and sat her in her lap. "How are you, little one?" she asked, smiling.

"You're a little grownup," said Isis.

"I am. I'm only 4'11" tall."

"You are much taller than that as a soul," said Isis. "You have a good, kind heart."

Rachel Reed looked at Isis and smiled. "Now how would you know anything about that?"

"I watched you," said Isis. "You are small, but you are determined."

"I am going to wake up very soon and tell everybody about the conversation I was having with a baby in my dream," said Rachel. "I'm pretty sure about that."

Isis reached over and tried to pinch Rachel. I could see what she was doing, but her little fingers weren't coordinated enough to actually get any skin between them.

"What was that?" asked Rachel.

"I was pinching you so you would know you're not dreaming," said Isis. "I'm thirsty."

"Well, let's get you some water, how about?"

"Gem," said Hemp. "You need some rest. I suggest you follow Bug's lead and get some sleep."

"Not until my girl here gives birth to that little papoose."

Charlie's face contorted as if on cue, and I saw the muscles in her legs tense. It brought giving birth to my son right back home.

"See? You're about to pop him out any minute, like a Pop Tart."

"Pop Tarts!" shouted Trina.

"She doesn't have any," said Taylor, rolling her eyes."

"She might," said Trina.

"I don't," I said. "It was an analogy."

"What do those taste like?" asked Trina.

"Oh, my God," said Taylor.

"Gem, why do you say him instead of her?" asked Charlie.

"I just doubt Isis is wrong about it," I said. "That's all. Doesn't really matter anyway, right?"

"You're right," said Charlie. "It doesn't matter what sex it is. But wake Doctor Jim, would you? I want him to check me again."

Jim had drifted off, too. Everyone was exhausted, and in the relative safety of the mobile lab they were able to give in to their fatigue. Despite how comfortable he appeared, and ignoring his soft snores, I awoke Doc Scofield, who came to life like he'd been sleeping for six hours.

"Oh!" he said with a start. "How long was I out?"

"Five minutes," said Hemp, smiling. "You are such a slacker. Your punishment is to measure my wife's cervix."

"Well," said Scofield. "Why'd you wake me then? I can do that shit in my sleep."

*****

317

Chapter Fourteen

I almost wanted to tether myself to something, the wind and rain was making it so difficult to keep my balance. Punch watched me from the truck, but what I was doing was a one-man job and he couldn't really help. Still, I thought my plan was a good one.

I fed the winch cable out and worked the crowbar's U-shaped end underneath the jammed VW wheel and axle. When I got it the way I wanted it, the long end of the crowbar stuck into the air, angled toward the Volkswagen.

I then slid the winch hook down over the crowbar and held it about ten inches from the base. I motioned to Punch to reel in the winch cable very slowly.

The motor kicked in and the slack in the cable began to wind into the winch. I held up my hand in a stop signal, and he did. I gave him a signal with my fist that I thought meant to give the motor a quick bump.

Punch got it the first time. He bumped the motor of the winch, and the cable tensed, keeping the hook where I had placed it, the tension between the truck and the crowbar perfect to hold the hook where I had raised it.

I fought the wind and rain back to the Toyota and worked my way to the driver's side.

"Okay, brother," I said when he opened the window. "It's ready. I don't want you to use the winch power. You gotta back this sucker up fast. Just a foot or two should do."

"You think it'll flip that fucker off the bridge?"

"That's the plan," I said. "Got it jammed under there perfectly. As long as the crowbar pulls straight back that rim's gotta lift up and over."

Punch looked at me. "You wanna give it a go?"

"Nah," I said. "If this doesn't work, I want to be able to blame someone else."

"I guess if passin' the blame is good enough for the POTUS, it's good enough for you," he said. "Okay. You wanna get inside? Don't stand out there, man. If that cable snaps off there it could smack you."

"Good call," I said. I went around to the other door and slid in. I was making a real mess of the upholstery. I was immediately glad it wasn't Gem's car.

"Ready?" he said.

"Cross your fuckin' fingers, Punch."

"We got this," said Punch. He put his foot on the brake and put the Land Cruiser in reverse. He looked at me. "Let me see 'em."

I held up my crossed fingers, smiling.

"Good," he said. He hit the gas without removing his foot from the brake pedal, and the Toyota shot backwards.

The cable held. The hook jerked the crowbar backward, and as the fulcrum created by my positioning of the steel rod engaged, the VW's wheel lifted up nearly three inches.

It was enough.

Just as the cable slid over the top of the crowbar shaft, the old Beetle flipped over the edge of the suspended train track bed and plunged fifteen feet to the fast-flowing water below.

We both watched as it bobbed away, reappearing three times before filling with water and sinking from view.

The tracks ahead were now clear.

I held up my hand and Punch gave me a nice high five. "Well, somethin' worked out, my friend," I said.

"We might just be a good team," said Punch.

"Well, we're all we got for now," I said. "I'll get out and feed that winch cable back in. Might get caught on the tracks."

"Good," Punch said.

I got out and was relieved to see the crowbar hadn't gone over with the car. I retrieved that, then lifted the hook and signaled Punch to reel it back in.

I walked it toward the truck and watched as it rolled up to the pilot, where I hooked it.

Then I heard something over the roar of the storm's wind and rain.

Punch began honking the horn, long and loud and nonstop. I looked around me, trying to see what the hell he was doing.

Then I saw it. A house.

Punch honked. I stared, petrified.

Then I ran. I don't even remember worrying about the narrow path I had available to me to get back in the truck – I just got my ass in and slammed my hand on the dashboard and screamed "Go! Go!"

Punch hit the gas hard and the Toyota jammed forward, jumping over the cross-ties now, probably rolling on the precariously high and narrow train bridge at fifteen miles per hour.

The two-story house, projecting upward from the water no less than twenty feet high, was coming toward us, twisting and turning in the churning current, only marginally breaking up as it bobbed in the raging floodwaters, making a beeline toward our bridge.

It would have to sink five more feet before we even stood a chance of it not smashing into the bridge itself, and it would have to completely disintegrate to avoid taking out at least two of the bridge supports.

The end of the bridge was now about 400 feet ahead.

The house was perhaps twice that distance from the bridge.

"Jesus, Punch, faster, man! Faster!"

He looked at the house, and back at the end of the bridge. "We ain't gonna make it there before that fucker hits, Flex!" he shouted, and pressed the Land Cruiser's accelerator firmly.

There was no sense in being cautious. If that house hit the bridge before we were clear of it, we were done for.

I hadn't buckled in and I was bouncing all over the cab, scrambling for handholds to keep from racking my head on the AK47 mounted to the ceiling of the cab. The house was now within about seventy feet of the bridge. We still had what appeared to be a hundred feet or more to travel, only we weren't going as fast as the house seemed to be.

"It's gonna hit, Punch!" I shouted. "Go, man! Fuck it! Give it all you got!"

His sudden acceleration threw me back in my seat as the roar outside grew louder and I felt the truck jar hard to the left. I swore, looking at the twenty feet ahead of us that remained, that I could now see the tracks no longer straight ahead of us, but now angling diagonally in the direction of the current.

The bridge was going to fall. The Toyota bounced over the tracks, eating up the remaining yards to the fixed, concrete side barriers, now ten feet away.

I looked back, but saw nothing because of the solid rear window. Now the tracks upon which we drove angled sharply and we were suddenly driving uphill. Only two yards to go.

As our front wheels hit the solid track bed, Punch smashed his foot on the gas pedal again and shot us up and over the edge, where bridge turned into terra firma again.

Once back on the fixed tracks, Punch drove like a bat out of hell to the end and slammed on the brakes.

I had to do it. I threw my door open and looked back.

On the other side of the vehicle, Punch did the same. As we watched, the narrow train bridge, now collapsed in the middle, slowly dissolved into the churning water immediately disappearing below. The house had broken up into a million pieces that now covered the entire surface of the Catawba River.

But we'd made it. As far as I knew it was our last major obstacle between me and my family.

Other than Buckfield.

It reminded me of another promise I'd made, and I intended to fulfill it. Cara was exposed to me, and I had been exposed to the little girl who had brought the Diphtheria. That meant any children with Cara were at risk, too.

I decided we'd stop on the way. It was just south of Buckfield and if I didn't give them what I'd promised, more people might die.

*****

We reached the gas station within a half hour after our ordeal on the bridge. In twenty minutes, we'd gotten the purple GTO started and both vehicles ready to roll homeward, all our gas cans back in the truck.

The Pontiac's battery didn't have enough juice to fire the starter, so we had to use the jumper cables hanging on the wall. I took them with us just in case the battery didn't charge or I had issues with the Land Cruiser.

Punch followed me out of the yard. He had a handheld radio, and we agreed to communicate with one another on channel three.

"You read, Punch?" I asked.

"Roger," he said. "Heading through Buckfield?"

"Unless you know another way around," I said.

"I don't."

"Buckfield it is, then," I said. "Maybe the hurricane will distract 'em enough so we can slide on through."

"It's doubtful," he said. "Make sure your roof-mounted AK has a full mag. One way or the other, we'll get the meds to your folks."

I knew that. Never doubted it. That's not how my mind works.

*****

"Gem, wake up," the voice said.

I heard the words, but did my best to ignore them. I didn't even know how I'd gone to sleep, but there I was, reluctantly waking up. Rachel stood in front of me with Lola beside her.

"The doctor needs to talk to you," whispered Lola.

I sat up, shaking away the cobwebs. "What's wrong? Where's Flexy?" I got on my feet.

"Not back yet," said Rachel.

"No, not him," I clarified. "My son."

"He's with the doctor," said Lola. "Behind the front curtain. It's what he wants to talk to you about."

I jumped to my feet and ran to the front of the lab where Doc Scofield had drawn the curtain across to separate the cockpit from the main cabin. He was sitting, holding Flexy in his arms, and he had a small oxygen bottle with a mask attached directly to it. It was currently over Flexy's mouth and nose.

"Jim, what's wrong? Is he okay?" A million thoughts ran through my head, but none of them meant anything. My own thoughts were a blur and included Flex, my son and that little girl who had been so sick the day before.

Jim looked up his eyes dead serious. "The Diphtheria, Gem," he said. "The little guy's having a bit of trouble breathing. It's one of the symptoms."

"And where does this symptom stop?" I asked. "Can it get better?"

Doc Scofield shook his head. "Without the antitoxin it only advances from here, Gem. Come here for a sec," he said, withdrawing a small, LED flashlight from his shirt pocket. "He's been yawning once every few minutes. It's been a while, and I think he's tired, but I need to keep oxygen flowing into him. I don't really want to let him sleep right now."

Flexy opened his mouth in a big yawn, and the doctor said, "Okay, come down here and look."

I knelt down and he shone the light in Flexy's open mouth. In the back of his throat was a scaly, dry area that looked like lizard skin. Fibrous and thick-looking. I knew from the girl who had brought the disease to us, Gina, that this was a symptom.

"He's having more trouble breathing with every minute that passes," said Scofield. "His airway's not closed off yet, and I don't think it will be soon, but if something doesn't happen within the next eight hours or so, I'm afraid we may have to give this little guy a tracheotomy to keep oxygen movin' to his brain."

"Jesus Christ, Jim!" I shouted. "Are you fucking kidding me?"

"Gem, I –"

I broke down into sobs, my sudden burst of anger now flooded with sorrow. The feeling that washed over me was completely foreign. It was the worst fear I've ever felt before, times a million. My baby boy was in danger of suffocating, and I was relying on my husband, who had left over a day ago for a destination that should've been a six-hour round trip at most, even in the storm.

"I'm sorry, Gem," said Scofield, rubbing a soothing hand on my back.

I took his hand and squeezed it. "No, I'm sorry, but I'm freaking out right now. I'm thinking how I can get us into the goddamned Crown Vic and get to where Flex is with that antitoxin."

"Your son needs to stay here," said Scofield. "Dry and safe with the available oxygen and other … things."

"Like a fucking scalpel to cut open his throat?" I asked.

Scofield hesitated, then nodded. "We're a long way from that, Gem," he said. "Flex has a lot to deal with out there. Downed trees, stalled cars, flooding. I'm sure he's doing the best he can. I expect he's well on his way back, Gem. Probably any time now."

The good doctor was filling me full of bullshit and I knew it. I couldn't begrudge him that, though. It was because he cared about me.

Lola came over. "Anything I can do?"

"I'd take you with me to find Flex if I thought Hemp would let me go."

"Gem," said Lola, "Flex has got to be on his way back now. Going out there doesn't make any sense."

"That's what he said," I said, nodding toward Scofield.

"The storm seems as though it's losing intensity," said Hemp, walking up. "Either the eye is approaching or it missed us completely and we're feeling the backside of it now."

"How's he doing?" asked Rachel, who walked up behind Hemp.

Doc Scofield gave Flexy over to me and I tucked him into my arm, holding the small oxygen container. After two breaths on his own, I put it over his nose and mouth and let him breathe deeply two or three times. "Let's just say he's been better," I said. "I'm so fucking worried with Flex out there and now this."

"Jesus," said Charlie, her eyes squeezed closed. "Wow."

"They're coming faster," said Jim Scofield. "Time to check you again." He moved between her legs as he pulled another pair of gloves on, then lifted the sheet covering her.

"Well, congratulate yourself, young lady," he said, snapping off his gloves and dropping them into a stainless wastebasket. "You're at seven centimeters. That's very good. With your contractions seven minutes apart, we need to get you up and moving now to hurry this along."

"Good," said Charlie. "I've been dying to stretch my legs."

Hemp kissed her on the cheek. "Well, then. Let's get you up." He leaned forward and she put her arms around his neck. He helped her remove her legs from the braces and swing them to the floor.

"You good?" he asked.

"Oh, yeah," said Charlie. She walked immediately over to where the music selection was, the Sex Pistols CD having long since played itself out. After flipping through for a bit, she settled on Aerosmith's Toys In The Attic CD. Seconds later, strains of the title track filled the room and anyone who slept was awake.

That included Nelson, who came to life holding an air guitar, ala Joe Perry. "Right on, dude," he said. "I dig old Aerosmith!"

"Wasn't my first choice," said Charlie.

"Did you have the baby dude?" asked Nelson, looking around the lab, as though the baby may have been tucked inside a drawer.

"Look at my stomach, Nel," said Charlie. "I'm –"

326

She stopped talking and put her hand on her stomach as she leaned on the stainless steel counter. She squeezed her eyes closed, fighting the contraction.

"Ah," Nelson said. "Still preggers. Sorry."

"Not as sorry as I am," she said.

Rachel had plopped down beside Nelson. She was so small that when she drew her knees up to her chest, she looked absolutely tiny. She glared at Nelson and smacked his arm. "She's stressing," she said.

Hemp rushed toward Charlie, but she held up her hand. "I'm fine, babe. Just another contraction. I promise not to fall."

"You were kind of lucky to have the zombie apocalypse come in advance of your kid," said Dave. "Toughened you up but good."

"Hard getting used to those red eyes, though," said Nelson.

Rachel smacked his arm again.

"One more time and you're gonna meet Subdudo," he said.

She hit him again, smiling. He smiled back. Love might be ridiculous, but fear sucked and I had enough of that to go around.

"You sure you're alright?" asked Hemp again.

Charlie nodded, and the contraction passed. She took a deep breath, then another. "Whew," she said, looking flushed. "I gotta see this."

She walked into the bathroom and switched on the light. I heard her say, "Wow." She stuck her head back out and she was looking straight at me. "These are some red eyes."

"Indeed," I said.

"Have I said anything yet that freaked anyone out?"

Hemp looked at her. "No, Charlie. Why? Did you … hear something? Feel some Impulse?"

"No ... well, maybe."

"Mothers and Hungerers," said Isis. "Near."

Bug went to her and knelt down. She had been clopping from one end of the lab to the other in her little shoes that looked unsuitable for walking, as most baby shoes were.

I had an idea, remembering something she did earlier. I went back to the cockpit passenger chair, which had been rotated around to face the main cabin, and sat, Flexy in my arms. He had fallen asleep, but I was still able to use the oxygen on him.

"Isis," I said. "Come here, please?"

Isis laughed and ran, utilizing the gait of a little toddler her age, tilting forward and back until you were certain she'd fall – only she never did.

She got to me and immediately tried to crawl into the chair opposite me. She found she could not, and turned, her lower lip quivering, and her face extremely sad.

It was a revelation to me. With all the abilities she had; all the telepathic powers and those of speech, too, she was still just a baby who cried when she was upset and frustrated.

"Hold on, I gotcha," said Lola, running up behind her and lifting her into the seat. Her frown immediately turned upside down and she smiled and clapped her hands.

Then she looked at me and said, "Yes, Gem?"

I'd almost forgotten what I called her for, but remembered a second later. I looked down at Flexy and back at her. She still smiled.

"Isis," I said, hesitating. I was afraid to ask her what I wanted to ask, because I feared her honesty. She would not lie to ease my mind. It wasn't in her.

"You want to know if I still hear Flex," she said.

"You are one scary little girl," I said, before I realized I'd said it. "Oh, my God, Isis. I'm sorry. You're not. You're sweet."

"I understand," she said. "I am different than you. But we are alike in some ways."

"Flex," I said. "Do you still ... feel him?"

"He is well," said Isis. "He is alone now."

"I thought you said he was with a man named Punch."

"He is no longer," she said. "Punch is inside purple."

I looked at her. "Inside purple? Where is Flex?"

"The same, only alone."

"Is he alive?"

"He is," said the little girl, trying to spin around in the chair but too small to manage more than a couple of inches in each direction.

"Where is he, Isis? We need him now."

"The storm passes," she said.

"Do you even know what that is?" I asked, shaking my head.

"All storms pass, Gemina," she said. "Only the wind is left." She said this as though distracted with the chair still, but I believed her – whatever she meant.

"Will he ... make it back to me?"

"I don't know, silly!" she said. "I see now, not next." Then she turned again to her father. "Daddy! Meat?"

I felt a tear roll down my cheek and I wasn't sure why. Was it because she put my mind at ease that Flex was still alive? Or was it because I wasn't sure if she couldn't or wouldn't tell me my husband's fate?

Trina and Taylor sat against the Plexiglas wall of the lab cage and shared iPod headphones. I'd pre-approved all the music on it and made sure it had the bubblegum artists that the younger kids loved; Miley Cyrus, Taylor Swift and Rhianna. I fully intended to scrub that shit from Trina's little brain by the time she was twelve. Maybe sooner.

I could tell by the way Bunsen kept pacing back and forth that she needed to go outside. She got Slider worked up, and they both paced back and forth, stopping by the door every once in a while.

Nelson got to his feet and said, "Okay, if you're not delivering this baby, dudette, then I'm taking those dogs outside for a pee and a poop."

"In good time," said Charlie, plopping back into her special chair again. "Now would be a good time."

"A watched pot," said Hemp.

"Need backup?" asked Dave. "I'll go with you. I think it's time for a sweep anyway."

"Me, too," said Lola. "I need to get some knife practice."

"Fuck it," I said. "Serena, would you mind taking care of Flexy for a bit?"

Serena grunted to her feet. She had been sitting for hours and I could see her muscles were stiff. "God, the accommodations, while life-saving, suck," she said.

"It wasn't built for comfort, I'm afraid," said Hemp. "Functionality was its purpose."

"Got a leash?" asked Nelson.

"She's not going anywhere," I said. "Lead the way."

Nelson opened the door and Bunsen ran by him, tossing him aside like a lanky, rag doll. He yelled "Hey!" and followed her.

Two seconds later, before we had the chance to follow, he was scrambling back up the steps. "Bunsen!" he shouted. "Bunsen, get in here now!"

To yell was so unlike Nelson. I ran to the door and looked out.

Red-eyes stood in a line around the mobile lab. They were an arm's length apart, almost perfectly spaced. To a number, they stared at the lab. None turned their heads to watch us.

A low vibration began emitting from them.

"Bunsen!" I yelled, and she came running. She bounded up the two retractable steps and was back inside. She was not wet.

The rain had stopped, but another storm had gathered.

*****

About five miles outside of Buckfield I pulled the Toyota over. So far the electrical system, while far from perfect, wasn't disabling the vehicle. In fact, a couple of the electronics had kicked back in.

Unfortunately, one was the goddamned digital speedometer and I didn't happen to give a shit how fast I was going. Not too many speeding tickets being handed out these days, and speed traps were all but ancient history. Punch pulled up beside me and hand-cranked his window down, a smile on his face.

"I can't even tell you how much I enjoy rolling a window down again," said Punch. "Oh, yeah. Give me a smoke so I can flick my ashes out the wind wing."

"You must be thinkin' that I pulled over for a reason, right?" I threw him a smoke.

He reached down to the dash and looked back up at me. "Anyway, sorry. Just excited. Thanks for stopping to get it."

"We needed to get the gas cans and top the tank anyway," I said. "My pleasure. Now we need a plan to get through Buckfield. I doubt they'll just be hunkering down."

"On the bright side, they don't necessarily know we're comin' back this way," said Punch. "Nobody left alive to tell 'em."

"Maybe," I said. "But we need a good plan if you want to get this big, purple beauty past 'em." I reached out the window and patted his car.

"Yeah, it's not exactly camo, right?" he said.

331

"Nope. You're military. Any ideas?"

"Nothing conventional," he said. "But that cow catcher of yours has sparked a couple of ideas. It's strong, bolted right to the frame. I was checkin' it out at the garage."

"How many did you say there were in Buckfield?" I asked.

"We killed some," he said. "When they were chasin' us. After we took out the two at the barricade, maybe seven or eight left – maybe more, if anyone else joined them."

"What would they do," I asked, "when they found their guys? You know 'em. How would they respond?"

"They like retaliation, which is why they came after us."

"So no chance they'd just pack it in and lick their wounds?"

Punch shook his head. "Not likely. We're gonna be comin' across where we ran 'em off the road in about a mile. We can see how many bodies there are."

"Wouldn't they just come and get them?" I asked.

"You don't know these guys," said Punch. "Plus, they'd likely turn into fuckin' zombies before they found them."

"Good point," I said.

"Anyway, as long as Erik Krauss is still alive, he'll be on high alert for a day or two, come hell or high water. He's never let an attack go unanswered."

"We met Cara and her people a few miles before we got to you," I said. "Seem like good folks. Scared of Buckfield."

"I made myself useful by hunting and pulling guard duty," said Punch. "Nobody ever came by but you, but Krauss insisted on the barricades. I can tell you he was looking for women." Punch shook his head. "Anyway, they're scared of Krauss," he said. "And I can tell you he

332

wouldn't have put himself at risk by being in the group that came after us. He wasn't there, I can guarantee it."

I looked up at the sky. The wind was still blowing good, but nowhere near hurricane force. The rain was just big drops but widely spaced. "Looks like the storm's slidin' by," I said. "I'd almost prefer a full-blown hurricane for driving through there."

"Look," he said. "Fuck what I said. I know the layout of the town. We can just get to within a mile and pull the cars off the road and cover them or something. Then we hike in and take 'em out. Covert, nobody except them gets hurt."

I shook my head. "Too much time. I got a bad feelin' and I need to get home. What was your other idea?"

"You got a third-row seat in this thing?" he asked.

"Yeah."

"Removable?"

"Retractable and removable," I said.

Punch nodded. "Okay. It's a start. Got rope in that thing?"

"Does Flex Sheridan have a ten inch cock?" I asked.

"I have no idea," said Punch.

"Well, just assume I do, because we got rope."

"Well," said Punch, smiling, "I hope you have more than ten inches of it, because we're gonna need it."

*****

It took us about a half an hour to figure it out. It wasn't so much the plan, but how to execute it. It wasn't bad, but it wasn't great, either. Basically, we were turning the Land Cruiser into a makeshift tank, minus any of the proper armor.

We had pulled all the shit out of the truck, removed the rear seat, then put everything but the rope back inside. Punch and I carried the seat around to the front of the SUV and opened it. We placed it over the windshield with the seatback leaning over the cab.

Now just the narrow gap between the back and the seat provided the driver a clear view of the street. When we were satisfied in its positioning, we roped it in place.

Punch yanked on it hard. It stayed put. "Okay," he said. "Now for the floor mats. You got duct tape?"

I'm sure the look I threw him was sarcastic, because he looked at me and shook his head, saying, "Forget it, man. I'll just look."

I laughed. "Yeah, in the right side compartment in back. You won't even have to take anything out. What are the floor mats and duct tape for?"

"We tape them over the side windows. Back window's already blacked out. When you drive this thing through, you're gonna duck down as low as you can. If they shoot, they're gonna be aiming for your head. It's what I'd do."

"Sure you don't wanna drive?" I asked. "I recall you telling me once that you were pretty good, remember? On the bridge?"

"I have to drive the purple people eater, brother."

"I'm shittin' you, Punch."

When we were done, we both stood back to examine our handiwork. We'd taped the floor mats on the inside of the glass to keep the remaining storm winds – that did have some significant gusts – from blowing them off before we even got to whatever blockade they'd set up.

The Land Cruiser looked ridiculous and foolhardy, and like something you'd find on any street in Tijuana, Mexico. Only it'd be blowing black-blue smoke out the tailpipe.

"Ready?" asked Punch.

"No, but I need to get home, and I need this payload with me."

"Then we go," said Punch.

*****

Punch positioned the GTO right behind me. While he didn't want to fuck up his new ride, he was willing to use his horsepower to help me forward if the barriers were fortified. He hung his super shotgun out the window and he had the passenger side window down.

For my part, I was ready at a moment's notice to drop the Land Cruiser into low gear, 4-wheel drive for extra torque if necessary.

We drove. A mile later, we saw the crashed cars from our trip out, but there was only one body with them. I didn't know whether the others had reanimated or if the guy named Krauss had disposed of them.

There were a few zombies around. Single stragglers. Hemp had figured out that if no distinct scent drew them, they just tended to wander along. If blood and flesh was near, they'd naturally congregate.

Punch and I were on our last wafers. We weren't food for the moment and I hadn't seen a red-eye the whole way back.

I hoped there wasn't another reason for that, but I didn't dwell on it, either.

I got on my radio. "So, best approach. Wait until we see the whites of their eyes and punch it?"

"Sounds like a plan, Flex," he said. "But fuck waitin' to see their eyes. Just wait until you see a gun. Then you get on that AK. Extra mags, buddy. On the seat?"

"On the seat. You right behind me?" I couldn't see shit from the damned floor mats over my windows.

"Yep," he said. "Duck down. Can you see okay?"

I sank as low in the seat as I could. "It's like Hemphill Chatsworth himself designed it," I said.

"You stalling again?"

335

"You're getting to know me," I said. "Okay, let's go."
I hit the gas and we drove. I kept my eyes peeled, and I had
one hand on the AK's firing handle. The GPS button was no
longer necessary. The GPS satellites weren't functioning any
longer. I didn't know why, only that we couldn't get a signal
any more. The GPS screen was just a gun sight for now.

Then I remembered. Hemp had set the rear camera up
to operate when the car wasn't in reverse. I hit that button
and saw the purple GTO behind me.

I was within a quarter of a mile now, and I could see
the barriers were back up. I couldn't tell if there were more
than before or if they were heavier duty, but either way I was
going through them.

Four men appeared behind the barriers and I saw guns
in their hands.

I reached up and gave the AK-47 a sight adjustment,
aiming downward, and gave it a quick pull. Just so they knew
that I wasn't someone's fuckin' grandpa.

Then I hit the gas. I brought it up to thirty, then forty.
I was approaching the barrier and saw that they were the
same ones the guys had set up before. Through a gap, I saw
traffic cone orange, but taller.

They had supported the back with those huge water
drums. Fucking stupid, and fucking perfect. I was never
worried about the barriers.

I was now doing fifty miles per hour and their guns
began to blaze. Sitting low in the seat, I saw the GTO no less
than a foot off my rear bumper, keeping pace. I heard the
shotgun from behind me, and a moment later, the guns from
in front of me could be heard, only more of them.

Explosions rang out one after the other. I reached up
and yanked the AK's rope and sprayed from left to right.
Then I let go, quick-ejected the magazine and slammed
another in. I was now fifty yards from the barricade.

All four heads dropped when I fired, but now they reappeared. In my peripheral vision I saw the GTO swing off to the left and heard the explosion of his shotgun. How he held that sucker and fired straight ahead, I had no idea, but I hadn't been in Afghanistan, so it wasn't my field of expertise.

The guy on the far left had a sudden headless problem. I saw the blood fly away and he dropped from view.

I was reloaded and ready, and I was now just feet from the barrier. The men leapt out of the way as I barreled through, smashing into the thin plywood and tin, impacting the orange barrels, the water blasting into the air and being whipped into heavy drops and mist by the still high winds.

Glass showered my face as the windshield exploded in front of me, a round clearly making its way past our makeshift armor. I felt rather than saw the round tear through the seat just to the right side of my head, which would have penetrated my shoulder had I not been practically reclining in my seat. My face stung from the glass fragments, but I floored the accelerator and pressed forward.

I glanced at the rear camera and saw the purple GTO still on my tail, giving me inspiration. If these assholes hadn't already done so, they'd likely take all of their frustrations out on Cara and her clan, and that wasn't something I could live with.

I grabbed the radio from the seat beside me and pressed the button. "Punch, in five seconds, drop off my tail and spin your car around!"

He came right back. "I don't see any of 'em, Flex!"

"No, but they're there," I said. "I'll slide around to the right and you slide to the left. When we stop, open up with Tony's gun."

My side passenger window blew out then, followed by my driver's side window. I reached up and blindly spun the AK-47 around, emptying the magazine. The floor mat had a single bullet hole in its center, and as I shot a glance to my left, I saw where it had exited on my side.

I was perhaps fifty yards past where the barrier had been set up when I saw the GTO drop back. I immediately slammed on my brakes and cranked the wheel hard right, fishtailing the rear of the SUV in a clockwise direction.

I could no longer see the GTO, but the side of my car was now facing them, even though I could see nothing. I stayed low and reached up to eject the AK's mag and slam another one in. I had the magazine almost locked when I heard shots and felt a stinging pain in my left arm. I felt the warm blood immediately.

It had missed the bone, but the pain was intense. I completed the installation of the AK's magazine and turned it, sitting way down, only my right arm reaching up to pull the rope trigger, my eyes on the GPS screen gun sight.

A man emerged from my left and I swung the gun around. Before I could pull the trigger, I heard the boom of Punch's shotgun and while it was in black and white, I saw the man's chest explode as he flew backward off his feet.

More rounds peppered my truck, and I prayed they wouldn't penetrate the thin sheeting of its exterior and blow through my chest, neck or head.

I fanned the AK again and gave the trigger quick pulls until I saw the GTO in my screen. There was Punch's sawed-off shotgun barrel, out the window firing one shell after another.

I didn't know how many bad guys were left, but any remaining were probably more intent on taking out the driver of the more dangerous-looking vehicle – and that would definitely be me and the AK-47-equipped Land Cruiser.

"Flex, go!" shouted Punch. I didn't wait. I floored it and spun the wheel left, straightening back out on the road. I saw Punch behind me and breathed a sigh of relief.

Up ahead about a quarter of a mile, I saw something that didn't make sense. Another roadblock. But this one was crowded with people. The barrier itself appeared to run from several feet off the left side of the road to an equal distance off the right side. I recognized the dull, white lane dividers, typically used during construction. They were made of the heavy plastic and usually filled with sand or water. I didn't know which it was in this case, but with all the people in front of it, I sure as hell wasn't going to try to blow through it.

I grabbed the radio. "Punch, get ready to stop. Another barrier."

"Can you run it?" he asked.

"Not this time," I said. "Oh, by the way. I'm shot."

I stopped the truck and spun the roof-mounted gun around to get a view of all sides. No men with guns came into my sights.

I grabbed the Bushnells out of the glove box, wincing at the pain in my left arm as I leaned over. I opened the door and jumped out, my Daewoo K-7 in my hands, but giving me more trouble now that my left arm was trashed. I found I could hardly support the heavy barrel.

Punch ran up to me, holding his side, blood leaking from an apparent wound. "You ain't alone, brother," he said. "I caught one, too."

"Jesus, Punch," I said. "Serious?"

He shook his head and lifted his shirt. The entry wound was on his left side. He had torn off a piece of his shirt and stuffed it in the hole. He turned and I saw the exit wound. Only slightly larger, but fairly clean. He held out another piece of cloth.

"I couldn't manage this one in the car, man. You mind?"

I snatched the cloth from him and said, "Grit your teeth."

He did, and I quickly stuffed the cloth into the hole, leaving a strip hanging out like a human Molotov cocktail.

He nodded and lowered his shirt. "Thanks. You got it in the arm? You okay?"

"Better than you," I said. I pointed. "Got company."

I held the binoculars up and panned the crowd from side to side. Not humans. Fuckin' walkers. Like thirty of them.

"Zombies," I said. "They're not the real problem. It's the barriers."

"Got a plan?" he asked.

"Yeah. Get back in your car and let's go up there. We've got a trick that Krauss doesn't know about."

At the mention of his name, we heard a gunshot behind us. We turned to see four men running toward us. They were still a good distance away.

"Go!" I shouted, and Punch ran, holding his side. I hopped back inside the SUV and threw it in gear. I wasn't cutting the motor since the electrical problem. Couldn't chance it.

I punched it and the GTO fell in beside me this time. We ate up the quarter mile and instinctively pulled the vehicles sideways, giving ourselves plenty of room to crank them back onto the roadway without backing up.

The zombies came toward us, interested at the movement. I checked my watch. We had about two hours of WAT-5 left. I grabbed the radio again.

"Come on, Punch. Get out."

"But … man, they're everywhere."

"Not a problem for us," I said. "Just watch for females and take any you see out just to be sure. If the others start coming at you, *really* look for females, only the red-eyed variety. You know the drill."

He was out and beside my truck. We'd left our pursuers a bit back, but now two of the men had mounted motorcycles and the other one was running toward us.

"Quick, Punch! Into the middle!"

We pushed our way into the center of the crowd of rotters, the smell assaulting me instantly. I had gotten used to wearing long sleeves, even in warm weather, to avoid the long, black fingernails a lot of the rotters had – because while fingernails don't keep on growing after you die, the fingers shrivel beneath them, making it appear they do. Short story, they can scratch you good. Many of their nails had been pulled or rotted off, but it only takes one out of ten to scratch you.

We looked back and saw the men on the motorcycles had stopped and now had binoculars to their eyes. They propped their bikes, their feet on the ground. I guessed they were waiting for us to become a meal to their blockaded horde of abnormals.

Punch's mouth was fixed in a grimace as he fought the pain from his bullet wound. He eyed the creatures on all sides of him, but when they bumped him, they kept milling around.

He doubled over and lost his lunch. I walked over to him, pushing through the horrid-looking crowd.

"So this is what Woodstock must have been like, you think?" I said.

He looked up at me, then glanced at our pursuers, who weren't that anymore. Now they were gawkers. I could see all their mouths open, and none took any pot shots at us.

"Yeah," said Punch. "I'd have probably been puking there, too. I take it you've got another plan?"

"Come with me." We pushed our way slowly to the barriers and I reached down to pull on one of them. It didn't move much, but felt as though it shifted. I gave it a strong pull, and it slid toward me. Then I threw my hip against it like a hockey player checking a winger at center ice.

It moved a foot. The fucking things were empty. This was enough to stop the rotters, and create the illusion of an impassable barrier, but that was it. I looked at Punch.

"Let's blow through this, then," I said.

Suddenly an engine revved in the distance, and from the tall brush on the side of the road, a massive, sand-colored vehicle burst into view, its enormous front knobby tires bouncing onto the pavement and heading straight into the crowd of biters.

"Run!" shouted Punch, and I did. He was military, so he likely knew the capabilities of such a vehicle, whereas I didn't know shit from Shine-Ola aside from what I'd learned about automatic weapons.

The huge truck plowed over three or four zombies and pushed the others into the crowd. Before long, a pile of writhing, undead men, women and children were stuffed under the front of the vehicle, their bodies being torn apart by the truck as they twisted and scraped along the asphalt.

We were still separated from the killing machine by twenty or so zombies who had not yet been flattened.

"No doubt that's Krauss," said Punch, his breath coming in short puffs. "It's a transport vehicle, not combat, Flex. With the three guys back there and the ones we've taken out, there's no way he's got anyone else in there."

So if he couldn't fire at us, Krauss was using the truck to crush us. We stayed low, hiding behind all the upright rotters. "So what now?" I asked.

"He can't turn too sharp!" said Punch. "Duck and run back toward him! If I can get underneath it I know where it's vulnerable!"

"Underneath it?" I asked, but followed him anyway. There were still rotters between us and the three men, who were closer, but not within accurate range with their weapons. We pushed back toward the vehicle, which had now plowed over at least fifteen more walkers, but had clearly lost track of us.

"Can you do it?" I asked. "Punch, you've got a bullet wound, man!"

He didn't listen. He held his sawed-off and drew up alongside the heavy vehicle. The wheelbase was significant and now that Krauss was driving it through the pile of bodies, it was moving pretty slowly.

Like a thirteen-year-old girl gauging a skip rope held by two of her friends before leaping in for a round of Red Rover, he dove between the mammoth tires and rolled onto his back among the smashed zombie bodies.

I couldn't watch the rest because now the other three men were all firing at me.

I dropped to the ground and rolled, tattered feet hitting me in the head, along with feet sheathed in ragged, deteriorating tennis shoes and boots. I pushed myself into position on my stomach, raised my weapon and started unloading back toward the men.

I heard three shotgun blasts in rapid succession, and the truck exploded as it rolled over the last cluster of zombies it had crushed beneath its wheels.

The huge truck, now billowing smoke and flame, continued its trek forward, but stopped when it knocked down three more rotters who ended up as human wheel chocks. The engine sputtered as the fire consumed it.

I scrambled back to my feet, slung my weapon over my good shoulder and grabbed a rotter by each arm, keeping him between me and the other four men as I walked him sideways back toward the area behind the burning vehicle.

There was Punch, lying on his back, staring up at me.

The dead zombies with destroyed faces and features lay all around and beneath him. One or two were in the last throes of gnashing before the deadlight went completely out of their eyes. As individuals they were disgusting; lying in piles with their dead brothers and sisters, they were a downright horrifying sight.

"Do yourself a favor and don't turn your head," I said, holding out a hand to him. The head of the zombie whose arm I clutched onto exploded, splashing my face with his putrid death-blood. The round whistled just about five inches over my head.

I pushed the collapsing body away and dropped down, simultaneously locating and grabbing the pant leg of another zombie that I pulled toward me, forcing him between us and our attackers.

"You okay, man? Good fuckin' job on that truck!"

"I'm fine," he said. "And yeah, I knew the right spot where the fuel tank is exposed. The fire from the barrel ignited it more than the shell. Give me a hand. My stomach muscles are screaming."

"Gunshots'll do that shit," I said. I gave him a hand and pulled him up. Once he was in a sitting position, he was able to get to his feet.

A hatch on top of the truck that had tried to run us down opened, and a man scrambled out. The gunfire started again from our north and Punch and I crouched behind any zombie we could find and circled around the backside of the vehicle.

Rather, I did that. Punch walked brazenly toward the man who had fallen to the asphalt. He had thrown his weapon to the ground to free his hands while he exited the vehicle from the top, but before he was able to get to it, Punch reached him and kicked him in the face – hard.

I skirted to the left and started firing on the other men. At least one of my rounds connected; a true, red mist of blood sprayed into the air behind his head and he went down, flipping backward off his motorcycle.

The man without a motorcycle ran into the forest that bordered the roadway, and the other guy fired up his bike and rode fast in the opposite direction.

"Clear, Punch!" I shouted.

Punch drew his leg back and kicked the man in the face again. Then he moved forward and planted his boot a third time.

"Krauss, you piece of shit," he said. "There won't be an inspirational speech this time."

"You fucked us, you prick," the man gurgled through his blood-filled mouth. His hair was spiked gray, and he stared up at Punch with steel blue eyes, filled with hatred.

"Well, here's your final fucking," said Punch. He put the shotgun in the man's mouth and fired. The blood hit the pavement like a well-aimed paintball splattering its intended target. Afterward, Punch turned toward me. His eyes revealed no regret or sadness.

The rotters, apparently feeling the vibration from the explosion, turned toward Krauss's body. They instantly crowded around and fell upon the man's corpse, ripping into him with the intensity of wild animals. In seconds the bullet wound to his head became an access panel to his brain, and the rest had his abdomen opened in mere seconds, pulling out intestines and other innards, stuffing their horrid mouths with the entrails. I turned away. I'd seen far too much of it already.

We stepped back. Punch watched the feeding frenzy for a moment, then looked at me. "Sorry, Flex. No redemption for a son-of-a-bitch like that."

"No need to apologize," I said. "People who use a catastrophe like this to gain power can't change. Now get back in that purple beast. I need to get home."

"Roger that," he said. We glanced once more up the street, but the other men apparently weren't very inspired now that their leader was zombie food.

We got back in our vehicles and cranked them around. There was still room on one side of the disabled, burning military transport, but the pile of bodies in front of it made that path impassable. I used the cow catcher to strategically nudge the piles of bodies to either side until we could work our way to the barrier.

The blockade was easily pushed aside. When we got back to the bridge, we stopped and waited for Cara's group to find us. I wanted to give her the antitoxin before heading back home.

I didn't want to come back to Buckfield – or anywhere near it.

*****

Chapter Fifteen

The low hum was intense, like an enormous, deep-toned tuning fork. It was interrupting my thoughts and convincing me that if it did not cease soon, I would literally go insane. I worried for Flexy and checked repeatedly to be sure the soft foam ear plugs – torn in thirds to fit into his tiny ears – were in snugly.

I couldn't wear the plugs for fear of missing something crucially important. The sound emitting from the red-eyes was grating and purposeful; it rooted its way deep into my brain and the drone absorbed through my very skin and rattled the bones within.

Charlie was so annoyed, she even asked that Lola turn up a Billy Joel CD almost to full blast just to try to escape it. It didn't help.

Serena stood and went to look out the window. "The window's loose in its frame," she said. "Wasn't like that half an hour ago."

"Why?" asked Rachel, walking over to where Serena stood. She moved it, and I could see it shifting from the other side of the lab.

Hemp spoke. "We encountered this in Concord. If you'll recall, the same thing happened at Three Sisters Bar. The red-eyes were essentially dissolving the mortar through some sort of coordinated vibration."

"Shit," said Dave. "Not good."

"They're trying again," Hemp said. "Only this is a bit different. Essentially, there's a gel coated, fiberglass exterior shell on this lab, and the plastic sheathing that you see on the inside. Unfortunately, all they have to disintegrate is the foam between the two, and it significantly weakens the structural integrity, making us vulnerable."

"Didn't you tell us they started to use the same trick when you had them trapped inside the Concord State House basement?" asked Dave.

"Exactly," said Hemp. "And they are likely the same group that went from there to Three Sisters. It appears to be an instinctive ability."

"How many goddamned tricks do these bitches have?" I asked.

"Do you feel something?" Rachel asked.

"What?" asked Charlie. We all looked around.

"I do," said Serena. "It feels like the trailer's moving," she said.

"*Moving*, moving, or just being knocked around by the wind?" asked Lola.

Nelson got up and went to the window. Bug followed. "Bummer," said Nelson, continuing to stare through the glass. "They're taking advantage of the improving weather."

"Must be a couple hundred out there," said Bug.

Hemp moved to the door and pulled back the curtain there to peer through. He looked for a moment in silence and said, "I can't even see the red-eyes. I think they're hiding behind the others, putting only the males at risk."

"Typical chicks," said Dave. Serena smacked him on the arm.

"I agree with Bug," said Hemp. "There are at least two hundred out there now. We can't open the door at all at this point. If we do, and they gain a handhold, we could quickly be overrun."

"Guys," said Bug. "There's gotta be a way for us to get the hell away from 'em. If we put our heads together, we can think of something. I can assure you we never thought we'd get out of my place in California, either. What are our options, Hemp?"

"As I recall, you had WAT-5 in California, too," said Hemp. "Unfortunately, we don't have that advantage."

"*Give the baby,*" said Charlie.

I jerked my head around to look at her. She sat up in her birthing chair, her expression one of horror. The color had drained from her face, and when our eyes met, she broke down into tears.

I went to her and put my arms around her, holding her tight. "Charlie, don't worry. Was that them?"

I felt her nod, because I wasn't ready to let her go yet.

"Did you feel the urge to do anything?"

Hemp rushed to her other side. In the midst of her tears, she had another contraction that lasted about a minute. We waited for her to get past it.

"No," said Charlie. "I didn't want to do anything. I just felt like this … this buzzing in my head. Not like words or anything. But the next thing I knew, the words were coming out of my mouth."

"Which baby do they want?" I asked. "Can you tell whether it's Isis or yours?"

Charlie shook her head. Hemp squeezed her hand. "Sweetheart," he said. "We're going to keep a close eye on you. Please stay in this chair for now, okay? If you get up, we're going to have to put you back in it and restrain you. You understand, right?"

Charlie looked at Hemp, who had tears in his eyes. Relationships were hard enough without having to tie down those you love and hope they understood the reasons for it.

"Hemp, it's not like this is the first time we've played with restraints," she said.

I wonder even now what the zombies and red-eyes thought of the laughter that came from the inside of what should have been to their minds, a doomed vehicle filled with doomed souls.

But laugh we did. If her son would've been born at that moment, I'm pretty sure he'd have been born laughing.

"I've got an idea," said Rachel, after our laughter subsided.

She looked up. Above her head was a crank-open ceiling vent that was around 14" x 14". "I can fit through there."

Hemp looked at her and back at the vent. "Rachel, you're small, but that vent is just over a foot square."

"I won't be able to do it with any clothes on," she said.

"Woah, Rach," said Nelson. "You can't go outside naked, babe."

"It's not like we've got neighbors to worry about," I said. "It's what she does once she gets out that's the question. Rachel, have you got a plan?"

She looked around. "I'm open to suggestion."

Remembering what they did in California, and knowing what inspired the red-eyes to move their horde our way, I said what nobody else dared say.

"Isis will fit through that hole, too."

"No fuckin' way," said Bug. "She's been through enough." I could tell by his expression that he was dead serious.

"Bug," I said, "we'd have to have a good plan before anything like that happens. Like the one you had in California."

"That was a crazy plan that happened to work. Even then my baby girl almost got eaten by one of them red-eyed bitches. I'm afraid I'm gonna have to say no way, José this time."

I didn't blame him, but it didn't leave me with any other ideas. "Anybody else?" I said. "Ideas?"

"Oh, God,' said Charlie, and this time she doubled over good. Scofield went to her and said, "No time like the present," he said. "I've been timing your contractions, and if you're not there now, you're damned close."

He moved between her legs again and positioned the sheet to protect her modesty. After snapping on another pair of gloves, he reached in, moved his hand around a bit, and withdrew it again, nodding.

"You're at ten centimeters, my dear Charlie," he said. "I can confidently predict you'll be a mama soon."

The sounds from outside the mobile lab increased. I ran to the window behind the stainless steel counter and drew back the curtains and lifted the blackout shade.

My car was visible, but just barely. The male rotters stood on top of the hood and trunk. They hadn't made it to the very top of the car where the AK-47 was mounted, but every small gap between the car and the mobile lab was jammed with rotters.

I raised my eyes. Red spots stared at me from beyond the Crown Victoria. They were side-by-side, about an arm's length apart. Between them and us were dozens and dozens of the dumber male variety, as well as young children and old men and women, but they pushed into one another as they pushed toward the mobile lab.

It was like watching a slow motion, human stampede that had hit a wall. Like mindless animatrons with no freewill of their own, and no reverse switch when the path forward became impassable.

The vibration had not stopped since it began, and I reached up to push gently on the wall around the window.

No resistance. My fingers pushed through until I could feel the interior paneling touch the exterior sheathing. All of the foam insulation that had once provided the center layer was gone, disintegrated.

I turned around. "Charlie, hurry the fuck up and deliver that baby. I need you recovering already. Guys, we need to take action now. Sitting here is stupid. Rachel, if you have even half a plan, I suggest we get started."

She nodded. "Get me through there, then," she said. "Urushiol-soaked bullets, blow darts, whatever. You guys just be thinking of something I can hit them with and I will."

*****

We stopped the two vehicles before the bridge, but nobody came out to greet us as they had when Tony Mallette and I were on our way north. It had been pretty instantaneous on our way out, and Cara and her clan would surely recognize us. After all, there weren't a ton of Land Cruisers with top-mount AK-47s.

I heard Punch's voice through the handheld radio on my seat. "Wanna get out and have a look?" he asked.

I picked up the radio. "Yeah," I said. "I know where their main group was hanging out last time."

I checked my watch. It was just after six o'clock, and the sun was waning. I needed to get home, but we were here now, and it wouldn't take too long to drop the stuff to Cara.

We exited our vehicles and locked them both. I wasn't positive the other survivors from Buckfield wouldn't make their way down.

"Hold on a sec," I said. I went to the back door of the Toyota and unlocked it again. I tore the floor mat off the side window and threw it in. Then I reached for the bag of meds and dug around inside it until I found what I was looking for; the Diphtheria antitoxin.

I took four containers of it and stuffed them into my pocket. I closed the door and re-locked the SUV.

"Let's go," I said.

From the bushes to my left, a staggering rotter burst toward me and I stumbled away from him, swinging my Daewoo toward it and firing a single shot into its forehead.

It toppled backward. The clothes looked familiar, though his face was vastly inhuman. I analyzed his corpse for a moment.

"He's from Cara's group," I said.

"Don't know 'em by sight," said Punch. "I made excuses to sit it out when Krauss sent guys down to fuck with 'em."

I looked at him. "I'm still not sure why you stayed," I said. "Seems to me a guy like you could've outsmarted a bunch of pricks like them."

"Krauss wasn't as dumb as you think. Like I think I told you, he suspected me from the start. He took leaving as an insult – which to him, was punishable by death. Or undeath."

I shook my head. "I'd rather die than live like that."

"I made my move when the time was right Flex," he said, rubbing his hand over his short-cropped red hair. "Please don't mistrust me. I'll prove myself if that's what it takes. Been lookin' for a good group to settle in with, and so far, I like what I see."

I nodded. We looked down at the ground for the path and continued our progress along a flattened area of grass. It was so tall and overgrown everywhere, that if any group passed through an area frequently, the mashed down foliage was all that was needed to find one's way.

We stayed on the path for a good ten minutes. Ahead, we saw some clothing hanging from some trees, a couple of tents and a few camping tables with lanterns on them.

Punch threw his arm against my chest. "Hold up, Flex."

He bent down and began moving some leaves away, revealing a tripwire, like the one Hemp had used with his snares.

"Good defenses against the zombies, but not bad against Buckfield guys, either," said Punch. "Over this way." He moved about three feet away and I moved with him, making sure to stay in his path. He looked around, then poked at the tripwire with the stick.

I heard something spring in the distance, and a large, cut branch hanging from a rope high above our heads pivoted down, a 10" railroad spike protruding from the end. It swung back and forth and finally fell still.

We both stood. The metal spike had been sharpened to a fine point. It would have penetrated at a height of around 5'7". That would get the average person in the head, though it might miss the brain of a taller person.

"Good," said Punch. "They're careful. Now if we can get through without another one of these to the head."

"I don't like this," I said. "I don't hear anything, and – "

"Flex, look," said Punch, interrupting. He pointed ahead. I could see a body, partially obstructed by low branches. I say it was a body even though it was standing. It hung limp.

We walked toward it, sure to step over any ground abnormalities. Before we reached the person, I said, "Oh, God."

"Who is this?" asked Punch.

The woman with the spike through the top of her skull was not human at the time of her death. This particular trap was designed to come down at an angle, but utilized the same railroad spike technology, if it could be called that.

The branch had pivoted downward, the long, sharpened spike entering at the girl's ear and coming out of the right side of the base of her neck. The blood that had run from the exit wound was black and crusted.

It was Cara. In the center of her chest, a swarm of flies had lighted, milling around what I could see was a wound likely made by a shotgun. She had apparently reanimated shortly after being mortally wounded, and had walked into her own trap.

A sound came from our right. Punch swung his shotgun around and fired in one motion. The creature flew off its feet and sank into the bed of leaves. We walked over to have a look.

"That's Cara in the trap," I said, nodding my head toward her. "This is her brother. Can't figure out why Krausse's guys did it this way."

It made no sense to me that the Buckfield people would leave them in this condition, only to possibly threaten them in the future.

Punch said what I was thinking. "Krauss looked at this like punishment. Eternal punishment. He was more frightened of living people than he was of the goddamned zombies."

"So he never went for head shots?" I asked.

Punch didn't answer. Instead, he turned and started inspecting the campsite. "Here," he said.

I walked beside him. Five bodies lay together, all riddled with gunshot wounds. Head shots, too. These people would not be coming back.

"If showing mercy is killing you good and dead, he did it here," said Punch. He pointed. More leaves had blown on top of the corpses since their deaths, but the scene before us was as gruesome as it was horrifying in its complete devastation of a family.

Cara's two sisters lay on their backs, their faces staring blankly toward the treetops. Their eyes remained open and their mouths, as if in the middle of a silent scream, hung open as well.

Their gray skin was showing early signs of decomposition, but it was not riddled with the streaking veins of the abnormals.

Holes peppered their blouses, tinged with black, bloody stains. The younger of the two girls had lost her eye in the battle – a telltale pistol just out of the reach of her fingertips, half-buried in the leaves. I bent down to pick up the revolver and opened the cylinder. I dumped the rounds into my hand and found them all to be expended.

On the ground beside her was a box of ammo, spilled out among the pine needles and leaves, along with the urushiol bottle we'd given her, smashed on the ground, the top popped off and the bottle empty. She likely never had the chance to use the spray because her attackers weren't susceptible to its properties, what with being human and alive and all.

Cara, at least, appeared to have been ready to reload when all of their lives came to an abrupt end. I could see only this gun. A knife lay atop one of the men, but it was a useless weapon against Krauss and his marauders.

The girls and their brothers had fought until they had nothing left with which to defend themselves. Either way, Cara Blake was dead now and the remainder of her family had suffered brutal, and more immediately permanent deaths.

Then I remembered something. "Hold on Punch. We gotta go, but there's something we need to do first."

"Sure," he said. "You alright, man?"

I shook my head. I realized I was crying as I walked back to where Cara stood, the spike splitting her skull. I looked down at her stomach. Not sure why I hadn't noticed it before.

The baby within the pregnant woman churned and roiled beneath the thin material of her maternity top.

I was no doctor, and I didn't even play one on TV. I could no more deliver a baby with a Cesarean than I could beat Gem in a game of Battleship.

"How long you figure they've been dead?" I asked Punch.

Punch went to one of Cara's brothers and rolled him over. He cut his shirt and looked at his back. A second later, he came back to where I stood before the hanging Cara Blake.

"About a day, I'd guess," he said. "Just a rough estimate, though."

"So right after we blew the barricade they probably came over here and just fuckin' attacked them."

"Yeah, sounds like Krauss. Why?"

"So the baby inside this girl's stomach can't be alive," I said. "Right?"

"It's a pretty good bet," said Punch. "She was pregnant, huh? I didn't even look at her belly, I was so focused on the rest."

"Dead a day or not, I'm compelled to check to make sure," I said. "I'm guessin' the baby would've died the moment Cara did."

"Trust me," said Punch. "Whatever's in there, it's dead. Now put a final end to it and let's get our asses back to your place."

Punch was right and I knew it. I was fighting the guilt for the fact that her entire family was dead. Had we not blown Krauss's barricade and killed his men, it likely wouldn't have been the case.

But the big son-of-a-bitch had shot Tony, so I'd have never chanced a second of my time with the man in charge of men like the ones who had manned the barricade.

I stood back and raised my Daewoo. I fired for a good three seconds into Cara's stomach. Her body danced from the spike as the bullets ripped through her, and black-red blood leaked from her stomach wounds.

Eric A. Shelman

The baby within her womb fell still.

A sound came from our right and we both swung our weapons toward it.

I looked at Punch. "That sound like a radio to you?"

"It did," he said, walking toward the sound. I followed.

Beneath a branch, we found a low, one-man tent. It was the type shaped like an A that stood less than three feet from the ground, and it had been hidden pretty well. Wires streamed from a hole in the top of the tent, and we followed them to see them snake up the tree.

"Wonder what this is about?" I said, picking up the wire.

I lifted the front flap and looked inside. There was a Ham radio setup on a low, plastic table. Beside it were two of the two-way radios that Punch and I carried. Both of their short-distance aerials were connected to the wires leading in from outside.

I ducked into the tent and pulled my radio off my belt. I switched the channel to 16 and pressed my button.

"Test," I said.

My voice came out of the other radio. I turned to Punch. "Charged and working."

"Should have good range, too," said Punch. "Looks like they're wired up to that antenna over there," said Punch, standing upright again.

I got out of the tent. He pointed. "There, see?"

About ten feet away, an old TV aerial stood around twelve to fifteen feet tall. It was in a clearing and guy wires anchored it to the ground. They had dangled leafy branches from it, most of which were now on the ground at its base, but some remained hung from the aerial rods.

It had apparently been installed very securely to withstand even the hurricane force winds that George brought with him.

"They must've been here a while," I said. "I assume these other wires lead to solar panels or something?"

Punched looked up. "Don't see 'em, but the wires run high enough in that tree to make sense," said Punch. "Want to see if you can get your family on the Ham?"

"I may not need it with that antenna," I said. "Hemp did something similar at my old place, and we could talk on it for miles."

"Go for it," said Punch.

I slid back into the tent and picked up the small, two-way handheld. Even with the solar juice available, it was my best shot if they had lost generator power back home.

*****

My baby boy struggled to breathe. It was darkening outside, and soon would be night. With the heavy cloud cover, the moon would be nonexistent and the black would be pure.

I now had to keep the oxygen on Flexy all the time, just to force the air into his lungs. Hemp came to me.

"How's the little guy doing?" he asked.

I looked at him. "He's struggling, Hemp," I said. "I don't want to … to cut him, Hemp. Isn't there another way?"

"I need to check his throat again," he said. "Doc, come here, please?"

"Yeah, Hemp," said Scofield. "What can I do?"

"Well, you could deliver that baby right now, but barring that, I need you to shine that flashlight here."

Scofield pulled out the flashlight and I removed the oxygen bottle from Flexy's nose and mouth. Hemp ran his finger down my infant son's lower lip and he opened his mouth wide in a yawn, attempting to pull in air that he could not get.

We all saw why instantly. The black, fibrous area in his throat had grown, now extending so far down we couldn't see where it ended.

"Oh, my God," I whispered, even though I wanted to scream it.

"Is he still struggling when you give him the oxygen?" asked Scofield.

"No," I said. "He seems okay. As long as the pressure's there."

"Then we have a bit more time before any drastic measures," said Hemp. "Doc, do you agree?"

"From what I know about it, when the time's here, it'll be pretty clear," he said. "But Gem, we can't hold off too long. The procedure takes a few moments, too, so he can't already be in trouble when we start."

While all of this was going on, sapping me of more of my resolve and inner strength, the vibration from the red-eyes had grown so intense it no longer just assaulted our ears. It rattled our goddamned teeth and our brains, not to mention that it felt like I was using a pocket rocket vibrator all over my body.

"I can't fucking take this anymore!" shouted Charlie. "I didn't want to have my baby this way!"

We had intentionally kept from Charlie the seriousness of Flexy's condition. And with the noise from the vibration, sound didn't travel very far within the mobile lab, so she could stay blissfully unaware.

Hemp squeezed her hand. "Charlie, there's nothing we can do about it. You need to remain calm."

"Dude, I got my weed," said Nelson. "I know it's not like an epidermal or anything, but it'll help."

"Epidural," said Hemp. "And yes, I believe it will."

"Will it hurt the baby?" asked Charlie.

"Not in the slightest," said Hemp. "One or two tokes should take the edge off and relax you. I'm sorry I don't have more drugs in here. I keep them in a cooler inside, and there was no time to fetch them."

"Ha ha," said Nelson. "Tokes. Reminds me of the Steve Miller Band. Anyway, you sure you don't mind? I could use a hit, too."

"Get over here, Nel," said Charlie. "Like yesterday."

I wanted to join them because I was about to lose my shit, too. I didn't. Charlie had an excuse and Nelson functioned like a well-oiled machine on weed, but I'd just be stoned and useless. And likely more paranoid.

In five minutes, Charlie actually turned toward me and smiled. "How are the walls holding up?" she asked.

"Yeah, like you care," I said, jealous. "I'm almost afraid to check."

"It's starting to get dark," said Rachel. "If you're going to let me go up there, I need to do it before the walls are so weak they won't support my weight."

"It's a good point," said Hemp. "But you still haven't presented us with a plan for when you get up there."

"Dude, I can help her," said Nelson. "She's my chick anyway, so I should go with her, and if you haven't noticed, I'm pretty skinny. I'm pretty sure I got through some smaller holes that than one in my time."

"Nelson," said Rachel. "There's no reason to go."

"As much as there is for you to go," he said.

"I ... Hemp's right," she said. "I don't even have a plan. I only knew I could get out."

"Let's make a plan, then," he said. "Hemp. You're the professor. What all kills them? Gunshots to the brain, urushiol for the dumb ones, and what for the smart ones?"

"Gunshots still work," said Hemp. "But they're sharp and they hide behind the others."

"Not if we take the others down," said Rachel. "We take out all the regular rotters and we can shoot the red-eyes."

A voice came over the radio on the counter. "Gem? Hemp? Do you read?"

It was Flex. My heart stopped and I ran to the counter and grabbed the radio. I mashed my thumb on the button and said, "Flex? Baby, is that you?"

I knew it was, but I wanted him to acknowledge it. I needed to hear him say my name again, and I needed to know he was almost here.

"Gem!" he said, relief in his voice. "Gem, how is everyone? How'd you make it through the storm?"

"Flex, it's not good," I said. "The house … it's gone. Destroyed. Rogue tornado tore it to shit and we got caught in the basement for a while."

"Where are you now, Gem? Is everyone safe? Is Flexy okay?"

"We're in the mobile lab, but it's disintegrating. Flex, he's showing some advanced symptoms. Where are you? Please tell me you're close. You're on this radio, so you have to be close, right?" I could hear the desperation in my own voice.

The door shifted in its frame, and the wall suddenly began flexing inward and outward, as though it were a cardboard house with no roof.

"Jesus Christ, Flex," I said. Then: "Someone get that door! Hold on to the door!"

Dave and Serena were already there. Dave held the handle, and Serena pushed on the wall next to it to prevent it from flopping inward, its sandwiched foam center likely dissolved to dust.

"What the hell is goin' on there, Gem?" asked Flex, his voice rising.

"We're trapped, Flex. Charlie is having her baby, the red-eyes are outside vibrating our walls into nothing, and we're trapped in here. All of us. Can you get here? Can you do anything?"

"Give the radio to Hemp," he said. "I got some stuff he told me to get. The estrogen blocker. I just need to know how to use it."

"I love you, babe," I said. "How far away are you?"

"I can be there in half an hour if I drive like a motherfucker."

"Then you need to drive like a motherfucker, babe," I said. "Our situation is deteriorating like this goddamned lab."

"Babe, put Hemp on, please. Hurry."

I gave the radio to Hemp.

"Yes, Flex," he said. "Did you get the estrogen blockers I asked you for?"

"I did, buddy. That's why I'm still on this radio and not already on my way. What do you want me to do with it?"

"We need a delivery system," said Hemp. "Something that can disperse in a wide pattern, but penetrate deep into the skin when it hits."

"Got any ideas?" asked Flex.

"Blow darts keep coming to mind, but it's not like it's a practical solution," said Hemp. "Whatever you come up with Flex, it needs to completely coat the needle or whatever is used. I only tested the estrogen blocker once, but it worked like a charm."

"How much did you use?"

"A lot. Probably more than I needed, but it ate her away like acid."

"What exactly is the situation there with the red-eyes, Hemp? Gem said the lab's disintegrating. They doin' that vibration crap?"

I could hear that Flex had so many questions he could barely spit them out. Hemp took them in order.

"As far as we can tell, if there was a red-eye within a hundred miles, she's here. To your second question, yes."

"How's that working on a Gel coat motor home?"

363

"Flex, I don't know. The foam insulation between the interior and exterior walls must have dissolved into particles."

The wall beside Hemp bent inward with the weight of the zombies outside. He leaned back against it and eyed me nervously. Then he said, "Everybody get up and go stand against the walls, front to back. Jim, you stay with Charlie."

"Jesus, Hemp. Fuck it," said Flex. "I'll be in range with the other radio within twenty minutes. I'll tell you what we've come up with then."

"Gem!" shouted Lola, who had been holding Flexy and keeping the oxygen flowing into him. "Flexy's in trouble, Gem. He can't breathe." Her eyes were filled with fear.

I ran to her.

Jim and Hemp were there in a flash. "His color's not good," Scofield said. "Gem, we can't wait anymore."

"No, Jim," I pleaded. "Are you sure?" But I looked at my son's face, and it was turning blue.

"We gotta do it now, Gem," said Scofield. "Hemp, I'll need your help."

"Everybody stay against the walls!" shouted Hemp. "And make sure your weapons are loaded and at hand!"

From behind us, Charlie screamed. "Oh my God!"

She had her eyes squeezed closed and her mouth in a grimace. She threw her head back and I could see her pushing.

Charlie was giving birth at the entirely wrong moment.

*****

Chapter Sixteen

I dropped the radio and charged out of the tent, almost barreling into Punch, who stood just outside.

"Flex, I heard what your friend said. I might have an answer."

"Tell me while we run, man."

We took off down the path, eating up real estate with each leg extension and footfall. The vibration of our feet pounding the trail must have drawn rotters, for several of them emerged from the thick growth of trees on either side of the path.

A quick shot from my Glock took some out, missed others. Punch used his multi-round shotgun on a few, blasting them back to hell.

I didn't have time to make sure any of them were dead. I ran full out, with Punch right beside me.

I hit something with my toe and flew face first into the wet dirt and leaves with a thud. It knocked the wind out of me, and as I rolled onto my back to catch my breath, I saw a branch swing down, its sharpened spike biting only air.

My momentum had saved me, and Punch must have cleared the trap. The tripwire had been all but invisible. Punch held a hand out to me, and I grunted back to my feet. After bending down to take two of the first deep breaths I could muster since my tumble, we ran again, this time keeping our eyes aimed at the ground.

"Tell me about your idea, man," I wheezed.

"I have four boxes of Flechette Shells," said Punch. "Total of 20 rounds. They used them during the Vietnam war to draw snipers out of trees. Called 'em beehives, among other things."

"What's different about 'em?" I asked. The vehicles were in view now, and I ran faster.

Punch kept up. "Flechettes are like little spears, but small. These rounds have like 20 or so inside. You want penetration, you got it. They even have little fins on the tail to make 'em fly true, at about 2000 feet per second."

We reached the car, and since we still had to hash this shit out anyway, I caught my breath while Punch ran through the details.

"Okay," I said when he was finished. "So that fits the bill. Now I gotta figure out how to impregnate 'em with the estrogen blocker."

"We can't get the gunpowder wet, Flex," said Punch. "But the flechettes are well above it, so if we were to dip them somehow, or inject the stuff into the end of the shell, that ought to do it."

"We got syringes," I said. "The ones from the pharmacy and more that Perry threw in the bag."

"Okay, okay," said Punch. "So we maybe pop the needles off to make a bigger hole, and inject the stuff right into the shells."

I unlocked the SUV and opened the rear door to get to the bag of medications. After digging around in the bag for what felt like ten minutes, I finally dumped it inside the Toyota and sorted through the bottles.

"Got 'em," I said. I popped the cap on one and tapped it into my hand. "Fuck!" I said.

"Capsules," said Punch. "We need to mix it with something. Something thick, like a gel."

"We'll need to crush them, though," I said. "These are like time-release beads or something."

"Anything will work. You got tools in here. Got a scraper or anything like a putty knife?"

I looked around and found a flat file, about an inch wide and ten inches long. Punch grabbed it. "This'll work. We'll just crush it like a junkie breaking up meth rock."

We both jumped as lightning struck somewhere to the south of us, followed by a crack of thunder, almost right on top of it. The storm had appeared to pass, but now, as we looked up, more ominous clouds were rolling in.

"Hurricane Georgie ain't exhausted yet," I said. "Okay, ideas. You said we need something like a gel."

"Yeah, something that will coat the flechettes," said Punch.

It hit me. "Fuckin-A," I said, and ran around to the passenger side door. I opened it, reached inside and popped the glove box open. I pushed the Bushnells aside and pulled out a bottle of Aloe Vera after sun gel.

I held it up. "Punch, this'll work, right?"

"Hell yes, it will. Get the syringes, man."

He reached into his cargo pants pocket and pulled out four five-round boxes of flechette .12 gauge shells, and dumped each box in the back of the truck. "Things are illegal in a bunch of states," he said.

Punch flipped the carpet away to reveal a hard, plastic surface, and I started breaking open the capsules and dumping them in a pile. Punch used the flat file to crush them into a fine powder. One side of the file was smoother than the other and didn't take too much of the powder into its grooves.

Another bolt of lightning hit a tree that could have been no more than a thousand feet away. As we watched, it caught fire and half of the tall pine split away, crashing to the ground. The strike and explosion had been simultaneous, telling us we needed to get our asses under cover and moving.

"Let me know when to add the gel, man," I said. "I only hope this shit doesn't neutralize the chemical properties of the blocker."

"It's our best shot," said Punch. "Go ahead and put it in."

I squirted the gel on top of the now fine powder, and Punch found a small, straight stick on the ground to mix it together. The medication did dissolve into the gel, and soon it looked like it would be enough. I'd gone through two of the bottles containing thirty pills each.

"Let's get injecting," he said. "But not too much. Just enough to coat the projectiles."

"Can you open them and re-close them?"

"Of course I can," said Punch. "I had lots of time on my hands when I wasn't fighting for my life."

I could feel my wife and son's lives slipping away as we prepared to save them.

It was a horrible fear that I never want to experience again.

*****

"You're crowning," said Scofield. "Jesus, girl, you're timing is impeccable. Can you do me a favor, Charlie, and not push? Just try to breathe deeply and don't push for now, okay? Just until we take care of Flexy?"

"I'll try," she breathed, and it was followed by a whimper as she tried to control her muscles.

Trina and Taylor were terrified now. Their mostly organized world had deteriorated, and they weren't handling it very well. I thought of what I could do to occupy them.

"Girls, go to Charlie and I want each of you to take her by the hand and help her stay calm, okay?" I said. "Can you do that for me?"

Charlie held out both of her hands and the girls went to her, their tears still coming, but now there was something to keep them occupied. Something important.

"I've never done this," said Hemp. "Doc, you'll need to talk me through it."

"I can do it," said Doc Scofield, eyeing Charlie. "You stay with your girl there, and I can do it. Gem, would you prefer to look somewhere else?"

I was holding my son in my arms, pressing the oxygen tight against his face. His color was worsening, but his eyes were still open and bright. He would be crying at that moment, I knew, but he couldn't get enough air in his lungs to do it.

"I'm not going anywhere," I said. "I'll sit in the captain's chair and hold him. Will that work?"

"Sure, I just need him still," said Scofield.

I went to the captain's chair and began spinning it around, but movement outside the windshield caught my eye.

Red pinpoints danced as though floating through the air. The sun had sunken to dusk and they were clearly visible in the distance.

I held my son more tightly as I finished turning the chair and prayed to myself.

"Hemp, where are your scalpels?" asked Doc Scofield, snapping on a clean pair of nitrile gloves.

"Second drawer from the left," said Hemp, even as he ran to open it himself. He pulled out a small, plastic tray encased in a baggie and unzipped it, sliding it out. He held it out to Scofield, who took the scalpel from the tray.

Hemp said, "It's already sterilized and ready for use."

Jim came back to where I sat with my son and knelt down. "Tilt his head back, can you?" he asked.

I did. Flexy didn't even fight me. I could feel how weak he was.

Hemp checked Charlie again, then went to the cupboard, which was now leaning sharply forward because the wall to which it was attached had lost its rigidity. He pulled out four towels and tried to close the door three times before abandoning the effort. The remaining towels fell out onto the floor.

He spread one towel out on Flexy's chest and the others he stacked on my leg, ready for Scofield should he need them.

The doctor felt my son's neck right in the center, where a man's Adam's apple would be. Then he ran his finger down another half inch. "This should be the sweet spot," he said.

"Should be?"

"It's an expression, Gem," he said. "I actually showed up for med school the day they taught us this."

"Ha ha," I said. "I'm freaked out enough."

The pounding outside grew more intense. The walls flexed in and out, and I started to smell something on fire outside. I guess the doctor could tell I was on the edge of losing it.

He patted my shoulder and said, "Gem, I'm going to make a horizontal incision right here, about a half an inch wide and approximately a half inch deep – just enough to enter the airway. Then I'll insert the pen and we'll tape it all up securely. Can you handle it?"

"You can handle it," said Charlie. "Right everyone? She can handle it. If I can sit here with a half-birthed baby inside me, Gem can handle her little boy getting a tracheotomy."

I looked up at Charlie. "I didn't know you realized this was going on," I said.

"Jesus, Gem," said Charlie, looking exhausted, but smiling. "I'm fucking stoned, not stupid. We're in a box the size of a school bus. He'll be okay, sweetie. Isis practically said so."

I laughed, despite my terror. Charlie had a way of doing that to me. "Got it," I said.

Nelson said, "Right on, dude. You can handle it, Gemmy."

"Have you ever done this before, Jim?" I asked. I didn't want to distract him; I wanted to make conversation and look anywhere except at the spot where there would soon be a hole in my son's throat.

But I knew the answer. Jim Scofield wasn't an ER physician or an EMT. He was just a small town doctor who delivered a lot of babies.

My son was a baby, so that was good. I held my breath anyway and nodded. I found I couldn't find my own voice anymore, so I shut up.

"Okay now, Gem," said Scofield. "There's gonna be a little blood, but it'll seal up when we get the tube in his airway. Plus, he's gonna cry because we don't have any anesthesia, but I'll make it as fast as I can, okay?"

I nodded and looked Jim in the eyes. "Just go," I said. "Be careful."

He nodded. Jim pressed the scalpel blade to my son's neck and drew it straight and cleanly from left to right, his fingers steadying his hand against my son's neck.

It felt as though he were dragging the blade across my heart.

As the blood flowed from the wound, Flexy struggled in my arms; I held him still.

Hemp had taken apart a pen and cleaned the hollow tube with alcohol. He came over, took the scalpel from Scofield and gave him the pen.

"Here goes nothin'," said Jim.

The pen had been a ball point retractable, but the cone-shaped end looked as though it would fit more easily than the old Bic pens you saw people use on television.

The pen slid right in. Blood immediately sputtered out of the end, then there was none. I could hear my son's breath, fast and free. His color began to improve immediately. Amazing.

Hemp held out some cloth tape he tore off a roll and Scofield took it, taping it around the pen protruding from Flexy's neck.

When he was satisfied, he looked at me. "He looks good, Gem," he said.

"Thank you," I said. "Now go take care of Charlie."

"What's that smell?" asked Lola. She looked out the side window. "Jesus Christ! We're on fucking fire!"

"What?" said Bug, jumping up and running over. "Where the hell?"

"That tree must've been struck by lightning," said Lola, pointing out the window. "Big branch caught and dropped against the lab." She practically pressed her face against the glass. "I can't see what's on fire, but it does smell like fiberglass or something."

Serena went over to where Lola looked out. "Yeah," she said. "That's plastic of some kind. Rachel, I know this is getting to be a habit, both in California and here, but we need you now. Can you get up there and douse the flames before we're engulfed?"

Bug looked out again. "One good thing is, the fire's cleared the walkers away from this side, but that won't do us any good if we –"

He stopped talking, staring at Trina and Taylor, who were still holding Charlie's hands and being brave. They stared at Bug, willing him to finish his sentence.

"Give me a boost and start filling buckets," Rachel said. "Bug, you're a big guy. Dave, you get my other foot."

"These walls are ready to fall in," said Dave. "Will this thing even support your weight?"

"It should," said Hemp. "The exterior shell is pretty strong despite the fact that the overall structure is faltering. If the walls don't shift sharply to one side or the other she should be fine."

"*Should* be fine?" asked Nelson. "I'm going with her."

"Let her get up there first to see how well it supports her," said Hemp.

Nelson shook his head and I didn't remember seeing him that agitated. "Nel, once you get her up there, take another hit of weed. You need to be sedated."

I looked down at Flexy. He was still upset, but he was calming in my arms. I would not relinquish him to anyone else until my husband got back home.

Bug had knocked the sky vent out and had ripped the flange piece off in two quick motions with his big hands. The pieces clattered to the floor and immediately, he said, "Come here and step up."

Rachel stripped off all but her bra and panties. No modesty, no hesitation.

She shot me a quick glance and I nodded and mouthed the words, "Thank you."

"Let's go," said Bug.

Rachel was used to taking orders. She did so immediately. Bug lifted her right foot and she fed her left arm and her head through the small, square hole. Once she pulled her right arm up and through, the rest was just Bug using brute strength to push her up and out.

Nelson was there immediately, holding up a bucket of water. The ceiling of the mobile lab bent inward with her weight, but no splintering or cracking sounds interrupted all of us holding our collective breath.

"I'm okay," she said. Then: "Oh, my God."

"What?" asked Nelson.

373

"Red dots everywhere," she whispered. "Oh, my God."

"The fire," said Bug. "Rachel."

She took the bucket of water from Nelson and we could see her walking across, each footfall bending the ceiling inward. She was a foot from the edge.

I heard a hissing, which was a good sign. Seconds later she was back.

"More," she said. "Two or three more should do it."

"Push now, Charlie," said Scofield, sitting again between Charlie's legs. "Nice and steady, and don't forget to breathe."

"I'm right here, darling," said Hemp. I watched him watching his Charlie, and I loved him. I loved that he loved her. I loved that Flex and I found her and brought her home to him.

Charlie blew out, then drew in a big breath and pushed with all her might. She screamed and the girls cried and I smiled and cringed at the same time.

"Here he comes," said Scofield. "Okay, the head's out."

I wanted to go over, but Flexy had fallen asleep in my arms finally, so I sat there and watched, tears rolling down my face.

"Yuck!" said Trina, looking at me with a look of disgust on her face. "Is that what I looked like?"

"I'm sure it's pretty close," I said. "But I wasn't there, sweetie."

Scofield worked his hands and said, "Shoulders are out now." He gave the baby an easy twist, and with one hand, took the towel from across his leg and filled it full of brand new baby. He looked at Isis, who had walked clumsily over to where he sat. She was smiling.

374

Jim examined the newborn as Hemp gave him the scissors. He clipped the umbilical cord and quickly wrapped a rubber band around it.

"Is he okay?" asked Charlie, sitting up on her elbows, the girls still squeezing her hands. Her brows were raised, and there was love and hope in her eyes.

"Good lookin' boy," said Scofield. "And he'll be fine, once we get him crying."

Doc Scofield carried him quickly to the sink and lay the child inside, rubbing it briskly with the towel. A moment later, we all heard the tiny cough, followed by the new cry of a living, breathing baby.

"So it is a boy?" asked Charlie. "Isis? You did know."

"I knew you would be happy," she said, her mouth opened in a big smile, her oversized teeth gleaming. "His name's Max."

We all stared at Hemp and Charlie for confirmation.

*****

I drove as fast as I could down Highway 72. We'd made quick work of saturating the flechettes within the shotgun shells with the estrogen blocker-enriched aloe vera gel. Now we just had to figure out how to efficiently take down all the red-eyes with our limited rounds.

I got on the radio to Punch. "Tyger River's coming up," I said. "We had it cleared on the way here, but I don't know if Cara and her crew blocked it off again."

There were a lot of rotters crossing here when Tony and I were heading north. I didn't see any now. We'd done our little part to decimate them, but that didn't mean much; there were nine times as many of them as us.

I knew at that point that I was a mere five miles away. The trip north had taken much longer, but most of the work we'd done to clear the roads on the way north was still in effect. No new crashes, no washed out roads other than what we'd already dealt with.

The bridge came into view, and we could see all the cars on it that we had pulled out of the way to allow us to pass. The hurricane's force must have been tremendous for a while, anyway. As I approached the bridge, I saw one car on its side against the rail, and as we looked down, we saw another two had somehow been blown off the bridge.

Maybe from that tornado that Gem had told us about.

"Must be a good feelin', Flex," said Punch.

"It is," I said. "How's the grape runnin'?"

"Sweet," he said. He zigzagged behind me as I maneuvered around the cars, following the sole open path of roadway across the bridge.

The river below was nothing like the Catawba had been. It still churned and roiled, having overflowed its banks by probably ten feet on either side, but I could see where it had already receded around three feet from where it had been at full tilt boogie.

I got that from Janis Joplin's last band name. Always liked it. To me, it's always been the equivalent of "the max," and describes pretty well how Hurricane George blew through the Carolinas at exactly the wrong time.

Once we cleared the bridge, we were open again. Within another two miles, the parade of walking dead came into view.

Staggering shamblers in filthy, rotted clothing, their sunken eyes and skeletal bodies reminding me of their goddamned immortality without a bullet or ninja star or knife to the brain.

They emerged as if materializing from the woods on the sides of the road, and I slowed the Land Cruiser to fifteen miles per hour and just mowed them over. I yanked on the AK-47's firing rope, blasting the crowns of their heads into a chunky mist until I was out of filled magazines for the weapon.

They pushed against the vehicle and slid away as I rolled past them, some of their legs slipping beneath the Toyota, and I'm sure the GTO behind me. I ran these over like bleeding speed bumps. Bleed bumps.

"Another mile, Punch," I said, pressing the pedal down more. Ahead was some kind of natural wash. The zombies that had been moving along the street had bunched up there, and I saw that some had moved into the forest, probably taking a deer trail.

The draw to Whitmire, where my family was, was undoubtedly stronger than their ability to ignore it. Some stepped into the wash, which appeared to be around three feet deep, and were whooshed away by the flowing water. I was fairly certain I could get through, but I wasn't sure about the GTO.

I got on the radio. "Punch, park that thing. You won't make it through this, and I can't stop to hook you up to the winch cable and pull you across. Too big a hurry."

"Not a problem, Flex," he said. He pulled the car off the road and hopped out with his shotgun and backpack. He got to my car, opened the rear door, threw his pack in and got in front.

I looked at him. He stared back, on his face what I might call a grateful smile. Sure. I recognized it. We'd saved quite a few people along the way since the zombie problem started, and it was a familiar look. Maybe Punch, with his military skills, had only been a prisoner in his own mind, but Tony and I showing up that day had flipped some switch that made him realize that inaction was his only barrier to obtaining freedom again.

"You're gonna have to pardon the first impression you're gonna get there," I said. "Sounds like the shit has not only hit the fan, it's smashed it. Being a Marine, you know

377

where shit rolls, and you and I are downhill, brother. It's on us."

He hefted his Saiga and said, "All twenty flechette rounds are in here." He reached to the floorboard and brought up the super soaker. "And we filled these at our last stop. We're good to go."

"We'll play it by ear when we get there," I said.

"You should call them," said Punch. "Tell 'em we're almost there."

"Good idea," I said. I picked it up and pressed the button. "Gem, Hemp? You there?"

"You are so not military," said Punch.

"Flex?" came a voice. It was not very familiar, but sounded kind of like Dave Gammon.

"Bug?" I asked.

"Yeah," he said. "Flex, we thought we had the fire out, but I guess a wheel caught, and now the undercarriage is burning. Floor's starting to get hot, man."

I floored the vehicle and if a zombie got in my way he'd just get cut in half. I made a left onto our access road.

"I don't see any flames, Bug," I said. "I'm coming down our road now."

"It's underneath," he said. "We can't even see it, but we can sure smell it. We're getting choked up in here."

"Nothing Lola can do to draw 'em somewhere else?"

"Maybe there would be, but she's trapped inside, and she can't fit through the ceiling vent like Rachel can."

The house came into view. I stared. Punch said, "Wow. They were inside when that happened?"

I pushed the button again, a million things on my brain, and I just started spewing them. "Bug? How's my son? How's Gem? How's Charlie? Did she have her baby yet?"

"They're fine," he answered. "We're all lying on the floor now to stay out of the smoke. Floor's hot, Flex. We gotta get out of this thing or we're all roasted."

He was keeping his voice low, but I knew the girls were listening to everything he said.

We rounded the corner of the house and a large tree had fallen in our path.

"End of the line, bud," I said. "Grab your toy gun, your shotgun and every handgun you have. And remember to preserve the flechette rounds. Only use them on red-eyes." I threw the SUV in park.

"Got it," he said.

"Hold on, Bug," I said into the radio. "We're coming around the corner. I smell the fire, too." It smelled like burning plastic and rubber.

"You should be in here," he said, his voice strained.

We approached the corner. I reached into my pocket and drew in my breath.

I'd never been called on to estimate a crowd size. I'd put the one in front of me at a thousand. Hundreds must have been pressing in on the motor home.

It was now full dark, and the moon was trapped behind a thick cloud cover. The wind still blew at probably twenty-five miles an hour, but it was like mere trade winds compared to its former power.

"Put Gem on the line," I said into the radio.

"I'm here, babe," she said. "I couldn't help myself. I had to crawl over to get the other radio."

There was a pause. "Flex? I'm so glad you're back. My mind was beginning to do stupid stuff."

"I wouldn't leave you guys," I said. "You're what got me back. Is Flexy okay?"

"You'll see. What's your plan?" she asked.

"Hold on, Gem."

I talked it out with Punch. We moved through the rubble of the house and worked our way to the only remaining wall; the one that stood five feet from the mobile lab. Both of us were on WAT-5, so we didn't worry about detection from the masses. The red-eyes had a sixth sense, but so far, none had turned to spy us.

"They need out of there," said Punch. "Only one door, right?"

"Yep," I said.

"Okay. I got something."

He told me his plan.

"That might work," I said. "Fastest way to get them out."

I got on the radio and told Gem and Bug what needed to happen. Neither argued.

*****

The generator had died, and there was no ambient light except for several LED flashlights that some of us had in our pockets. It had become a staple item in our survival inventory. I had a headlight on, as did Hemp and Dave Gammon.

"Everybody, lie as flat as you can on the floor. Girls, no heads raised, not even an inch, you got that?"

"Yes, Gemmy," the girls said together.

"And keep Bunsen and Slider down, too," I said. "It's very important."

"I got Slider here," said Dave. "Serena's holding Bunsen down."

Rachel and Nelson had taken a far corner. The floor was hot, and I swore it would burn through and scorch us all if something didn't happen soon. It was easier to breathe down on the floor, but not by much.

The rain had stopped, and now only the wind whistled past the open vent above us. Some of the wind made its way to the interior, helping move the air inside, but it wasn't enough. There were too many of us consuming oxygen and the fire below us seemed to pre-heat it before it reached our lungs. It felt like I was breathing through a smoldering sock.

A huge explosion sounded, and the mobile lab dropped on one end, throwing the floor on an angle.

"That was the tire blowing out!" yelled Hemp. "Front left, from our angle."

"That's where the fire I couldn't get to was burning," said Rachel. "I'm sorry, but I couldn't lean out that far."

Then we heard hissing, popping and muffled, animalistic shrieks. The walls began pushing in farther, for we could no longer hold them back and be on the floor at the same time.

In the light of our headlamps and LED flashlights, we watched the walls in flux, moving in and out, cracking and bending.

The hiss-popping continued, and above our heads, water began to pour in on us.

*****

"Spray it up as high as you can, Punch!" I said. "Make it rain, buddy! The more you wet 'em the more we take down and the quicker we can get to the red eyes!"

"Got it," he shouted back, and we separated. I saw a red-eye to my right and spun my Daewoo toward her, firing as I turned to avoid giving her a chance to make a defensive move. I'd seen that trick in the waiting room at the prison in Concord and so many other places.

The rounds blew her red eyes through the back of her head and she collapsed into the crowd of melting zombie bodies. The three-round burst punched the same number of holes in the mobile lab's now thin sheathing. I hoped everyone was on the floor as we'd instructed them.

I told myself I didn't have to worry, but I backed toward the destroyed house again and pulled the radio from my clip as I watched Punch water down another twenty or so rotters.

"Gem, are you guys down?"

When she came back, her voice was shaking and she sounded frightened. Not like my Gem. "Yeah, Flex. That last one rattled the blinds, but that's all."

"Stay there. It's gonna get messy. When we give you the go-ahead, I want someone to kick that fucking door open and you all get the hell out of there as fast as you can, okay?"

"Yes!"

"Just wait, then," I said. I put the radio back on my belt.

"Get over here, Punch," I said. "Right in front. Hurry!"

Punch had done well. Most of the standard-issue rotters were now on the ground, bubbling like the La Brea Tar Pits. As they melted, bubbles in their muck would expand larger and larger before popping, sending small spatters into the air.

"Clear enough?" he asked, moving beside me, his eyes ever watchful. More of the zombies moved in where their brothers and sisters had fallen, and now it seemed the majority was of the more intelligent variety.

"Time to try this fucker out," he said. "Flex, is that one over there?"

I followed his pointing finger. The creature stood with her back to us, but her straight hair blew in the wind, untangled. She was five feet away.

"My guess is yes," I said. "Don't shoot her in the head. Hemp says just introducing the blocker into her system should be enough."

"Good," he said. "It'll tell us if this shit is gonna work."

He raised his gun. She turned and launched herself toward us simultaneously.

"Fire!" I shouted.

Punch fired. The booming explosion shattered the night, dominating the howling wind and the hiss-popping of the melting zombies around us. What happened next amazed me.

She dropped in mid-flight, smashing into the sticky, wet pile of the dead creatures around us. Seconds later, she pushed herself from the muck that clung to her hands and arms like rubber cement and got back to her feet.

She looked downward, her attention on the wound in her distended stomach, and as we watched, the skin there peeled away and the fetus within her slid from its cold, dead chrysalis, dropping with a sodden thud into the mass of melted, black-red slime at her feet.

From her belly, she began splitting up to her chest, her neck, then her face. Her skin peeled away, revealing only her skeletal framework beneath, and finally, her oh, so lovely hair and scalp fell from her frame and slid down what remained of her body.

The bones began to disintegrate, and she dissolved into the ground. She had not made a sound. Her destruction was complete.

I slapped Punch on the back and said, "Let the fucking flechettes, fly, but focus on a path out of that goddamned lab first."

I pushed the button on my radio again. "This is it! Everybody flat on the fucking ground! Stay below the one foot high mark!"

Punch stood back dead center from the entry door to the lab. No more of the standard issue walking dead remained, having been reduced to a sea of goo.

All that were left on their feet were red-eyes. It seemed that they turned toward us all at once. Punch stuck to the plan.

"Now!" I shouted. He let flechette round after flechette round fly. I took as many out with the Daewoo as I could, until we had cleared a path about ten feet wide, centered at the door.

The goddamned mobile lab started to look like Bonnie and Clyde's 1934 Ford on the day they died. I hoped everyone inside had followed our instructions or they'd be dead, too.

*****

As Flex and Punch fired away outside, the blinds, upholstery and walls blew into fragments that rained down upon those of us cowering inside. The side window had blown out with the onset of their attack, and directly in the line of fire, the chair Charlie had just used to deliver her baby was peppered with bullet holes. Tiny metal rods stung our exposed skin as they hit the opposite wall of the lab, bounced off and dropped. They were hot and sticky and I had no idea what they were at the time, but they didn't seem to pose a threat.

The onslaught continued for at least five solid minutes before things outside fell silent. The smoke was thick and smothering and I could hardly breathe. I worried for my son and all of us inside, but mostly for him. The little tube in his neck was his only airway, and what he had to breathe wasn't what I'd consider up to the EPA's clean air standards. I also worried for Charlie's newborn son, facing this battle in his first minutes of life.

"Gem!" came Flex's voice over the radio. "Get out of there! Kick that fucking door open and prepare to step in some sticky crap, but keep going. Got me?"

"Everybody!" I shouted. "You heard. Up, up!"

"We just go?" asked Lola. "I still hear them," she said. "Still in my head. There's lots of them," she said.

"Flex is right," said Isis. "They have cleared a path."

Nelson, skinny as he was, scooped up Trina, and Dave grabbed Taylor. Neither child cried or argued. Their expressions were fixed, determined and watchful.

Our girls had come quite a long way over the past months, and almost seemed unfazed by anything that happened. Sometimes they lost it emotionally, but we were seeing children grow up in madness for the first time in our lives. They were adapting.

I wondered if it was similar to what children went through when the wild west was the destination of early settlers seeking their version of the American dream; wagon trains attacked, children and adults killed by the natives of the land who did not welcome the invading white men and women.

I suppose they had as much a chance of talking themselves out of trouble as we did. Their children were taught that it was one of the hazards of their world, just as ours were told about the strange humans with pink and red eyes who hungered for their flesh.

I'd rather have taken my chances as a child in the old west.

Bug held Isis and I held Flexy, careful not to bump his new breathing tube, and Charlie held her little Max.

They had always intended to name a boy Max to honor Max Romero, Hemp's friend from the CDC whose death I detailed in my chronicle, and the man who had allowed us to take the very RV we were currently ready to escape from. Strangely, Isis had known his name before he was born.

Had the baby been a girl, her name was to be Emma. Not after anyone – just because Charlie loved the name.

Charlie was on her feet and I could see the pain in her face.

"Are you okay, Charlie?" I asked. "Can you do this?"

"I don't have a choice," she said. "Hemp needs to be ready to use his gun and there's no way I'm letting go of my son."

"How's your pain?" I asked.

"I had a baby a few minutes ago," said Charlie. "Worse still, I don't think I dropped the placenta yet."

"Holy, shit. You *are* one tough bitch," I said.

"You want tough?" she asked me. "It's a new world, Gem," she said, a twinkle in her tired eyes. "When it does come out, I'm curing it and making a Bota Bag out of it."

I laughed out loud, mostly at the image in my head, and Charlie stifled her laugh. Probably either because it hurt or she was afraid a placenta flying out of her might be a bit more extreme than an accidental fart.

Bug stood in front. "Everybody ready?"

"Yes!" everybody yelled in unison.

He stood back about two feet and kicked the door, which was already barely fixed in its frame. It ripped from its hinges and fell straight forward, landing so as to serve as a ramp and walkway over the first few feet of dissolving zombies who lay near and far, side to side as far as we could see in the darkness.

I looked up and saw a beautiful sight comprised of my Flex and another man who could only be Punch, about ten feet from the door. They scanned the area and fired their weapons intermittently. They used three round bursts rather than full auto, clearly to preserve ammo, and dangling from their belts were two colorful super soaker water guns.

Bug dropped out with Isis, walked across the door until it came to an end, and stepped into the gooey pile of dead walkers. The smell was horrific and assaulted me the moment the door fell, but I choked down the bile that threatened to force its way from my stomach.

Punch and Flex kept their eyes on us, still alternately turning and firing at the red-eyes moving in. The prize the

386

creatures wanted was now visible, and they came without regard for their own safety. Isis was a pull they could not deny, and I realized we were seeing the true intensity of the phenomenon for the first time.

I let Dave and Nelson go first because they were carrying our girls, and I needed to keep an eye on them. Hemp went out next, his gun in the firing position, and his left arm around Charlie's waist. He supported her through the sticky thickness at the end of the door until they stepped up on the piles of destroyed construction debris beyond.

When I got to the end of the fallen door and stepped off into the biological scum, my feet sank into it and I nearly fell forward each time I attempted to pull one foot out to plant the other. The reek was more intense and pungent and I felt myself getting lightheaded.

"Watch out!" yelled Nelson, who had turned around to watch my progress. He gripped Trina in his left arm as he did his best not to lose his balance and topple over into the slime at our feet. At first I had no idea why he had yelled, but even as he pressed Trina's face into his shoulder, he brought his arm back and flung it forward, the silver Ninja star whizzing past us at a distance of around a foot, angled sharply upward.

It was thrown so quickly I couldn't follow its flight path, but when I turned to look at the top of the burning laboratory, I spotted his target. Even in the swirling, black smoke billowing from the rig, I saw the red-eye's head whip backward.

When a sudden gust of wind blew the smoke away from her for a moment, I briefly caught her red eyes as they faded to black. The creature that had been standing atop the collapsing mobile lab, likely ready to leap on me and my child, fell and plunged through the roof, crashing into the interior of the rig, blasting sparks out the door as she hit bottom.

I must have been staring as though in a daze, because the next thing I remember is Flex taking me by the arm and pulling me along. I held onto my son, careful of his new, plastic appendage, and went to Flex.

"Hurry, Gem," he said, not mincing words. "You go to the SUV and lock yourself in," he said. "You and Charlie and all the kids. Here, take this."

He passed me his Glock.

"What are you going to do? Come with us," I pleaded.

"We gotta finish this," he said. "I want every last red-eye dead and gone. This estrogen blocker shit seems to do it, so no time like the present."

"I love you, Flex."

"Hurry," he said. "God, it's good to see you two." He peeled the blanket away from our son and gasped, seeing the pen sticking from his throat. He looked at me. "Gem, what happened? Is he okay?"

"His throat was blocked from the Diphtheria. You have the antitoxin, right?"

"I do," said Flex.

"Then he'll be fine," I said. "For now he can breathe."

He kissed his son on the cheek and kissed my lips briefly. "Go," he said. "Be careful."

*****

After Gem and our boy were out of the mix of things, I monitored the others. As Doc Scofield moved to step down onto the door, his ankle twisted and he fell forward, rolling off the door and into the slime.

I threw the Daewoo over my shoulder and ran up to him, pulling him up. I got him back on the ramp and past the dissolving zombie bodies.

"Thanks, Flex," he said. "You boys got here just in time."

"Earlier would have been better. Get to the truck with Gem and them. You can't help with that ankle."

"I'm sorry, man," he said. "Didn't want to let you down."

"You deliver Charlie's baby?" I asked.

"I did," he said.

I patted him on his slimy back. "Then don't apologize because you've had a good day, Jim. Now get over there."

He hobbled off and I realized that Dave, Nelson and Bug must've heard my instructions to Gem because they were running with the girls in their arms toward the Land Cruiser. Doc Scofield was soon behind them.

Everyone heading for the Land Cruiser had to skirt around the fallen tree branch that had prevented us from driving in closer, but I watched them until they all reached the truck.

Lola ran up beside me breathing hard, her long knife in her right hand and a Glock in her left. "I'm gonna do what I can, Flex," she said.

She stood there in front of me, her look unwavering, her blonde hair a crazy mess. Her red eyes held their own luminosity. I hadn't known her long, but I understood she had been a literal lifesaver to Dave and the rest of them in California.

I turned to fire at another red-eye who had appeared around the corner of the lab, the roof of which was now fully engulfed in orange-yellow, licking flames. I knew we had to get clear of it, because there were propane tanks inside that would blow as the fire progressed.

"Care to elaborate?" I asked, shielding my eyes from the flames that turned Lola into nothing more than a silhouette against them.

"That big field over there," she said, pointing. "Behind the lab. I can try to draw them in there, and you can get a firing squad together to take 'em all down."

Eric A. Shelman

"You'll be fighting Isis's pull," I said. "Can you compete with her?"

"I did before," said Lola. "Not at her advanced stage – I mean, she wasn't freaking talking back then, but it was only a week or so ago. So yeah. I'll try."

"Okay, but if shit gets sketchy, I want you to hightail it to my Toyota and get safe with the girls."

"Not really my style," she said, spinning her knife in her hand. "I'm a take action kinda girl."

"So was Gem," I said. "Sure you're up to it?"

"I'll get to the field and call them," she said. I asked no further questions, because Lolita Lane ran into the night, now ablaze with brightly burning flames.

From the corner of my eye I saw Serena pulling both of our huge dogs by their collars toward the Land Cruiser.

I hoped there would be room for them.

I searched the yard. Gem's car was nowhere in sight. I pulled my radio from my belt.

"Gem," I said. "Where's your car?"

She came back almost immediately. "Don't worry about that!" she said.

"I need it to put the dogs in," I said. "They're comin' your way, but they can't fit in the SUV with you guys."

"Shit, Flex, it's on the other side of the mobile lab, but it's probably on fire," she said. "We'll fit them in."

I didn't answer her. I ran on the outside edges between the melted zombie bodies and the rubble from the house, and cut right. I saw Hemp about fifty yards to my left, and spotted a huge horde of red-eyed females moving toward my SUV.

I had to abort my plan. Hemp was forty yards to my right. I called to him, waving my arms.

He looked over at me and called, "Yeah, Flex!"

I pointed at the advancing red-eyes. "Flank 'em on their right side! I got the left! Dave, if you can hear me

390

buddy, get that Crown Vic away from the mobile lab if you can!"

I lowered the radio and yelled into the night, "Punch! Where are you, Punch?"

The wind carried my words away as they fanned the flames before us. I ran toward Hemp and as I rounded the corner of the mobile lab, I saw Lola charging toward the open field. I hoped she would begin her call soon. Things were getting out of control. I had no idea where Nelson was.

I ran, my lungs burning, until I was about fifteen feet away from Hemp. He had been firing constantly, but at that moment his gun fell silent. I looked around and realized that the many red-eyes who were near us just minutes before were gone.

Vanished. Of course. They were hiders.

The wind had turned and the smoke shifted direction, now billowing toward our driveway and the SUV where Gem, Charlie and the children had retreated for refuge. The pungent, black smoke made it impossible to see not only where the intelligent females had gone, but the SUV itself.

*****

Jim Scofield had gotten to the truck last, so we were able to tuck him into the very rear of the SUV, still allowing room for others I hoped would make it to the vehicle.

It appeared that floor mats had been taped up over the front seat side windows, but I could also tell the glass was gone, so despite the fact that they limited visibility, we left them in place.

I was in the front seat holding Flexy, and Charlie sat in the middle with her newborn baby in her arms. She looked utterly exhausted. She was quiet and morose; so unlike my friend.

"*The child is there,*" said Charlie.

My heartbeat stopped and I stared at her.

"Charlie, are you okay?"

Tears rolled down her face and she held her child closer to her as though someone might take Max away from her.

"Charlie, it's okay," I assured her. "You took the wafer. You're fine."

I could do nothing more than put my arm around her and let her know that I was there for her. Always.

I glanced in the back seat. Both girls stared out of the window into the dark, smoky blackness, their haunted eyes reflecting the flickering, distant firelight.

A pounding came on the rear driver's side door, but we couldn't see out because of the heavy tint. Trina leaned over to unlock the door.

"No, Trina!" I shouted, but it was too late. The door flung open and to my relief, Bunsen jumped in, landing atop Trina and Taylor, followed by Slider. Serena followed the dogs, pushing with all her might to stuff them in and jump in herself. She yanked the door closed behind her.

"I'm sorry!" she said, hardly able to speak, her voice raspy. "There's so much going on out there that nobody focused on these guys!"

"Thank you, thank you, thank you!" shouted Trina, hugging the dogs' necks and crying. Taylor was also in tears.

"I dropped my goddamned gun so I can't go back out there," said Serena. "Did you see Dave anywhere?"

"No," I said. "Not since we got in here, but we can't see much of anything." I got on my radio and pushed the button. "Flex!"

There was no answer. I transmitted my message anyway. "Jim, Serena and the dogs are in with us!"

He didn't respond. The tension within the vehicle was palpable.

Right after we'd gotten to the Land Cruiser, Bug had run up and deposited Isis with us, who now stood on the driver's seat holding onto the steering wheel, peering through the gap in the shattered windshield, that for some reason was fortified with what appeared to be the missing third-row seat from the Toyota.

The thick smoke from the blazing RV blew directly toward us, killing our visibility. With half a windshield, the reeking soot was drifting into the interior of the cab, and it was hard to breathe. We might as well have all been blind.

The wind suddenly shifted again, clearing the heavy smoke away for the moment. As if by divine intervention, a break in the clouds above us allowed the faint light of the moon to illuminate the area in front of the Land Cruiser.

Nothing but rubble spread out before us except for the distant, leaping flames from the RV fire. I let out my breath. With the heavy smoke, I had been blinded. With it gone, I felt far more at ease.

Charlie seemed to have calmed. I slid my arm from around her and retrieved my Uzi from the floorboard. There was a Glock down there, too, but I knew I would not fire either one with two babies so close to me.

With a sigh, I placed the Uzi back on the floor and started on what might have been my fiftieth prayer of the longest day of my life.

Suddenly the scene before us changed from marginally serene to intense.

I gasped as directly in front of us, no more than twenty feet away, what had to be a hundred red-eyed females rose swiftly to their feet.

Charlie's hand gripped my wrist.

"Jesus, Gem, you see that?" asked Scofield from the back of the Land Cruiser. I adjusted the rear view mirror to see his eyes, wide, alert and frightened.

Eric A. Shelman

The monsters before us appeared organized – at least for them. Standing almost in an army marching formation, shoulder to shoulder, five zombies wide and maybe twelve or thirteen deep all in a row, the horde of red-eyes now advanced on us.

Aside from the differences in their clothing and heights, I could not have told one from the other.

I hit the headlights on the SUV, turning on the high beams in an effort to blind them with the light. Perhaps they didn't utilize their vision in the same way humans did, for they did not seem fazed. Now that I could see, however, it struck me that some of the bulges in their stomachs appeared to have been almost full term pregnancies at the time of their deaths and conversion into evil; others were in indeterminable stages of gestation.

"Mothers and Hungerers," said Isis. "Mothers want me," she added. "Hungerers want us all."

With that, the red-eyes moved in with a fluid motion, separating into two groups that began surrounding the SUV.

I reached up to pull the handle of the AK-47 on top of the Toyota, but Charlie stopped me, her eyes still red, but now sharp and focused.

"Gem, you can't shoot them!" she screamed. "The boys might be in the line of fire!"

She was right. I lowered my hand and situated Flexy in my arms, desperation in my heart, my brain racing like a freight train. "Girls, eyes on your knees, now!" I shouted. Then I turned toward the strange, beautiful infant standing in the driver's seat.

"Isis," I said, feeling my heart pounding in my ears. "Can you stop them? Can you send them away?"

"I can send them nowhere, but if I can allow them to see me, I can reveal to them who I am not," she said.

"What do you mean, who you are not?" I asked.

"As I said before," she said. "They believe I am their child. If I see them, as with the Mother in the basement, I can show them."

At that very moment, something changed. The many dead women before us started to turn away. As she watched, Isis smiled. "Lolita Lane calls them," she whispered.

"Lolita –" I began, then realized it was Lola. I had heard what she did in California.

"Where is she?" asked Charlie. "I don't see her anywhere."

"Oh, she's out there," I said, as the army of rotters turned their backs to us. "Thank God."

*****

Chapter Seventeen

I heard a thud and a grunt behind me and turned to see Punch pulling himself and his shotgun from the sticky zombie waste that coated the ground. It was a mixture of clothing, shoes and mottled bones mixed with the slimy, melted residue of those who once utilized them.

He got to his feet and joined me, Hemp and Nelson.

"What happened to you?" I asked, as he attempted to squeegee the slime from his clothing with one hand.

"I got fuckin' treed by four of 'em, so had to waste two critical rounds. Did the job, though."

"How many flechette loads you got left?" I asked.

"Around twelve," he said. "How we use them is a different question."

"Where's Rachel?" asked Nelson, his eyes filled with worry and his head practically spinning in all directions. "I haven't seen her since I left the lab."

"I don't know, man," I said. "I never saw her."

"Jesus Christ!" shouted Nelson, and ran back through the muck toward the burning RV.

"Nelson!" I shouted, but he ignored me. He sludged through the thick scum and got to the door, but in seconds he backed away, his arms up over his face, blocking the searing heat from the flames.

"She was in the back, man!" he yelled. "She was in the rear!"

"Didn't she come out?" I asked, but again, Nelson jumped off the now sunken door and trudged toward the rear of the mobile lab. The very back of the rig hadn't begun to completely burn yet. He yanked open a tail-end storage compartment and jumped inside.

"Flex, look!" shouted Punch. Hemp and I turned to see the red-eyes emerge from the ground like amphibious creatures from the black water of a murky swamp. There was an army of them advancing on the SUV where Gem, Charlie, Serena and our dogs and children waited.

"We can't fire on them!" I shouted. "Damnit, they're moving on it!"

The headlights of the SUV lit up, but the females continued to advance. No gunfire erupted from the SUV and I couldn't figure out for the life of me why. Some of the baddest ass women I knew were in that rig.

Suddenly the situation changed. As the clouds parted overhead and the wind took a shift, the red-eyes stopped and appeared distracted.

All at once they turned and changed direction, now moving toward the field where we had intended to keep the livestock and grow the food that would sustain our families into the future.

A wave of relief washed over me. "Let's go!" I shouted. "That's Lola doing that! She went to the field!"

We all ran to get ahead of the advancing horde of red-eyes. As we rounded the corner of the RV, the engine fired on the Crown Vic, the headlights came on and it shot forward, cranking hard left around the enormous, burning branch that had ignited the mobile lab.

We saw the driver then. Dave Gammon spun the car around and jammed toward the middle of the field. He reached Lola, who stood dead center, her red eyes like tiny beacons in the night, staring toward us.

Eric A. Shelman

I glanced back at the mobile lab and saw that the driver's side rear access panel for the storage area was open.

Nelson had entered from the passenger side, but I could now see all the way through to the other end of the rig. The compartment was empty. I said a silent prayer for my crazy friend and his new love.

Dave drove with the pedal to the metal straight toward Lola. When he reached the spot where she stood, he spun the vehicle behind her and pulled up on her side, stopping the Crown Victoria. I saw the gun on top of the Ford spin around, but he didn't fire.

Lola never acknowledged the car's presence; she stood as still as a column, her arms by her sides, staring, beckoning the powerful creatures. She held no weapon.

As we approached Lola, we slowed to a walk and turned to witness the fruits of her labors.

The brigade of red-eyed, female zombies made its way toward the field, their individual movements coordinated and far more surefooted than their dumber, male counterparts. The entire mass of them moved three to four times faster than the regular rotters.

Mesmerized, Punch raised his shotgun, flush with the deadly ammunition, in their direction. He didn't fire.

"Guys," said Bug, his voice a whisper. "Take a little spin around and check out this shit."

We all turned to see what he was talking about. Hundreds more tattered, shambling men, women and children emerged from the woods on all sides of us, moving toward the field from the forest beyond. They were slowed by downed branches and debris, not only from the surrounding forest, but pieces of nearby homes undoubtedly destroyed by the hurricane and tornado.

I heard shouting and saw Nelson and Rachel emerge from the Ford. They ran toward us and I smiled at the sight of them despite the rapidly deteriorating situation around us.

398

As they drew nearer, I saw that Rachel had smears of soot on her face and carried a one-gallon bottle in her hands.

"I got her, dude!" shouted Nelson. "She was trapped in there!"

"I didn't know about the rear hatch," Rachel puffed, her breathing strained. "I wanted to grab this bottle of urushiol oil before I got out, but the Plexiglas walls fell and I was trapped behind them. No way to get to the door."

"Look at all of 'em!" shouted Nelson. "We can't stop 'em all, Hemp! What do we do, dude? C'mon, man!"

Dave got out of the Ford and jogged up to stand beside us.

"You see all of them?" asked Dave. "Jesus, guys."

Hemp eyed the field and the partially completed fence. "Over there! The golf cart's there!" he shouted.

We looked where he pointed, and saw that against one of the posts rested the golf cart on its side.

"Follow me!" he shouted. We did, and he ran toward the overturned golf cart.

We reached it and Hemp practically dove to the ground and jammed his arm behind the seat into the storage basket. A couple of seconds later he pulled out a stack of quart-sized plastic buckets and four wood-handled paintbrushes that had somehow remained lodged inside.

He separated the three small buckets from one another and placed them on the ground, side by side. Then he uncapped the urushiol jug and poured an equal amount in each bucket, leaving about the same amount in the jug. "Flex, you have your pocket knife?"

I gave it to him and he cut the top off the jug, dropping one of the brushes inside.

We looked back. The red-eyes were a hundred yards from Lola and closing, and the horde was working their way over the fallen debris toward the fence, now staggering toward it from around about twenty yards away.

It was impossible to determine which of them would kill us faster. A fucking miracle needed to fall out of my ass pretty damned fast or we would all be dead.

I got on the radio. "Gem!" I shouted. I didn't wait for a reply. "Fire up that truck and get the hell out of here!"

Hemp went on: "We need to coat as much of that fence as we can with the urushiol oil, and we need to hurry! Divide into four groups and let's split the oil up and brush as much as we can on the top two wires. Let's go! We have to get there before they do!"

Hemp and I went to the first section of fencing on the east side of the pasture. Nelson and Rachel ran toward the south side, and Bug and Dave covered the west perimeter.

Now the mass of rotters was no more than ten yards from the fence. Even without the urushiol it would hold them for a moment or two, but we hadn't intended its design to be efficient without the oil coating, so they could get through with minimal effort.

Hemp held the bucket and I dipped the brush, running it along the fence and slopping it on the top wire. As he ran toward the next section, I ran back the opposite way and coated the second wire.

To give me a rest, I held the bucket this time and we repeated the process for the next section with him doing the running. There was no looking back to see what kind of effect our work was having; we had to get as much coated as possible.

Battling these creatures while not on WAT-5 was something we hadn't done since Hemp had discovered the compound. I quickly decided I didn't like it much at all.

I glanced over to see that Rachel and Nelson had utilized the same procedure as Hemp and me. They were making progress, but the horde had now reached the fence. In the section they had not yet coated, the zombies were pushing through it, hitting the clean section of fence, falling backward among their fellow rotters, and once down, crawling below the two installed rows of baling wire.

Nelson improvised. He ran toward them and gripped the brush tightly, flinging the coated bristles at them and splashing their emaciated bodies with the caustic oil. They stood briefly, then dropped to the ground and began the melting process that ate them away.

Nelson's response might have been more effective than Hemp's original plan. Each drop that hit them was like a bullet to the brain and took them down by the dozens.

The situation on our side was the same. I would have yelled for Bug to do the same thing, but he was no fool. He had glanced at Nelson and had begun to fling his brush at them, too. I saw Dave dipping his fingers in and flinging the oil toward them as well.

Soon, there were piles and piles of writhing zombies melting inside the fence line and just beyond it. The others, trapped behind them, were significantly slowed by the mounting, degrading mound.

I had time to look toward Lola. The creatures were now ten feet away from her and closing. She moved for the first time now, backing toward the Crown Victoria.

I hadn't known if she had even been aware of its presence; she had never looked away from the advancing horde of females, and I had believed Lola Lane was in a trance of sorts.

When she reached the Crown Vic, she opened the door and slid inside. Even from across the field I could still see her red eyes within, never averting from the females who surrounded the car to the point that I could no longer see the Ford at all.

*****

As soon as the radio cut out after Flex's brief order to evacuate, I looked at Charlie.

"Do you want to lose Hemp?" I asked.

"Hell no," she said. "No, Gem." She looked at her son and back at me.

"Serena, you want to lose Dave?"

I looked back at her and she shook her head. "You know I don't," she answered.

"Well, I'm not losing Flex either," I said.

I grabbed my Uzi off the floorboard, jumped out of the SUV and ran around to the driver's side door. I slapped on it and Charlie leaned past where Isis stood and unlocked it. I pulled it open and picked up Isis, placing her on the other side of Charlie.

"Isis," I said, "You'll need to plant your bottom on the seat and use those little fingers to hold on to something. Now."

"Yes, Gemmy," she said., scooting next to Charlie who put her right arm around the toddler as she held Max.

I turned the key, and it clicked. My heart sunk into my stomach. I closed my eyes, said a little prayer, and turned off the headlights.

I turned the key again and the starter wound once, then twice, more slowly. I released it and dropped my head against the steering wheel, feeling the tears rolling down my cheeks. I sat there and wondered if Flex had forgotten who I was. He and everyone else knew I'd rather die than leave my family and friends to do the same.

Using every bit of the powers of the universe that I could lasso, I focused my thoughts on that key and the electrical signals it would transmit when turned. I clicked it forward and turned it again.

With a quick, single wind, the engine turned over. I revved it twice, hit the headlights on the high beams again, and threw it in gear.

"Hold on, guys. Those bitches went somewhere and I don't think it's to a fucking Tea Party Rally."

*****

I heard the engine of the Land Cruiser fire and my heart and breathing settled, even as I splashed each and every zombie that made it past the fence line. It wasn't all that difficult. If you've ever flung a paintbrush against a wall, you know how much paint flies off and the amount of spatter you can expect.

We had the advancing horde well under control.

Static sounded on my radio and I grabbed it in time to hear Lola's voice. Dave had a radio in the car and she had felt the need to let us know some more bad news.

"I can't do this much longer," she said. "I'm doing the best I can, but I'm exhausted."

"I don't know what to tell you, Lola," I said. "You got 'em away from Gem and the others. We'll think of something."

When I heard the engine whine and saw the Land Cruiser bouncing in the rough terrain on the outside of our pasture, I nearly shit myself. I pressed the radio button again and yelled, "Gem, get the hell out of here!"

"Not gonna happen, baby," she said, her voice calm but determined. "None of us think that's a very good idea."

"I say it is, Gem! Tell them I think it is!"

"Isis can handle this," she said. "She's working on it now."

With that, Gem cut the SUV hard left and the front end of the Toyota hit the baling wire at the first section on the east side. The zombies who had melted there were squirming in their own muck as they died, and Gem powered that 4-wheeler right over them, snapped the baling wire and bounced into the field, where she floored it again, heading straight toward the surrounded Crown Victoria with our tired Lola inside.

*****

I drove to within twenty yards of the focused crowd of red-eyes. I had seen Flex, Hemp and the others using paint brushes on the fence and the creatures who had gotten by it, and it appeared to have really helped, from the number of bodies just outside the fence.

As for the red-eyed females, they appeared to be in a huddle, and after a moment of staring, I realized there was a machine gun just above their heads.

They were around the Crown Victoria. I pushed the radio button. "Lola, are you in the Ford?" I asked.

"Yes," she came back. "I'm here, and I'm calling them. But I'm goddamned tired, Gem."

"Hang in there," I said.

I looked at Isis. "Isis. Can you show these fine ladies what you are not?"

"I can," she said.

"Then I respectfully ask that you do so right now."

Isis stood on the seat again as I put the SUV in park, leaving the engine on to avoid a repeat of what I'd been through when trying to start it.

"I must reveal their children as I did before," she said.

I knew what was coming. "Girls, please keep your eyes down," I said.

Isis peered through the broken windshield and brought her fingers to her own stomach. With both hands this time, she made scratching motions, as though she had a rash from poison ivy itself.

In unison, the females turned their attention from the Crown Victoria and its inhabitant to our vehicle.

I picked up my radio. "Lola, you can stop calling them," I said.

"I have," she said.

The rotting women did not move toward us. Instead, as Isis continued the clawing motion with her little hands, each of the females before us began clawing into their own distended bellies, tearing the flesh away.

Their decayed skin peeled in flaps and shreds, the almost deep purple liquid flowing like molasses down their hips and legs. As we watched, newly visible movement began to emerge from within them, and in many cases, tiny arms or legs slid out of them.

"Your babies," said Isis, her red eyes focused intently on the standing creatures outside of the vehicle. "Your babies are with you. I am not of you."

Not one pair of red eyes watched us now. To a one, they all looked down at their own bodies at the emergence of their living dead babies.

Some of the squirming fetuses dropped onto the ground at their feet, prompting their deceased mothers to lean forward to try to pick them up. Coordination and proper care of a baby eluded them, however; many of them merely clutched the squirming infant by the arm or leg, which in its deteriorated state, was not enough to support the weight of their undead children.

The arms and legs pulled from their sockets, leaving their babies to drop back to the muddy ground.

Others were more successful and were able to take their grey-faced babies in their arms, still connected to them by a shriveled umbilical cord.

I watched this for too long. For the first time in a long, long time, I remembered that these were once women who were excited about their forthcoming children, putting together wardrobes and nurseries and hanging musical mobiles above cribs, anxious for the moment their beautiful children would gaze up at them with wondrous eyes, smiling at the sweet melody and so fascinated with the many, many things to discover in their new world of light , sound and love.

I raised my radio to my mouth and pushed the button. "Whatever Punch was doing with that gun of his before, I think he should do it again … like now," I said.

I turned to see Flex say something to Punch, and the man ran toward the horde of red eyes. He planted himself between the Land Cruiser and the dead women and their offspring, and placed shot after shot into the crowd.

What happened was nothing I could describe. I had believed nothing would affect them like urushiol, but the estrogen blocking agent infused into the shotgun rounds was the hammer of Thor to these creatures.

The skin peeled away from their legs, hips, rib cages and breastbones. It worked its way from top to bottom, exposing their skulls and popping their red eyes out, to extinguish forever, becoming dark and lifeless.

By the time they fell among their own remains, only their shining hair was recognizable as potentially human.

I don't know how many estrogen blocker-soaked rounds Punch had to start with, but in the end, it had been enough.

I got back on my radio. "Get the hell in that Crown Vic, you guys. The rotters at the fence line are making progress now."

From the outskirts of the field, the horde of standard-issue walkers that had backed up against the piles of their melted and fallen brethren crawled over one another. In some cases their hands or feet melted away in the process, hindering their forward movement; others avoided contacting the oil altogether and came through unscathed, now advancing in their slow, jerky way toward our kind.

To my great relief, all of our friends had slogged through the biological muck and now crammed into the

Crown Victoria with Dave Gammon at the wheel. Two apparent diggers had made their way in front of the Ford, and Dave accelerated, flinging them both out of the way with the car's cow catcher.

Everyone was alive. Now I needed to get the antitoxin, Doc Scofield and Hemp in the same room with my son and Charlie's new baby. Isis would also be immunized, whether or not she felt it was necessary. Sometimes a baby had to be put in her place.

*****

"Flex, man," said Dave," tell me it wasn't like this the whole time we were in California."

With Gem, Jim Scofield, Trina, Taylor, Serena, Charlie, Flexy, Isis, the dogs and the newest member of our brood, Max, crammed in the Land Cruiser behind me, we kept our speed to a cautious minimum as Dave carted the rest of us down to Tony Mallette's house in the Crown Vic. Punch introduced himself to my partners in the zombie war and they all thanked him for taking down the red-eyes.

"Well, Dave," I said, "I don't mean to insult anyone, and this definitely isn't a slam on Bug, but this shitstorm – and the hurricane – all started when you guys got back."

"No offense taken," said Bug, from the back seat. "My girl does what she does. I'm just glad we're all alive."

"Anyway," I said. "We *were* gettin' ready to live like the fuckin' Waltons before all this."

"I'd take a little freakin' house on a prairie about now," said Nelson.

"Punch," I said, "We'll see about gettin' the grape GTO back here in the next couple of days," I told him.

"No hurry," said Punch. "Pretty distinctive color. I think I can find it if it gets jacked."

Tony's house was roomy, centrally located, and it was built out of brick. We hoped it had been missed by the tornado and spared substantial damage from the hurricane.

As it turned out, Tony's house was intact. On the way there we passed Doc Scofield's place, and it had not done so well. The path of the tornado was clear, and his home had been dead center. It was more rubble than our place.

Just after we went by, the radio kicked into life. It was Scofield's voice. With an audible sigh, he said, "There goes my resale value."

Bug grabbed the radio and pushed the button. "Easy come, easy go Doc," he said. "I'm starting to miss my bunker."

"If only anything came easy these days," said Jim. "I wasn't there all that long, but it sure started to feel like home. I was ready to grab a club and go out huntin' for a good woman."

"Hey, bro, give it here," said Nelson. Bug did, and he pushed the button. "Grampa Jim," he said. "Any chick would be lucky to snag a guy like you, man. You're smart, about the same height as a woman, and you got a nice beard. What else do chicks want?" He paused a moment and said, "Wish I could grow a beard."

I didn't hear Scofield laugh, but I'm sure he did. I imagined just knowing that his grandson was alive had to give him some peace.

A huge oak tree had fallen at a home about an eighth of a mile up the street, and it nearly blocked the entire road. As we drove up on a lawn to get around it, two straggler zombies staggered toward us so Bug tried his luck at shooting with his left hand. He wasted three rounds, but eventually took the rotters down.

Dave turned into Tony's driveway and we got out. I went immediately to the Land Cruiser that pulled in right behind us. Everyone piled out and I lifted Flexy from Gem's arms. "Let's get this boy inside and give him the antitoxin. I don't want my boy breathin' out of any goddamned pen tube any longer than he has to."

Gem put her arm around my waist. She didn't say anything right away. Just the feel of her beside me was all it took to tell me that despite the fact that we lost everything yet again, we had what was most important.

We still had one another. I looked up at the house and thought again about Tony. He was the sole casualty of this harrowing couple of days. He was a great loss and a character who would be greatly missed.

"Tony Mallette is dead," I said. "Long live Tony Mallette."

I don't know why I said it. There would never be another Tony.

*****

Epilogue

It's been almost a year since the hurricane. Since the Whitmire house we lived in was completely destroyed, we got back on the road and drove. You'll never believe where we went.

Yep. Back to my home in Lula, Georgia. We'd come full circle.

We had quite a group now, and I know you're probably thinking that we'd already had a bad experience there, but we had just been exposed to all this crap back then. Our knowledge base and our ability to protect ourselves had come a long way since the days right after this mess began.

I knew of a couple of local distilleries as well, so it was a good bet that we could set up a good processing plant for urushiol. Once we got more of the regular and red-eye zombie vapor, we'd have our WAT-5 and the specialized variety of wafers for our pregnant women – should the pregnancy epidemic continue, and Serena's condition seemed to indicate it would.

Hemp wanted to make a run by the CDC again to see if any of the mobile labs remained in the garage. He had been big-time depressed to see his burn to a crisp, and there had been a total of six of them on our first visit. We'd taken the best of them and Hemp had told us that the worst one they had was still a hell of a rig.

410

Flexy responded almost immediately to the Diphtheria antitoxin, and shortly thereafter, his tracheotomy incision healed. It's almost invisible now. We were able to immunize Flexy, Max and Isis, though, as we suspected, Isis told us it wasn't necessary.

We let Isis know that no matter what she thought about her need for vaccines, we didn't care. She was around fifteen months old, so she would have to obey the grownups for a bit longer. I was actually very interested in seeing her grow up so that we could watch her develop. If she were walking and talking at that age, it was anyone's guess what she would be able to do later.

Speaking of that, since it is now a year later, Isis is just over two years old. She is far taller than the typical two year old – she looks around four – and carrying on complex conversations with her is commonplace.

For Hemp, that is. Hemp can keep up with her and even surpass her. The child is amazing and can articulate and share what she is capable of with anyone, if they care to know.

One thing that Isis can do is something she wasn't able to do in Whitmire at the time all this stuff happened. Had she been able to do it, we might have saved the mobile lab. The house still would have been turned to kindling. Isis can't control the weather.

Isis can now block the impulses that she sent out as a younger child; the ones that call the red-eyes to her. She relates it to drawing down a shade and preventing others from seeing in. She keeps the shade drawn at all times, but she explained that it's only with a conscious effort that it is possible.

Isis also believes there are other things she will be capable of as she gets older. She has indicated to Hemp that when she achieves puberty, the changes in her body will trigger powers of which she cannot even conceive. It's strange, because I both look forward to and fear what may be to come.

I don't sit around and freak out like a little pussy about it, but it does cross my mind now and then.

Let's talk about Max Chatsworth for a moment. He's one now, and almost as chatty as Isis was at that age. Max also has red eyes like Isis, only he can and will eat things other than meat. Like Isis, his teeth are also oversized, and he does prefer meat to anything else. Max never cries, but Hemp believes he knows why. As a baby, he was very good at pointing very specifically to things he wanted. A rattle. A toy. A piece of beef jerky. Now he possesses the vocal skills to simply ask for what he wants, so he has never had a need to cry, which is, essentially, an unspoken demand for something a child wants.

Max, like Isis, does not sleep. I imagine there will be some marathon chess matches as the years go on, so long as these two remain near one another.

Hemp has run blood tests on his son and has found nothing really out of the ordinary. He and Isis are like brother and sister, and as far as anyone knows, they are unique to the world.

Isis seems protective over him, and that can't be a bad thing, considering what the child seems to be destined to grow into. Goddess Of The Zombies. It's what I picture when I see her as a young woman in my mind. I say this because of a dream I had.

In the dream it is near dusk and the sun is setting in a brilliant, yellow-orange sky. The dark clouds leap from the horizon to the heavens, and everything on the ground is bathed in its unearthly glow.

Gem and I are sitting on the front porch at what I recognize as the Lula house. We are in the swing, and beside us, in the Adirondack chairs, are Hemp and Charlie.

Out in the yard, wearing a long, flowing white dress, is Isis. She stands facing the tree line, her arms outstretched to the sky, the final warmth of the day touching her skin.

In the distance, all along the edge of the forest, zombies appear. Diggers, rotters, men, women and children.

Hungerers.

There are mothers among them, too, as always, remaining behind the front lines, protected by the vulnerable flesh of the hungerers.

Suddenly, Isis lowers her eyes from the sky and stares straight ahead. We turn to see the creatures as they fall to their knees and avert their eyes, unworthy of the gaze of the Goddess, Isis.

Her eyes change from light red to a dark, burning red, no less intense than Mars through a telescope. As this occurs, the zombies, in a motion they are incapable of, rise smoothly to their feet and retreat once more into the cover of the forest.

In my dream, at that moment, Max walks up beside her, a boy of perhaps thirteen or fourteen. He wears jeans and a white shirt, and over his shoulder is a crossbow.

Isis takes his hand and they walk toward the trees, leaving two beautiful young women in their mid-twenties staring after them.

Trina and Taylor, I know.

A boy stands in front of us on the porch and calls, "Go get 'em, you two!" and he is smiling and excited at the coming confrontation, for he knows Isis and Max will reign supreme. Over Flexy Jr.'s shoulder is a Daewoo K-7 like his pop's. Yeah. The boy is good looking in my dream, just like his old man.

So that was it; either my dream or a premonition. Not sure which it was just yet.

So at this point, we're hanging up the chronicles and just moving on with life. I think it's been long enough since the apocalypse hit that the world has become a place where most people know the story. If anything happens to us, our stack of notes and stories will remain here.

Who knows? Perhaps as the years pass, Isis or Max, maybe even Trina or Taylor will write their stories down. As the years go by, I'll be slowing down, when possible.

I might just get a kick out of reading the adventures of Isis.

The Goddess of the Zombies.

THE END

A WORD ABOUT THE DEAD HUNGER SERIES

When I sat down to write the first Dead Hunger book, it was the first time I'd written any fiction for over a decade. I had, for some reason, abandoned something that I really enjoyed.

I had never written post-apocalyptic fiction before, and had not been a huge watcher of zombie films. Sure, I'd seen about as much as the average guy who likes movies, but I wasn't a fanatic. So essentially, this was me capitalizing on a craze. I'm not ashamed to admit it, and I'm damned glad, because by doing it, it brought me out of my writing graveyard, so to speak. I was dead as a writer.

Writers write. That's what they do. If you ain't writing, you ain't a writer.

So in 2011, I sat down and wrote Dead Hunger. I thought of how I would be in a world where REAL zombies were coming at me at every turn, and I tried to draw the characters as me and my friends would be – freaked out, cursing up a storm, but fighting to maintain our defenses and seeking out others who could help.

I found the experience of writing that book was amazing. It poured off my fingertips onto the page, and I had a blast doing it. Then, after joining zombie group after zombie group on Faceboook, paying for ads here and there, and promoting like crazy, I realized that I had achieved … something.

People were reading it! And they were liking it.

So naturally, when it ended with the cliffhanger, there was always going to be a book two. The others just show that I'm still having fun with it and my readers are still demanding more.

Eric A. Shelman

I wanted to touch on Charlie. I had never seen the TV show "Revolution" before. I created "Charlie with a crossbow" out of thin air. Then this damned show comes on, and what do I see?

Freakin' Charlie – yes, blonde – with a freakin' crossbow. I'm only saying ... I came up with her first!

Anyway, my plan is to jump ahead fifteen years now, and have Isis and Max grow up – two unique human-creatures who may or may not have special communication abilities with the red-eyes – perhaps with even what Isis has termed The Hungerers. (Love that name, by the way – it may someday be the name of a book!)

Keep a watchful eye out, okay? Not only for zombies, but for my future work. And ... seriously. Try something of mine that ain't zombie. You'll dig it.

~ Eric A. Shelman

ABOUT THE AUTHOR

Eric A. Shelman lives in Southwest Florida with his wife since 1986, Linda. They have the best dog in the world … a Chihuahua mix named Bella. No, not yappy. Loves people. She's mixed with a yellow lab, ya see.

Eric was born in Fort Worth, Texas, leaving there as a teenager in the early 1970s when his widowed mother remarried and his new stepfather moved the family to southern California.

Eric first took on zombies as a genre in 2011, but has been writing poetry and stories since he was in elementary school. In fact, when he was a young longhair living in Laguna Beach and Dana Point, California, in the late 70s and early 80s, he'd write ridiculous short stories with no plot and no end, all with his friends' names in them. In fact, you'll find the names of many people Eric knows today in his stories and books.

Eric is also the lead singer for The Caloosa River Band. That band, plus one guitarist, used to be called The Mood Zombies, at which time they released their one and only album, Breaking Ground. Ten original tunes, all with their own charm. You might just like "Zombie Bar." David A. Simpson used it for a movie sizzler he was making for his series, Zombie Road, which if you recall, is IN THIS BOOK. Right before Tony gets killed, they pass a sign where someone wrote those words over another street sign.

That's where David got the title to his series. Trivial, you say? Eric's quite proud of that. Like David says: "Don't get hit by a bus."

Eric has an author fan page on Facebook – and it's the best place to find out when his next release is coming – just search for Eric A Shelman Author, and you should find it just fine. You can find him on Goodreads, too. Last resort, you can also check out his website – www.ericshelman.com.

Eric A. Shelman (A pain in the ass.)

Bella Shelman, 2020 (Also a pain in the ass.)

MORE BOOKS BY
ERIC A. SHELMAN
AND DOLPHIN MOON PUBLISHING

1999: Out of the Darkness: The Story of Mary Ellen Wilson
2005: Case #1: The Mary Ellen Wilson Files
2011: Dead Hunger: The Flex Sheridan Chronicle
2011: A Reason To Kill
2011: The Witches of Laguna Beach
2012: Dead Hunger II: The Gem Cardoza Chronicle
2012: Dead Hunger III: The Chatsworth Chronicles
2012: Dead Hunger IV: Evolution
2013: Shifting Fears
2013: Dead Hunger V: The Road To California
2014: Dead Hunger VI: The Gathering Storm
2014: Dead Hunger VII: The Reign of Isis
2014: The Camera: Bloodthirst (Book 1 of planned trilogy.)
2015: Dead Hunger VIII: Peace, Love & Zombies
2015: Scabs: The Gemini Exception
2016: Scabs II: The Quantum Connection
2016: Dead Hunger IX: The Cleansing
2017: Scabs III: Humans, Gods, and Monsters
2017: Emma's Rose: A Zombie Tale, Book 1: The Cave
2018: The Camera II: Alive & Dead in Texas
2018: Onslaught: The Zombie War Chronicles, Book 1
2018: Convergence: The Zombie War Chronicles, Book 2
2019: Judgement: The Zombie War Chronicles, Book 3
2019: The Camera III: Final Exposure
2021: Dead Hunger X: The Remnants
2022: Time Killer: A World of Monsters
2023: Time Killer II: The Hunters & The Prey

Remember to review these books … it helps!

**If you enjoyed this book, please do the author a BIG
favor and visit Amazon.com to write a review!**

Try retyping this damned link: (You *will* have to sign into
Amazon.com to actually write a review!)

http://www.amazon.com/s/ref=nb_sb_noss_1?url=sea
rch-alias%3Ddigital-text&field-keywords=eric+shelman

www.ingramcontent.com/pod-product-compliance
Lightning Source LLC
Chambersburg PA
CBHW051543250626
47157CB00001B/169